WILLOW'S WALK

RUSTY BLACKWOOD

Copyright 2015 © by Rusty Blackwood
All Rights Reserved.

ISBN - 10: 1516987276
ISBN – 13 9781516987276
LCCN – 2015913677
CreateSpace Independent Publishing Platform
North Charleston, South Carolina

This is an original work of fiction. Names, characters, places, and incidents used throughout are either the product of the author's imagination, or are used fictitiously, and any resemblance to any actual person, living or dead, events or locals, is entirely coincidental.

The title of Lord Alfred Tennyson's poem, 'The Lady of Shallot,' is used purely in an innocent manner, and in keeping with the storyline of this novel. Miss Blackwood claims no hold whatsoever upon this poem, its creation, revenue from its sales, or its Rights.

No part of this book may be reproduced or transmitted in any form or by any means, electronic or mechanical, including photocopying, recording, or by any information storage and or retrieval system, without written permission from the copyright owner..

Lovingly dedicated to my mother:
'Norma Irene Webber-Beecroft'
December 25, 1921 - September 18, 2015

'A mother's love is unconditional,
A daughter's love is eternal,
For everything you gave me,
I thank you, and I love you.'

OPENING THOUGHTS

What drives a person's train of thought, impelling them toward detrimental, often licentious acts that often bring nothing but heartache? Does lifestyle matter, or the way in which one is brought up? Could the lack of too little, or too much cold, hard cash be a relating factor? The answers may be found by tracing a family tree, studying the roots of those whom came before with hope of finding some element of explanation pertaining to choices made long before, of which still guide the present, remaining in the shadow of the one moving forward?

Studies have been conducted throughout the ages, trying to arrive at some acceptable answer, or plausible reason why people do as they do. What is really mind-boggling is the fact that people choose to walk a path of which they know will be destructive, yet they forge ahead, and the rest be damned. One should learn from mistakes made, and not repeat them. But what is the excuse for continuing down the same destructive path, repeating over, and over what you should have learned the first time through? If these answers were truly known it might explain the reason behind the course one chooses to take. Yet that is part of life's mystery, and what allows each and every one to walk their chosen path.

Chapter 1

WILLOW SUTHERLAND-CROSBY

When trouble faces you down you have two choices — fall in defeat — or stand and fight. Willow Lane Sutherland-Crosby always chose the latter. One might say the Celtic blood in her veins provided the grit to stand her ground when the need arose, and it would have certainly shored-up her determined outlook to prevail at all costs. It could even be said that up until now her entire life had been that of a woman on a mission, but every mission eventually comes to an end, and Willow, now well into her fifty-fifth year, was finding more adversity with each newly risen sun. But do not make the mistake of under estimating her, for she could still hold her own with the best of them, at least in her mind. For quite some time she had felt her age, but was still blessed with a youthful appearance, something her vanity had given thanks for many times. It had even brought her accolades when the fact was divulged that she was a grandmother - three times over - having reached that plateau for the first time at the ripe old age of forty-four. She had often pondered the reason for this fortuitous blessing, as well as the reason she had been chosen to receive it. This unexpected fountain of youth could possibly be attributed to the tireless energy of her grandchildren, for they consistently tweaked her interest, and never settled for the excuse 'not right now, dear, Grandma's too tired'. But the long Canadian winter of 2003 was taking its toll on her body, yet she rose each morning to face whatever that day threw her way.

Her job as a residential home cleaner was not an easy one, and from Tuesday, through Friday, she diligently cared for each client's home as if she were tenderly caring for her own, leaving them spotless on departure. She had conducted this service for many years, but the last few had grown increasingly difficult. Her health was no longer co-operating, and she often found herself sitting, more than standing, yet she carried on, for she had no choice. The prior year had witnessed her twenty nine year marriage to Jonas Crosby hit the rocks in the same fashion a storm-tossed vessel smashes upon a hidden reef. For quite some time she had felt its approaching demise - they both had - yet neither cared enough to secure the help required if they were to salvage even a minute fragment of what they had once shared. Stubborn actions toward an amiable compromise can be a terrible flaw within a personality, but when it's doubled, the result is complete and utter gridlock. They might have considered marriage counseling, yet to Jonas, who considered his every cent further lining to his impenetrable coffer, marriage counseling seemed a frivolous waste of hard-earned money, but to Willow, who had tried her utmost to make the marriage work at whatever means possible, it simply admitted failure, something her pride would not allow, so they did nothing. Up to this point their marriage had been a fairly good one with Jonas at the helm, and Willow doing her best as first mate. Never once did she look upon that role as secondary in any way, in fact many times it was she who did the main navigating when the marriage waters got rough. But even her best laid plans could not hold them on course once they realized the ship was going down, and the most heart wrenching reality of all was the blatant fact neither cared.

For three despairing years they had labored, trying desperately to salvage the bond they had once thought unbreakable. The early years of their marriage had been hard, yet regardless of what came and went they remained steadfast and loyal, realizing that all marriages go through trying times, even the best of them. In that regard they were no exception to the rule, even though they had married in their early twenties when their friends were still diligently furthering their education, and with the minor exception of a twelve-month separation ten years in, they had managed to jump the largest hurdles and carry on. They endured, not because a marriage license instructed them to, but because they loved each other.

Looking back over the years it had not always been that way - at least for Willow – for her life leading up to her first encounter with Jonas Crosby had been anything but serene, or free of un-needed mistakes. Born in 1949 to Shay and Mary Sutherland, Willow was the second of two children being raised on the diary farm owned by her paternal grandfather, Benjamin Sutherland, on the outskirts of Smith Falls in the Upper Ottawa Valley. Like the majority of 1950's farm children, Willow's life centered on daily chores which consisted of gathering eggs, feeding chickens, and the hardest of all, assisting her older brother David with the cleansing of stainless steel milk separators before, and after school. It was strenuous work, and while city children spent their summer holidays carousing at the local baseball diamond, the Sutherland children spent theirs working in the fields, tending numerous chores assigned them. Many nights they tumbled into bed so exhausted they were asleep before their head hit the pillow, but when the morning dawned the daily ritual began once again, for this was normal life upon a farm, whether it was cash-crop, dairy, or livestock. Farm families were a tightly knit lot, everyone pulling together, doing their part, for without consistency the farm could not function, and the families could not make a living.

Many of them had emigrated from the British Isles, some settling in the Ottawa Valley and surrounding district, some in other areas, but regardless of their proximity, they all shared the same common link of hard work. However it was not all work without play, and come Saturday night the Sutherland family, along with their neighbors, would happily come together at community dances, where they'd kick up their heels to the rousing jigs and reels provided by the lively fiddles and guitars. As a small child, Willow often remained with her aged grandfather while her parents attended these local functions, but on occasion both she and her brother would accompany them. She dearly loved spending time with her grandfather, listening to his tales of youth in the Valley, the way it had once been, and the importance of family. She tried her best to understand the meaning of it, as well as the necessity, but small children don't always understand the importance, or what makes it so, yet Willow, young as she was, realized a very unique bond with her father.

The years passed, and as childhood gave way to adolescence, Willow, who considered her life boring, found the need to experience exciting new things, often yearning for the desired outcome she had envisioned they would hold. She would frequently ask to accompany her parents to the Saturday dances where she would sit with other young ladies, watching their parents dance the different style each musical selection required, and it wasn't long before she was learning the numerous techniques of Celtic dance, among other things. It was on one of these occasions when her drab life was about to change.

Chapter 2

BERNARD WHIDBEY

During a bitterly-cold, yet rousing Saturday night in the winter of 1964, Willow was sitting beside her best friend, Megan Patterson, when the front door of the ancient hall opened wide, letting in a chilling gust of wind, and to the girl's delight, a group of young men whom instantly swarmed the white-hot, pot-bellied, wrought-iron stove in the hall's back corner like a hive of frozen bees seeking warmth. Among them, innocently standing behind the rest as though he were desperately trying to remain inconspicuous was a young man with smooth dark hair, tight-fitting jeans, worn leather jacket, and black biker boots. Willow let her huge eyes sweep over him with burning interest, hardly believing what she saw, for he was without a doubt the handsomest young man she had ever seen. Her cheeks instantly flushed, which enticed Megan to inquire why her friend had suddenly become so crimson.

"Well geez, Meg, can't you see what just walked in the door?" Willow questioned while her scarlet glow intensified.

"What are you talking about, Low?" Megan inquired with interest, her eyes scanning the entrance for a minute clue. "I don't see anybody other than those dumb jerks blocking the heat."

Shaking her head in a disgruntled manner, Willow exclaimed, "No, Meg, not them, the boy with the luscious dark hair!"

Megan's eyes had already zeroed-in on the intended source of interest. Pointing her finger straight at him, she inquired, "You mean that boy right there, standing away from the others?"

Embarrassed beyond belief, Willow immediately thrust her hand upon her friend's outstretched digit, stating, "For goodness sakes, Meg, don't *point* at him! He'll think we're a couple of hicks that have never seen a man before!" Then leaping behind her friend in exasperation, gasped, "Oh no! He's looking straight at us!"

"Not only that, Low," Megan replied with surprise, "he's walking straight toward us!" and she practically tripped over her cowering friend now in a crouching position behind her.

With the realization of her skin's brilliant hue, Willow moaned, "Oh, I can't believe this. My face must look as if somebody slapped me." With this revelation an idea suddenly sprang to mind, causing her to madly seize her friend, while she spit out, "Do it ... Hurry!"

Confused, Megan inquired, "Do what?" though in actuality had already surmised what it was.

"Slap me across the face!" Willow ordered in haste. "Come on, he's getting closer!" and braced for the impending blow.

"I can't slap you," Megan replied apprehensively, shocked beyond belief at such an outrageous request from the one person whom meant the world to her.

Willow Sutherland and Megan Patterson had been best friends from the moment they first met at age six in grade one. Their parent's properties sat adjacent each other, which allowed the girls as much time in each other's company as they fancied. They loved each other like sisters, always there for each other, never failing to defend one another in whatever the scenario might entail.

"Hurry up!" Willow ordered, for she could see the boy moving closer with each passing second. It was imperative she be ready.

With apprehension clouding her voice, Megan said, "I-I can't hurt you."

Willow was beside herself with embarrassment while her adolescent hormones screamed their need. The object of her desire was inching closer; she was fast running out of time. Action was required, and fast. "If you don't slap me right now," Willow threatened, "I'll tell your mom where you hid those dirty magazines of your dad's that we found last week!"

Bristling in horror, Megan gasped, "You wouldn't dare!"

"Oh wouldn't I? Just try me," Willow managed to squeak-out, just as her left cheek was met by Megan's right-handed wallop. She could have sworn the impact rattled her teeth as she rubbed the burning area, and thought, "Well you didn't have to slug me quite that hard!"

The excited girls jumped up, almost colliding with the interested young man, as he sternly questioned, "Hey-hey, what's going on here?"

Megan's startled expression was as obvious as Willow's, yet neither would relinquish the reason when the young man politely gestured them to sit, but beat them to it, settling himself upon a chair in between them. "My name's Bernie — I mean Bernard - Bernard Whidbey, but all my friends call me Bernie, the ones that aren't call me *Nerd*. Needless to say they aren't standing long after they do," he said with a half-cocked grin, and then proceeded to inquire their names.

"Willow Sutherland and this is my best friend, Megan Patterson," Willow replied, her hand making a slight gesture toward her friend as she spoke.

"Pleased to meet you both," Bernie replied in an inquisitive tone, "but I got to say that best friends don't usually hit each other."

Not wishing to divulge the particulars, both girls replied in unison, "It was nothing!" and then burst out laughing.

Bernie shook his head, as he chuckled, and said, "Didn't look that way to me."

"Well it was," Megan replied, quickly adding, "I'm going to get something to drink. I'm absolutely *parched!* See you later, girlfriend."

The remaining couple sat in silence, feeling rather awkward as they watched her walk away, for they both realized the reason she left, not to mention the opportunity it now provided.

Clearing his throat in a somewhat inept manner, Bernie said, "You've got a pretty good friend there."

"Yes ... yes I know," Willow replied, trying hard not to falter.

"Have you two been friends long?" Bernie asked in an interested manner, his dark eyes traveling deeply into hers, their color vibrantly capturing her attention the deeper they went. They were the most intriguing eyes she had yet to see – though in actuality she hadn't seen many – but they had something about them that somehow put her at ease. The anxiety she'd been feeling instantly vanished, and letting her eyes return his gaze, she gently answered, "We've been best friends since first grade."

"Hey, I think that's cool. My best friend couldn't make it tonight; his dad's got a horse down with a touch of colic. The vet was going to stay for awhile, but my pal had decided to stay too so his dad could bring his mom to the dance - gives them a bit of a break that way," he explained as his eyes continued their intoxicating hold.

"That's good of him," Willow replied in kind. "I love horses too, and I know how serious colic can be. Hope he comes along alright – the horse that is." She grinned at her remark, but couldn't help noticing his stare had not left her face. Suddenly he asked her to dance. "It's a slow one," he explained, "so I can do that. Sorry, I'm not much good at the faster stuff - all feet it seems but I can slow dance – that is if you want to … Do you?"

He stood up, extending his right hand which somehow beckoned her to take hold. Before she knew it she was in his strong arms, letting him hold her as they swayed to the fiddle's soft lilt. The dance ended far too soon, as did the evening, but not before he asked to escort her home. As much as she would love to jump at the chance, she was hesitant with her answer. "Gee, I don't know, Bernie," she said, her answer emitting sudden caution, "I mean, I'd love to, but I'm only fifteen and, I'll have to first ask my dad."

Willow knew this would not be an easy task, for she was her father's only daughter; his pride and joy. He doted on her; had from the day she was born and the feeling was mutual. For as long as she had memory her father had been the center of her universe. He would often protect her from her mother's harsh tongue, intervening to the point where a full-blown argument would erupt pertaining to the way in which he was bringing her up. He was an extremely gentle man, not prone to violence in any form, nor could he bring himself to discipline his children, even if they required it. Willow's mother, on the other hand, would not tolerate any form of nonsense from either of her children. She was a firm believer in the adage 'spare the rod and spoil the child', and she was not about to let this well-instilled knowledge be lost when it came to her own.

Willow longed to accept the invitation from this handsome, doe eyed Adonis who set her heart aflutter with a mere glance, yet she knew the chance was slim to none, still she would chance it. It might prove more difficult than first thought, for even though she had a special way with her father, this was a far different area than the usual requests to go to town with Megan and her parents, or have girlfriends for slumber parties where their silly giggles kept her parents awake to all hours, which often resulted in her mother putting the kibosh on the party, and possibly Bernie's present request - that is if her dad even gave his permission – for even if he did her mother would most likely change it. She also realized that it would not hurt to summon reinforcements; somehow she felt the need to summon all the help she could muster. "Where's Meg when I need her," she stated under her breath, thinking it must appear ridiculous to this young man who was no doubt used to immediate acceptance, not the run-about of a dizzy, under-developed fifteen-year-old who, at the moment, appeared as if she were trying to prove herself worthy of his attentions, but was in fact too young for them. But she was not giving up. Megan finally appeared, and was instantly commandeered to Willow's side.

"Where have you been?" she questioned, gripping young Whidbey's hand in such a way it must have given Megan the impression they'd become engaged during her absence.

"Oh I was having a wonderful conversation with Jenny," Megan confessed with a snicker, glancing back in the direction from which she had just come.

"Yeah, I bet," Willow stated snidely, "more like gossip if you ask me. But never mind that now. I need your help."

With her right hand stiffly holding a salute that would make the Armed Forces proud, Megan snickered, "Private Patterson at your service, Miss Sutherland! And what, may I ask, do you require this time?"

Willow rolled her eyes at this dramatic gesture but knew she could count on her friend, as she stated, "I need you to come with me to ask Dad if Bernie can drive me home, okay?"

"Sure," Megan answered, then putting her lips to her friend's ear, whispered, "Come on, kid, you don't really think you'll get to go do you?" Without need of answer, Willow shook her head in a negative manner as she approached her parents, whom had just finished a waltz and were about to sit down, but before she could open her mouth, her father spoke up, inquiring the young man's identity.

"Dad – Mom, this is Bernie ... err ... Bernard Whidbey."

Shay Sutherland hardly acknowledged young Whidbey's outstretched hand, but lost no time in noticing the boy's obvious interest in his daughter. "How do you do?" he asked in an inquisitive manner, but continued to ignore the boy's hand. This gesture did not go unnoticed by Willow, and it instantly informed her of her father's intentions, causing a quiver to ensnare her voice, as she said, "D-daddy, Bernie has asked if ... if he can drive me home."

It was obvious her father was not impressed by this young stud; furthermore his possible intentions and he made no secret of it, as he said, "Princess, you've only just met this young buck tonight. You don't even know him."

"But, Daddy —"

"You heard your father! You will be silent!" Mary Sutherland snapped, instantly stifling her daughter's request.

The floor could have opened right then and there, swallowing Willow whole, for that was the way her mother's direct order made her feel. It was embarrassing enough to have been refused her request in front of this young man, but to top it off she had been spoken to as if she were nothing more than an impertinent child. A reprimand like that would be difficult for anyone to accept - regardless of age - but a young girl like Willow could not understand the reasoning behind her parent's words, only that they were not the ones needing to be heard. In desperation, she blurted, "What if Meg comes with us?"

Always true-blue, Megan promptly remarked, "Oh yeah, Mrs. Sutherland! It's alright with my parents," but she lied; further more Mary knew it.

The situation appeared to be intensifying, causing Bernie to speak up. "Excuse me," he stated in a respectful manner, "I don't mean to interfere, but I can certainly understand your reluctance to let her come with a guy she's only just met. But I really would like to escort them home, if I may," and if in after-thought, he added, "If it's any consolation, sir, I am a good driver, and I promise I'll take them straight home."

But Shay Sutherland was not to be convinced so easily, and his steel-blue eyes bore down on the boy, as he said, "Haven't seen you around before. From where do you hail?"

The young man did not falter in the least, instantly answering, "Carleton Place. My dad has a hardware store there."

Seemingly amused by the boy's intrepid response, Shay stroked the fresh whisker growth upon his chin, as he said, "Well you're certainly a ways from home tonight, Mr. Whidbey – and I might add it's a bit stormy to be out and about."

Not missing a note, Bernie replied, "Well, sir, I have to agree with you about the weather, but you and your family are out and about. I'm sure the snow was not about to deter you from an evening out with your lovely wife."

Willow couldn't help but smile at the boldness of it all, and she inwardly praised this young man for his forthrightness - if not a tad ill-placed - but it was obvious he knew his mind and was not afraid to speak it. It hadn't gone amiss, for Shay replied, "Well I must admit you've got a good point there - by the way - what's the name of your father's store?"

With an air of pride, the young man stated, "Whidbey Hardware, sir, the finest of its kind."

"Then tell me, Bernard," Shay openly inquired, stepping closer to the young man, "would your father by any chance stock a decent assortment of separator parts? The local hardware has not been able to get a part I've been waiting on for a dog's age. I'm down one separator every milking. It's getting a bit annoying - to say the least - and every time I call about it I get the same redundant answer," and with what could only be described as an exasperated swing of his arm, motioned them all to join his wife at the table.

Young Whidbey gently took Willow's hand and guided her to one of three vacant chairs located near the end of the table, all the while motioning Megan to sit on one side of her friend, while he pulled back the third chair for himself. Plopping himself astride it, he then casually folded his arms across his chest, and leaned against the chair's back.

"I'm sure it does," he announced in a nonchalant manner. "Actually he carries quite a large stock of stuff like that. I wouldn't be afraid to bet he's got just what you're looking for, Mr. Sutherland, or if he doesn't he wouldn't be long in getting it. He did a lot of research on this area before we moved from Halifax. He ran a hardware store out there too, but after my mother died he didn't want to stay on, but he still wanted to remain in hardware, so he decided to come to a farming community where his business would be in greater demand. He did some looking, found the store in Carleton Place, and bought it. We've lived there ever since."

"Well," remarked Shay in a matter-of-fact way while he continued to rub the stubble upon his chin, "I guess I'll have to take a drive up there. Maybe the first of the week, if all goes well," and he casually rose to his feet while studying the stalwart boy, causing a small eternity to pass before finally extending his hand while inquiring the boy's age.

Clasping the older man's hand in a tight grip, Bernie answered, "I turned eighteen this past June, sir."

"Well, Whidbey, it appears you're a conscientious young man, so I've decided to let you escort my daughter and her friend home," Shay replied, though he made a point of adding, "But straight there."

"Oh, Daddy, thank you!" Willow exclaimed joyously, even though it would mean she and Bernie would not be alone.

Mary Sutherland's brooding dark eyes shot a look of disapproval toward her husband, and in a no nonsense manner, she stated, "I don't think that a wise idea, Shay. The storm seems to be growing worse, and I think we should be leaving for home together."

"Now-now, my dear, there's no need to go ruffling your feathers," Shay replied in a rational manner, and he coyly winked at the boy, and continued, "I somehow feel I can trust this young man with my princess — besides we'll be following right behind."

"Thank you kindly, Mr. Sutherland," young Whidbey remarked politely. "But you need not worry about your *princess*. I'll be exceptionally careful." Stepping back and grasping the young ladies' hands in his, he respectfully bowed his head toward the Sutherlands, and bid goodnight.

Much would follow, but that was to be the first of many delightful evenings Willow Sutherland was to spend in the inviting company of the dashing Bernard Whidbey.

Chapter 3

YOUTHFUL INNOCENCE OR CHOSEN IGNORANCE

Three delightful years passed with Willow and Bernie spending every free moment they could find together. This was not an easy task, for school was always a problem, but from Monday through Friday evenings, after Willow had completed her homework, they would burn-up the telephone line, whispering sweet-nothings into the receiver as if it were actually into each other's ear. But when the weekend arrived they would spend it however they could, doing whatever they could, and enjoying every second. What wonderful times they shared. Youth is such a fantastic blessing, energy never leaves, anything is possible, regardless of the endurance required to see it to fruition. Willow had never been an easy child when it came to making the right choices, but she had been raised to respect herself, and conduct herself accordingly to the inexplicable rules laid out in each women's monthly periodical of the time, each bolstering instructions as to the reader's stellar conduct of one's self when being courted by the opposite gender, especially when that young gender is feeling his wild oats, and hoping to sink his throbbing manhood into his young lady's moist, inner sanctum.

It was an on-going problem for Willow, for how could she hope to hold her young stud at bay and still grasp his love in her hands without giving in to his wonted needs - worse still - the possibility of his finding it elsewhere if she did not bend to his will? It had been a quandary every woman since the beginning of time has had to figure out. Willow was no exception in this area, and she not only grappled with Bernie's desires, but her own. Each time their hungry lips touched, the fire burned hotter, fanning smoldering embers into full-blown flames within each of them. Yet they held fast. Mary Sutherland could be proud of what had been instilled in her rebellious daughter, as well as the determination being shown in her conduct. One could only hope that the late Mrs. Whidbey's pride shone brightly for her son's conduct as well.

Time moved on, and as it did it brought the young couple closer to experiencing all love has to offer each time Bernie's searching fingers found their way up Willow's quivering inner thighs. Should he touch what he wanted, or slide his probing hands back down? Willow was no further ahead, for each movement of his fingers found her clit hoping they might inquire entry, and if they did, could she accept what she so desired? Torture can come in many disguises, and trying to choose the proper one to evade is the pure and utter result of the game. Surely no-one would know if they succumbed to the enormous desire to explore what love is all about, a nip, a taste, a quick emersion into lust - lust of the flesh - the total essence of what everyone shouts about. Still they restrained, knowing that the wedding bed must be the first to witness the dance that ends in the ultimate carnal act.

The spring of 1967 arrived, and with it sadness to the family by the death of Willow's aged grandfather. She found his passing difficult to endure, much more so than she ever thought she would, for she had come to understand the true meaning of his teachings, and the difficult time following his death often found her memory recalling their wonderful times spent together. Though hard in many ways, they had been happy times, bringing with them a feeling of safety and love that could never be broken. Through her grandfather's unyielding guidance and enduring love she had come to understand the true meaning of *family*, and all which that encompasses. It evoked many emotions, most import of which is the unbreakable bond that blood kin share, and the immense pride in knowing this bond can never be broken. Willow knew her grandfather would never be truly gone, for his spirit remained within all of them. It brought her ever-closer to her father, and if her earlier connection to him had not been intense by way of measure, it had now cemented to a consistency beyond breakage by anything.

Willow sat at the sewing machine, completing the final touches on her graduation dress for the anticipated ceremony being held in the high school gymnasium in less than two weeks. While the machine hummed its placid tune, she found herself retracing her childhood, savoring with wonderment each memory conjured, and smiling when each one began its performance. All the fun she'd had, the delightful times spent with Megan and her cousin Will during their assorted escapades about the farm, as well as the countryside, but these memories always brought her back to her grandfather, their time spent together, his passing, and how little the hurt had actually lessened during the time that had since lapsed. Still, as much as sadness weighed heavy on her heart, it could not suppress the joy she felt in becoming Mrs. Bernard Whidbey when the coming summer presented itself. The dashing, dark-haired Bernie was everything she had ever hoped for. He even doted on her as much as her father did - which may not have been the wisest decision on his part - but he loved her as much as she loved him, and would do whatever was required to insure her happiness.

Summer was not long in coming and with it stifling heat, little rain, and a most anticipated wedding in the white-washed Methodist Church of Smith Falls. Family, both Sutherland and Whidbey, filled the pews to capacity as Megan Patterson, tossing wild flowers, preceded the bride down the aisle. Holding tightly to her father's arm, a nervous Willow stepped cautiously toward her handsome groom, who was standing confidently at the altar with his best man standing in support beside him. Willow was eighteen. Bernie was twenty-one. They were young, in love, with their entire lives ahead of them.

The first few months of their marriage was like a dream come true, for every day spent in their own living quarters in the back of the Sutherland house was pure bliss. Bernie was Willow's first lover, wild, lustful, passionately removing her virginity as if it had been created solely for his taking. He took her often, and she couldn't be happier. His touch was pure magic, the magic of a young man in love with avenues to discover, areas to explore, and total fulfillment between the thighs of the woman he had captured. Willow, whose idea of marriage was like something out of a fairytale, was living her dream. All was grand. Why wouldn't it be? She was Bernie's wife, as well as her father's daughter, with the best of both worlds at her feet. What more could she hope for?

The following summer brought another delightful chapter to Willow's life in the form of her first child, a son, whom she named Benjamin Bernard. She may have been a mere nineteen, but she was bound and determined to be the best mother a child could ever hope for. Everything seemed perfect. She was living what appeared the perfect life, yet in reality all is not always as it appears. The strain of living under someone else's roof was beginning to take its toll on the young couple. Bernie had not been happy for quite some time, yet he never let on anything was amiss. Daily activities carried on as though nothing would ever change. The farm continued to function, and Bernie continued to do what was expected of him. He wanted to please his licentious wife because her happiness resulted in his own. Still, regardless of how he tried, it just wasn't working; furthermore he knew it. Living with their in-laws - though they were extremely good to them and did their best to afford the young couple privacy - was not the same as having their own home with their own privacy. Many times Bernie tried imploring his young wife to come away with him to a place of their own, yet as much as she loved being his wife, she loved being her father's princess fully as much and could not bring herself to leave. Innocence is not always as it appears, for she knew a wife's place first and foremost was at her husband's side, and though she wanted to be there, knew she was not yet ready to leave her father's home. She may have been innocent in many ways, after-all her age was not that of someone who had experienced life to any extent, yet she was old enough to realize that the way she felt was wrong. But ignorance is often chosen, even a mere nineteen year-old knows this, still she turned a blind eye to the situation, and chose to ignore the most important problem facing her.

Before long they were on each other's nerves, fighting almost daily. They couldn't even do that in private, but try as they might an amiable solution could not be found, and during a hot July night in 1969, while the first man walked on the moon, Bernard Whidbey, son, or no son, walked out of Willow's life.

Chapter 4

LIFE AFTER BERNIE

The hazy days of summer transformed to autumn, and with it came a nip in the air accompanied by Willow's completed divorce papers. The divorce from Bernie Whidbey had come quickly, the final decree being granted on September 11, 1969, wrapping everything into a neat little package, very much the way the entire marriage had been — in-fact the more Willow thought about it, the more she shook her head in dismay with the realization that she had dated Bernie longer than she'd been married to him, and the only positive issue that had sprung from their union was their son. The entire marriage raced through her mind, yet regardless of the bitter taste it left in her mouth, Willow had to admit that she could not blame Bernie for leaving, after all it wasn't like he hadn't tried to be a good husband and father, but he could not be *her* father. She knew this, yet the realization of it didn't change her present mindset, and though she understood his departure, she was not sorry for the choice she had made.

One late autumn morning Willow was sitting at the kitchen table, sipping lukewarm coffee, happily watching her young son attempt to crawl as he pulled himself along the cedar plank floor toward her. She smiled at his bravery, while applauding his success, and as she did she found herself wondering how she would ever raise him alone, yet she was determined to find a way, and like everything with Willow, she would find it.

"Oh, Benny," she sighed with tender emotion, "I don't know how Mommy's ever going to do this, but I promise I will," and she half sighed while her arms encouraged him into them.

It seemed odd in a way, almost as if the child sensed her uncertainty, for as she cuddled him against her breast, his little hands affectionately caressed her cheeks as he softly cooed while banging his face against hers in a gentle manner.

"Oh, my little darling," she sighed affectionately, her voice cracking with emotion as she kissed his tiny fingers, "I love you *so* much."

He gaily chuckled as she nuzzled him. "Nothing could be this precious," she thought, for regardless of what she may face, this child brought her a comfort like no other before. She could not fail him.

The chilling days of winter on the farm meant endless cups of steaming cocoa topped with fluffy marshmallows, hot apple cider with fresh cinnamon sticks, and the reading of storybooks before a roaring fireplace. Willow whiled the hours away with her son; constructing block castles encased with cardboard fortresses, certain to defend the most ferocious dragon attacks, and creating countless crayon masterpieces that Picasso himself would envy. Whenever a break was required she could always rely on her parents, yet it never ceased to fail that her son appeared a little more spoiled upon her return. She never complained or resented it, for she had never forgotten the way her own grandfather had spoiled her. My how she missed him, yet she knew he was never far away, no doubt bursting with pride of his great grandson whom carried his name.

The boy also carried his father's name, and Willow found herself missing him too. She had never refused Bernie access, but for some unknown reason he chose not to remain in his son's life. "His loss," she thought in sadness, yet she couldn't help feeling resentment toward the possible void it could one day leave, especially if other children boasted the magnificent feats of their fathers. If they did, little Benny wouldn't be able to boast about his, and Willow regretfully hung her head as these suppressing thoughts consumed it.

Benny's possible predicament was not Willow's only concern; her need for male companionship – especially his penis - always simmered at the ready, even though she lived in consistent denial of her carnal needs. After all she was only nineteen years old and the majority of her friends were still sewing *their* wild oats. But regardless of this fact, Willow felt she was now reaping the rewards of the ones sewn with Bernie, possibly long before they should have been. Yet this acknowledgement did little to extinguish the fire smoldering within her loins. Countless nights, long after her son was in bed, she would cry herself to sleep with the wonted need of a man's touch, his endowment buried deep within her, but more importantly his love.

Four years passed, and with them a few male encounters, but nothing serious. It appeared another adage 'here for a good time not a long time' rang true, for as long as Willow was willing to put out they were willing to stick around, but as soon as they discovered Benny they were gone faster than lint in a windstorm. "There's the goddamn door hope it hits ya on the way out!" she would exclaim in disgust, anger getting the better of her as she watched yet another spent penis lunge for the door. It was an unfortunate, eye-opening lesson, but she was quickly discovering there weren't many guys keen on raising another man's child, regardless of how much they may fancy the mother. Willow had already surmised this fact; still she hoped to find that special someone who just might love her little boy as well as her. This was only one problem she faced; the other she lived with and locked horns with on more occasions than she cared to mention. But when the dust finally settled it was Mary Sutherland who reigned supreme.

Born in 1923 to Flynn and Agnes Whalen, the raven-haired Mary had grown up in a time much different than that of her rebellious daughter. The great depression had not been an easy era for anyone existing throughout it, and being the eldest of eight furthered that difficulty more than it otherwise might have, for she was expected to carry a by far heavier load than most, and at a much earlier age. Still, when it came to the care of her younger siblings, she was her mother's right hand, completing her assignments with no complaints. Mary's father was an unyielding man who believed in hard work with no complaints when muscles got sore or backs got stiff, you simply did the work if you intended to eat when the end of the growing season rolled around. It was a hard life, but Mary grew up knowing no different. She had married Shay Sutherland in 1942, and moved from her father's farm to her husband's, yet her choice had been a good one, and it showed in the solidity of her marriage.

Willow was like her mother in many ways, possessing the same drive and ambition - not to mention hot temper which seemed to surface rather frequently during the past few years - yet she always held an immense respect for her mother, though at times felt none in return. She had a difficult time understanding this, for she had been taught that in order to generate respect one must first give it, and she gave endlessly of hers, yet couldn't help but wonder why she never received much back, especially when her mother belittled her in front of her son, or reprimanded her as though she were a mindless child with no sense in the least. It hurt, and it hurt deeply. She often wondered why her mother never saw this, further wondering if she even cared, but deep inside she was certain that she did.

Part of the problem may have stemmed from Willow's exalted place within her father's eyes, because to him she could do no wrong, even if she did. It may have been the fact that he took her part in what seemed endless confrontations with her mother, which only resulted in her mother becoming even more domineering than she otherwise might have been. Either way it wasn't easy for them, and it became even worse when it was centered on Benny. It was on such an occasion in late February 1973 when the phone interrupted yet another heated argument between mother and daughter. Maybe it was a Godsend – perhaps luck - but whatever it was it was Willow who managed to arrive at the phone first and snatch the black receiver from its cradle.

"*Hello!*" she hollered, shaking with anger as she clutched the doorframe for support.

For a brief moment there was silence, before a man's voice laughingly said, "Well, *ha-ha*, hello to you too, cousin. What in hell's the matter?"

"Is that you, Willy?" Willow questioned in earnest, her temper slightly easing in the hope that it might be. Mary had left the kitchen, leaving her daughter to speak in private. "Good of her," Willow sarcastically thought, but immediately felt remorse for thinking it.

"Yeah, it's me. What are you doing?" Will questioned.

"Talking to you," Willow answered in a smart-ass manner, trying her best to tease him. "What in hell does it sound like?"

In a faux English accent, Will said, "By the sounds of it you were - shall we say - a bit heated when you answered. Having a little tiff with Mummy again are we?"

Figuring he'd surmised the answer without need of confirmation, Willow answered, "Well, let's just say you've caught me at a rather *difficult* moment. I haven't seen you in awhile. How have you been?"

Of all of her cousins William Sutherland was her favorite. They had grown up on adjacent farms, and though he was eleven months Willow's senior, his mother had held him back from school until Willow was old enough to attend with him. It was always said Mrs. Sutherland did this so the cousins could walk together to the same one room schoolhouse their fathers had attended many years earlier.

"I'm managing the best I can," Will answered in a matter-of-fact way.

"That's good," Willow replied, finding her anxiety lessening. "Hey, I miss you since you moved up to the big city. How's life been treating you in our fair capital?"

Willow truly missed him, for along with Megan he was her best friend, and even though he was her first cousin, she could always confide in him, knowing he'd be there come-what-may, for he, more than anyone, knew what it was like to have his better half walk out the door leaving him holding an infant. Willow had tried her utmost to be there for him throughout his troubles, for she knew only too well how it felt to be without a mate and back on the market with a child where no one wanted either.

Her eyes, for want of something to do while awaiting his response, traveled the worn kitchen counter, until he said, "Oh it's okay; I guess, lots to do for a backwoods boy like me. But in all honesty I really don't have a lot of time to get out. I'm working long days. By the time I take Dane's babysitter home and get supper ready it's time for us both to crash. Now enough of that, I want to ask you something," and as he spoke his little boy's voice could be heard cajoling in the background.

"Sure, what is it?" Willow inquired with interest.

"Well," Will said as though he were hesitant to speak, "I was wondering if you might like to go out with a good friend of mine from work." On conclusion Willow could hear him speaking to his son over the receiver, assuring him that he wouldn't be much longer. His statement triggered the always present thought within her mind of what it would be like for Benny to hear his father speaking to him that way, and remorse consumed her until the thought once again diminished.

"Yeah, who is that?" she asked while her interest piqued, somehow feeling that this person must be alright in order to be a close friend of her cousin.

"His name's Jonas Crosby," Will replied. "He lives in the city here, not far from me actually. I met him the first day of work. He's a bit younger than we are - couple of years I'd say - but he's a great guy. Bottom line, he asked if I knew any chicks that might like to go out with us this Saturday night. I already asked this girl I know and she agreed, so I told him all about you and he seems really interested in meeting you. I'm sure my sitter would look after your boy if you can catch the train up here. Besides, Low, I thought you might like a weekend away from the old homestead, maybe catch up on old times. Hey, it'd be a blast, so how about it?"

Willow sensed that he was not only trying to provide a break for her, but was no doubt requiring a shoulder for himself, much in the same way he had when his wife first left. There was just something beckoning in his voice, and before she thought further, she blurted, "Yeah, sounds like a plan, man! But how much does he know about me – I mean – I assume you've told him about, well … you know?"

"Yeah, I do," Will confirmed, "I told him you're divorced — and before you get your back up I also told him you've got a kid, and guess what? It doesn't seem to matter; he just wants to meet you."

Once again he could be heard in compliance with his son. Not wishing to further detain him, Willow said, "Look, Willy, I can hear you're needed, so I won't keep you. Benny and I will be on the eight-thirty train out of Smith Falls on Saturday morning. I'll get Dad to drive us to the station. Can you meet us when we get in?"

"Don't worry about that. I'll be there," he answered with relief, and in a joyful tone, added, "Thanks, Low. See you Saturday."

She couldn't help but smile at the tone in his voice for it obviously meant a lot to him; besides she could certainly use the break.

Willow had often thought about taking Benny and jumping on the first train going *anywhere*, but she knew that was a senseless idea, not to mention the inevitable reprimand she was bound to receive if her mother ever caught wind of it. She remembered being told she was free to go any time she wished, but her son would remain with his grandparents. That was not an option, for come what may the one thing she would never do was abandon her child. That night during supper she prudently informed her parents of her intended plans, inquiring her dad if he would drive them to the station then return for them Sunday evening. To her amazement there was no disagreement, no questions, no 'why do you need to go there', and she almost found it too good to be true, yet she was not going to question it. However there was one particular item she purposely kept to herself. This way, if it was ever found out, one could never accuse her of lying, for it really wasn't a lie if it was just information that had been discreetly left out, and she was not about to divulge what that was.

Saturday morning dawned to find Willow putting the finishing touches on what little packing was required as two, tiny worn suitcases lay open upon her bed, while she flit about in great anticipation of what lie ahead. Never once did the thought cross her mind that she may encounter a situation that would be too difficult to handle; if anything she found herself unable to wait. After all she knew her cousin would never allow harm to befall her; even if it did she was a big girl who could take care of herself.

The sun was well up as she looked around for any last minute articles that may have escaped the awaiting suitcases. "Hope I haven't forgotten anything," she thought aloud, her eyes scrutinizing the room for clues after having stayed up half the night planning their wardrobe. But she had to be sure she wasn't leaving important articles behind. Her closet remained open, revealing the few faded dresses she possessed, and even though her wish to acquire a few of the latest fashions could finally be realized, she knew it was impossible, especially if her son was to have what he required. Few articles fit him as it was. She could hardly believe the speed in which he was growing; stretching up before her soft green eyes like a weed from well nourished soil. But oh was she proud of him. He was her world. Yet as much as he gave her he could not fill the void left by his father. As she stood reminiscing, her boy came barreling through the large bedroom door, almost knocking her down as he ran.

"Mommy, Mommy, when can we ride the choo-choo?" he asked excitedly, awkwardly tugging at the bottom of her worn yellow sweater.

Beaming with admiration at how handsome he looked in his spanking new outfit, she answered, "Pretty soon, honey. Are you excited?"

His mood was plain enough for a blind man to see as he jumped up and down, waving his hands wildly, as he joyfully replied, "Yes, Mommy! Can we go now — can we — huh? Oh please, Mommy, please!"

"Yes, Benny. I'm almost ready. I must not forget anything, so I've been checking to make sure that I haven't. I'm just as excited as you!" she gleefully remarked, just as the click of her suitcase echoed throughout the room.

The little boy bound out the door with as much energy as he had on entering, calling for his grandfather to come have a look at his new suit as he tore down the hall toward the stairs. Willow couldn't help chuckling at his excitement, but had to admit to his right in feeling that way. After-all he never got too many places, and she knew exactly how that felt as she slipped her purse strap over her shoulder, picked up the suitcases, and hurried out the door after him.

They arrived at the Smith Fall's depot just minutes before departure time. They were cutting it close, and the train would certainly not wait for tardy passengers. Willow took her excited son by the hand and walked into the lobby as her dad followed close behind with the minute luggage in tow; in fact it was so minor that they could have kept it with them instead of having it taken to the baggage car. But none of that mattered, because they were finally embarking on a journey to *anywhere*; possibly a new life. Willow's right foot tapped slightly as Benny gave his grandfather a gigantic hug, adhering to the man's chest as though he'd become an outer appendage. Then Willow took her turn, holding her father tightly against her body while she firmly kissed his weathered cheek.

"See you Sunday night, Dad. Now don't forget to come for us," she stated with excitement as she held Benny's hand, and climbed aboard.

Chapter 5

JONAS REGAN CROSBY

The sun was shining brightly; though the temperature cold enough to freeze your tongue to a lamp-post, should you be silly enough to try, when the train arrived at the Ottawa station late Saturday morning. Will Sutherland, along with his tiny son Dane, resembled two frozen Eskimos, dressed in their winter best, standing in wait upon the platform. Their misty-white breath, floating in the air before them, appeared frozen in time, as they continually stamped their feet in attempt to keep their circulation moving, while passengers took their sweet time disembarking. It must have felt as though eternity itself had lapsed by the time their intended passengers finally stepped off the train.

"Hi, Willow! Oh it's so good to see you! Hi there, Benny! How did you like the train ride?" Will Sutherland inquired with excitement, playfully rubbing the boy's woolen-clad head, while his eyes darted from mother to son. Immediately turning to Willow, he lost no time in throwing his arms around her slight body, embracing her tightly as he affectionately kissed her cheek.

"Hi, Will, it's good to see you too!" Willow remarked in a lovingly manner while anxiously returning his embrace.

The two little boys did a stare-down, much like children are known to do when they first meet. After all they didn't know they were cousins, and they must have wondered at their parent's outlandish performance, but just as Will secured the luggage, the wind suddenly picked up, forcing the merry group toward the warmth of the station. As they neared it, a tall, slender, flaxen-haired man, dressed in a worn brown corduroy coat, stepped from beneath the roof's over-hang, and extended his hand to Willow.

"How do you do, miss, my name is Jonas Crosby. You must be Sutherland's cousin Willow," the man inquired while a broad smile engulfed his rugged face, but before she could respond, he extended his hand to her son, and stated, "And this stalwart young lad must be Benny."

The little boy, uncertain of the man before him, pressed inwardly against his mother. It was obvious her teachings about strangers had sunk in, and he was certainly not going to be courted by this one.

Acknowledging the man, Willow replied, "Pleased to meet you, Mr. Crosby," and held one hand to him as she embraced her son's head with the other. Realizing her boy was trying to disappear inside her coat, she said, "You must forgive him. He's a bit shy."

"Nothing wrong with being cautious," Jonas replied in a knowing tone. "It's good to see he's not quick to be taken in — and the name's Jonas."

Clearing his throat while scoffing sarcastically, Will barked, "Yeah! Too bad all of us weren't a bit more cautious when it comes to things like that. If we were we might not get taken for a ride so damn easily, *ha-ha!*"

Willow shot a knowing glance toward her cousin, and nodded in agreement just as another bone-chilling gust slammed into them, causing her to say, "We'd best get the kids out of this cold wind, Will," and searching about, asked, "Where's your car?"

"I managed to find a spot out front. It's not far," he answered as he glanced at his friend, and asked, "You want to come along now, or meet us later?"

Another chilling gust forced Jonas to turn-up his collar, as he answered, "Well I wouldn't mind catching a ride, if that's alright. You're going right past my boarding house anyway, so you can just drop me out front."

Will agreed as he motioned them all toward his car. Getting the children fastened in their seatbelts was a bit of a chore, as neither wanted to be separated from their respective parent, but persistence finally prevailed. As she settled herself, Willow inquired the evening plans.

"Thought we'd take in a show," Will answered as he carefully maneuvered his car out of the icy parking lot. "There's a good one playing at the Mayfair which is not far from my place. My date said she'd just meet us there around eight. It works out fine; it'll give me time to get Dane settled into bed before we leave."

Thinking about her evening departure, Willow hastily injected, "Hopefully Benny too! Though I'd like to hang around until he's asleep - strange bed in all," she explained, rubbing her son's head in a loving manner, and as she glanced around, she couldn't help but notice Jonas' expressive blue eyes smiling her way.

Dinner was a treat long-overdue. Willow had forgotten what a good cook her cousin actually was, and she enjoyed every morsel. It was a good feeling for both of them to sit around the table with their children, enjoying ice-cream, and laughing. In a lot of ways it must have swept them back to their own childhood and many meals spent just this way. But the evening was warring on. The sitter arrived, and though it took awhile, the children settled into a sound sleep which put Willow's mind at ease. Everything appeared to be moving along fine, with the exception of the noticeable absence of her intended date, but just as she was about to comment on this fact a knock sounded upon the door.

"Must be him now," Will said, and he opened the door to reveal his friend nervously clutching a colorful bouquet of flowers. "How utterly lovely, are these for little-ole-me?" Will questioned in his best southern-belle accent, dramatically fanning himself with his hand as he did. "My-my but aren't you sweet. You really shouldn't have!"

Jonas laughed in a good-hearted way as he lovingly shoved his friend aside while handing the beautiful arrangement to a surprised Willow, who couldn't help but smile as she accepted them. Holding them to her nose, letting their rich fragrance fill her senses, she replied, "They're lovely. Thank you, Jonas; it's really kind of you."

"Glad you like them," he replied, his gaze revealing interest as she walked to the kitchen with intent on arranging them in a vacant, over-sized beer mug she'd spotted a few moments earlier. As she moved along, she found herself catching his amused stare. He obviously intrigued her, and her smile openly revealed this fact as she fussed with the flowers, and silently watched him.

Originally from Nova Scotia, twenty-two year old Jonas Reagan Crosby had spent the last four years in the Royal Navy as a Radio Seaman, stationed on Canada's Vancouver Island. He'd recently received an honorable discharge, and had lost no time traveling to Ottawa in search of employment in the field of Automatic Machinist, of which he held a Masters. It was obvious he knew his mind, as well as where he wanted to be, and this intrigued Willow even further for she had always been taken with a man who was in control of his life; the very opposite of the way she was in her own. They had a wonderful time that night, discussing anything and everything until the wee hours of the morning. Willow found Jonas delightfully exciting, and ultimately hard to leave, but her life was in another place, and even though she realized this discerning factor, she would never forget this incredible night.

It is said time flies when you're having fun. Willow could certainly attest to that old adage for the weekend was almost over; it would soon be time to leave for the train. She knew her dad would be anxiously waiting to hear all about her adventure, just like he always did when it came to anything she ever did; still she didn't want this weekend to end. It had been delightful. It was everything she had hoped it would be. Jonas Crosby was everything she had hoped *he* would be. He was polite, gentle, interesting, in fact she found him fascinating in every possible way.

She had no sooner donned her coat, having already buttoned her son's, when the phone rang. Will answered in his jovial fashion and spoke for a moment while his playful eyes traveled to Willow's, but the spark in his voice soon faded, along with the smile on his face, and as it did Willow's heart skipped a beat. Will's face held a somber look as he held the receiver toward his cousin, and said, "It's for you, Low. It's David." She instinctively knew that something was wrong by the fact that he had referred to her brother by his given name. She also knew she should take the call, yet shook her head in denial. "Low, you better talk to him. Come on," Will coaxed, but she still refused, until he demanded, "Take the call, Willow, you have to talk to him," and pressed the receiver into her trembling hand.

Willow knew her mouth opened but was certain nothing came out, yet it mattered not that her voice appeared frozen, for her ears heard her brother announce their father's death perfectly. The universe stopped revolving. The room darkened around her. Will quickly embraced her, trying his best to support her for her legs had completely given way. She could hear Benny crying, yet couldn't go to him. In the confusion of the moment his young mind could not understand what was happening, only that his mother was lying on the sofa, barely breathing. He cried harder, and laid his little head upon her stomach while his small hands tried in vain to comfort her. Jonas, his impassioned eyes full of concern, knelt beside the sofa.

"Willow, everything is going to be alright," he said in a soothing tone while stroking her chestnut hair. "I'll stay with you, and I won't leave. Everything will be fine. I'll take care of you and Benny, don't worry. I realize you don't really hear me at the moment, but that's okay. You just rest. I'll take care of everything. I promise."

Chapter 6

DOWNHILL SPIRAL

Twenty nine years had passed since the train carried Willow and her son to Ottawa that cold, frigid morning. They had passed quickly, as Willow, now fifty-four years of age, stood thinking about them, shaking her head in dismay with the realization of just how fast they had actually passed. "Where did they go?" she wondered, for so much had happened since that long ago day. She could still remember the excitement they felt as the train pulled away from the station while they waved goodbye to her father, standing on the platform, fading into the distance. Sadness gripped her heart as that image now engulfed her mind, for how was she to know it would be the last time she would ever see him alive. No-one can change the course that is set before them, and fate awaits each and every one of us, whether it is good or bad, and as Willow's mind regressed to that time long past, she couldn't help wondering that if she had it to do again, would she change anything? But it was something she could not answer. That was a question no-one could.

The early years with Jonas Crosby had been some of the best in her life. As she thought about them, a smile tugged the corners of her mouth, flourishing into a full blown-laugh the more she dwelled upon it, for though they could scrap like wildcats, the one thing he could always do was make her smile, and no one had ever touched her so tenderly, or with as much passion; the irony presently facing her was the fact that he would no longer touch her at all. The more her mind dwelled on the way they had once been, the more she could taste the intensity of bitter-sweetness growing in the back of her throat. They had once been strong, young adults, taking on the world at a time when anything seemed possible, whether it was attainable or not. They were happy. They were in love. Times were good.

One of their happiest moments had been realized in 1975 with the birth of their son, whom Willow named Shay Reagan, and even though they would never meet, she knew her father would be pleased with the name she'd chosen. This thought always summoned tears, but it was her way of honoring the man whose unconditional love had taught her so much. She inched through her elegant living room, letting her eyes drink deep of its tasteful, welcoming décor, wondering how she and Jonas - who would have walked to the ends of the earth for one another - could drift so far apart, but they had. The blue damask walls reflected the mood she felt as she paused in reflection of it all. Somewhere throughout this lengthy journey, they had forgotten the way it had felt along the way, let alone in the beginning. She let her memory travel back to the way his knowing fingers enticed her lower lips. The way they had encased his rock-hard penis while it thrust within her, climbing fully into her welcoming chamber until it was lost in total climax, surplus cum oozing from her encompassed vagina as he withdrew, only to rise again. Many nights they made love until sunrise, when tireless energy would kick in to carry them through another busy day as they diligently pulled together, moving ever closer toward their goals. "Why has this all come to an end?" she thought, and as these memories saturated her mind she strolled from one area to the next, feeling the loss, the loss of a life she had cherished. It was all there, lined in perfect rows upon the mantel, pictures of their children, pictures of Jonas himself, pictures of them all together, each a reminder of a life now over.

It had reached its long awaited climax in the form of a doubled-fist barely missing Willow's delicate chin, while she adamantly, yet foolishly stood her ground, feeling the wind of her husband's hard-knuckled thrust slap her face with nightmarish reality to the present situation. Willow may have been many things, but stupid was not one of them. She knew she would lose this battle should she retaliate in any way, but far worse than the loss of her front teeth was the sobering realization it might well be her life. "How could it have come to this?" she wondered. "Where did we go wrong? More importantly, where did I go wrong?" She tried in vain to reason with him, but his ability to reciprocate had closed like a steel trap upon a helpless victim, and regardless of what she said he would not be reached. Instead he let his fist do his talking. Nothing was worth that, and definitely no man.

From the time of early childhood Willow's mother had taught her to stand up for herself regardless of the outcome. 'Any woman who would let a man walk all over her is nothing more than a spineless jellyfish,' her mother would state on occasion as she drove her well-meaning point home. The irony was that somewhere within the previous moments Willow's terrified mind could swear it heard her mother's voice emitting those same imperative words. But her giver of life had never faced impending death at the hands of the man who vowed to love her come what may, but could no longer stand the sight of her and would willingly remove her face if she dared move against him.

WILLOW'S WALK

Their once cheerful dining room held no comfort as they stood glaring, grimacing faces set in stone, and Willow feeling as if her feet were set in quick-drying cement. Where was the gentle, compassionate friend she once knew? How could someone, whom she had lived with for so many years, become a total stranger — worse still a terrifying attacker? It was inconceivable, yet regardless of these thoughts her feet remained clued to the well-polished floor, awaiting the final blow. "What's keeping him?" she thought in silence, though inwardly grateful for the reprieve afforded her, as she further thought; "Could there possibly be one measure of my former lover still hidden deep within what now stands before me, unable to do me in?" She stood fast, holding her head high in the knowledge she was the mother of their two sons, grandmother of their three grandchildren, but no longer keeper of his heart. But she wasn't to know what had caused him to reconsider his prior intention, because he suddenly whirled around, and stomped out of the room. Willow remained still, watching him go, while rivers of relief slid down her pale cheeks and dripped upon the floor. As fear crowded her insides, the tell-tale moisture falling from her eyes displayed the emotion of a dying love in its final throe. Their marriage was dead. They had just managed to kill it completely.

With remorse in her heart, Willow somehow found her way to her cold bed and silently lay upon it, no longer thinking, or crying, only existing. The morning would surely come with the rising of the sun, just like it had countless days prior, but regardless of whether it shone or not it no longer mattered, for the world she had known for so many years had just been blown apart, now all that remained was the numerous chunks of fallout. She knew life continues despite death - she learned that wrenching lesson years earlier - and though her father's untimely death had happened twenty nine years prior, in her mind it always remained yesterday, though in actuality had only happened a few months prior to her marriage to Jonas. Now, like the painful steps that had followed her father's death, she would again pull up her boot straps, and walk on.

The bed held little comfort as she stretched her slender body full length upon her back, snuggling beneath its pink satin sheets, wondering if Jonas was finding any notion of warmth within the guest bed directly above. She could hear him moving, tattletale springs gave it away, and she couldn't help noticing just how *much* he was stirring. "No doubt he's as wound up as I am," she pondered in thought, while tired eyes stared blankly at the ceiling, wishing she could will her tortured thoughts deep into his mind. An eternity passed before the night slowly opened to bleak daylight, peering through lace-draped windows, announcing the arrival of her first official morning alone. On a normal day she would rise, stretch, and amble out to the coffeemaker to enjoy her first cup of the morning stimulant of which Jonas always had waiting in the kitchen - sometimes within their bed - but not this morning. Instead she rolled onto her back, embracing a solid body pillow between her arms and legs. Her marriage may be dead, but her sexual desires where anything but, and as ludicrous as it may seem, she found herself craving his touch, but knew it would be quite some time before she'd let anyone in her bed again, let alone within her. A long sigh escaped her throat as she scrunched her knees into her tummy, and let her desires turn to dreams.

She slowly awoke to find herself positioned on her back with her husband's intense eyes ogling her satin-draped outline in the same exotic way he had so many times prior. Many was the night she would be awakened to a lustful organism, the satisfying result of which was brought about by her husband's unique ability to finger-fuck her until she pleaded for him to fully enter her, and ride her until they cried-out in unbridled ecstasy upon climax. It was the only joy she found in his choice to work night shift.

"What the hell!" she thought in surprise, immediately retreating against the headboard. Clutching the sheet against her, she said, "What do you think you're doing?"

"Nothing," he replied flatly, though his eyes stared boldly at her covered clit. "I just came in to get my work clothes."

Returning his accusing stare, she awkwardly pulled herself into a sitting position, and asked, "How long have you been standing there?" but her inquisitive glare could not remain locked with his and instantly fell away. Jonas said nothing, instead turned to open the closet door. He stepped inside but quickly reappeared with a fresh navy uniform in his hand. Laying it upon the mattress, he stooped down to open a drawer beneath the bed, but as he did she thought she heard him mumble something obscene, and in an impertinent tone, she said, "I beg your pardon?"

"What?" he coldly inquired as he resumed his prior position.

"I asked what you just now said," she answered, her nervous fingers pressing the glossy fabric against her bare chest in a protective manner.

Firing an obstinate glare her way, he bluntly replied, "I didn't say anything *really* ... least nothing worth repeating ... besides it doesn't matter any longer," then he turned and walked out the door.

How she hated that! He always did that whenever he wanted to piss her off, and knowing the mood she'd be in after the previous night made it that much worse, for she wondered what he actually did say, or whether she even cared enough to be bothered. Yet she was. She also had a fantastic memory, and the thoughts from last night still left a bitter taste in her mouth, but at least it was only a fictional taste; not actual dried blood. She was just in the act of rising when he returned.

"I'm leaving as soon as I take a shower and I won't be back," he coldly stated. "This is nuts, and it can't go on. It's gone on far too long as it is so, whatever you have to say, you can say to my lawyer. I've decided to take his advice and leave. I'll send for my things later."

Willow sat in utter silence. She knew it was over last night, but his present words just clarified it. What kind of reply could she offer? There may have been a hundred words to be said, argued — screamed, but for what, and to what end? But it no longer mattered, for she too had come to the end of the line, and as he was making the final move it meant she didn't have to, but it also meant she would be the one left behind, again. For an elongated moment she felt as if she'd been thrown into an instant replay of a scene played-out nineteen years earlier. That may have been a different scenario, but the present hurt was fully as bad – if not worse – because since that time they had managed to forge another nineteen links into the marriage chain. It was almost beyond reproach. She may have fallen out of love with him, but there was still something alive, begging to be heard. She was certain he felt it too; how could he not? But they had crossed the line where once you do there's no turning back, so she said nothing, but her heart said plenty.

The shower sprayed away as she lay in dead silence, not saying a word, but thinking just how empty, used, and tossed away he made her feel, much in the way a forgotten toy which no-longer gives enjoyment must feel. She had felt that way the first time he left, and now she found history repeating itself, but like before, she would survive. It wouldn't be easy this time, for she had gained nineteen years and had lost a good portion of her youth and vitality. As she sat thinking about these added strikes she couldn't help but wonder how she'd manage. "Where there's a will there's a way," she said aloud, just as the shower ceased. The decision to forge ahead alone had been made, but it was not merely her choice; it was the final choice they had both made. Now they must live with it.

A few agonizing moments passed before the bathroom door opened. As it did, Willow slid beneath the sheets like a turtle withdrawing into its protective shell. But she need not have, for her husband never entered the room, and she was left in an onslaught of tears when the front door finally closed. He was gone, along with the marriage. Twenty nine years of her life was gone. Now she would face alone however many more awaited her. The lingering seconds stretched to minutes as she found herself remembering feelings of nineteen years earlier. How extremely present they now felt. But she was no longer the same woman, and even though the situation was different the pain remained the same. One would think it too would change - at least to some degree - grow older – better - yet if it changes in any way it is to grow worse, and she somehow sensed it would grow far worse.

The afternoon sky was even darker than the morning had been as she sipped her dish-water coffee, and let her puffy eyes study an ominous cloud building in the west. She sighed in disgust, figuring it wouldn't be long before snow again flew past her windows to pile even more whiteness upon the ever-growing mounds out front.

"Guess it's not that bad, is it?" she questioned herself aloud. "No, guess not … at least it keeps the drab covered up," she answered, chuckling in surprise with the realization she was carrying on a conversation with herself. Maybe it wasn't as bad as it seemed, for she found herself half decent company, and one thing was certain, if the conversation ever got a bit out of hand she could always end it. She liked that idea, for like her mother she relished the last word and would gamble anything to get it.

She no sooner stepped into the kitchen when the storm hit full-on. Listening to the voices speak within its driving force, she found herself recalling her latest thought, wondering if she hadn't inherited her mother's ability to argue tooth and nail then maybe she wouldn't be in the present predicament. The known reality of this might well be proving true, for she was now reaping the bitter rewards of this unfortunate habit, but on the other hand the best trait inherited from her mother was her fierce independence, and as her mind deciphered this she already knew the answer without need to delve deeper. The difficult part was taking that first, unknown step. Still, regardless of how complex it was, she would somehow take it.

The coffee had grown cold. As it passed her lips her facial expression voiced her displeasure toward the ill-tasting brew, but this neglect of her beverage happened often, even when Jonas brewed his delicious blend. His sterling touch made Willow decide not to learn the delicate art of brewing Columbia's famous treat, he always did it, and he enjoyed doing it, so she let him. One might think it easy - it certainly isn't rocket science - but it takes the correct application to achieve proper balance and perfection, still, regardless of what it took, Jonas certainly had it. His wife, on the other hand did not, and the sorry remains found their way down the drain. As the last bit seeped away it suddenly dawned upon her that learning to properly brew coffee was the least of what she'd have to master. A half-hearted laugh escaped her throat when she gazed at the pot, resting triumphantly upon its moorings as if it were mocking her inability. Oh how she longed for a decent cup of coffee, but she knew it wasn't to happen that day.

A sudden gust of wind wailed around the back of the house like a banshee in flight, causing her to whirl around and gape out the window, eyes wide in fright. When it finally eased back, she realized her fingers were caught in a death-grip upon the silk lapels of her unforgiving robe, while her eyes watched the driving snow fiercely lash her favorite tree. How frigid it looked. It even appeared to quiver, as if it was actually shivering, causing her to feel the same bone-wrenching chill it must be experiencing as the frost crept deep within its sleeping bark. She couldn't help but feel sorry for it, why it almost appeared to summon her attention. She moved closer to get a better look, but as she did her reflection in the windowpane stared back, revealing something she wished she'd never seen. She could not believe the pitiful creature she'd become, so small, thin, so incredibly frail. She realized the last few years would had taken their toll, but she hadn't truly looked at herself in a very long time, yet as she did, she couldn't help but be moved to tears when she witnessed what she'd become. "Is this how Jonas sees me?" she thought with despair. Had things deteriorated to the point where she had deteriorated right along with them? Maybe it was no wonder he left. But how could he walk away from that pitiful atrocity living in the windowpane? "That's not me," she thought aloud. "It just can't be."

Chapter 7

INTRODUCTION TO DESTRUCTION

One morning in mid-January of 2003, a frenzied blanket of white swirled past the kitchen window as if it were doing its utmost to obliterate the entire back yard. Willow stared-out at her sleeping garden, wishing she too was as fast asleep as the frozen landscape she so dearly loved. Her hands clutched her favorite cup, and as her eyes fell upon it, a smile touched her lips when she fondly remembered the Valentine's Day when she had received it as a gift. She could still envision her eldest son Ben, rushing through the front door of their low-rent townhouse with a wide smile upon his face, his hands clutching a white ceramic coffee cup filled to the brim with red and white roses surrounded with lace ferns, all of which were dwarfed by a silver heart-shaped tinsel balloon bobbing gaily above. But what had caught her eye the most was that of a colorful adornment painted on the vessel of two red teddy bears engaged in a tender embrace. How sweet it was, and how thoughtful her son had been to remember his mother that special day, for Jonas had again forgotten to remember his wife.

She sighed with fondness; mist clouding her eyes as she sipped her morning coffee from this same cup. She had to admit the java wasn't too bad; she even finished it and decided to pour another. Over the past year she had learned to do many things, some rather well. "It still doesn't taste quite like his, but it's gaining," she thought aloud, still her best companion, now astute critic. She continued her window vigil, pondering what to do, and feeling thankful it was her day off so she wouldn't have to battle the hazardous roads. The wind had again picked up as she lean against the counter, stirring her brew, and letting its intoxicating aroma fill her senses. Then with favorite cup in hand, she ascended the stairs to her private loft where her laden desk stood in wait, laboring beneath a stack of ever-growing bills.

The past year had not only been difficult for Willow by way of menial chores having to be learned, it had also brought enormous amount of anxiety. Her husband's refusal of support until the marriage could be dissolved had brought her to the brink of a nervous breakdown. She even found herself wondering if that was his goal. But she would not be forced out of her home nomatter how much grief he threw her way. She may not hold his Machinist's Degree, but she had decided long ago that *she* would be the master of her destiny, not Jonas. She may have faced disappointments over the course of the year, but she also celebrated accomplishments, and the most significant was that of an old dial-up computer of which Jonas had left behind. She had become fairly knowledgeable about it, self-teaching herself the ins and outs and though far from the preverbal computer *geek*, the term used for someone who is proficient in every aspect of the field, she wasn't doing too badly. Trial and error had confronted her every step of the way, some resulting in costly repair, but she was determined to travel abroad, something in actuality she had always wanted to do yet whose luxury could never be afforded. Since funds for that – anything else for that matter - were non-existent she could still travel to exotic destinations via the Net, the abbreviated term for the world renowned *Internet*.

Jonas, before his untimely departure, had spent countless hours upon this technological marvel, seeking pleasure, or simply spending time. Willow often wondered if it was for the entertainment it provided, or a plausible excuse to be away from her, but regardless of the answer, she found herself resenting its constant occupation of his attention. Still as much as she resented it she had to admit that she too found the infernal machine intriguing; so much so that during the increasing time spent alone found herself navigating its interesting pathways with as much interest as her husband had enjoyed. "And why not?" she would often ask herself as she settled before its beckoning screen during the evenings Jonas was at work.

As the lonely nights wore on she'd board the cyber-jet to numerous destinations of choice, some exotic, some intriguing, but all entertaining. There were times she would surf briefly, other times her attention would be captivated for hours, which annoyed family and friends alike because they could never reach her via the phone, for the line was always engaged supplying her latest Net-fix. But just as world travelers have desired places to visit, so did Willow, the only difference was her journey was made from the comfort of home. One particular *site* of choice was dedicated to a favorite celebrity where she could check out the endless supply of gossip, or sigh in awe at the latest photographs captured by the relentless paparazzi. Numerous times she would simply don a disguise and sign into the site's chat room. As time went on she befriended a few who habited this chat, no doubt seeking a friend to talk with in the same innocent manner as she.

Snow presently pelted the back dormer as Willow sat at her desk, writing checks on a badly over-drawn account, yet bills must be paid, regardless if it leaves enough funds with which to purchase food. It had become a relentless merry-go-round, but she refused to knuckle under, so she continued her juggling act until day faded to night. But the loss of daylight was never mourned, for the illicit cover of darkness provided a refuge where she could find solace on the other side of the computer screen. Many people came and went, very much like they do in a one on one situation where you might stop to chat with a friend at the local Mall, have a few laughs then carry on until you meet another familiar face. The only difference between the two is the ability to actually touch in the flesh.

The storm raged on as Willow fixed a peanut butter sandwich accompanied by a soothing cup of Chamomile, and then upon return to her desk, settled comfortably into her chair before the lifeless screen. It wasn't long before the computer's delightful song was heard signaling life within. "Now what will it be tonight?" she thought in amusement as her hand guided the mouse across cyber universe. The first click led her on a wild goose chase - so it appeared - for nothing seemed of interest. "Oh no, have I finally grown weary of cyber-space?" she thought in animosity, while she laughed, certain her family would be ecstatic - if only they knew - yet she was certain it was only a matter of time before something of interest revealed itself, and she was right.

An impulse to check out her favorite site would prove to be one that would lead her down the most destructive path to date. Had she only the foresight to what was waiting she might better have gone to bed, but the wild child of her youth still dwelled deep within her, not to mention the carnal needs of a woman without a man. The site opened, but rather than just mill about endless photographs and interviews viewed countless times, she decided to pop into the chat room to see who might be there. The familiar blue screen opened, and she immediately scrutinized the list of names, the majority of which she had spoken with numerous times, but tonight there appeared a new one. In all honesty one could never be sure of the identification a person would use. Often times it had no connection whatsoever with the person using it, and Willow had come to learn that most everyone, herself included, used an identity of which they may or may not be, but rarely did they use their own. This made perfect sense, if not common sense, because this was the Internet, the way the world now communicated where anyone could be whoever or whatever they chose to be. No one would be the wiser, for how could they be found out when no one knew who they actually were, unless you told them. This was the main reason Willow donned the persona of *Left in Limbo* and never used her real name, nor rarely spoke with anyone who did. However this night the rules would be tested when she found herself intrigued by the newest name taking great pleasure in the usual female conversations, yet in-fact was a male, using the persona *Dream Come True*.

One might say he had come from nowhere, appearing instantly among the regulars, and stirring up great commotion among the ladies. He appeared polite, something unheard of in this day and age, and definitely not put into practice in a place like this. He was a refreshing addition to the usual fare, never failing to enlighten the sometimes heated conversation with daring input. This often ruffled the feathers of the resident males, who fancied themselves cocks of the walk among the assorted ladies that kept appearing nightly. A good time was assured whenever the name *Dream Come True* signed in, and it would not be long before someone would bombard him with questions, some of which enticed bold answers. Not much escaped him - not even Willow - who now found herself looking forward to his name appearing in the nightly lineup.

WILLOW'S WALK

A couple of enjoyable weeks passed with Willow signing-in nightly along with *Dream*. They both participated in jovial discussions, the topics ranging from A to Z, none of which found *Dream* encountering difficulty in the slightest. He had no problem holding his own, in-fact the more in depth the topic, the more insightful his comments, and no-matter who posed a challenge he was up for the cause, showing no worry in the slightest that he may faultier. This delightful fare continued for a few more nights. Once in awhile the mysterious *Dream* would take part in a conversation Willow would be having, as she did her best to keep up with the fray. One night, while the words appeared on-screen faster than rapid gunfire, Willow was swept *upstairs*, a term used in chat rooms where one instantly finds them self within a private chat-box separate from the main discussion area. It is often used when two people wish to speak in private - supposedly only after an invite to do so has been accepted - yet before she realized what was happening, she found herself in a one on one with the charming *Dream Come True*.

Chapter 8

THE MIGHTY QUINN

Declan Eamon Quinn was a strapping, nineteen-year-old rugby captain from Ireland's beautiful coastal city of Galway, heir to Quinn Distilleries Incorporated, and the youngest son of the town's wealthiest family. Though young in years his thoughts and practices were well advanced beyond them. He was a likeable sort, always looking for a good time, whether it was hanging out in the local pub with mates, or flirting with the staggering line of young ladies falling at his feet. There was no deigning he loved to be where he felt special. This was not merely because he belonged to the town's wealthiest family and could buy any one of them as much as they wished to drink, but simply because he was consistently trying to prove he was just one of them. But in actuality, he was a very troubled, lonely, young man.

The youngest of four rough and tumble boys, Declan could often be found smack-dab in the middle of many Galway fights of which he usually reigned supreme, though in all fairness one never knew if he actually did win, or if the opponent simply let him. He was proud and arrogant which often got him into trouble more times than he cared to mention. Many was the night he would down one too many in the local pub of which left him loud and obnoxious, yet he wouldn't be suppressed, and not many tried for everyone knew what to expect, and not many wished to wear his anger upon their jaw. Still when push came to shove they'd fight back, often finding themselves victorious in their plight, but only until the Quinn brothers came looking for their youngest sibling. It was then all hell would break loose. Bloodied teeth would fly along with handfuls of hair. Bones would get broken as the Malay continued, that is until the local police arrived to crack a few skulls while bringing those responsible to justice.

On many occasion, Declan, along with his brothers, faced the music after having paid restitution for the establishment they ruined. But the youngest Quinn was more prone to reprimand, which landed him on the wrong side of the law more than any of his brothers, but because of his tender age jail time would often be relinquished; instead applied through hours of community work. This even bothered him, for as much as he loved a rousing donnybrook; he cared more about the sullied reputation it was bringing him as one who loved escaping retribution. He may have had a short fuse, but it was equally balanced by a tender, gentle heart, especially when he wished to show it. In many ways he was a kind boy, generous to a fault – if he liked you – the problem was he didn't find many that he did.

He'd grown up getting his way most of the time, which compared to the majority, might have contributed to his massive ego and overly inflated image. The exact reason for this might be attributed to just about anything. Possibly an irrepressible amount of illness as a child - he'd certainly had his share - or it might have been the fact that he was the apple of his mother's eye. This of course did not sit well with his siblings, for regardless of what he did, in her eyes he could do no wrong, therefore got his way when he otherwise should not have. Yet none of these factors provide an acceptable excuse for an inflated ego, accompanied by an abundance of attitude and arrogance, because as he grew, so did the idea that whatever you do, be it right or wrong, money will buy your way. By the time he came along the family's wealth had reached lavish proportions and he, being the youngest, was born into a life most people can only read about. Suffice it to say that if Declan's rose-colored outlook failed him in any way, it could be attributed to the department of personal revenue, and the pitfalls which that can bring about.

The name Quinn was well known in Galway. The family's history stretched back as far as the city itself. It was also a name to be reckoned with, for not only was it known for toughness, it was known for extreme measures in diligence. Shamus Quinn, Declan's great grandfather, founded the area's first distillery which primarily brewed its liquor from the juice of pressed potatoes. It was handed down to his son; Darcy-Shamus, who carried on his father's brewing tradition while expanding the distillery to accommodate the addition of fine lagers and ales. The town flourished in size and population, and with it grew *Quinn Distilleries Incorporated.* As Galway became known worldwide for its exportation of exquisite oysters, the name Quinn became known for the finest spirits money good buy. Though deteriorating health plagued him, Darcy overseen the daily production, carrying on his father's personalized touch while working grueling hours teaching the business to his two sons; James, and Derek, the latter being Declan's father.

Derek Quinn was indeed a wild Irishman. No moss gathered upon his black patent leather boots as he kicked up his heels at the local dances – one in particular – where he met the feisty Cailen Cathlain O'Brian, the woman of his dreams. She was the most striking lass he'd yet to lay eyes upon, with flowing chestnut hair, and skin the color of alabaster, but the one feature in which he could never get enough of was her striking eyes of ocean-blue. They found their way into his heart, capturing his very soul. Derek and Cailen married, and as the years rolled by their blissful union produced four sons: Derek Jr., Daniel, Delaine, and Declan. They were a happy, tight knit family, but this happiness would soon change.

One bright morning in late June 1989, Derek kissed his wife goodbye, and headed off to work in his usual, high-stepping, grandiose manner, whistling a Celtic melody, as he danced out the door. Cailen stood at the mansion's front entrance, watching him finish his jig, leap into his silver sports car like a man possessed, and roar down the lengthy tree-lined drive. She continued her vigil long after he'd disappeared, until her concentration was broken by two of her sons roaring past with the slender nanny scurrying behind, trying her best to corral them to the breakfast room for their morning meal.

"Matilda, could ye be not speaking to me boys so harshly?" Cailen questioned in her jovial Irish lit, just as her youngest came thundering through the foyer, eyes wide with terror, shouting, *"Mummy, oh, Mummy, there be a clown!"*

"There-there," Cailen soothed, "hush now, precious one, and don't be fretting so. Mummy be right here."

The boy's wide eyes remained locked upon his mother as he pushed against her, whimpering, his hands clinging tightly to her green silk skirt and twisting the smooth material within his long, slender fingers, but no matter how much she soothed him, he would not stop quivering. He appeared extremely nervous, and the more she tried comforting him, the more he refused to be calmed.

"Mummy, the clown ... the clown's going to get me! Don't let him!" he screamed, now cowering behind his mother's legs.

"I really do feel that child is far too nervous about the slightest thing, Mrs. Quinn," Matilda Prichard remarked in her stiff English accent as she smoothed a recent crease on the skirt of her drab navy suit.

"Aye, Matlida," the Quinn matriarch stated boldly, "that may very well be, but 'tis not for ye to be worrying on. Furthermore I would be appreciating it if ye not be speaking with such a course tongue round me Declan. He cannot be helping that he gets as nervous as he does." It was frightfully obvious that she wished the subject changed as she held the little fellow to her stomach, stroking his thick black hair, as she asked, "How be the other children doing with their breakfast?"

Prichard, lending the appearance as one whose patience had been stretched to the limit, stiffly replied, "They've finished their meal and have left to prepare for class. I was just coming to fetch the young master as he hasn't eaten as yet, and he too must ready himself. Mrs. Donnigen is keeping his plate in the warmer, but you cannot expect her to hold it indefinitely. You *know* how she gets if her schedule is thrown off in the slightest. Now do come along, Master Declan," but as she proceeded to step toward the quivering boy, he shouted, *"Clowns today, Mummy! No! I don't want to go!"*

No sooner had he completed this outburst when his ocean-blue eyes darkened to indigo, and he fainted dead away, collapsing against his startled mother.

"Declan!" she gasped, proceeding to drag him across the great foyer to a satin-covered settee. Laying him upon it, she awkwardly glanced toward the nanny and in a displeased manner, stated, "Yur assistance could well be used, Matilda," and immediately retrieved a vile of smelling salts from her skirt pocket, and proceeded to wave it beneath the boy's nostrils.

His eyes popped opened, and in a sad tone, he whimpered, "Da is gone away now. The bad clown came."

"What silly nonsense is he speaking?" Prichard questioned in an agitated tone, staring over the horn-rimmed glasses pinching her elongated nose.

The little boy repeated himself, but just as the strange statement crossed his trembling lips the telephone rang, causing the staunch nanny to hurry toward it, catching it on its third ring. "Quinn residence, Matilda Prichard here, may I ask who is ringing?" but as she intently listened the color drained from her face, and she swiftly motioned her employer toward the phone.

Continuing to stroke the boy's hair, Cailen inquired, "Would ye come and sit with me boy, Matilda?" then proceeded to the phone. "Hello? Ye must speak up!" she demanded. "Aye, this be she ... Me husband? What about me husband? I'm sorry, but I not be understanding — blast the noise! What are ye to be saying? There seems to be interference on the line and I not be able to hear — What's that? What be this about me husband? I be begging yur pardon, but what are ye to be telling me? *What?* He ... He be ... *Oh!* ... Saints above! *No!*"

Her agonized scream pierced the silence. Dropping the polished receiver upon the marble floor, she bolted straight for Declan. The other children, upon hearing the sudden commotion, rushed into the foyer. They may have been children, but the second they saw their mother's ashen face they knew something was terribly wrong. She sat before them, struggling to hold her emotions in tact all the while searching for a way to inform them. How could she tell them what she had just learned? Where in Heaven's name could she find the proper words when she couldn't even find them for herself? She took a few moments to gather her thoughts, but time was running out for they inched closer.

"What is it, Ma?" the two eldest inquired in unison.

Clutching Declan to her breast, Cailen sat with her back as straight as the pain in her body would allow. She must tell them, but her voice had left her. Her lost eyes traveled about the handsome foyer until they came to rest upon the tall oak doors. She couldn't help but recall the dance her husband did on that very spot before departing for work that morning. She must gather herself. She must breath. She must be strong.

Taking a labored breath, she said, "Boys, that call just now be about yur da. I-I need to be telling all of ye that … that he be in a terrible car crash and … and I must go where they be taken him. Ye must be staying with Miss Prichard, and I'll be returning as soon as I can." She stopped to locate what bit of breath she'd managed to summon but was no longer sure there was any left. Finally she continued, "Now while I be away, I need ye all to be watching over Declan. He be having another of his spells – just like yur da." Her tear-drenched eyes looked upon each son as she motioned them to gather round, and as she gently embraced each one, she said, "I must be telling ye something and … and it be the most difficult thing I have 'err to do." One more breath - she was running on reserve now - emotions engulfing her mind, as she softly uttered, "Yur da did not survive the crash. He be killed instantly."

Money can buy many things, but it cannot buy life, and regardless of the amount one might acquire, it may as well be nothing, for the entire Quinn fortune could not replace what had been lost that day, and in the blink of an eye, Cailen, and her four sons, were left without a husband and father. For a moment no one said a word. They just stood, staring blankly, eyes not really focusing yet moisture still welling within. Cailen held young Declan to her breast, embracing him, almost as if she were preparing to nurse him like she had when he was an infant, the way she had with all her boys. At that moment she couldn't help but remember each of them in that respect, as her eyes looked imploringly into theirs, one son at a time. Ironically it brought her comfort to do this, comfort in a time that only these children could provide - *their children* – the children she and Derek had conceived through their immense love for each other. Now the children were are all that was left of it. Still, with all the pain she felt, Cailen knew her husband would never be gone. He would continue to live within their sons, one in particular.

Chapter 9

CAILEN – THE RESULT OF STRONG IRISH STOCK

The day of the funeral was, as expected, the most difficult time for all concerned. Cailen would not allow weakness, and though she was dying inside, would not reveal it, nor would she allow it to be shown by her sons, especially the elder ones. They stood side by side, as if in regimented line, accepting heartfelt condolences from a line of well-wishers that stretched on endlessly. Cailen, her sons, the nanny, and the housekeeper, soberly took their seats before the closed casket. The service had no sooner begun than little Declan broke down in tears. Even though he was the youngest, his mother knew he sensed things far more deeply than her other boys. He was frail, and regardless of numerous tonics, and appetite stimulants, he remained pale, and anemic.

The service wore on, never seeming to end. It was sheer torture for the Quinn family yet they would endure. The priest carried on his speech about life, sin, and death as though he were campaigning for public office. One would think he would have dwelled a little more on the living, let alone the family who was now left without its guiding light, instead of the one direction he was determined to lead the congregation down. Derek Quinn had been a wealthy man, but he never failed to give of himself nor his love. He adored his family, never once letting the chance escape to reassure them of this one simple fact. His wealth had provided them anything they could desire, yet the most important things in life are things that no amount of money can provide, and Derek had made certain each of them received as much of this as he could possibly give. The priest spoke not of this, but of the spiritual part of Derek's life as though that was the only subject of importance. Maybe all we achieve or give of ourselves in life counts not for the place awaiting us in death, but if angels really do exist by virtue, then Derek Quinn had definitely earned his wings of gold.

The service finally ground to its anticipated halt, and the bereaved family followed in their own limousine behind the gleaming black hearse. The long-winded priest, no-doubt anticipating another rousing performance at the graveside, may have been a bit miffed, for it was cut short at Cailen's insistence. She was a devout Catholic, but she'd had enough and she knew her children - especially her youngest - could not stand much more. It was stifling hot. The sun blazed unmercifully upon those present, while the hapless chauffeurs, hoping to provide shelter for the weeping family, dutifully held umbrellas above them. But the umbrellas were black, which allowed the sweltering heat to penetrate even further, yet it must be endured, for everyone knows that black is the official color of death. A slight breeze afforded them a much welcomed reprieve, but only temporarily, for it left as quickly as it had come, but not before young Declan began to crumble.

Prichard immediately encased him within her grasp as she stood erect, refusing to show any form of weakness.

"Stand fast, young master," she quietly remarked, doing her best to support his sagging form. But nothing escaped Cailen's astute eyes, and neither did this.

"Is he to be alright, Matilda?"

"We are holding our own, Mrs. Quinn!"

"I ask ye to be bringing him to me now," Cailen instructed while extending her strong arms.

But the determined nanny continued her task, as she remarked, "Mrs. Quinn, you have enough on your mind without the addition of more. I am perfectly capable of handling this situation, and I will prevail!" Quickly retrieving a tiny vile of smelling salts from the left pocket of her tweed suit, she waved it beneath the nostrils of the semi-conscious boy. The pungent smell swiftly brought him to awareness, just as his wide-eyed mother proceeded to snatch him from her grasp in a determined attempt to not be out done. "Thank ye kindly for yur merciful aid to me wee boy, Matilda," the Quinn matriarch firmly remarked, "but I be taking him now!"

Cailen had been raised within an unpretentious family, but the life of a wealthy man is viewed in a far different way than one who is poor. Cailen knew this, and though she never celebrated the life of wealth, as such, she still acknowledged what it stood for, as well as her husband's hard work to realize it. Her arms supported her son, holding him upright while the long-winded priest put the finishing touches on his condensed service, yet her attention no longer remained upon the words emitting from the crimson-nosed papist, but rather on her pallid boy. At that moment she couldn't believe how alike to his father he actually was, and this recent spell only reinforced her worries, for Derek had been prone to them from the time he too had been a boy. Thinking about that, Cailen remembered how he would often bring her heart to her mouth with the way in which he drank, the speed he drove, and the reckless way he lived. She could never do much about that, but she could control Declan, and come hell or high water she would. She would somehow find a way to be both mother and father to all her boys, but as she left the cemetery her hand gripped that of her youngest tighter than she ever had before, as she smiled, and watched his huge eyes look about with innocence. Declan may have possessed her breathtaking eyes, but the soul of his father shone brightly within them.

Cailen O'Brian-Quinn had not come from money, but she was a strong woman, having come from solid Irish stock where times had been hard, yet never once did she give into the pressures it brought. Her happiest years had been spent with Derek and her four sons, and she vowed she would make her husband proud of the men they would one day become. She realized it would not be easy, for even with the mass fortune at her disposal, she'd had the foresight to realize that the fortune itself may be more of a burden than help.

Her childhood had been spent in the quaint village of Claddagh, located on the eastern shores of Galway Bay. It had been a tough life and many was the night when her belly ached for the want of something more, but there was nothing. Unfortunately this happened more often than she cared to remember, but even though her daily menu had been limited, she never once complained about it. She had remembered sitting at her desk in the one room schoolhouse she attended, learning about the great potato famine of the mid 1840's, when a million people died, and a million more found nothing but rot in their fields, and bare cupboards in their larder. It was the main reason so many left their homeland in search of a better life. But some stayed, determined to make a life. Among those were the Quinn and O'Brian families.

During the long evenings of her youth, Cailen would sit upon her grandfather's lap listening intently as he spun his tales of Irish folklore, and marveled when the leprechauns danced their merry jigs and reels while daring anyone to touch their magical pots of gold; for it was always said that if you could catch a leprechaun at the end of the rainbow he must then give up his treasure, but many was the time when Cailen would follow a newly-formed rainbow in search of the mystical little fairy, yet regardless of how far she traveled, the path would always end before the rainbow ever did. Her grandfather would laugh at her adventures, but never once did he fail to assure her of the love to be found within the stout walls of their thatched-covered abode. She could never listen to his spellbinding stories enough, and as he relayed them, her vivid imagination would carry her to the faraway places of which he spoke. She loved him dearly, but the stories he told of Ireland's great famine were ones she wished he would avoid, for they were heart-wrenching. He knew how she felt. Not only could he see it in her eyes as they gazed imploringly into his, he felt it, as she would snuggle in his lap and sob against his chest. These stories filled her mind with horrid images of death and starvation. She never forgot the wretched images he'd described, or the way they had made her feel, and though she had never been asked to endure her ancestor's plight, she was always mindful to never complain for the want of something more, and she never did. Instead she would listen with great interest each time he would reminisce about the O'Brian history. If anything it provided her with the knowledge of where she had come from, who had been born into her, and what she would one day pass on to her children.

Chapter 10

FIRST CHAT ENCOUNTER

Excitement ensued Willow's senses with the realization of who had pulled her *upstairs*. Though it was the first time with *Dream*, it wasn't her first time in the private chat, for she'd often found herself being hauled into a one on one with someone she wished would simply leave her be, for it made her feel like an unwilling pawn in a ridiculous mind game so many loved to play for their crude enjoyment. Still she always tried to be polite, that was the way she'd been raised, yet the majority - with the exception of a select few - didn't seem to know the meaning of the word. But *Dream Come True* appeared different, and even when the room's conversation became heated, he remained polite-fully respectful. Willow couldn't help noticing this unusual trait, and she often found herself smiling at his thoughtful comments and unique ability to speak his mind, injecting his views whenever he wished.

Suddenly the words *knock-knock* appeared on the screen; somewhat in the same fashion as if someone were rapping upon your front door. Willow typed a simple *hello*. The previous words again appeared but this time in a smaller screen which had suddenly appeared inside the first one. She typed her previous response on this screen, but still no response. She thought this dance most strange and again typed a response, but instead of a reply an information box appeared informing her that the required respondent had left the private chat. "Well, this is odd," she mused aloud, feeling a bit let down, but just as she proceeded to depart *Dream* reappeared, along with the words *knock-knock*. She couldn't help wondering what was going on yet quickly typed an inquiry all the while expecting him to leave, but delight consumed her when he simply typed *hello*, prompting an instant conversation.

Left in Limbo: *How are you?* These few words had actually caused a slight flutter within Willow's chest. She wasn't sure if she should have typed anything, yet she was somehow glad she did.
Dream Come True: *Is it alright if I chat with you?*
Left in Limbo: *Why wouldn't it be?* While typing this reply Willow couldn't help but think him extremely well-mannered.
Dream Come True: *Well I just thought that maybe you wouldn't want to converse with me.*
Left in Limbo: *Why would you say that? I'll talk with you; in fact I think it's nice that you want to talk to me.* As she typed she couldn't help thinking her choice of words somewhat redundant.
Dream Come True: *Of course I want to talk with you. I just wasn't sure whether you'd feel the same, but I'm glad you do.*
There was something about the way in which he phrased his words that made Willow realize he was sincere, and she found herself wanting to converse more, as she typed, *Oh really?*
Dream Come True: *Yes! I find you interesting. You don't seem like the others. You express yourself differently than they do and I find you interesting.*

His typing abruptly ceased, somewhat as if it had been strategically planned at this particular part of the conversation, leaving

Willow to ponder why she seemed to stand out from the rest, but there was something about his words which made her feel glad that she did, and she swiftly let her fingers express her thoughts. *I must say it's nice to finally meet somebody in here that likes to discuss all sorts of topics, not just the usual silly chit-chat. Do you know what I mean?*

Dream Come True: *Yeah I do. I get tired of that. A lot of the stuff they talk about gets boring after awhile, that's why I find you interesting. You don't seem to act like the rest. It's nice.*

His response brought a smile to Willow's lips, as she typed, *I suppose that might be because I'm so much older than they are; no doubt you too. How old are you, by the way?* She felt the need to know just in case this might turn out to be no different than any other time she'd been pulled to private chat.

Dream Come True: *19. You don't find me too young to converse with, do you?*

"Sweet Jesus!" Willow thought in sudden surprise, yet there was something about his directness that she couldn't help admiring. It appeared that he was trying to be honest. After-all he could have typed anything, but he hadn't, and he certainly seemed much older than a mere nineteen, as she typed, *Not at all, in fact I think it shows a sense of maturity on your part that you're so open and honest with me about your age.*

Dream Come True: *Why?*
Left in Limbo: *You could have typed any number. We're online here, you could have easily lied and I wouldn't be any the wiser, would I?*
Dream Come True: *Guess not. But I don't want you to get the wrong impression. How old are you, if you don't mind me asking?*

A coy smile pursed Willow's lips. She somehow felt he was apprehensive in asking what he just had. She also wondered that if she could actually see his face would it be blushing with anxiety, sort of like hers was doing. Again she admired his forthrightness, for the more they typed, the more she felt she might have finally found someone who cared enough about the person they were conversing with to actually get to know them, so she answered his question. She was not ashamed of it; in fact she was proud of what her maturing years had brought her, even if they now found her alone.

Dream Come True: *Cool. My mum's not much older than you.*

Left in Limbo: *Oh really, how old is she?* As Willow typed, the realization suddenly hit her that she was conversing with a man nine years younger than her youngest son. "This is ludicrous," she thought. There was a brief pause, maybe he was thinking. Willow couldn't help pondering a few thoughts of her own when his reply appeared on the screen. *My ma's 57, but she's really young for her age. Although she's kind of had it rough since my da died. I don't remember him that much.* Willow was positive that if he were standing before her he might need a hug, but her words were all she had, and she typed, *you don't have to tell me if you don't want to - though I do know what it feels like to lose your dad.* Sorrow instantly pierced her heart with the words just typed.

Dream Come True: *Yeah, it's tough. Ma tells me I'm a lot like him.*

Left in Limbo: *How's that? Are you like him in personality, or looks?* Willow was actually interested in the way he would answer, but for a few elongated moments he typed nothing, making her wonder if this topic might better be left alone. But just as she was about to type this thought his words flashed across the screen. *It's hard to say. Ma says I'm very much like him, but Mrs. Donnigan always tells me I'm my own person - though I do look like him, but I sometimes wish I didn't, y'know?*

Left in Limbo: *Why's that, if you don't mind me asking? By the way, who is the lady you just mentioned?* Willow was finding her interest increasing with each word he typed.

Dream Come True: *Na I don't mind. She's our housekeeper. She's really neat, been with us forever, she and Miss Prichard. Prichard's on staff too as our nanny and tutor. About my da, I just look like him. A couple of my bro's do as well, but Ma always says I remind her more of him than the rest. Sometimes I think I give her grief. I don't mean to, but I like to have fun.*

As *Dream* typed he surprisingly found himself feeling a kind of relief he'd never known. He wasn't exactly sure what it was, but this woman made him feel more at ease than he had ever felt; little did he know that Willow was feeling the same. Her life was in such turmoil, had been that way for a very long time, yet she actually found herself anticipating the next words he would type. She wasn't kept waiting, for his next sentence instantly appeared in the form of a question. *Where are you from?*
Left in Limbo: *Ottawa Canada. How about you?*
Dream Come True: *Galway.* He didn't type anything else, but Willow could not wait. *Well judging by the way you form some of your sentences it leads me to believe that would be in Ireland.* She suddenly felt foolish the second she'd finished the idiotic sentence, but there was no retrieving what had been typed.
Dream Come True: *Yes, miss.*
Willow sensed that he somehow felt amused at the insertion of her foot into her mouth, as she typed, *How nice. I've always wanted to go there. My ancestry is there.* She had rapidly typed these words in hope of reprieving herself, as well as thankful that he couldn't see the color her face had become with the embarrassment she now felt.
Dream Come True: *Is it really now, where about?*
Left in Limbo: *Londonderry, and the surrounding area.*
Dream Come True: *That's a long way from where I live, but Prichard moved there from England not long before Da hired her. She still lives with us; tutors me as yet. I don't know how long she'll stay after*

I graduate - or at least I should. But I suppose it depends on how well I stay out of trouble. It appeared he was teasing her, grinning with wonder if she might be smiling in amusement at his impetuous remark.

Left in Limbo: *Do you get into trouble a lot?* Willow couldn't wait to see if he would be as forthright with this answer; she didn't wait long, as he typed, *I try not to, but sometimes I can't help it, especially if I've been in the pub and gotten too bollixed. I often get into fights, but I usually win – btw my name's Declan Quinn.*

Willow found his name fully as intriguing as she did in knowing he was Irish, and the anachronous word he'd just used was fully as amusing, as she typed, *Bollixed, ha-ha! That's a good one. I never heard that word before. What's the meaning of it anyway? And my name's Willow Crosby.*

Dream Come True: *Drunk - after all I'm Irish!* At that moment Willow was certain he'd have a wide smirk on his face, could she see him, as she typed, *Well, Declan Quinn, I'm sure you have a barrel of fun turning all the young girls' heads while you're getting that way.* She chuckled as she typed and was just in the act of furthering her remark when her eye caught the time. It was late, and it angered her to not only know it had sped by as swiftly as it had, but that she would have to leave this fascinating young gentleman, but work waited in the morning, and she must be ready for it.

Dream Come True: *Willow, are you still there?*

Left in Limbo: *Yes, but I'm afraid I have to say goodnight. I have work in the morning and it comes early, unfortunately.* She sighed in discontent, wishing he could actually hear it.

Dream Come True: *It's been a pleasure, miss. I hope to be able to chat with you again soon. You have a grand night and a good day at work tomorrow. Ok?*

Left in Limbo: *Thanks, the same to you, and don't be giving Miss Prichard a hard time in class tomorrow. Bye for now.*

How she hated to go but she must, yet something told her to wait; as she did another sentence appeared, a simple one, but one that sweetly touched her heart. It simply said, *Goodnight, sweet Willow.*

She sat staring at these three words long after he'd left. They were merely a simple goodnight sentiment, yet they held a tenderness that she hadn't felt extended to her in a very long time. That night, as she lay upon her mattress, she felt a new friend had been added to her heart, and as she drifted off to sleep she could hear her voice whisper, "Goodnight, sweet Declan."

Chapter 11

ANOTHER LOST DAY, BUT ON A CHEERFUL NOTE

The harassing buzz of the alarm woke Willow from a sound sleep. Extending her arm from beneath warm covers, her groping hand swiftly seized the culprit, stifling its annoyance as quickly as possible. She lay back, yawning in sleepy haze while stretching her body its full length. The howling wind that was racing across the porch told her that another stormy day had arrived, but it was warm and cozy within the confines of her bed, so much so that the idea of going outdoors made her shudder at the very thought. How she wished she could just snuggle deeper into her covers and drift back to dreamland, but that wouldn't pay the relentless bills doing their best to set a record growth upon her desk.

Glancing at the clock, Willow noticed that she had a few spare minutes before she had to get up. Thankful of the reprieve, she lay yawning, her thoughts traveling back to the prior night's delightful conversation with her charming new friend. There had been something about him that tweaked her interest. She didn't know what exactly, but whatever it was it was bringing a pleasant smile to her lips and it felt damn good. Her thoughts remained upon the charming young Irish lad as she rolled onto her side. As she did, she thought about how long it had been since she'd actually smiled about anything. She laid her head back, closing her eyes tight in order to relive the prior evening when it suddenly occurred to her that her sleep had gone unbroken. She'd not slept that sound in days – months in fact – for her mind could never shut down long enough because of the constant thoughts running rampant throughout it. Worry had become a constant staple, but no matter what she did it never seemed to leave.

A strong gust of wind hit the house, flipping the porch chairs on to their side, causing Willow to jump in the process. "Wow!" she exclaimed, throwing back the covers in haste. She quickly secured the heavy robe from the foot of the bed in hope of it holding the bed's warmth against her bare body. How she hated winter, the exact opposite of the way she had once felt, for there had actually been a time when she liked it. But that seemed so long ago it was as though it had never been. She still held a fondness for snow for its whiteness blanketed the stark, rancid death lying beneath. Everything remained alive if it were covered in fresh snow, for the snow itself was alive - that is until it touched the ground - but how she wished it would remain off the road, as well as her car for it meant another morning of scrapping ice. It might not have been so bad had her car the pleasure of a garage to rest in, but that wasn't the case, so cold or not she would endure as always.

The morning ritual slipped by without a hitch everything falling into place like clockwork. Surprise tapped Willow's shoulder with this realization, yet she couldn't help wondering about it. Something was out of whack every morning, so why should this one be any different? As she stood at the kitchen counter sipping hot coffee and dreading the outside elements the phone rang, causing the cup to eject from her hand sending its contents airborne. "Damn!" she remarked in disgust. The phone continued ringing while she hastily grabbed a dishtowel to soak up the spilled contents. "I'm coming - I'm coming!" she called with annoyance. Finally abandoning her plight, she scurried to the phone. "Hello?" she inquired, all the while extending her foot as far as she could to gingerly aid the poor soaked towel, that of which was fast-becoming a sticky, brown blob.

"Good morning, Willow! How are you this nasty day?" Winifred Brown inquired in her cheerful English manner. "It's certainly dreadful out there, which brings me to the reason I'm ringing. I don't think you'll get down my road. The plow has not yet been through, and the drifts are dangerously high."

Even though this news meant she didn't have to venture out, Willow sympathetically replied, "That's too bad, Winnie, because I was hoping to get those cupboards finished for you today."

A chuckle reached through the lines, as Winifred gaily replied, "Oh that's alright. They certainly aren't going anywhere. I've not a doubt we can catch up another time. What day do you next have free, dear?" and as she spoke a giant gust of wind shook her house at the precise moment it shook Willow's.

Glaring out the window with eyes wide, Willow regretfully replied, "Not until next Monday, I'm afraid. But if this storm keeps up it's highly unlikely I'll be getting to anybody for a few days. Are you alright? How's your hydro holding up in this wind?"

Of all the people on Willow's cleaning roster, Winifred Harris-Brown was her favorite. She was getting well on in years, and was Willow's eldest client. They had enjoyed each other's company for eighteen years; fully as long as Willow's cleaning service had been in existence. She had been the first lady to answer Willow's advertisement all those years ago, and had become a fast-friend in no time. Having accompanied her husband from England many years earlier, Winifred was now a widow, living alone, her only companions being that of four cats and Jeeves, her loveable little terrier. Willow always worried about her for she no longer drove, having given up her license a few years earlier, and she knew how much Winifred had come to depend on her, maybe more than she should, and more than ever when the weather was presently like it was.

Jovial laughter again tickled the line, as Winifred replied, "Still holding fast, dear, though I think we shall lose it before the day is through. I've candles at the ready, should I need them, and enough water drawn to last indefinitely. The worst, of course will be the loss of the furnace, should the hydro default, but should the need present itself; I have extra blankets standing by in which to wrap the animals and myself in warmth. How are you faring there, my dear?"

Gawking out the window, Willow answered, "Well it's terribly windy. The snow's still coming down, but so far everything's alright. I must say though that I'm glad not to have to come out in this. I just hope the hydro continues in this wind, because the temperature's really dropped over night. You just stay put in the house and whatever you do don't venture outside, okay?"

Somewhat chuckling, Winifred replied, "Oh you need not worry, I'll be fine. I just didn't want you on the roads, and if we must wait 'till next week then that will be fine."

Realizing her friend's intention to disengage, Willow quickly stated, "Now remember, Winnie, don't be going outside. Just let Jeeves out on his short rope so he can't get off the porch. Trust me, he won't want to stay out long, and he can be reeled in when he's finished his business. I don't want you going out there."

Still chuckling, but in a stiff tone, Winifred replied, "Very well, my dear. Jeeves and I will hold down the fort! Not to worry! I'll talk to you soon!"

"Okay, but if you need anything please call," Willow stated, but before her friend could leave, added, "I don't know how I'll get it to you, but I'll find a way."

"Right-o, Willow, bye-bye for now!"

Willow's thoughts remained upon her English friend as she returned to the mess on the floor. She was grateful not have to venture out, but sorry because it meant a day's lost wages that were badly needed. She also felt sorrow at not being able to partake of her friend's eccentric, yet wonderful outlook on life. Willow often wished she could share Winifred's audacious way of looking at things. She knew her friend had faced tremendous difficulties throughout her life, but had risen above adversity in every aspect. She had survived the London Blitz of World War 2, and had fought to win her rightful place within the dog-eat-dog world of publishing, primarily dominated by men in a time when women - regardless of their qualifications - were considered secondary. She had then carried on achieving success in that field while enjoying a successful marriage along the way. She was certainly a prime example of what a woman can do when she sets her mind to it.

Since the day was to be hers, Willow looked about while deciding what she'd do with it. Going anywhere was certainly out of the question, for even though she lived in the city, the rate in which the snow was descending the streets would soon be turned into a driver's nightmare. There was always endless chores to be done, after all the house didn't run itself, yet she didn't wish to waste her newfound holiday doing menial tasks that wouldn't be going anywhere, so she decided to just see where the day would lead her. The first order on tap would be the coffee cleanup. That sticky glob couldn't be let lie, and in no time at all it was removed. She hadn't dressed as yet, but since the day was to be a lazy one she decided to simply remain in her soft, pink, terry robe, a Christmas gift from Jonas back when times were better, a time that now seemed a lifetime ago. Maybe it was, for her present life seemed useless, its path going nowhere but deeper in debt, and long, lonely nights spent alone. But she refused to feel sorry for herself regardless of the ever-present desire to do so. She realized she wasn't the first woman to feel this way, nor would she be the last, and she also knew she was far better off then some. At least she still had her health and a roof over her head, she should give thanks where it was due, yet self-pity can become a bottomless pit that sucks you deeper, if you let it, dragging you to depths you'd never believe possible. But Willow was bound and determined that would not happen to her.

The kitchen clock read 9 a.m. The day was well under way but she felt like it had been going on forever, as she refilled her favorite coffee mug, thankful it had survived the recent fall. "Good thing we never put in ceramic," she muttered aloud, just as the toaster signaled its content's readiness. As she sat enjoying hot butter upon her tongue, thoughts again drifted to the previous evening, bringing a smile to her lips as she thought about the words she and Declan typed to each other. She found her mind filling with images of what he might look like. Would he be tall and dark, or short and fair? "How could it even matter," she sarcastically thought, "he's years younger than my own children, so regardless of whether his physical appearance is fully matured or not he's definitely too young for me. Yet age is only a number, one can be as old or as young as one feels, couldn't they?"

Willow had known a few men in her day who shared this same opinion, but when she actually applied serious thought the realization suddenly dawned that her interest in men - with the exception of Bernie Whidbey - had always been in younger ones. She never bothered analyzing the reason, it was just the way she was, and the outlook she had. After all Jonas was two years her junior - but only two - not thirty-five. That was ridiculous, yet as ridiculous as it was it felt intriguing. It had been a long time since Willow Sutherland-Crosby had been intrigued by anything. Maybe it was time she was again.

Chapter 12

THE STORM RAGES ON

The morning drifted, along with the roads. This was fast becoming the worst storm of the new century, but since the century was merely three years old, there as yet wasn't much to compare it with. But regardless, it was bringing traffic to a standstill, and downing power lines across the province. Living in the city had its drawbacks, but it also had its advantages, for if Willow's dream of again residing in the country had been realized she too would be without power, for it was now lost to its stricken residents. Emergency crews had been dispatched to numerous outlying areas, but the power within the city of Ottawa remained. That was a miraculous feat in itself. Apparently the previous government's plan to increase the city's reservoir allotment hadn't been a waste of tax money after all, for if it wasn't for the added reserves the city would also be without power - good on Parliament's stalwart members who had pushed it through - as unscrupulous as they might have been in doing so.

Willow, just like everyone, knew what reserve meant, and she always used her power wisely, however today it didn't seem as important. She knew she mustn't waste it, but surely a few minutes on line would not harm anything. She wouldn't stay long; then she too would fill the bathtub with water reserve, refill her grandmother's aged kerosene lamps, and make sure her candle supply was ample. Should the power be lost the furnace would continue producing heat for it was a hot water system generated from natural gas. Once the old radiators got hot they would carry on warming the house for hours. It was another plus in Willow's book of advantage, and it wasn't long before she was flying into cyber-space with a delightful wind beneath her, but before surfing the web, she decided to check her e-mail. A few quick clicks of the mouse took her straight into her mailbox where she was, per usual, presented with a ton of junk mail. "This is as bad as regular mail," she silently thought while sifting through endless advertisements from soup to nuts with a huge amount of vulgarity in between. Luckily she knew how to delete it as fast as it came in, for she was not only disinterested, she didn't want her grandchildren, during an unexpected visit, coming on-line and finding X-rated material looming before their innocent eyes.

With finger poised upon the delete key she scrolled through an assortment of unfamiliar names, shaking her head in dismay at the amount of nonsense associated with each before being sent to the recycle bin, but her eyes lost no time in retaining a glorious sheen when they happened upon a familiar name tucked discreetly within the list. Her heart did an instant flip when she read the subject heading, *something pretty for a pretty lady*. The message it contained was accompanied by an attachment of which she couldn't wait to open. She nervously wondered what it could be while pondering the reason why he would be sending anything. Furthermore where did he get her address? She didn't recall giving it to him, still her heart accelerated with each beat. What would he have to say? More importantly, he was writing her. And as she pondered these thoughts her hand began to quiver as if she'd suddenly been stricken with palsy, causing her to question the extent of her nervousness while steadying her hand long enough to open his message. But her question was instantly answered as soon as she opened his letter.

Hello Willow,
I hope all is well. Been watching the telly and it says there's a major snowstorm happening in your area. It says the lines are down and it's expected to get worse. I'm concerned about you. I'm hoping your electric is still on and you get this message as soon as I send it, but mostly I hope you're okay. I'm sending you something (btw don't open it 'till you've finished reading) with hopes it might brighten your day; also to say thank you for chatting with me last evening. I had a really good time and I kind of got the feeling you did too. I'll be seeing you soon.
Declan x
    P.S. I got your e-mail address from the fan site's message board we both go to. I found it in your profile there and copied it. Hope you don't mind. You take care, pretty lady.

Willow immediately opened the attachment which revealed a photograph of a delicate pink rose. It was simple, yet exquisite, and it stole her breath entirely as she sat in awe just staring at it. She was completely over come. "What a beautiful gesture, and this young man is a mere nineteen," she thought in total amazement, her quivering fingers caressing the screen. Her fingertips continued to glide over the image as her imagination felt it. Here it was, the dead of winter, everything dormant, flowers nonexistent except in greenhouses, yet this image presenting itself could not have touched her deeper had the real thing been freshly delivered to her door. Even if this young acquaintance was nineteen, he was certainly knowledgeable within the realms of what it takes to enlighten a woman, and she quickly saved the image to a private file. Soon the delicate rose was hidden away, preserved in time as if it had been freshly pressed into a remembrance book where it could be viewed whenever she wanted, and she knew that would be happening often. She quickly secured his e-mail address, the desire to reply enticing her, but she decided against it. She was uncertain as to why, only to follow her instincts which at the moment were telling her to wait. Before she realized it the time read 1 pm, well past lunchtime, and much longer than she had originally planned to be. Guilt immediately consumed her. She knew the power it took to remain online might literally mean the difference between life and death for someone, and even though her hydro remained, she knew there were those who had none. Winifred Brown was the first to come to mind. Willow couldn't help but let her mind travel down that old country road to the green gabled farmhouse where her friend lived, and before she knew it she was on the telephone, dialing the familiar number. It rang, and continued to do so, but no answer came.

"Please answer the phone," Willow begged impatiently. The phone continued its signal, but to no avail. "Oh, God, please let her be alright," she pleaded as she unconsciously manipulated the phone cord around her trembling fingers. Still it rang, yet nobody came. Willow's anxiety grew, along with her concerned thoughts as they centered on images she hoped were not true. "Surely she wouldn't have ventured outside," she nervously thought, fighting to remain calm, yet her mind was remembering an earlier incident where Winifred had lost her balance and fallen down the front steps. Luckily for her, the young couple who were spending the night at the B & B directly across the road was on the porch swing, enjoying the warm summer evening, and had immediately come to her aid. But it could have been an entirely different story had they not been there, or had the day been like the present one. These thoughts kept pummeling Willow's mind as the phone carried on ringing. *"Come on, Winifred, answer the frigging phone!"* she remarked sharply, just as the receiver was picked up.

Sounding slightly out of breath, Winifred inquired, "Hello?"

With an enormous sigh of relief, Willow remarked, "Thank God you're alright!"

"Of course I'm alright, Willow. Why on earth would I not be?" Winifred questioned, sounding somewhat concerned.

Willow was so relieved to hear her friend's voice, she instantly blurted, "I was certain you'd gone outside and fallen!"

A familiar chuckle absorbed the line, before Winifred answered, "No-no, my dear, all is well. I was rather indisposed. I tried my utmost to cut it short - the telephone ringing off the wall and all - but nature was not co-operating. I got here as fast as I could. 'Tis a wonder it didn't discontinue before I got to it, such is the case far too often, as you know! But you will be pleased to know your little friend was *barking up a storm*, trying to alert me to the fact I was being summoned, *ha-ha!*"

"Tell Jeeves I'm grateful to him," Willow replied, but as her suspicion grew, she asked, "By the way, you haven't ventured out have you?"

"No, dear, I have not," Winifred replied in jovial rebuke. "I've jolly-well been a good girl and not stepped one foot out the door. Poor Jeeves needed to do his business, but when a gust of wind struck him he refused to venture forth. I had to prod him with my walking stick! Needless to say he was not out long, *ha-ha!* The cats are faring well, but feeling the wretched chill of course, and are gathered on the chesterfield, huddled for warmth. I really wish I could light a fire —"

"*No!*" Willow exclaimed hastily. "Oh, Winifred, don't do that!"

"Of course I won't!" Winifred remarked sharply. "I jolly-well know better in this strong of wind!"

Feeling rather embarrassed, Willow sheepishly replied, "Of course you do. I'm really sorry for snapping at you, but I'm very concerned about you up there by yourself."

"But I'm *not* alone, dear. I have my furry little family with me. Everything is fine, and I will be alight. I have all I require, and I'm certain the storm will blow itself out by sundown; if not then by morning," Winifred relayed, trying her utmost to convince Willow of her safety.

The wind continued its mournful wail as ice pellets splattered upon Willow's kitchen window, causing her to shiver when she watched them freeze upon contact. Returning her attention to her friend, she said, "Well I'll let you go. Now remember, if you need help of *any* kind don't hesitate to call. As I stated before, I don't know how I'll get out there, but I'll find a way. Okay?"

"Of course I will, dear, you already know that. But I've no doubt everything will be fine. Not to worry, and we shall chat later," Winifred replied with confidence, and then hung up the phone.

Willow's gaze remained upon the icy window while she continued thinking about her old friend long after she'd gone. "My, but she's braver than I would be," she said to herself, and turning to refill her coffee cup, suddenly realized how lucky she actually was, for even with the growing stress that each day managed to bring, she couldn't help but feel fortunate to be safe and sound within her own home. Daylight had now faded, yet the transition had been so gradual it was barely noticeable for the entire day had been on the dark side. "Wonder whether this wind will go down with the sun," she nervously thought as she gazed about. The house was beginning to feel a little on the cool side, urgently propelling her to the nearest radiator with fear it had given up the ghost. Feeling warmth still emitting, she sighed with relief, though it was hard to say how much longer it would continue. "No doubt it's because of this damn wind," Willow thought in aggravation. Just then the lights began to flicker in a precarious manner, and like any mother in-tune to the moment, her concern instinctively turned to her children. They lived not far from her, yet that knowledge was little comfort when a mother is worrying about her child.

Lifting the receiver, she quickly placed a call to Ben with hope that he and his brother had left work early. Both were graphic artists employed by a prestigious design firm located three blocks east of Parliament Hill, one in a senior position, the other in junior with both offices affording a commanding view of the Rideau Canal. It was an entertaining sight upon any given day, but this time of year the activities upon the canal were especially active because of the upcoming Winter Festival, slated to be held in its usual mid-February slot. Ben Whidbey often commented about the musical selections chosen for the daily skaters who braved the frozen surface, and whenever his wife could find the time she would join him for a lunchtime glide, laughing, and carrying on as though they were young lovers on a first date. Willow affectionately smiled, thinking of the way her two boys adored their wives. It was the way it should be, and each had chosen well, proving that at least *someone* in her family could choose a mate wisely. It was a good thing they had not decided to follow in their parent's footsteps; if they had it would have been highly unlikely their mother would have enjoyed grandchildren.

"Hello?" Catharine Whidbey inquired.

Realizing that deepest indigo had now swallowed the daylight, Willow anxiously inquired, "Hi, Cathy, how are things over there? Has Benny gotten home alright?" While awaiting an answer, she could hear her daughter-in-law speaking to her daughter across the receiver, asking her to let the dog in. Coming back on the line, Catharine answered, "Yeah, Mom, he's here, got home about a half hour ago. Do you want to speak with him?"

Breathing a thankful sigh of relief, Willow answered, "Yes, dear. I would."

A couple of minutes passed before Ben came on the line, stating, "Hi, Mom, how are you? Sure been a hell of a day, hasn't it?"

She could hear him speaking to their dog, telling him to lie down, as she answered, "Yes it sure has. I'm fine, how was your drive home? Do you know if Shay left when you did?" She knew her youngest son often stopped for a pint of the bitters at the pub around the corner from their office building, and she was hoping that Benny could advise her on this.

"As far as I know he went straight home," he answered.

"Well I hope so, Benny, but I'll give a call over there to make sure," she replied then added, "What are the streets like?"

With a touch of smartness, he replied, "Mom, you worry too much. You're almost as bad as Grandma. Pretty soon you'll be telling me to wear double socks, especially if the snow gets any deeper. And don't be worrying about Shay. He's a big boy, just like his bro here, he'll be fine. Are you sure everything's okay with you?"

"Ha! Ha!! Very funny about the grandmother thing there, sweetie, but I'll have you know it's a mother's prerogative to worry. I'll stop fretting when I know it's safe to," Willow replied with a touch of reprimand, though she had to admit she probably did worry needlessly. But it was her right, as she had told her son, and it wouldn't have made any difference what he said because she'd worry regardless. Tightening her grip on the receiver, she continued, "Well I feel a lot better knowing you're home safe, and all is well over there. I'll talk to you soon, son."

"Okay, Mom. If you need anything just call," Ben replied, then quickly added, "Love you."

A smile lit Willow's face, as she answered, "I love you too, Benny," then as a joke, quickly injected, "Don't forget your double socks for the morning!" She could hear laughter, then a click as the dial tone resumed, assuring his departure. She couldn't help but smile while her fingers punched in familiar numbers, as she mused, "Now to make sure number two son is safe and accounted for."

"Hello?" Deborah Crosby inquired.

"Hi, Deb, it's Willow. I was wondering how you're fairing over there in this storm? Is Shay home yet?" Willow asked as her eyes narrowed to slits toward her reflection staring back from the window.

Deborah answered, "Yes, we're doing fine here. Actually he just came in the door as the phone rang. Are you okay?"

Relief again flooded Willow, as she replied, "Yes, I'm fine. The lights are ducking periodically but so far they're hanging in. Do you have power?" she inquired, certain she could hear a hissing sound growing louder in the background.

"So far we do," Deborah answered, "but it's been flickering every so often. I've already got candles burning just in case it goes out. Listen, Willow, I don't mean to rush but the kettle's on the boil and I have to tend to dinner. Shay wants to speak with you anyway, so I'll say bye for now."

Willow could hear her son inquiring his wife over the receiver as to when dinner would be ready, before he came on the line, stating, "Hi, Mom, how are you getting along over there?"

"Well," Willow answered, grateful for his voice in her ear, "I'm a lot better now knowing you're home safe. But it really has been a wicked day. I'm glad I didn't have to work. Mrs. Brown cancelled.

I figured she might, and I'm thankful I didn't have to brave the roads. I've been talking to your brother and he informs me the streets are getting pretty heavy, so you could about imagine what the country roads must be like by now."

"That's for sure," Shay answered, "I'm glad you didn't have to go out there. I know I was damn glad to pull into my drive just now. Saw a few fender-benders on the way home but nothing that looked too serious. Anyway, I'd best go for now. I'm starving, and Deb's got supper ready. Talk to you soon. Love you."

"I love you too, son." Willow softly answered, setting the dead receiver upon the cradle while nerves tried their best to upset her, but she would not give into them. Apparently she had been more nervous than first thought, but her family was safe, and so was she. "Be grateful, Willow," she mused to herself, feeling a bit unsettled yet experiencing a satisfying calmness as she climbed the stairs to her loft.

The computer beckoned her once more, and since the hydro continued she would take advantage. In no time at all she was online preparing to select her nightly destination when her mail icon signaled the arrival of a letter. "No doubt more junk," she thought in disgust as she opened the inbox, but as she did her eyes twinkled with delight at the awaiting message. With wild excitement at the prospect of what the hidden words might say, her stomach felt as if it had suddenly been invaded by a swarm of butterflies. She thought this rather phenomenal, if not a bit strange, yet their wings thrashed about as though they were hopelessly trying to escape a spider's web. Her nervous finger clicked on the mouse, and the message instantly opened.

Hello my pretty lady,
I went to the chat hoping you might be there but you weren't. I got to admit I'm disappointed. I miss you. I hope you come soon and we can chat because I really like the conversation between us, it's not like the usual stuff with the others, y'know? I really do hope you're getting along ok in the storm and all. Come soon.
Declan. X

Willow's eyes stared at his words as if they were reading the Holy Grail itself. There was nothing extraordinary about them - certainly nothing to be considered classic - yet she hung on them as though she were a moth drawn to a hypnotic flame, reading them over, and over again. The urge to again answer sprang to mind, but just like before thought better of it. The one thing she didn't want to do was lead him on. After all their extreme age difference prevented anything other than friendship, but the feeling she felt when reading his words touched her in a way she had never before experienced. There was nothing wrong in this feeling, many friendships are forged between different generations - often times with favor - so why should this one be any different? The wind had not gone down with the sun; if anything it was blowing harder than it had all day. The lights ducked, sending Willow scrambling for matches. She had no sooner lit a candle than the lights went out completely. "Great," she groaned in disgust, "so much for that." As sorry as she was to have lost the hydro, she was more perturbed in knowing she could not meet Declan for a chat, and her excitement faded into the awaiting blackness as she held the candle before her while descending the stairs to bed.

Chapter 13

THE ABSURDITY OF SOME

The bedside phone rang shrill, startling Willow into an upright position so quickly her head swam. She gasped, clutching her chest as she grabbed the phone on her way back down upon the bed. "My God!" she remarked in pissed-off surprise, grasping the blue receiver in a death-grip while snuggling further beneath the covers in an attempt to warm the sudden chill in her bones. Gathering her wits, she answered the call, all the while noticing the air in the room feeling cooler than it had the previous night. "Surely the furnace will continue its entrusted task," she thought, still nothing was certain, and she knew it. "Who did you wish to speak with?" she asked; then abruptly snapped, "He doesn't live here anymore!" Anger quickly rose within her. She caught herself on the verge of emitting a few choice words when she thought about the sound sleep she'd been enjoying just to be startled awake for this, as she disgustingly thought, "You'd think after this amount of time people would realize that the person in question doesn't reside here any longer," picturing her husband's face as she did.

The morning, so it appeared, was a repeat of the previous for the sky was so overcast one would hardly know it was morning.

Willow's indignant thoughts remained glued upon her estranged husband, wishing he would let his new number be known so people would stop harassing her. She cursed, and rolled to face the bedside clock whose neon face was blank. With the realization of this she openly cussed before scrambling to the dresser for her watch. The tiny hands read 10:35 am, making her realize just how late for work she was, but a mere glance out the window soon changed her mind about going. "Damn, not another one," she thought in dismay, for it meant not only another workless day, but another day with no pay. Her job was the only source of income she had, and regardless of whether she was the only one living there, bills required paying, and she still needed to eat. Sitting up, staring into the mirror, her eye was suddenly caught by the flashing of a red light behind her. It appeared life had been restored to the bedside clock. With the realization the power was back, relief flooded her thin body, and she lost no time making tracks for the kitchen and the empty coffee pot awaiting its morning duty. Before long the stimulating aroma filled the air, along with her cup.

Standing at the window, savoring the delicious liquid, Willow found it amazing that her upper-crust client of the day hadn't already phoned to inquire her whereabouts. All it would have taken was a mere glance out the window to know the answer, yet there were certain clients - regardless of weather conditions – who expected her to arrive undaunted, ready to delve into whatever they threw her way. On the whole the majority of clients were respectful, never expecting anything they themselves wouldn't do. However there were those who took her for granted, expecting the impossible, and demanding unreasonable perfection for little compensation in return. Since the beginning of Willow's service she had encountered an array of people, as well as countless situations, but one fact in which she had long come to terms with was that human nature never ceased to amaze her, yet through it all she did her best to handle whatever came her way.

The wind, though lessened measurably from the day before, continued to bear down. Even with plows on the roads it wouldn't be long before drifts filled them in. Many of the roads Willow had to travel meandered through winding hills, and deep ravines with dangerous drops on both sides. The scenery might have made for a spectacular drive, especially during the summer months – winter - however was a far different story. She may be in dire need of money, but she valued her life more. With these thoughts rambling through her mind she inched toward the phone with expectations of an impending hassle, but regardless she wasn't venturing out. If all her clients were as thoughtful as Winifred Brown then her job would be a piece of cake, but unfortunately they weren't. The phone continued to ring, giving Willow the impression no one was there. "Good," she thought with instant relief, "I can just leave a message when their machine picks up." But luck was not to be hers that day for the call was finally answered.

"Hello?" Nancy Richardson's staunch voice inquired with apprehension. By the woman's tone, Willow couldn't help thinking, "Well here we go," as she took a deep breath, and answered, "Hi, Nancy, another miserable morning we're having."

"Yes, so it appears," Nancy relayed in an authoritative manner. "Tomas is overseeing the clearing of our drive as we speak. We've employed a new company; the previous one changed their policy which no-longer met our requirements." As she yammered on, Willow couldn't help thinking, "Changed their policy, eh? More likely got fed-up being bullied by your outrageous demands," but she kept her thoughts to herself, as her employer condescendingly said, "And I suppose *you're* calling to inform me you're not coming to work today."

With tension growing, Willow replied, "As a matter of fact that's exactly why I'm calling. Your road is so narrow that I don't like the thought of trying to get down it to your driveway."

There was a pause – no doubt for dramatic effect - before Nancy replied, "As you are well aware, we have an extremely capable generator to carry us through emergencies such as this, and Tomas switched it on yesterday as soon as the power was lost. I *need* you to come. I'm hosting a dinner party for ten of my husband's business associates tonight at eight, and I require the house thoroughly cleaned and prepared. Surely you can get here. Our drive will be clear, so I fail to see why you cannot come."

It was exactly as Willow expected. Why people cannot simply accept something at face-value without need of explanation was beyond her ability to comprehend, but selfish people - especially those who consider themselves above the norm - seldom see beyond their own raised nose. Taking a deep breath, Willow replied, "Because the roads *getting* to your road are as narrow as yours. Should I start to slide I don't particularly relish the thought of ending upside down in one of the ravines," and not giving her client the chance to intervene, injected, "Besides if this wind keeps up all day it's highly unlikely your guests will get through either." She felt like adding, 'regardless of whether your lame driveway is clear or not,' but she didn't.

With exasperation, Nancy inquired, "Then *how* will the house be cleaned and ready for my guests if you cannot find your way clear to do it?"

Willow felt like telling her she could always do it herself, but she knew that would go over like a lead balloon - heaven forbid she might get her lily white hands dirty - worse still - break an overly-priced salon nail. It was becoming obvious Nancy Richardson was bound and determined to brow-beat her cleaning lady into coming, as she remarked, "I hardly feel the weather inclement enough to prohibit you from coming. But if you are finding the roads too intimidating to maneuver then could you not have one of your sons drive you?"

Willow had no intention of endangering anyone's life — most importantly her children's, as she blatantly replied, "Mrs. Richardson, I am not going to ask *anyone* to drive me *anywhere* today. The weather is far too severe for people to be on the roads unless it is an *emergency*, and a dinner party is not! I will see you on the usual day next week unless you would rather make other arrangements."

Not losing a second, Nancy vigorously snapped, "I cannot possibly cope with the menial chores I pay you to do! If you refuse to come when I require you the most then I shall no longer require your service at all!"

There it was! The number one intimidation tactic practiced by millions everyday to get their way when they otherwise would not. However it was not working for Nancy Richardson today.

"Well I'm sorry to hear that, Nancy, but I'm not coming. You'll just have to manage as best you can. Good bye!" Willow replied in an adversative tone, for she refused to be chastised any longer by someone who thought more of her social standing, than for the safety of the person who had faithfully come week after week to clean up after her.

Willow didn't wait for a response but instead hung up the phone. The only thing she felt remorse about was the loss of a weekly paycheck. Yet when she actually thought about it the monetary loss was not all that much. For a woman whose financial means were the least of her worries, Nancy Richardson was one of the most frugal clients Willow had. She may have needed the money, but she did not require the price that went with it. It would just mean tightening her belt a little more. But at the rate she was going the belt itself would soon be non-existent. "What else is new?" Willow stated to herself as she ventured to the front door to see if the mailman had gotten through. She shuddered when she stepped out on the porch, for the wind blew fiercely, driving the cold deep within her aching bones. Quickly retrieving the box contents, she hurried back inside her warm house, wondering in amazement at how the mail - especially the bills - always managed to come regardless of the weather. They were hand-delivered if need be, and they could always be counted on just as sure as the sun rising in the east.

The mail landed in a heap upon the dining table as Willow went to fetch another cup of coffee. Maybe the added caffeine was doing little to help her frazzled nerves, but it tasted good, and that was all she cared about. Returning to the table, she pulled out a chair, flopped upon the seat, and began sorting the usual array of junk, that of which consisted of colorful advertisements singing their praise of whiter whites, softer towels, and the peace of mind in knowing that if you added more fiber to your diet you were not only assured a more thorough clean-out, but your chance of developing colon cancer might lessen. "Guess that's a good thing to know," she thought, "yet does it really matter?" Then laying them aside, her eyes fell upon a white business envelope from the hydro with bold red lettering stamped on the exterior, which read, **Attention: Final Notice!** She quickly tore it open, and proceeded to read the contents.

February 6, 2003.

Mrs. Willow Crosby,
Our records show your account is in arrears. To avoid disconnection of service, plus collection proceedings, payment in full must be received within seven days of the issued date on this notice.

A $200.00 re-connection fee payable in advance will apply. Payment can be made at any financial institution, online banking, *by mail, credit card, or money order. If payment in full has been made, please disregard this notice.*

Regards,
Ottawa - Hydro.

Before she could fully absorb the message the phone rang, enticing her to jump out of her skin. "Damn it! What in hell now!?" she thought in frenzied confusion, racing to see who it was. Some time earlier she had installed call display on the main phone as the amount of unwanted callers - charities in particular - had totally gotten out of hand. When she came to think about it, she herself had become her biggest charity, and she again cussed when the earlier call for her dearly departed husband came to mind. Too bad she hadn't come to the primary phone in the first place; had she it may well have spared the unneeded aggravation it had caused, not to mention additional stress. This was certainly turning into a banner day, for the call was from her attorney's office.

"Hello."

"Hello, Mrs. Crosby, this is Timothy Breen's office calling."

"Yes?"

"I realize this is short notice, but Mr. Breen would like to know if you could possibly come by the office at four thirty tomorrow?" the secretary questioned in a polished manner. "Something must be up," Willow thought, as she answered, "I suppose so. What is this about?"

"Mr. Breen has just received the latest offer from your husband's lawyer. He would like to review it with you if you can make it in."

Willow's interest elevated with the news of this latest development, though in actuality it remained to be seen whether it warranted the interest it encouraged. So far there had only been one offer, and that wasn't worth the paper it was written on, yet she knew she must explore all avenues if she was to end up with what she wanted. The most important issue was the house, and though it no longer meant one iota to her husband in the way it once did, it had become a sanctuary for her, a safety-net - for lack of a better word - for regardless of what the world threw her way she could always return to her little house with its charming burgundy door.

As Willow pondered the previous offer's content, she replied, "I'll be there. I would also like to discuss the present financial situation. I just received a final notice from Hydro, and as Jonas is not giving me one dime of support I would like this case into court as soon as possible. I've been trying my utmost to keep my head above water, but it's gotten to the point where it's impossible."

"I understand your concern, Mrs. Crosby, but you'll have to discuss that matter with Mr. Breen," the secretary announced in a tone which gave the impression she could care less one way or the other.

With a tired sigh, Willow replied, "Very well. I'll see you tomorrow."

Chapter 14

FURTHER DISMISSAL

Just as Willow placed the receiver upon its cradle a gust of wind swept by the living room window but died as quickly as it came. Parting the curtains, she peered through the frost-etched glass to find the storm had subsided. There was even promise of sunshine as a few filtered rays were valiantly trying to stab through the heavy cloud cover. They would certainly be welcomed, especially by those who'd been without heat since their hydro had been lost. With this thought in mind, Winifred Brown's current situation popped into Willow's. She had planned to call her in a minute anyway, but she would wait until her anxiety subsided. The sorted, bitter events of the drawn-out morning sat like a lemon wedge in her mouth. She hated confrontations, regardless of whom they were with, but as her eyes fell upon the hydro notice she decided she would endure yet another, and call her husband.

"Hello?" Jonas Crosby inquired in a sleepy manner.

Feeling anger rising, Willow answered, "Hello."

There was a pause - possibly an intended hesitation - as he said, "Oh, it's *you*. What do you want?"

"Well good morning to you too," she remarked coldly.

Yawning, he stated, "I hope you realize you woke me from a sound sleep," and Willow could hear him fiddling with something which sounded not far from the receiver's mouth piece. "No doubt one of his never ending cheroots," she thought in disgust. She swore he smoked so many his fingers were stained as brown as the paper embracing the tobacco. It was something she hated. She had lost track of the times she had implored him to quit - if not for his own health then hers – and if not that then certainly the grandchildren's. Ever since they had come along she tried even harder; still he was relentless.

"Sorry about that," she announced, though he knew she lied and so did she. Under normal conditions lying was something she never did, but at that moment it was providing enjoyment.

"I bet you are," he replied in a surly tone. "What brings you out of your lair on a morning like this?"

His curt remark stung, and before she realized what she was doing, she blurted, "Your lack of humanity — let alone responsibility!"

She could hear him cuss under his breath then in a curt manner, ask, "What'd I do now?"

"It's more like what you *don't do!*" she remarked bitterly.

With as much warmth as her words had held, he shot back, "Like what? Look, Willow, I don't know what this is about, but whatever it is, talk to my lawyer about it."

The hackles instantly rose along the back of Willow's neck, for of all the people throughout her life that had ever rubbed her the wrong way, Jonas Crosby could set off her temper faster than anyone – even her mother - and he utterly made it explode whenever he brazenly inquired if she as yet had her *Irish up* when he knew full well she did. He too was of Irish descent, yet according to him he always kept his anger in check. She shook her head in annoyance toward the entire situation as her thoughts returned to the present, and she snapped, "Well I'm talking to *you* about it! So open your goddamn ears for once and listen! I'm calling about a hydro bill that's way past due!"

"Not my problem, sweetheart," he replied with arrogance.

The palms of Willow's hands grew sweaty as she gripped the receiver tighter, thankful this was not happening in person. If it was the outcome would certainly spell disaster. Drawing a deep breath, she retorted, "No, it seems nothing ever *is*, is it!"

"Look, Willow," he replied haughtily, "you're the one that wanted space. Or have you conveniently forgotten that?"

His words were true, as much as Willow might have wished differently, for she had found the need to secure an area all to herself where she could cope with the changes happening within her body. She had tried on numerous occasions to talk to Jonas about it, tell him how she felt, and try to explain feelings that she too found impossible to understand, let alone accept. But he appeared disinterested, and above all never there for her when she needed him the most, though years earlier had faithfully promised to stand by her come what may. She had convinced herself that his promises had only been words, for when the going got rough he was anywhere but where he should have been.

But the ongoing turmoil was taking its toll on Jonas as well, and it was beginning to show. He too had gone through a change, no longer the virile stud of his youth, but rather an aging baby-boomer now in his early fifty's. It was hard to let go of the days when his strength was never spent, nor his ability to satisfy a woman. Willow had been the centre of his world, everything he had ever hoped to find in a mate. She had given him the ultimate gift, that of which any woman could give a man, and every time he looked into his son's eyes he could see his own looking back. It was no secret that the early years of their marriage had been stormy, but they had also been filled with a wondrous magic as they found their path together, day by day, until the days turned to months, and months to years. Throughout that entire time Willow remained ever stalwart and true. She had stood by Jonas through thick and thin, hardship and death. Jonas, in his own way, had tried his best to understand and be supportive, that is until Willow's surmounting problems made it impossible for him to cope any longer.

The sun pierced the clouds as Willow fought back the flood of emotion threatening to break loose. "No," she said in a forlorn tone, "I haven't forgotten. But you seem to forget the reason I needed it in the first place. You never listened to me, or cared how I felt. *I needed you, Jonas*. I needed your support but, mostly I needed your understanding. Why can't you see that?"

Another pause while he lit a cigar. A few more minutes passed before he resumed the conversation. "All I know is the way you treated me," he answered in a subdued tone. "Half of the time you wouldn't *let* me touch you — hell you acted like a frigid statue one second then the next you were all over me like your fucking ass was on fire! I didn't know how to take you. What was I suppose to think, let alone do, Willow? I haven't forgotten the way we once were *or* the way we felt about each other but ... Hell, I don't know ... you ... well, you just changed, and not for the better. Not what I want anyway."

Tears clouded her green eyes and her voice choked, as she replied, "I - I didn't change, Jonas. Inside my head I'm still the same woman I always was. The change happened within my *body*. It felt like part of me died — part of me did - and I grieve that part that's no longer alive, but what I find so hard to accept is the failing strength of your love after I became ill, and was no longer able to work as much or, be what you wanted in bed. Where was your compassion for me when I needed the man I loved? I never turned my back on you, but you pushed me away when I needed you the most. You walked away from me. You left me with hardly any income except what I manage to make myself, and you refuse to help me. What did I ever do that was horrible enough to be punished like this?"

"Save it, sweetheart," he replied heartlessly. "Save the sob-story for the judge, you're going to need it. Now go away."

Willow stood crying, holding the receiver in her sweat-laden hand while the dial tone hummed away. Once again she had been dismissed, and the hydro notice floated to the floor as she soberly walked to her bedroom. The wind howled past the window, its voice picking up then fading back as it told of its latest adventure, and any other time she would love to have listened, but this morning her heart was not in it. She lay upon the bed, her husband's acrimonious dismissal still echoing in her mind. She wondered why he did that. Why he treated her like a dog that had failed to carry out its latest command therefore banished from the room for disobeying. She wondered if it somehow brought him pleasure to treat her this way, or possibly make him feel more superior in the trying situation between them. Maybe it was simply for spite. Whatever the reason, the pain it caused was none-the-less real, regardless of the reasoning behind it.

As she laid thinking, her mind wandered to better times, back when their children were still boys playing in the huge backyard on her father's farm. She laughed in an ironic manner when she thought about the way history consistently seems to repeat itself. Whoever came up with that old adage had been right. The first year and a half of their marriage had been spent in a small apartment located in the downtown core of Ottawa. Willow had been happy there, though it hadn't been the best place for Benny for the backyard was almost nonexistent, and the only playground within any reasonable distance was that of the elementary school he attended a block away. When she had become pregnant with Shay they moved to her dad's farm. Jonas secured a machinist's job in local Smith Falls, and for ten years life was good. Then it hit a snag. Thoughts of that derivative time returned, invoking a laugh along with it for here she was, nineteen years down the road, with history once again repeating itself. The only difference was the cold, hard fact she would never let it happen again.

Chapter 15

SECOND ENCOUNTER

A new day dawned with extreme brightness, and though it was early February, the sun already held warmth in its cheerful rays. The alarm sounded, rousing Willow from a restless sleep and she laid, stretching tiredness from her aching body, wincing as her bones voiced their stern complaints. But it did them no good, for she threw back the covers and rose to face the day, hopefully a better one. It had finally reached the point where each new one had grown more negative than the previous. She could scarcely remember when days had been happy, life not a constant battle, or the stress level anything but over the top. Today would be no different, but at least it would bring much needed revenue for the roads would be plowed, meaning she could safely get to work. She briefly thought about the previous day's events, trying not to dwell on the fact that she was now one day short of her weekly income, yet she refused to be taken advantage of by Nancy Richardson or anyone else.

"Why couldn't she be more understanding, or considerate of my needs, let alone safety, why couldn't she be more like Winnie?" Willow questioned aloud while she poured morning coffee into her favorite cup. The plans to call her friend the prior day had gone array, but better late than never. The phone rang its usual amount of rings, at least the amount where she wasn't worried of the count before the ring was answered.

"Hello?" Winifred's cheerful voice inquired.

"Hi, Winnie, how is everything with you today. Is your power back on?" Willow inquired, trying her best to sound as cheerful as her co-conversationalist.

"Good morning, dear!" Winifred exclaimed with fervor. "Aren't you thoughtful to ring an old woman to check on her? I must tell you how silly your little friend has been throughout this entire ordeal with the electric, *ha-ha!* He's been a perfect *rascal* whenever I tried nudging him out the door, and of course he was jolly-well determined not to go. So I had to apply a right-old prod to his behind! It was all a great-to-do, but I managed to get him out long enough to cock his leg! He bolted back in as though the Devil himself was after him and tunneled aside the hearth beneath the knitted throws. I had laid the fire last evening in hope of somewhat warming the house, as it had gotten rather chilly, but it was far too windy, as you know. The electric was restored just before daybreak, and of course already being up with my animals, I lit the fire to assist the furnace in warming the house. How have you been managing, my dear? Fine, I hope."

At that moment indelible thoughts of Nancy Richardson, along with the newest stress fix from Jonas, pummeled Willow's mind, but she replied, "Yes, everything's fine. I was unable to get to work yesterday but hopefully I can make it up another time. I'm off to work later, but I wanted to see how you were doing. I'm sorry I didn't phone yesterday I … I meant to but, well, you know how it is with good intentions getting off the beaten track? I feel bad that I didn't call you sooner, but I have been thinking of you."

She realized she must sound redundant - maybe she was - but her intentions were stellar regardless of her lack of action.

"Oh that's perfectly alright, dear," Winifred replied, her voice still as cheerful as when she'd first answered. "And my furry little friends and I have ridden out the storm rather well I might add. After all when one dwells in the country one must be prepared for winter blows, such as we have recently endured."

With that remark Willow shook her head in admiration, wishing Winifred could actually see it, as she replied, "You are amazing, Winifred Brown. I wish *all* my clients had your outlook. I'm glad to hear the hydro is back, and the house is warm, but mostly that you're fine."

In an appreciative manner, Winifred replied, "That is most kind of you to say, Willow, but it's only commonsense. However I do know what you mean. Yet if all people were the same, the world would be a very dreary place, do you not agree?"

"That's for sure!" Willow remarked auspiciously, feeding off her friend's admirable outlook and finding her contemptible mood of late quickly improving. "Well I have to get ready for work, Winnie, but you take care, and I'll see you soon."

"Right-o, my dear," Winifred remarked with as much gusto as when she'd first come on the line, "do take care, bye-bye for now."

The time read 8:15 am as Willow swiftly donned her day's apparel before racing to the kitchen just in time to grab the toast as it flew out of the toaster. Still feeding off her friend's cheer, she poured another coffee then ascended the stairs to check her computer mail. The screen instantly sprang to life, and she lost no time opening the mailbox. The cheerfulness she was enjoying soon exploded into full elation when her eyes fell upon Declan Quinn's name awaiting her attention.

Morning, pretty lady,
Hope you woke to a better day there in Ontario. I've been watching the telly ever since that storm began, and I've been kind of worried. I really hope you're fine and got heat and electric and all that stuff. I missed you last night in the chat. I waited for a long time hoping you'd come but the kids there started bugging me. I don't know what it is, but ever since I met you their conversations seem childish. I like talking to you about stuff. I don't know why, but you seem more interesting. I know I've said that before but sometimes I get a bit tongue-tied and don't know what to say. I don't want you to look at me like a kid — 'cause I'm a man, and you talk to me like I am. I really hope you will come to the chat when you get this.
Take care,
Declan X

Willow stared at his words as though they were the first she'd ever seen in her life. This young man was doing something to her - touching her – touching her heart. He barely knew her, yet she felt as if she'd known *him* all her life. It was nice. She found herself smiling, feeling as though she had finally found a friend, a very unique friend, one who was looking for a special friend as well. The longer she gazed at his words the more she found herself wondering what he looked like, and her mind instantly comprised an image of a tall, slender, dark-haired, brown eyed young man with very pale skin, the type of man she'd always been attracted to. She quickly made a mental note to inquire this when next they chatted. He always called her *pretty lady*, yet he had never laid eyes on her. But if he asked she would try and describe herself the best she could without evoking a false image. She even wondered if she would exaggerate - just a smidgen - yet she never lied, so if he asked she would be truthful and hope his mental image of her wouldn't be shattered by the description she would give. Her eyes traveled to the computer's clock which reminded her that if she didn't soon get the lead out she would be drastically late for work. This could not be let happen for she could not run the risk of another lost client.

All that day at work Willow thought about Declan, picturing him over and over in her mind as she went about her duties. She had to hurry; the lawyer's appointment would not be long in coming, but regardless of this her thoughts kept returning to Galway, and the young man who tugged at her heartstrings. In many ways it was ironic, for it never seems to fail when one dreads an impending circumstance or the need of extra time to prepare, it's gone before you know it, yet when it's in reverse and you're wishing the time gone it just seems to drag. So it was for Willow. Finally three o'clock crept around and she found herself speeding for home.

Four thirty would not be long in coming. She couldn't help but wonder what her husband's latest offer would be. If he remained true to form it would not contain much worth writing home about, but there was always the possibility his conscience would remind him of the years she had given him. Yet she was not holding her breath. Had she done that from the first day he had walked she'd be dead from suffocation, for according to the begrudging offer thus far it was obvious he had given it no thought at all. By three forty-five she was ready with time to spare, and what better way to spend it but to take a little trip to her favorite chat with hope a certain someone would be there.

She was pleased to find Declan present along with the usual lineup of names. But today a new one appeared, a female, using the persona of *Sweet Sue*. Willow wondered at this, but soon dismissed any unsavory notion other than the fact it was a very busy chat room. Everybody there was a great fan of the talented actor the site honored, so the array of female names were a constant staple, yet she found herself remembering the increase in female population ever since *Dream Come True* had become a permanent fixture. She lost no time in saying hello to everyone with growing hope *Dream* would soon click her name, pulling her upstairs to the private chat.

The usual nonsense was well underway with different names insulting others with silly nonsense that only a glutton for punishment would enjoy. "No wonder Declan says what he does about these kids," Willow thought in dismay for she too couldn't get over the idiotic sentences, ill-spelled words, and senseless salutations being batted back and forth. The monotony stimulated the brain about as much a monochromatic color scheme lifts the spirit. Each day seemed to bring an even larger array of lame conversation, and an even greater assortment of idiots to type it out. Willow realized she was not the most informed, well read person, but compared with the present group languishing in this chat room she must have appeared a rogue scholar.

Dream Come True: *Knock-knock!* With this Willow mystically found herself whisked away to a world of splendor, as she typed, *Hello Dream,* trying her best to make her words smile as much as she was, yet striving to keep them as simple as possible as to not appear overly anxious of receiving this wonderful gift.

Dream Come True: *Hey-hey, pretty lady, 'tis Declan, remember, your Irish lad? I wrote to you a few times. Have you forgotten me already?* His content of words made her eyes gleam. "Forget him," she thought in apprehension, hardly believing he could think such a thing let alone express it, as she quickly typed, *certainly I remember you. Thank you very much for your e-mails, and your thoughtfulness, and your concern, and your kindness.* She immediately wished that she hadn't formed her sentences as though she were still in primer grade making him think her a brainless twit.

His reply instantly appeared on the screen. *De nada, pretty lady, I was really hoping you'd write back, but I guess you wouldn't want to write to someone like me.*

Left in Limbo: *Why on earth would you say that, Dream – sorry - I mean Declan? I really like that name, it's very Irish isn't it? Oh, and by the way I need to ask what de nada means.* She truly loved his name. It was very unique, totally unknown in her circle, but something told her it was most befitting. She also found some of the words he used intriguing.

Dream Come True: *It's Spanish for 'you're welcome'. Prichard has taught Spanish to my brothers and me for years. She calls it the language of love. It's funny to hear her speak it 'cause she's got this very formal English accent. But I like Spanish a lot and speak it fluently. About my name, it's Irish. Ma made it up. It's really a combination of my parents' names. It's okay I guess. It's just a name - nothing special.*

Willow instantly picked up on something within his words, as well as the way he typed them – sadness perhaps? They were mere words, yet it was as if his hands had come through the screen, touching her own with fragile innocence, as she typed, *Well I really don't think many people like their name all that much. If the truth be known most would change it if they could. I never liked mine very much, though I don't mind my middle one, in fact I quite like it.*

Dream Come True: *What is it?*

Left in Limbo: *Lane.* Willow found herself hoping he might fancy it as much as she did.

Dream Come True: *It's different, pretty too, but I like Willow, it suits you. Why don't you like it?*

Left in Limbo: *I really don't know. Maybe it's because I feel it means nothing special, like the way you feel about yours. But that's what*

WILLOW'S WALK

I mean about people not caring much for their names. By the way, Declan, I'm curious to know why you think it suits me. You've never seen me, you don't even know me. His words, seemingly as if he'd already had them lined up and ready to go, appeared swiftly. *Don't know, I just do, possibly the way you talk. You seem to be so open and honest. It's refreshing, and I like it. So will you describe yourself, and I'll see if it's like I picture you?*

She could almost feel him quivering. How well her senses served her, yet she quivered as much as he thinking of the answer she would give; more importantly how well it would be received. The scenario that she had earlier contemplated had finally arrived. How she wished she could tell him she was a young, supple, vibrant woman, fresh out of school, ready to take on the world and anything that came her way. But she wasn't. She was old enough to be his mother and then some, coming from a generation he could only read about in history books. She well remembered how it felt to be nineteen, but it was a far cry from *his* nineteen with many pitfalls in between. In many ways the world that she had known at his age would seem totally alien to him, certainly something that couldn't help but cause awkward problems if they were discussed, yet regardless of all of this she would not be dishonest.

Left in Limbo: *Well you already know my age so that doesn't need repeating. I'm just slight of 5' 5", weight about 120 lbs. I have fairly long chestnut hair, fair complexion, green eyes and I actually manage to stay fairly slim - which isn't too bad for having birthed two kids.*

As she typed, her stomach felt as if it had become bound by a thousand knots. One might think this a first date, where approval is desperately sought, yet little did she know Declan was feeling the exact same, as his trembling fingers quickly typed, *you're beautiful! You look exactly like I visualize you and you take my breath away.*

This revelation brought Willow to her knees, and she blushed like a schoolgirl, regardless of the fact she was a middle-aged woman. It had been so long since she felt this sensation that it felt like the first time she had ever experienced it — or had she ever experienced it until now? She found herself looking over her shoulder; half expecting prying eyes to emit their disgust at her carnal behavior. For a brief moment she paused, and then typed, *Thank you, Declan. It's been a long time since I was ever asked to describe myself. Come to think of it I don't think I ever have, until now.*

Dream Come True: *You sure did a great job. How do you picture me?*

With this request Willow froze. She so wanted to know, yet a part of her liked the mystery of him. What if he was nothing like she had pictured? When it came to herself she had to admit to the sin of vanity, but when it came to others she did not judge how much she liked someone simply by their physical attributes, regardless of how much they possessed or how little. What is within a person is what counts, and that's the way she saw Declan, no matter what her mind's image of him may be, still she wouldn't be sorry if he was as she had pictured. Taking a breath, she typed, *well you're Irish, so I feel you have dark hair - possibly black - and because you're so young your skin is taunt and pale. I feel you're rather tall, slim, muscular, and you have huge, interesting dark eyes - brown perhaps.*

She couldn't help wondering just how close she was, but his response was almost instant. *Wow! You're not far off the mark — except for the color of my eyes. They're blue – which is no big deal in Ireland except mine are kind of ocean blue, which would make them not a normal blue at all, but everything else you got right — almost exact! Do you want to see how close?*

Oh how she did, but she took her time as to not appear overly anxious, as she typed, *I should have realized your eyes would be blue — but ocean blue, now that's different, and how nice! I agree with what you say about blue eyes being common there, after all you are Irish – I am as well — well of Irish descent. Most of the people in my family have blue eyes so I guess it is pretty common, yet I don't know what happened to mine. I always wanted brown, that's my favorite eye color.* She stopped at that, wondering what he would type next.

Dream Come True: *Yeah blue eyes are nothing special here. Mine are the color of the sea, unless I'm really tired, or about to faint, then they go really dark, almost black. I just sent you my picture. Now you can see how close you are.*

Willow's heart thumped loudly as excitement bubbled within her. Her mail notification instantly signaled his photo's arrival. She nervously grasped hold of the mouse. Doing her best to remain calm she began to guide the cursor toward the attachment, but the damn thing wouldn't move, and fearing the computer was beginning to act up, thought, "Don't freeze now," and pleaded, "Please move," while she willed the cursor forward. Finally it relented, and her finger immediately clicked *open* while she sat, eyes consumed with splendor. He was sitting erect with his back pressed firmly against a window of which flooded his firm-muscled shoulders with brilliant sunshine. His black hair was rather short, though styled most becomingly as it lay loose and wispy upon his high forehead with a few strands almost covering his eyes. His dark, brooding stare looked away from the camera's lens, giving the illusion he did not wish his photograph taken yet knew he would be captured by the prying eye set upon him. He wore a form fitting, white sleeveless undershirt which openly revealed his muscular chest. He did not smile; instead wore a look of elusive sadness upon his full, succulent lips. He looked well beyond a mere nineteen years, and he simply took her breath away. She just sat staring, so enthralled by his image that she hadn't noticed his awaiting words upon the screen.

Though Willow was unaware of it, Declan was sitting in a tense, anxious manner hoping she would like what was being revealed. His computer held many images, some more revealing than others, and at that moment he couldn't help wondering why he'd chosen the one that he had. Maybe it was because it was his favorite, and presented him the way in which he wanted to be seen. But regardless of what she saw, Declan felt that he had found what he'd hoped to find in this woman. It didn't seem to matter that she was thirty-five years his senior, for he felt a rapport with her like no other before, as he anxiously awaited response to his pre-typed words. *What do you think? Huh? I think I look like a dork. It was taken on holiday last year in Morocco. I had just come from the pool. Prichard used my brother's cam to take it when I wasn't looking. She says I have an interesting profile, though the angle's not really from the side. I was looking away at something else.*

His explanation gave Willow the impression he was feeling the need to somehow apologize for not looking directly into the lens, but before she could type her response, he quickly asked if she liked it. She adored it, but simply typed, *it's very nice, Declan. Thanks* for sending it. It's also nice to hear that your family includes your nanny in your holiday vacations.

Dream Come True: Yeah, we take both she and our housekeeper. Ma says they are part of our family now because they've been with us so long. I wouldn't know what life was like without them. For as long as I can remember they've been there. I always laugh 'cause they both rattle when they walk.

His interesting words filled Willow's screen with a spell-binding presence, as she thought, "What an odd remark," and typed, *what do you mean, rattle?*

Dream Come True: It's the bottles of my medication and smelling salts they carry around in their pockets.
Left in Limbo: Why? Do you tend to be ill a lot? Willow's interest suddenly heightened.
Dream Come True: No not really. I have asthma and I tend to faint a lot. I'm anemic, and I have to take iron injections. Prichard injects me when required.

Declan had fired off his answer as though it were a recorded message, but Willow's heart had instantly gone out to him, and she found herself wishing she could hold him close. Anemia really isn't life threatening, but it certainly would be a nuisance in the same way asthma could be. She had experienced her share of that with Benny who had coped with asthma all through his childhood, thankfully outgrowing it by the time he'd become an adult. Yet when the hot, hazy days of summer rolled around she could still detect a bit of wheezing whenever he was near. He often wondered why she would become concerned, yet little did he realize a mother's protective instinct does not cease once childhood reaches its end, nor did the familiar sounds go undetected by a mother's astute ears, and she typed, *I'm sorry to hear that, Declan, it certainly would not be the best feeling, especially never knowing when an attack might happen, or the need for medication. I've had a fair amount of experience with this as my oldest son had asthma quite bad when he was a child, but he's outgrown it to quite an extent. He still gets wheezy if the air's really humid, but he copes with it. Sounds like you do too, sweetie.* She was hoping he would find her words encouraging for that was the way in which she had meant them. Before she continued she glanced at the time, finding it hard to believe where it had gotten to so fast. Her appointment was almost upon her, and she quickly typed, *I'm sorry to cut this short, Declan, but I have a lawyer's appointment in a few minutes concerning my separation. I'm not looking forward to it but I have to take care of it. There's nothing I'd like more than to stay here with you, but I can't. I hope you understand.*

Dream Come True: *Oh, I didn't know you were married. Hey maybe I shouldn't be talking to you,* and as he typed he found his heart experiencing a horrid letdown.
Left in Limbo: *Declan, if you bothered to read the words I just typed you would see I was separated. I've been that way for quite some time now, but things are still up in the air as far as any settlement is concerned. That's what I'm discussing with my lawyer today — btw do you have a girlfriend?*

His dampened spirits rose with these encouraging words, and he quickly typed, *nope, no bird, just the occasional fuck when I need it from this girl I know in town, but she's nothing to me.*

Hope your appointment goes well, miss. I really wish there was something I could do but I don't have any experience with what you're going through. Did he abuse you? Sorry for asking, it's really none of my business.

His question had vividly brought that horrid night to Willow's mind, and she swore she could still feel the thrust of Jonas' rough knuckles brushing her chin. For a brief moment she sat gathering her thoughts, before she typed, *No, Declan, he never hit me, but there are many kinds of abuse and I really don't want to go into that right now; besides I haven't time.*

Dream Come True: *You don't have to tell me anything if you don't want to, Willow. But I don't think I could do that — especially if you were mine. I want you to know that! But I know you'll handle things ok at your lawyers - you'll be cool.* His words had appeared in rapid succession, and Willow was about to type a response when he quickly added the fact that he'd be thinking of her, and asked if she'd return to the chat in order to let him know how she'd gotten along.

Willow was thoroughly impressed by this young man, and inwardly touched by the gentle nature he was projecting. With the exception of Megan, Will, Winifred, and her own immediate family, it had been a long time since anyone cared what happened to her, let alone took the time to tell her, and she typed, *You are very thoughtful, Declan, and I want to thank you for that. I'm going through a really rough time and your words help more than you realize. I'll try my best to return after dinner, but I can't promise, so I won't.*

Dream Come True: *That's okay, Willow, will you write me?* With those words he instantly found his thoughts consumed by her. He wanted to spend as much time with her as he possibly could; he just wasn't sure she wanted the same.

Left in Limbo: *I'll try, sweetie. Now I have to go.*

As the screen faded to black, she secretly blew him a kiss then raced down the stairs. She didn't want to leave, but the clock had reminded her she must. As it was she would be cutting it close, but tardy or not, she could not miss this appointment.

Chapter 16

LET THE BATTLE BEGIN

The streets were somewhat slippery as the day's travel of cars, combined with the unusual warmth, made them slick. The tires fought to hold their grip upon the pavement as Willow drove along, her mind remaining upon the young man she'd left mere moments before, yet knowing she must clear her mind of any unnecessary thoughts if it was to become the steel trap she would need. As she turned into the crowded parking lot her eyes scrutinized the endless rows of cars with hope of locating a single space. Finally one presented itself, and none too soon for her watch now read 4:29 pm. She had arrived with one minute to spare. Realization of this preciseness actually made her chuckle, for it brought to mind a story her father used to tell about the days in which he worked at a welding shop in Smith Falls. Each day he would arrive at his job with exactly one minute to spare, followed by the same reenactment after lunch, which over the course of time brought him the nickname of *Minute Man*. He always laughed when he related this story, and she laughed the more she thought about the way in which she was repeating his habit.

Once inside the courthouse, she hurried along the main corridor of the aged building, listening to the echo the huge wooden doors made closing behind the latest client's arrival. As she pressed along, she couldn't help feeling a bit reserved, wishing with each step taken this appointment over and the entire ordeal finished, for the end of this black tunnel was becoming more elusive with each new day, leaving her to ponder the amount of time she must yet endure. Passing each door in search of the required one, she tried her best to train her thoughts upon the reason she was there, but try as she might, she could not rid her mind of Declan Quinn. "One thing's for sure," she affirmed under her breath, "He certainly knows how to lift a girl's spirit. He thinks I'm *cool*. It's been a hell of a long time since anyone thought of me in any way, let alone that way, but he does, and from this day forward I will be just that." This thought remained glued in her brain as she reached for the brass doorknob leading into her lawyer's office, and as she stepped inside, the decision had been made that come what may she would hold her head high, and never look back.

The Edwardian reception desk stood adjacent to the office entrance. Behind it sat Timothy Breen's secretary, wearing a beige suit, and sipping a cup of tea as she diligently worked away. As Willow approached the desk, the woman glanced up, smiled politely, and said. "Good afternoon, Mrs. Crosby, please have a seat. Mr. Breen is presently on the phone, but should be with you momentarily."

Nodding her head in agreement, Willow settled into an emerald wingchair and picked up the latest issue of a decorating magazine. As she began thumbing the pages her eye caught the time upon her watch-face, and along with this discovery, found she was dreading this appointment even further when the realization dawned that it would be dark by the time it ended. Hopefully they could move through the legal jargon in a timely fashion and cut to the chase. After all that was the reason she was here, but if everything ran true to form it should not take long, for her husband's limited offer to date was anything but acceptable. She failed to understand how he could manage to escape so many issues, ditching every obligation along the way, but he had. Over the past year he had managed to shirk every responsibility he possibly could, which left her footing the bill for everything, bills of which Jonas himself had rung up. She was certain it was his calculated way of forcing her out of her home, for if he made it impossible enough, she would have no alternative but to knuckle under. So far she hadn't, but she knew that if something did not happen soon she was as good as on the street. The most upsetting fact was the knowledge that her husband could care less.

She leafed through page after page of unique furniture designs, and current wallpaper trends, wondering how in hell Jonas could change so much, and toss all those years away as though they'd never happened. She even found herself thinking about days long past - even meals they'd shared - all the while thinking how ironic it all seems, or what little is actually left at the end of the day. Another fresh page revealed exotic flavor in fabrics, explaining how their touch can stimulate the inner senses, and arouse the sleeping tiger within. Her thoughts centered on this page, wondering how parallel the field of design actually reflects life, for had she and Jonas added a bit more spice to their marriage then maybe she wouldn't be sitting here waiting to discuss a new way to dissolve it.

"Mr. Breen will see you now," the secretary announced, snapping Willow upright.

Timothy Breen greeted her at the door, and summoned her inside. "Please have a seat, Mrs. Crosby," he said, sweeping his hand toward two chairs standing before his desk. "I'm glad you could make it in this afternoon. Quite the storm we had, wouldn't you agree?" he asked, settling himself into a huge leather chair behind his mahogany desk while opening a large paper file awaiting attention.

"Yes, it certainly was," Willow answered; settling comfortably into the leather chair assigned her.

Breen studied the contents of a legal document, while Willow gazed about the room, finding the walls lined in multiple books bound in beautiful leather, many boasting gold lettering along their rigid spine, signifying the legal content within, while the wall directly behind Breen's desk proudly displayed assorted diplomas from university and law school. A few more minutes passed before the lawyer addressed his astute client.

"Mrs. Crosby, I received your husband's latest offer from Patrick Doyle the day before yesterday, which is why I wanted you to come in today. I have it here for you to go over, and as usual you're free to write anything in the margins you may wish to discuss or disagree with. I'm sure there will be numerous items that you will no doubt take issue with. I have spoken with Mr. Doyle about your husband's negligence concerning the utilities, and reminded him of the original agreement stating he would carry them until this matter is resolved." Looking over his glasses toward his client, he stated, "Now my secretary informs me there is an outstanding hydro bill. I will discuss this matter with Mr. Doyle. Hopefully he can immediately speak with his client about the urgency of the matter."

"Mr. Breen," Willow stated seriously as she placed the hydro notice on the desk before her, "my husband has no intentions of paying *anything*, he as much as told me so yesterday. I phoned him about this hydro matter and, well he just swept it aside like he does everything else. Somehow he's managed to divert everything into my name and continues to pay nothing. All I have is my own income - which is not much - and I recently lost a client so that takes away even more. I need assistance and soon. Hopefully this matter can immediately get into court because I feel that's the only way Jonas is going to give me any kind of help whatsoever."

Breen intently listened while scribbling notes upon a thick pad. It was obvious his work was cut out for him. Patrick Doyle was one of the best divorce lawyers in Ottawa, well known for his shrewd business ventures and under-handed tactics to prevail for his clients at all cost. However when it came right down to brass tacks Timothy Breen was no slouch. His reputation for unyielding performance in the courtroom preceded him, and he had stood in victory more times than defeat. Years earlier he had gone to bat for another woman who had found herself in a similar situation to Willow. The woman's case took awhile to settle, but when she finally walked out of the courtroom she was walking toward a brighter financial future. Willow was hoping to do the same.

"Now according to this latest offer, Mr. Crosby remains adamant about the sale of the matrimonial home. It also appears that Mr. Doyle has inserted a retribution clause for suffering and abuse," Breen stated, his right eyebrow rising slightly higher than the other at the last few words on the document before him.

Willow could hardly believe her ears. "Abuse?" she questioned in disgust. "Is he serious? That is a joke if I ever heard one! From what I've read so far the entire offer is a joke. It's absurd! There is absolutely nothing here that's any different from the last one — with the exception of that ridiculous innuendo. It's a lie! He sure has a short memory when it comes to who abused whom! What's it suppose to take to prove it, the loss of my front teeth — or worse?"

Breen shifted about in his chair, somewhat as if he were sitting on hot coals. "Of course not, Mrs. Crosby," he stated. "Try not to become upset. I do understand how infuriating this must be, and that is what they are banking on. I've got a few tricks tucked neatly up my sleeve, so try not to let it get to you."

"I'm afraid that's easier said than done, Mr. Breen. Especially when you have people breathing down your neck for money you haven't got. *It's embarrassing!* You know in all the years that Jonas and I were together we never once let things slide. Gaud I hate this! But I'll try and stick to your advice, if I can. I'll take this offer home and read it over in depth, but from what I've seen thus far you already know my answer," Willow stated as she folded the document in half, and shoved it in her purse.

Breen removed his glasses and stood, extending his hand, as he said, "Read it over carefully then make an appointment for the first of next week. I should have some news by then."

With obvious concern, Willow said, "Very well, but will you contact Hydro about this problem?"

"I can't guarantee anything, but I'll phone them," Breen replied as he hurriedly shook Willow's hand, before bidding her good day.

A light snow fell as Willow drove along the well-lit street toward home with her lawyer's words still fresh in her mind, and her husband's latest offer gnawing at her stomach. Her car sped over the wet pavement finding no difficulty holding to its course. But as she approached the required intersection with intent on making a left turn onto her street the light changed to amber, but there was no time to stop. The oncoming traffic had slowed to a crawl with full intention of stopping, but a fairly-new, dark blue pickup was traveling at a much faster pace than it should have been. The amber light was threatening red as Willow tried her best to brake, but the newly fallen snow had transformed the intersection to a skating rink, causing her to slide out of control. She frantically fought to turn the wheels in the required direction as the fast moving pickup bore down on the intersection, bound and determined to make the light. At the last possible second it swerved to the left, barely missing Willow, who slid around the corner and into the curb on the far right side of the snow-lined street.

She sat upright, breathing hard, heart pounding in her chest. A young man, who appeared to be in his late teens, was walking up the street and had witnessed the entire event. He approached Willow's car, and instantly began knocking on the window as he spoke in a loud voice, inquiring if she was alright.

Trying her utmost to gather her wits, she lowered the window, and stuttered, "Yes – I - I think so." Upon impact her purse had slid to the floor, and she nervously unfastened her seatbelt to reach for it. Retrieving it and locating a tissue, she dabbed her eyes, glanced at the young man, and said, "Thank you for your concern, but I'm okay. It's a good thing there's a fair amount of snow piled up, otherwise I'm sure there would have been some damage."

Shaking his head discontentedly, the young man remarked, "That son-of-a-bitch should have known better! Could have caused a serious accident with a fool move like that. Huh! There's never a cop around when you need one, is there?"

Willow couldn't help but chuckle, as she answered, "No, it always seems that way. But the main thing is I got out of the truck's path in time. I figured he wasn't going to stop. It's so icy I couldn't get stopped either, all I could do was pray he'd miss me," and she reached for another tissue.

"Well," the teen said, "the asshole purposely sped up to make the damn light. I watched him, but unfortunately didn't get his plate number. Are you sure you're okay?" With this question he smiled at her.

She returned his smile, but as she did she found herself delightfully riveted to his face in disbelief of how much he resembled

Declan Quinn. She actually gaped in awe before regaining her senses, and stuttering, "I-I'm s-sorry."

The young man look puzzled, as he inquired, "About what?"

"To stare at you like I've been doing," Willow answered. "It's just that, well, you resemble someone I know - well - I don't actually *know* him in the sense of the word - what I mean to say is you look very much like a young man I just met online. He recently sent me his picture, and I guess I can't get over how much you look alike."

"Well, I've heard my grandmother say everybody has a twin somewhere, so maybe I'm his doppelganger, this guy you're talking about."

"Yes I've heard that too. Anyway I'm glad you came to my assistance – by the way what's your name?"

"It's Dolan Quran."

Willow sat dumbstruck, staring straight at him as she looked him over. "You must forgive me," she stated, rather flustered. "Really, this is astounding. Your name is even similar. Talk about coincidence!"

Her mind instantly pictured Declan standing before her, and she couldn't help wondering what the rest of his body looked like. After-all his picture had only revealed him to his well-developed chest, but if the rest of him looked in any way of what now stood before her then he would be nothing short of model material. Returning to reality, she said, "Well I really need to move from this spot before I do get hit - or cause somebody else to - but I want to thank you again."

A broad smile parted the teen's full lips, as he replied, "You're very welcome, though I really didn't do much except check to be sure you were okay."

As Willow started the engine she again returned his smile, and said, "Well it's commendable, and in this day and age that is something to be proud of. Besides, it's nice to know that chivalry is not completely dead. You take care now."

The warmth of her little house instantly greeted her as she stepped inside the door, feeling as if she'd been away for years, and had finally returned to the safe arms of a loved one. Her nerves were still on edge from the close encounter with the pickup - not to mention the charming stranger - but it wasn't long before a mild sedative, accompanied by a steaming cup of Chamomile settled her down. Before long she was comfortably seated before her electronic friend, summoning its interior to suck her in and whisk her away to parts unknown. Her mail indicator immediately signaled another waiting message from Ireland of which she instantly opened.

Hi pretty lady,
How are you doing? How did your appointment go? Hope your news was what you wanted to hear, but even if it wasn't I bet you were cool the entire time. I can feel it. I think you're the coolest lady I've ever met - not that I've met that many - but I think you know what I mean. I was just wishing I could have said something more useful before you went, but I hope I helped somewhat. Guess you're not coming back tonight and it's getting pretty late here, but maybe you could come to the chat room for just a little while and see me when you get this mail — that is if you want to and you might not even get this before the morrow, but you know what I mean. Hey I'd really like to see you and maybe we could laugh or something. Anyway, Willow, I'll be there for you if you want to come by. Take care.
Declan. X

Her eyes read then re-read his words over and over until she could have recited them in memory class. There was something about the way he wrote. It was nothing spectacular, certainly nothing her high school English teacher would have given a whopping one hundred percent for, yet his words held an innocent honesty about them, so much so that she felt totally compelled to answer.

Hi Declan;
I hope these words find you well. I really want to thank you for your encouragement, as well as the support you freely give in a situation that must be totally removed from anything you've ever experienced in your young life. It really helps to know someone cares enough to say so, even though they may be far removed from the situation, meaning you of course, but I really appreciate it more than I can say. Since we've met I'm finding the mornings not quite so cold, and whether the sun is shining or not, it is, you know? This budding friendship between us is something very special and unique. I hope it's the beginning of a very long one. I won't be coming to chat tonight because I realize there's a five hour time difference between us, and I really can't expect you to stay up to all hours of the night for me. I hardly think your mom would appreciate that, let alone Miss Prichard when you're falling asleep in class. Besides, I'm not really in the mood to laugh, so I'll say goodnight and hopefully catch you in chat early tomorrow evening. Take care. Willow.

As she sent it off a twinge of sadness touch her insides, somewhat like a yearning for something that can't be gotten at the moment, but she had been correct in sending a reply instead of going to the chat, and she hoped he would somehow realize that her intentions were genuine. The last thing she wanted was to give the wrong impression, but she felt a mysterious hand gently nudging her forward. Yet regardless of this feeling she would not be propelled too quickly. That would be all she'd need, especially if Jonas found out; then she'd really be up a creek without a paddle. She made a solemn promise to herself that that would not happen. Just having the friendship of another man at this time would be bad enough, let alone one thirty-five years her junior. People would have a field day with it - especially Jonas - yet setting all jokes aside she found this synthesis not all that unsettling. She had never been one to judge people, let alone their age, regardless of the circumstance surrounding the issue, but as she thought further she could almost hear her sainted mother's remarks, and the reprimand would be something entirely its own. Still she didn't care, for she had found a friend. The delicious scenario might make a wonderful read in a risqué novel; then again her entire life had been a walk on the wild side, so what made this venture any different? The night wore on, bringing a chilling coolness to the house as she made her way to bed. It was warm there, and it made more sense to cuddle beneath the blankets instead of increasing the heat. She realized that tightening her economic belt meant decreasing not only the heat, but the hydro as well which meant time consumption on the computer. With this thought an anguished moan escaped her throat, causing her to snuggle further beneath the warm blankets.

Little did she know, but across the sea Declan lay coaxing his dreams to deliver him to the arms of the woman he found so intriguing, the mere thought of her aroused his senses to a level he had yet to experience. He had read her reply mere moments before leaping into his satin draped bed, with excitement encompassing his heart, and a smile upon his lips. Willow was different than the assorted young ladies he spent his time pursuing. They, like him, were only interested in a good time. They were much too young to think about anything else. When one is in their teens they have their entire life before them, and when their thoughts project the future they are filled with adventures and fun, not serious involvement and demands. Declan's world was a far different one than Willow's, where the entire world was his oyster. But when he thought of her, his insides fluttered as if a thousand butterflies had been set free within it. He wanted her to like him, wanted her to look at him like she must look at other men. Yet in so many ways he was still a boy, and he knew it. Still his wildest dreams aroused hope within him that she would one day fall madly in love with him; somehow give him an existence he only read about in steamy novels where the younger man purses the older woman until she's caught; then enraptured by his essence until it consumes her very soul. It always worked in fictitious settings, so why couldn't it be realized in real life?

Willow continued to consume young Declan's mind as his thoughts took them to wild, exotic places, where their days were spent swimming nude, their evenings spent sipping cocktails beneath the stars. He could well afford it; his family's distillery had grown to one of the largest in the world. Thanks to his father's sound business investments he and his entire family would never know a hardship or the meaning of one. He knew nothing of a life where one did physical labor to earn a living; it was assumed he would grow up and take his rightful place aside his brothers in the management of their company. The older Quinns had already tasted the assorted flavors of the difficult business world, but young Declan was not yet convinced it was what he wanted to do. It wasn't fun to think about serious ventures. Besides he had yet to finish school.

The time in Galway had grown late; still Declan - even aided by nightly ordered sedation - would not sleep for confusion had consumed him as to why he was beginning to feel the way he was. He'd had girlfriends, even a couple that he sexually desired and whose virginity he had stolen, yet somehow it was not the same as this new emotion nibbling his heart. He suddenly felt the need to write her once more, but the hands on the clock forbid it, and even should he disregard the time, he knew the morning reprimand from Prichard would not sit well when reported to his mother, especially should he be found face-down upon his lessons. It seemed hopeless, yet nothing would deter him. He had come from proud Irish stock where they got what they wanted, and would fight any person threatening their cause. Like his father, and grandfathers before, he was determined to pursue this woman who so intrigued him. He would make her see him as a man, and capture her heart. As sleep finally took him an enraptured sigh escaped his throat as he silently blew a kiss to the west.

Chapter 17

THE WRATH OF PRICHARD

Morning dawned in Galway to the thrilling calls of hungry gulls in search of a morning meal. Patches of ice formed upon numerous portions of the Bay's pristine water, but the determined scavengers would not be deterred, for their hunger was great, and their stomachs empty.

"Declan Quinn, get ye lazy self out of that bed!" Cailen Quinn snapped in her fun-loving manner. "Mrs. Donnigan be having yur breakfast waiting so long the pots be boiled dry!"

"Mmmm — what?" Declan questioned in a sleepy tone.

Walking past his door, Cailen sharply replied, "'Tis well past seven, me darling, and ye best be getting yeself upon yur feet! I don't want ye late for class again! Ye been dragging yourself these last few morns as it is. Miss Prichard be anything but amused by it – I not be either! Ye best be pulling up yur socks if ye know what be good for ye!"

At the sound of his mother's lively conversation with Prichard in the hall, Declan figured he'd best drag his tired body out of bed. He couldn't distinguish what was being said, but judging from the tone figured it was serious. "What'd I do now?" he muttered to himself as he went about preparing for the day. Time filtered away. It wasn't long before a knock firmly sounded upon his door. Before he could respond another rap sounded along with Prichard's stern voice, stating, "Master Declan, are you about? It is well past the hour and we are fast approaching class time. You have yet to consume your breakfast!"

With toothpaste oozing from his mouth, Declan hollered, *"I'm coming, Miss Prichard!"* and under his breath, groaned, "Geez," as he swish-away the sticky paste. He quickly rubbed a bit of styling wax through his tousled hair, creating spikes where he wished, grabbed his shirt, and tore out the door almost knocking his mother to the floor in his haste.

"Declan, watch where ye be going! Ye almost bowled me over!" she exclaimed as she swatted at him with her hand.

"Sorry, Ma, I got to run - I'm late - again. Miss Prichard was just here calling after me," he explained reverently while he steadied his mother on her feet, brushed her cheek with his lips, then continued his tear toward the stairs.

Cailen laughed toward the heavens as she shook her head, and remarked, "Oh my but that boy be a handful, Derek darling. He be so like ye in so many ways - aye but ye be proud of him. But I not be knowing what be on his mind of late. He be forgetting everything. Maybe he be falling in love, after all it be coming that time," and as she spoke she clutched her rosary while a sudden sadness consumed her.

Declan bound into the kitchen, sliding half way across the floor before coming to a stop, as he exclaimed, "Top-o-the morning to you, Mrs. Donnigan!" all the while flashing a daring grin her way before flopping himself before his place-setting at the large, glass topped table.

"Aye, 'tis about time ye showed yurself!" the portly housekeeper retorted sharply. "Ye breakfast be almost burnt to a crisp — and don't be telling me to make another! 'Tis ye own fault, sleeping so late ye be missing out! The other boys be on their way long ago, but ye still be sleeping the grand morning away like a dosser!" But he could see her cheerful smile waiting to burst forth, as she muttered, "Now get on with ye, and be eating yur breakfast!"

With the morning meal consumed, Declan finally sauntered into the spacious elongated classroom his mother had converted out of an unused drawing room. She had found no use for the room's prior function after Derek's untimely death, so had it converted to a traditional classroom complete with blackboards, books, and desks. Matlida Prichard had taught all four Quinn brothers from primer grade through high school. She'd had her work cut out for her, but never once did she falter in her duty as a teacher, or to her entrusted students. However with each passing year the youngest Quinn had become more of a handful than any of his siblings prior, and try as she might she felt she was not only losing her patience, but in fact control over him. It appeared the more she tried stressing the importance of an education, the further he seemed to drift from it. She found this difficult to understand, she even found *him* more difficult to understand as each new day presented itself. There was a time when his young mind had been a virtual sponge, soaking up detail after detail of countless subjects and topics. He would even challenge her when the answer didn't appear to make sense, and she never ceased to marvel at the meticulous detail he gave to each and every area he studied, that is until recently.

"Now, Master Declan, are we ready to delve deep?" Prichard inquired in an uplifting tone.

Her charge sat slouched at his desk, looking dazed, his head supported by his right fist. His attention seemed lost; it was anywhere but in the classroom for he didn't even appear to hear his tutor's voice, and she was completely annihilated when a dreamy smile consumed his lips while his eyes closed fully.

No longer withholding her pent-up annoyance, Prichard bellowed, *"Master Declan!"* and slapped her clipboard upon the desk at the precise moment her foot stomped the floor.

Startled, Declan jumped, knocking his open textbook off his desk. It slammed upon the floor, ripping a couple of pages in the process which then tore completely out when he hastily tried to retrieve them. The more he fumbled, the more disheveled the mess became.

"Fuck!" he exclaimed in frustration, his long fingers desperately scrapping everything together into an unruly mess. The uneven pile took no time in collapsing, papers sliding everywhere, which caused him to scream, *"Blast it! The bloody thing can damn-well sod off!"*

Prichard's mouth fell agape, as she remarked, "I beg your pardon! You will not take that tone here or anywhere else, young master! You will gather that outrageous mess, place it in the trash-bin, and return to your desk immediately! Do I make myself clear?"

The boy snapped to his feet, and quickly began to carry out her wishes, as he remarked, "Aye, Miss Prichard, I'm sorry! I just seem to be all thumbs this morning!" The wastebasket appeared a mile away but he made it with record speed that would make a sprinter proud. Then sitting erect in his chair, awaited his tutor's initial instruction of the morning.

Prichard approached him, stopping just slight of his desk as she began the lesson's instruction. The morning wore on, as did Declan's patience as he sat fidgeting, twirling his fountain pen around his fingers until it suddenly flipped out of them, and landed upon the marble floor, splitting open, ink splattering everywhere. He opened his mouth to cuss, but nothing was coming out and Prichard was growing near, her eyes expressing her abhorrent thought without need of verbalization. She scurried to grab paper towels, and on return handed him a partial roll along with instructions to promptly remove the mess.

"Really, Master Declan!" she fervently exclaimed. "I do not know *what* has come over you! Your attention span is that of a piss ant! It is anywhere but on your studies!" As he diligently scrubbed away, she stood vigil above him, and continued, "I was speaking with your mother this morning about this very issue! And I really do feel that if you cannot listen to me any better than you recently appear to, then as much as it pains me to admit, it is best to have you sent to private school in England — further more I think it best to inform you that your mother agrees!"

This news could not have shocked the boy more than had it been an unexpected thunderbolt sent down from the heavens. He couldn't be sent away! He had never known any other home other than the house he'd grown up in *or* Galway itself. His mates were here. His life was here. He could not be banished!

"You can't send me away! I won't go!" he vehemently hissed, trying his best not to cry. He truly did admire Matilda Prichard, but for as long as he had memory she had always made him somewhat nervous. Times like this made it even worse. He fumbled and fussed with the inky mess, desperately wishing it would just disappear along with him. A tortured moan escaped his throat and he finally gave up, shoving the inky slime beneath his desk. He tried getting to his feet but the room suddenly spun, its brightness fading to black. He could feel himself falling forward, and he gasped, "Miss Prichard, I'm … I think I - I'm going to … faaa…."

She was already ahead of him, for she knew him like the back of her hand and had coped with these spells many times during the course of his life. Her arms came firmly around him, supporting his weight while guiding him to a daybed just back of her desk. She eased him down, silently giving thanks he had not lost consciousness entirely for he was no longer the tiny boy she once carried when these spells befell him. It had been quite some time since one had, and just as she had then, quickly retrieved the trusty vile of smelling salts from her pocket, and waved them beneath his nose, speaking gently as she did. "Master Declan, can you hear me? Come now, breathe deeply and just remain still until this feeling passes."

She swiftly poured a glass of water from her desktop container and held it to his lips, brushing his hair off his face as she continued to care for him as if he were her own child. The spell soon passed, allowing him to sit up. She instructed him to sit quiet for a few minutes and that she would be dismissing him from class for the rest of the day, provided he went to his room to rest. This request did not require coaxing, and before long he was in his room, supposedly in bed, yet he figured what Prichard or his mother did not know would not hurt them, so he quietly settled into the black leather chair before his computer. He somewhat felt disoriented, but this was nothing new for he always felt that way after one of his spells, but he felt the need to talk to someone who understood him. He needed to talk to Willow.

The screen jumped to life. Declan may have been lacking in the majority of his studies, but one subject in which he excelled was typing. He could surpass the world's most accomplished secretary in speed, and before long his message was completed and on its way. He knew the time in Ontario, he also knew it was unlikely his intended would be home unless he'd gotten lucky and she wasn't working. The only way he would know was if she instantly replied, which meant she was on-line. It also meant that she just might be in the chat. A quick click upon his mouse instantly transported him there where he quickly signed in to find an assortment of names, some familiar, some not, but the one he'd hoped to find was nowhere in sight. A surge of disappointment consumed him to the point of weeping; he so badly needed to chat with her. Time passed as he stared at the screen, but it wasn't long before he found himself whisked into the private chat by *Sweet Sue*. He really didn't wish to talk with anybody at the moment, especially if it wasn't the one he had hoped to find, and definitely not with the one commandeering him at the moment, so he left. No sooner did he arrive back in the main chat when he was again pulled upstairs by the same girl.

Sweet Sue: *hey dream how's it goin huh?* Declan was not up for this. He didn't wish to be rude yet he had no intention in passing the time with anyone other than the one he sought. Soon another message appeared on screen. *Hey I saw ya come in. I've been waitin 4 ya ta show, hows it been goin 'since we last hung out?*
Dream Come True: *What do you want? I really don't want to talk.*
Sweet Sue: *then why are ya here?*
Dream Come True: *I said I didn't want to talk — especially privately.* Oh how he wished she'd just go away.
Sweet Sue: *when are we gettin' together again, Declan? It's been awhile. I haven't forgotten the last time ... it sure was good, lasted longer before ya cum – yur gettin' better, boy! I was at the pub the other day lookin' for ya but old man barkeep said ya haven't been in there for awhile, but I told 'em I'd track ya down, seein' ya don't giv out your number soz I can call ya and at least have some fun on the phone – but wez here now may-b-we can cyber!*

Declan openly sighed while he read her choppy English, thinking for a girl who professed to be so well-spoken, she certainly never learned to spell very well, let alone execute her thoughts in a legible manner. But what could he expect; he was in an internet chat.

Chapter 18

WHAT COULD POSSIBLY LURK INSIDE A SIMPLE TELEPHONE?

Declan was used to girls giving him their phone number, but because of an unfortunate incident that had happened when he was three years old, he was left with an uncanny fear of telephones, and could never bring himself to answer one, or use one. As he stared at Sweet Sue's enticing request, his mind again envisioned the reason why he couldn't adhere. It had all come about on a stormy day in early fall during his older brother Daniel's ninth birthday. His parents had thrown a huge party complete with pony rides, streamers, balloons, ice cream, and a huge cake. The highlight of the party was to be a surprise visit from a renowned American ex-circus performer by the name of Marvin Lederman, better known in the field of entertainment as *Peepers the Clown* whose specialty was painting children's faces to match his own. He was best known throughout Ireland for his unique makeup technique, and was often hired for children and adult parties alike.

The celebration was planned for Saturday, September twenty-ninth, at one o'clock in the afternoon. The ponies had arrived early and had been taken to the stables where the children would be riding in the enclosed paddock situated directly behind. The little guests, along with their parents, began arriving just before one, and as each child arrived they were given a riding habit then escorted to the stables by the Quinn's groom. Declan, looking dapper for his age in a tailored riding habit and high topped patent leather boots, was among those patiently waiting their turn. He had ridden from the time he could walk, as did all the Quinn boys at the insistence of their father. Cailen also rode, and had taught each of her sons the fine art of equestrian horsemanship, including the stiff-spine discipline of English dressage.

While the children took delight in numerous rides, Mrs. Donnigan, assisted by Matilda Prichard were busy in the huge drawing room helping Cailen put the finishing touches to the last-minute preparations. The children would enjoy one hour of riding, followed by numerous games of chance in the drawing room before *Peepers* made his grand entrance, and on conclusion a sit-down dinner was planned for all, rounding off the afternoon festivities.

As the day wore on, ominous clouds continued to gather, threatening to spoil the party should they decide to open. The riding had concluded, and the children, awaiting the clown's appearance, were gathered in the drawing room enjoying the boisterous frivolity when the first clap of thunder shook the mansion. The lights flickered then partially ducked, sending Mrs. Donnigan rummaging for candles should they be totally lost. A few of the guests were heard commenting on the fun of it all, and how utterly ripping it would be to have a good old fashioned birthday party, the kind in which their grandparents would have enjoyed back in the day, but another horrendous clap soon diverted their mind from the good old days to the present, as they suddenly began calculating how intense the storm might become.

The wind picked up strength, driving torrents of rain against the huge, tapestry embossed windows. Derek, always the life of the party, was not one to be disillusioned by anything, let alone a mere storm, and immediately decided to entertain the guests by summoning the groom's assistance in the playing of assorted musical recordings. In the event the hydro was lost they would then resort to charades in candlelight. The storm grew worse, enticing Derek to weigh the possibility of sending his guests to the provided safety of the mansion's stone basement, or the massive steel-lined vault located back of his main floor office, but before a decision could made the strong gusts had lessened, and the crisis soon passed, but the rain did not let up, and the grounds were soon transformed to a miniature lake.

It was growing close to the time of *Peeper's* arrival, but instead of his anticipated knock upon the door the telephone rang. Everyone had become so engulfed in the activities that no one heard it ringing. As a rule Mrs. Donnigan answered, but she was busy keeping candles at the ready while Prichard and Cailen seen to the guests. Young Declan had wandered into the foyer following a stray yellow balloon of which gaily bounced in front of him. The phone continued ringing; still no one came to answer. Declan knew what a telephone was, but he'd always been used to seeing either the housekeeper or his nanny answer it, so he waited, watching for someone to come. Time lapsed while the ringing continued. Still no one came. Finally Declan approached the phone and lifted the receiver to his ear, but just as he did, a blinding flash of lightning seared the sky at the exact moment a piercing crash sounded at the front of the mansion. Everything went black! High pitched screams were heard shattering the darkness as frightened female guests thought the end had come. Mrs. Donnigan's earlier plight had proven successful, for candles were immediately set ablaze throughout the down-stair rooms, supplying much welcomed illumination to the otherwise Gothic setting.

In the commotion Derek soon realized that little Declan was not where he'd left him, and went looking for him. He no sooner entered the front hall than fists were heard pummeling the front door. Removing a lit, opulent silver candelabrum from the hall table, he held it before him and moved in the direction of the massive oak doors, but he had failed to see his son holding the ivory receiver in his quivering hand. As Derek opened one of the huge doors a brilliant flash of lightning, accompanied by a deafening crash of thunder ignited the sky just as *Peepers* frantically forced his way in, pushing past a startled Derek, and lunging in the direction of the phone. It was obvious that he had been caught in the deluge, for his face had been transformed to a grotesque mask of blue, green, red, and yellow oozing down it like a distorted river gone wild. He was out of breath, yet he railed ahead, spitting blood as he charged for the phone. Little Declan stood frozen to the floor, eyes wide in terror, tiny body shaking.

"Give me that Goddamn phone, brat!" *Peepers* hollered, and he pounced upon the quivering child and proceeded to pry the receiver from the child's stiff fingers. With blood oozing from his mouth, *Peepers* held the phone to his ear, and in a maniacal tone, shrieked, *"It's dead! The fucking thing is dead! Dead I say!"* If this wasn't enough to frighten anyone, the raging clown stared straight at the horrified child, and screamed, *"Then go ahead and die, you sorry bastard—Diiiiiiie!!!"*

Demanding an explanation, Derek rushed to his petrified boy just in time to break his fall. Some of the more adventurous guests had ventured into the foyer, and upon seeing what was happening, went straight to the aid of the injured clown who had also collapsed, almost knocking the concerned father off balance in his journey to the floor. A close friend of Derek's peered out the front door and saw *Peeper's* crumpled party van wrapped around a huge walnut tree, but the Quinn patriarch was far too busy tending his unconscious boy to take notice of the activity happening around him. Suddenly Cailen's terrified scream was heard the second she saw *Peepers*, but it instantly turned to hysterics when she saw her husband bent over their son's prone form. She tore to his side, screaming his name as Prichard came racing into the foyer. Part of her training as a nanny had been in the administration of first-aid, which is required when working with children as one never knows when its application may be required. Prichard was a strong woman who did not frighten easily, but when her eyes fell upon the ghoulish scene presenting itself she let out a deafening wail before speeding to the fallen boy. She could see *Peeper's* sorry condition as well, and following immediate instruction to Derek, went to the injured clown, but his condition did not appear life threatening for he was back on his feet, cussing a blue streak about the storm and the sorry condition of his van. The appearance of his face made things far worse than they actually were, still the nanny advised him to sit while she summoned help.

Mrs. Donnigan had arrived with a pan of cool water for the fallen boy when Prichard insisted a doctor be summoned immediately.

"Aye, Matilda, but the lines be down at the moment," Donnigan replied in an upset tone, setting the pan upon the floor before nervously wringing her hands.

"Then don't stand about fidgeting like a bloody ninny, Bridget! Do help Mr. Quinn with the young master! He should really be taken to his room instead of receiving treated upon the floor! I am certain this is merely another spell, but he has been unconscious too long for a mere faint. Try the line again!" Prichard ordered as she tended the wailing clown who was now openly sobbing into his paint-encrusted hands.

Cailen sat upon the floor, cradling her son's head in her lap while her husband continued sponging the boy's forehead with cool water.

"Declan, me poor boy," she sobbed, "please be opening yur eyes and be looking at Mummy. Please, darling one, ye need to be waking now." Looking forlornly at her husband, she anxiously asked, "What be wrong this time, Derek? He be in the faint far too long!"

"Hush, Cailen, calm down, darling princess, it really hasn't been that long, it just seems that way," Derek replied as he gently patted his son's pallid cheeks. "He'll be coming round soon, I'm sure," but his own concern was quickly growing.

Teetering on the verge of hysterics, Donnigan exclaimed, "The line still be down, Matilda!"

A look of realization suddenly crossed Prichard's stern face, as she asked, "Is Doctor Sullivan still about, Bridget?"

The frenzied housekeeper, now pummeling her hands within themselves, looked confused as she shook her head in bewilderment. Suddenly the fallen boy began convulsing, intensifying the situation, which caused Derek to summon Prichard's immediate assistance while he and Cailen fought to control their ragged emotions.

Abandoning any control she may have managed, Cailen screamed, *"Oh gaud, Matilda, help me precious boy for he be dying!"*

The huge foyer grew dense with rubbernecking guests trying to see what was happening. Prichard quickly seized the convulsing child and gently placed him upon his left side. "Someone fetch a spoon, or any firm object!" she snapped, just as an older gentleman, still attired in a riding habit and gripping a small leather satchel, rushed into the foyer.

"All will be well, Mr. and Mrs. Quinn, I be here now," Dr. Sullivan announced. Kneeling beside the fallen boy, he stated, "Ye son appears to be suffering a mild seizure. Everyone be standing back and give the wee one air! Miss Prichard, I be needing him kept as still as possible until this passes." Someone had brought a sterling knife which Prichard was preparing to put into play, as the doctor instructed, "Aye, that be it, place it squarely upon the tongue and keep it firmly suppressed so he not be trying to swallow." A few anxious moments passed, extremely long ones for the Quinn family, but it wasn't long before the doctor confidently said, "There now. The little fellow be relaxing. The worst be over."

"Oh, Dr. Sullivan, the Saints be praised for yur presence to still be about for me Declan. Is he to be coming round soon?" Cailen inquired in an elated manner as tears ran down her ashen cheeks.

The doctor looked deeply into each of his patient's indigo eyes before nodding his head with favor. Turning to Derek, he said, "Ye best be taking him to his bed. I'll be there directly. I need to be taking a look at this other fellow for a minute or two." As not to be over-heard, he took Prichard aside, and said, "Check the phone line again. I be needing an ambulance, especially for the little one, but if need be I will take him to hospital in me car. Would ye now be going and sitting with him 'till I come?"

Prichard nodded then immediately left as the doctor proceeded to check the angry entertainer. He couldn't help commenting on the bazaar condition of his face, and the fact that it was almost impossible to determine injuries until the macabre mask was removed. The irritated entertainer took immediate offence, but regardless of this, was assisted to a main-floor bedroom where the required privacy was adequate enough for an examination of which discovered a few minor contusions, a couple of chipped teeth, but no broken bones. The doctor advised X-rays, and suggested the man be driven to hospital where results could later be reviewed, but he must first see to the child. The miffed clown was lead away, but not before he was overheard stating his displeasure of the entire gig, adding that Derek would not only be billed an extra amount, but would be hearing from his attorney.

The small boy lay in the middle of a tiny bed covered to his neck with a dark blue duvet sporting leprechauns dancing a jig. His parents sat either side of him, hoping for some form of movement, any kind of sign their boy was returning to them while Dr. Sullivan, having begun an intensive examination, said, "It appears the wee lad has suffered a great shock. Nothing seems physically wrong, though I will need to take him to hospital to be completely sure."

Cailen gasped, clutching her husband's hand, as she cried, "Ooh no! Don't be taking me baby away from his home, Doctor! We can be caring for him here just as good as there. We have Miss Prichard, and Derek can be bringing a full time nurse to be helping. Please, Dr. Sullivan, I beg ye not to take him away," and her tears ran freely as she gazed upon her child's motionless form.

"Now-now, Cailen, me darling girl," Derek soothed gently, "the good doctor be knowing more than we, and if he be thinking Declan be needing to be in hospital then 'tis where he must be."

With imploring eyes she looked at her husband, and cried, "But, Derek, he be never away from home before. He be frightened if he not be in his own bed when he wakes. I not be letting him be frightened like that. I not be *allowing* it!"

Dr. Sullivan was busy taking the boy's blood pressure, but replied, "Mrs. Quinn, ye may be staying with yur son, if ye wish. I will order a bed readied for yur use so ye may remain with him at all times."

A smile lit Cailen's face as she breathed a sigh of relief, and said, "I be thanking ye, Doctor, and be taking ye up on yur generous offer for I will not be leaving me boy alone." Turning to Prichard, she kindly said, "Matilida, I would like ye to have Bridget prepare an overnight bag, and one for Declan. Aye, and by the way have her pack his favorite teddy."

The next morning found the young lad in hospital and still unconscious. His mother sat at his side, gently squeezing his hand while humming an Irish melody in her soft, sweet voice. One after the other she sang, all the while stroking his silken hair. Her huge, aqua eyes traveled the lengthy intravenous lines running to his slender little hands, and they filled with tears at the thought of the needles deeply inserted beneath the flesh. Her fingers lightly touched them, taking great care not to disturb them in any way, but trying her best to sooth away any discomfort they may be causing. For the life of her she could not understand what had caused this to come about, remaining further baffled as to the reason for his prolonged condition. But she was unaware of what he had endured mere moments before he lost consciousness. No one did, and so the reason for his condition remained a mystery.

Three days passed and still the boy had not woken. Dr. Sullivan had run numerous tests and the results always came back positive. Everyone was happy about this for it meant there was nothing internally wrong, yet he would not wake. Time was taking its toll on the little fellow, and it showed in his body, as well as his lips for they had become dry. Thin cracks were beginning to appear, yet he wasn't dehydrating for the intravenous kept needed moisture within his system. Cailen kept his lips as moist as she could with wet cloths, dribbled cool water upon them in her determination to keep them moist, even applied her own lip-balm, but nothing seemed to impede the dryness, and her tears spilled forth. Her determination may have been strong but her faith was stronger. At that moment she would have given her own life if only her son would open his eyes, and with his hands in hers, she bowed her head in prayer.

On the fifth day following the traumatic incident Declan regained consciousness. It was early morning, and his mother lay at his side sound asleep with her arm protectively over him. She was totally exhausted, but never once had she used the bed provided her for she refused to be an inch away from her son. His huge eyes opened and looked about in wonder of where he was. He wasn't frightened for he somehow felt in a cocoon of safety. In many ways he was. He gazed at his sleeping mother, smiled, and gently touched her face. She immediately opened her eyes, instantly fighting-back the joyous cry within her throat lest it frighten him. She could hardly believe he was awake. All she could do was smile as tears of elation streamed down her cheeks.

"Don't cry, Mummy," Declan said softly, "the bad clown died."

Intently peering into his eyes, Cailen asked, "What do ye mean, darling one?"

He reached for her, and as she embraced him, he softly whimpered, "Mummy, the bad clown holler at me. He holler so loud he scare me. He did not want me touching the ringing box. He called me bad names. He was telling me to die, Mummy. I try - I really did - but I'm still here with you - so the bad clown died instead."

That disturbing incident had happened sixteen years prior to Declan's present conversation in the chat room, but his memory of it was as fresh as if it were yesterday. Whenever the sound of a telephone was heard, the distorted face of *Peepers the Clown* leapt from his memory like a madman rushing at him, spitting blood, screaming at him, commanding death. When it had happened it had frightened him to the point of immobility, he could not even breathe, and before he knew it everything had gone entirely black. He had died - or so he thought - and even though he'd come to realize that a mad, death-seeking clown would not jump from within the receiver; he still could not bring himself to speak on the phone. He had tried, countless times he had tried but each proved as disastrous as the first, for it always brought that terrifying memory to life; often with dreaded results.

Sweet Sue: *hey dream, ain't cha gonna talk? Come on let's cyber? I'm up for it if ya want to!*

Her bold words propelled Declan to the present, but still he didn't wish to chat, as he typed, *I don't much feel like it!*

Sweet Sue: *whaz bout callin' me then? i givs u ma # if u want cuz i wanna talk to u.*

Dream Come True: *I said no! I'm not interested!* How Declan wished his typing could somehow relay his growing animosity, but again her jargon shot across his screen, *christ declan ya know what a hot bod I got – ya also know how much ya like ta fuck it so wuts up wit the cold shoulder?* Declan never bothered to answer, but she wasn't waiting for one. *I wanna knos whats goin' on ... is ur old lady still runnin' ur life ... WHAT THE FUCKS UP?!*

He could have left; maybe he should have, but instead he typed, *nothing.*

Sweet Sue: *what ya mean, nothin'?*

"Fuck! Why can't she just let it go?" he thought in disgust. He was in no mood to banter, but he realized she was bound and determined to hound him to sunrise, so he gave in, and typed, *I'm not getting into it with you right now. I'm not in the mood! Now I'm going to go.*

Sweet Sue: *givz me ur # and i can calls U.*

Dream Come True: *No!*

He'd had enough, and since it appeared Willow was not coming, he would leave. All he could do was hope she'd soon get his message and reply, better still come looking for him on her own. His head begun to swim, and he quickly retreated to his bed. The feeling soon passed as he stared anxiously into darkness, listening to his heartbeat, and envisioning the woman he so desired.

Chapter 19

SINKING DEEPER

The morning remained bright and cheery as Willow scurried about her duties at work. She had always loved this house; it so reminded her of her childhood home outside Smith Falls, and every time she stepped inside its solid walls it was like stepping back in time. Maybe it was the antique furnishings, the whitewashed cupboards in the rustic kitchen, possibly the wainscoting covering the dado portion of the walls, or maybe it was the house itself; whatever it was it embraced her as though she were a wayward child who had found her way home. The eccentric couple who owned it was among her favorite clients, for they always made her feel welcome, and treated her like family, not just someone who came once a week to clean.

Throughout her lengthy career in homecare she had encountered an array of clientele ranging from the eccentric, to the impossible, with an assortment of flavors in between. There were those clients, like the present John and Mary McCarthy – also Winifred Brown - who doted on her as if she were their only daughter. There were those in between who appreciated her service but kept it strictly on a professional level. There were those she never saw of whom she communicated with through notes and the odd phone call, and then there were those like Tomas and Nancy Richardson, who expected the impossible for the least amount of compensation in return. When she actually thought about this she had to shake her head in bewilderment, but regardless, she wasn't the least bit sorry to be finished with people who took advantage just because they knew her financial situation. She would have never considered asking anyone - let alone someone whom she might employ - to clean up after her in the ridiculous, often degenerate way in which that couple expected. She would have been thoroughly ashamed, but it goes to show that it takes all kinds to make the world go round.

John and Mary McCarthy were the exact opposite of the Richardson's. They had been born and raised in County Cork Ireland, and following the war, immigrated to Canada in 1946 where they settled on a one hundred and fifty acre wheat farm outside Saskatoon, Saskatchewan. Farming had been part of their heritage, but the harsh prairie winters had proven too much for them, and they sold this property in order to purchase a twenty five acre farm twelve miles west of Ottawa. John McCarthy was a tall, large-boned man, whom for many years worked as a conductor for the MYO Railway, making daily routes to and from Cornwall, Ontario. His wife Mary, along with their hired man Sean O'Grady, were kept busy with the demanding farm operation of which produced fifteen acres of assorted varieties of apples - one of which John had brought with him from Ireland - and ten acres of commercial Christmas trees.

Harvest time upon their farm was an exceptionally busy one, and one which created numerous opportunities for local children in which to earn much needed revenue for assorted books and school supplies. When Christmas approached, Mary, and the hired hand were again swamped, as people flocked from miles around to experience the country tradition of trudging in the snow until the perfect tree was located, marvel at the thrill of felling it themselves, and dragging it to their car, which in turn would transport it to its special place of honor within their homes.

Willow had been with the McCarthy's *and* Winifred Brown from the beginning of her service. She clearly remembered their response to her advertisement, as well as the first time she'd met them. It had been instant friendship all around, and even though Willow realized she'd been hired for her service, surmised from the very beginning that all three were looking for companionship much more than the need to have their house cleaned. Neither the McCarthy's, nor Winifred Brown respectively, had ever been blessed with children. They had once confessed that it was not by choice, but rather what nature intended. She felt saddened by this because she felt they would have made wonderful parents. They loved children, always doting on those who spent their spare time diligently working in the McCarthy's bountiful orchards, or tending the prize-winning roses in Winifred's magnificent English garden. Willow often felt these elders looked at her somewhat like a surrogate daughter, for she would be around the same age of theirs - had they had one - but at any rate she cherished her time spent with each of them.

As she gently rubbed wax into a century-old dining table, her thoughts drifted across the sea to her young Irish friend. As they did a smile consumed her lips with the very idea of him as feelings, long since dormant began to stir deep within. She hadn't checked her morning e-mail for she had overslept and was running late, but she couldn't help wondering if there would be something waiting. The more she thought about it the more excited she became, almost to the point of distraction. However that flimsy excuse would not hold water should she send a treasured heirloom to its demise. She prided herself on her expertise and high standard in which she set for all her clients, not just her favorites, and so far this standard had remained untarnished.

Finally the work day ended, and she found herself speeding toward home with anticipation of what may lie in wait. The roads were icy but she used common sense behind the wheel, even if it was somewhat lacking when it came to her newly aroused emotions and the man causing them. Her thoughts pondered on what his letter may say, possibly ask, or if it would say anything at all. But regardless of what it might contain, her overwhelming excitement at the very notion he may have written was enough to send her heart aflutter. She knew it was not a wise idea to let her emotions get the better of her, especially with someone so much younger, but regardless of her common sense withstanding, it was happening just the same. Before she knew it she was plopped before her computer, anxiously awaiting the mail. Her heart thumped so loud it actually echoed inside her head as her eyes scanned the list of messages waiting to be opened. Suddenly her eyes encompassed the name they so hoped to find, causing her already labored breath to further quicken with the realization his message was actually there. It was an accomplished feat in itself to make her trembling fingers do her biding, but as she held her fast-paced breath, her favorite son of Irelands' message opened before her dancing eyes.

> *Hi pretty lady:*
> *I find myself thinking about you constantly; so much so that I cannot seem to concentrate on what I'm supposed to do, y'know? Like this morning, I overslept. It took a long time to go to sleep thinking about you and wondering whether you were thinking about*

me. I was late for class again this morning, and Prichard was pretty pissed with me. Apparently she's been talking to Ma about sending me to boarding school in England, and she told me that today. I can't go Willow! I can't! I WON'T! I even got so upset I fainted in class. I needed you SO much when I felt that way. I wish you were here with me. I've been on pins and needles ALL day waiting for you and hoping you'll get this and maybe come to the chat. But I know you're probably too tired from work, but I miss you SO much. I hope you miss me too. I don't know what's happening 'cause I never felt like this before. I'm such a loser. I'm sorry to sound so desperate, but I kind of am. I can't help it, and I really hope you don't think I'm just being a knob, or anything like that, but I really like you. Please come soon. I'll look for you. D Q. X

P.S. Would you give me your address and phone number? I promise not to give it out to anybody so you don't have to worry — but I'd really like to hear your voice – even if I can't answer back. Do you think you could possibly do that for me?

Time ticked away as Willow stared at his words, almost entranced by the trapped feelings of desperation pouring forth, reaching out, and begging for her. As she did, she felt as if he was actually aside her, speaking in her ear. She could feel his anxiety, so much so that her body shuddered as if someone had just walked over her grave. As strange as it felt, she too was experiencing his desperation, but in an entirely different way. He was reaching for protection, understanding, and the need to be accepted for who he was striving to be. She too was in need of understanding, but also the desire to be touched, and the craving to be loved. Her rational mind demanded she listen, and not let her starved need for affection blind her to the harsh reality of the situation presenting itself, yet the magical bond that was forming between them would not be deterred by either toward the other.

A quick click of the mouse instantly swept her to the familiar chat room with its soothing blue walls, and familiar lineup of names. But tonight a few new names appeared who seemed to lose no time engaging in the rapid conversation filling the screen. The topic seemed to change as fast as a fickle mind, jumping from one idiotic notion to the next, and all the while Willow did her best to keep up as she patiently waited for Declan should he chance to drop by. The clock ticked away while the conversations continued to bounce about like multiple basketballs in play. The more time ticked away the lower her heart seemed to sink. She sat watching the screen, feeling tears well in her eyes as she wondered where he could be; more importantly why his absence was affecting her in the manner in which it was. After all their relationship could not go anywhere. She'd spent countless hours weighing the odds, and every time she sensibly came to what she thought was the right fork in this bewildered road, her heart would remind her of the way he made her feel. Time had grown late. She knew the five-hour difference between their countries would mean it was the middle of the night in Galway. There was no further chance he would be coming tonight, so she bid her farewells, and left the chat, but before going offline she decided to write him a brief letter.

Hi Declan,
Hope my words find you feeling better than when you wrote me earlier. I've been waiting for you in chat as you said you'd be there. I waited all evening but you never came. I guess that was kind of a lame sentence for you already know this fact. Anyway I wanted to tell you that I miss you too, and I was very sorry to have not been able to join you so we could spend some time together. I'm

concerned about the things you told me in your letter, as well as the way it's affecting you. I really hope that you're feeling better, and also what you overheard will not become reality. There's no need to borrow trouble before it actually presents itself, but should it happen I'm sure you will be just fine. And besides, sweetie, there will be computers there so you'll be able to chat with me, and you already know I will be happy to do whatever I can for you. I'd very much like to hear your voice, and even though I never give out my number I feel it's safe to do so with you. After all we've been chatting and corresponding for quite some time now, so I'll include it at the bottom of this letter. Tomorrow is another day and you'll see your morning long before I'll see mine, and I hope your eyes open to a sunny one filled with better things than yesterday.

She quickly typed the information he had requested and signed her name along with an added kiss, all the while envisioning the depth of his breathtaking eyes.

As she lay in bed, thoughts drifted while sleep gently touched her, whisking her across the sea to the Emerald Isle where she could frolic barefoot upon velvet moss, let it tickle her toes with delight, while she waited for her handsome prince to come. She could almost feel what she envisioned as voices of those who had gone before seemed to summon her. They too had danced upon this grass, their eyes sweeping the rugged landscape as each day awakened with newness and awe.

Chapter 20

CYBER-CIRCUS

Four months past, with Willow enjoying each free moment in deep conversation with her young Irish consort as they engaged in every topic imaginable, typing thoughts and comments back and force with perceptibility, but mostly affection. Each new day found them bonding even firmer than the previous. They couldn't wait to be together, for during the time they were the troubles of the world didn't exist for either of them, regardless of the fact that Willow's situation with Jonas was worsening, and Declan's fear of being banished to England loomed ever closer as he continued sinking deeper within the quicksand of his demanding studies. Yet none of this mattered, for they were together and completely consumed by each other.

One pleasant evening in early June, Willow sat before her computer, hopes soaring, and heart beating with wild passion as she traveled the cyber-jet to her young Irish love. It seemed she'd no sooner arrived in the chat than she found herself the centre of attention, and not in the most pleasing way. The majority of the time the resident names cordially greeted her as everyone exchanged pleasantries, but that was not to be the case this time.

WILLOW'S WALK

Sweet Sue: *whos u here ta speak wit as tho we don't know?* This ineptly spelled question was immediately followed by another impertinent person using the persona of *Anna Banana*, who scribbled, *hola it's the cougar! watza OLD persun like U doin hangin out herz 4 huh? we nos u jas lurkin fur hot guzs + the 1 ur chasin is dream come true, but hez here ta c me un maz g/fs not a dried up skuzbag liks U!*
Sweet Sue: *ya HO he liks US now — specially ME so ya maz well giv up cuz ur a loser boozer — LMFAO!!!!!*

The conversation – if one could refer to it as such - had come to a screeching halt the minute the two girls flung their impudent remarks into the ring. Willow was stunned, and for a few moments typed nothing while in surprise, thought, "What the hell is this?" She was honestly set aback at this sudden attack, trying her best to figure out who they were, and the reasoning behind not only their irregular use of the English language, but the viciousness behind the use. After a few passing moments, she typed, *yes, girls, you're right about who I'm here to see, but I hardly think it's worth 'laughing my fucking ass off' let alone any of your concern. Furthermore I resent the way you're both speaking to me. Neither of you know me, or the reasons why I come here, so I would thank you kindly to keep your inept comments to yourselves.*

Suddenly a rude response from *Anna Banana* shot across the screen like a star gone nova, *shuzt ur mouth ya scum bag — wez can say whtz we watz in here and thers nutin u kin du abouts it so don't b raggin on mas g/f ... HAG!*

Left in Limbo: *Look here, I never said or did anything to either of you to warrant being spoken to in this manner, so kindly have some respect for other people's feelings, if you don't mind.*

Sweet Sue: *well wez DO mind so watz ya gonna do about it?*

Before Willow could respond, another person, using the persona of *Hot 2 Trot*, jumped to her defense. *Look, you two, just knock it off! Willow is a nice person whose been coming to our chat for a long time. Whoever she's here to see is her business, so back off and leave her alone.*

Anna Banana: *u can fuk off 2 hot trot — nobodies talkin ta U!*

This had gone beyond reproach, not to mention getting everyone no-where fast.

Left in Limbo: *Look everybody, I don't mean to cause trouble for anyone. Yes, I am here for Dream Come True. We've become very close. We enjoy each other's company and there's nothing wrong with that.* Willow was fast becoming upset, her nerves getting the better of her.

Sweet Sue: *U is OLD enough ta b his GRAMMA — u shud b ASSHAMED ovs urself — hes cumin here ta b wit US now!* Before Willow could reply she found herself swept into the private chat by this same girl, firing, *I'm Declan's girlfriend! He luvs me cuz he said he duz and he laufs at U cuz he told me he duz. Hes been seein me for a long time so u can just start actin ur AGE and leves him ta b wit me – where he wunts ta b.*

"What the fuck is this crap?" Willow thought as her hackles rose, but she wasn't about to let this smart-mouthed girl away with anything, and she swiftly typed, *he never mentioned you any time we've spoken and we discuss everything. I asked him a long time ago if he had a girlfriend and he told me he didn't nor was he involved with anyone on a permanent bases. I didn't take him away from you or anybody else. I'm not like that! He's very dear to me and we've become special friends.* Willow had typed as fast as her fingers could manage in hope this girl would realize what she was saying and abort this ridiculous conversation, but it continued, as *Sweet Sue* shot-back; *u got ta b kiddin old HAG! — what would he see in someone as ANCIENT as U ARE! Yur a JOKE and he's LAFIN just as hard as me, so if u think he cud LUV u ur CRAZEEEEEE!!!*

This hurtful statement totally crushed Willow. This Sweet Sue person was blatantly telling her something she didn't wish to hear, yet the words were there in black type to read. It was obvious by the bait just typed that the girl was waiting for a response, but instead of giving her what she surmised would come, Willow fled the private chat just as *Dream Come True* signed in. His sudden arrival sparked an instant explosion of words upon the screen. Some people were cheering him on, others typing warnings to beware of hair that would fly when *certain* ladies became aware of his electrifying presence.

Dream Come True: *What's going on here? Where's, Limbo?*
Hot 2 Trot: *I guess she's gone, Dream. She was here a minute ago and was asking for you, but I don't see her name in the lineup.*

Declan remained in the chat hoping Willow might return, yet something told him if she had quickly left then something must have caused her to go — or *someone*. He was not a novice in chat rooms and knew the way they worked. After all that was the main reason one never gave their true identity. You didn't want strangers knowing anything about you other than what you chose to let them know, which was the main reason Declan never did, at least until he met Willow. He too had found himself thinking more and more about their age difference, yet it didn't seem to matter, for he had finally found someone who understood him, his needs, as well as his fears. For years he had battled with his problems, taking his temper out on whomever looked at him the wrong way, which in the local pubs had fast-gained him the reputation of someone to avoid at all costs. This certainly did nothing to boost his moral, or guide him in any direction except the wrong one. But when he was chatting with Willow his troubles vanished as if they'd never been. She touched him in a way he'd never been touched before; cleansing him like a fresh spring rain as it gently fell upon the awakening Irish landscape.

Hot to Trot: *If Limbo comes back do you want me to tell her you were looking for her?*

Declan felt as if the floor had suddenly let out from under him. He wasn't sure what he wanted to say, for this was not the person he had hoped to find asking him intentions that even he at the moment had no answer for.

Hot 2 Trot: *You just missed her, Dream. She came about 15 minutes ago, but I think she got pulled upstairs because she wasn't talking with people like she usually does until you come in.* This caused his nervousness to increase, as he typed, *do you know who pulled her up?*

Hot To Trot knew that Declan and Willow liked each other a lot, in-fact she thought it sweet, as she typed, *well the only ones that weren't talking in the main chat after she signed in were her and Sweet Sue.*

"Sweet Sue!" Declan thought in apprehensive surprise while a familiar twinge jabbed his gut. He wondered what this girl could be telling Willow — more importantly what Willow would think of what this girl might divulge. He had to chat with his special friend, but if what he was thinking turned out to be true then he may have just lost her.

Hot 2 Trot: *Dream?*

Dream Come True: *What?* Declan didn't wish to be rude but he was not really paying attention to anything other than his own thoughts.
Hot 2 Trot: *Any message for her if she returns?*
Dream Come True: *Well — nay — yeah! Tell her I miss her and ... well, never mind.*

Before more words could appear on screen Declan quickly closed the chat and opened his mailbox to see if there was any word from Willow. His heart raced with anguish as different names appeared - everyone wanted him - everyone kept bugging him - everyone except the one he needed to find. No message was there, and his heart sank lower than it ever had. He knew it wasn't all that late in Ontario, yet if she wanted to contact him she would have written, but she hadn't. "What had been said to make her leave so quickly," he thought, and his mind raced as fast as his pulse while his tormented thoughts continued, "I need to sleep and fast - least I can be with her in my dreams," and he opened a medication bottle, popped a few pills, quickly stripped down to his silk boxers, and jumped into bed.

Though unbeknownst to Declan, his mother was standing outside his bedroom door preparing to knock, while wondering why he was up so late after having had one of his spells. But before she entered she decided to go down to the kitchen to get him a glass of warm milk. Mrs. Donnigan had retired for the evening, but even if she hadn't Cailen was not about to demand such a menial task carried out when she was more than capable of doing it herself. A good ten minutes had passed by the time she returned. Gently opening the door, she softly called her son's name as she stepped into the darkened room. "Declan? Are ye settled for the night, me darling one?" but he was not responding, and she again spoke his name.

Finally, in a sleepy voice, he muttered, "Aye, Ma. I was asleep. What do you want?"

"Well I be wondering why ye was still up so late after yur earlier upset. I brought ye some warm milk to be taking yur medication with," she explained, and turning on the bedside lamp, inquired if he'd already taken it.

"Aye, Ma," he replied, the diffused light causing his eyes to squint while she checked the remaining amount. Not satisfied with the count, she confusingly asked, "How many did ye take?"

"Hmm, what?" he asked in a sluggish tone.

"Declan, I be asking how many pills ye be taking tonight. I want ye to be telling me," she demanded as she arranged the satin duvet over him.

Pushing the covering askew, he answered, "I don't know, Ma - a few. They're mild, you know that — I-I just took a couple of extra ones because I really need to sleep — please, I'm so tired. Just let me go to sleep."

Cailen knew the medication was mild, at her request, yet there was something not right about the entire situation. She didn't know what it was, but she could feel it, and she had to know.

"How many, Declan!" she sternly demanded, her hands shaking him roughly.

"Three, Ma!" he stated with exasperation.

"Then I be sitting here for a awhile to be sure. I not be needing a repeat of last year when ye be telling me ye only took a few. Can ye still hear me?" she inquired with concern as her strong hand patted his serene face.

He did not answer, but she refused to leave. She knew something was bothering him by the way he'd recently been acting, yet she couldn't put her finger on it. She realized his attention span was limited at any given time, yet for the last couple of months it was anywhere but where it was suppose to be. This was the main reason she'd approached Matilda Prichard with the idea of him attending university in England. It was a conversation she'd dreaded, for she realized it may well result in him having to live away from home, something she didn't relish for she was not yet ready to let go of him. He may be a grown man in a lot of ways, yet in many he was still a boy, a very high-strung one, and the spells he took made her worry that much more wondering what the outcome might be if she or Prichard were not there to watch over him when they happened. Her eyes settled upon the medication bottle, and she quickly opened it to count the remains. She hadn't counted them in a couple of days, but he was to take no more than two at bedtime. "He said a few," she thought, while lightly caressing his face. His breathing was deep, but steady, the way it should be and she found herself thinking that she may be making a mountain out of a mole-hill, but she had not forgotten the amount he downed a year before over the break-up with a girl. She had almost lost him, and though the doctor still felt the need for bedtime sedation, she hadn't forgotten the fear she felt when she found him that night, nor the anguish she endured at his side until the danger passed.

A few hours lapsed while she sat in the bedside chair, watching him smile in his sleep. She wondered what could possibly be making him so happy in slumber when he never smiled while awake. "How I wish he would confide in me more," she thought, but knew that a nineteen-year-old had their secrets just like anybody. As she gazed at him, pride flooded her insides along with thoughts of how alike to his father he'd actually become. Surely Derek would be bursting with the same enormous pride she felt - not just for their youngest - but of all their boys, yet he was so dominant within Declan. The boy looked peaceful, and as she looked upon him it was as if time had suddenly transported her back to the night she sat gazing upon her husband lying in eternal sleep before her. But Derek would never be lost to her as long as there was breath in Declan's body, and a strange sensation crept through her as she watched him sleep. It was very late when she quietly got up, kissed his forehead, pulled the duvet to his throat, and then quietly left the room. As the door gently closed behind her she heard a long sigh escape his throat, and he softly spoke an exotic name.

Far across the ocean, in a bed of no warmth, lay the dark-haired woman in Declan's dream. Sleep had finally taken her after hours of sobbing into the pillow held tightly in her arms. Outside her bedroom window the wind howled like a wolf with no mate, calling to her, summoning her attention, asking her to feel its despair. She softly whimpered to its commands, and as dreams took her away, tears slid from closed eyes, soaking into the pillow which had just managed to dry.

Chapter 21

SUNSHINE AT ELEVEN

Willow was awakened by a sudden crack of thunder, signaling daylight's arrival, as well as the first official storm of June. It startled her, causing her to leap toward the window to view the overhead sky. For as long as she could remember storms had made her nervous, especially the wind, for one never knew how strong it would become. Tornadoes were the worst; although not overly common in the area the last few years had witnessed a rise in turbulent weather, resulting in funnel-clouds becoming a more frequent sight in the skies above Ottawa and the surrounding valley. One could never be assured of an impending storm's intensity, regardless of the forecast, all one could do was wait to see, and take shelter if need be.

The sky to the west resembled twilight, yet a good twelve hours of daylight remained before that time of day would arrive. Willow, who always looked at things in a descriptive manner, had to admit she found it rather stunning as the sun rose higher in the east, striking the dark clouds with such intense illumination one would think they were being summoned to centre stage for an encore. As clouds rolled thick as blackened marshmallows, bolts of jagged lightning exploded from within, sending shards of patterned electricity across the sky. As entertaining as this was Willow's instincts advised her to keep watch just in case the entertainment should turn disastrous. She had witnessed a few tornadoes in her life, each in itself a fantastic show of nature's dark, unyielding strength of which questioned safe passage to anything in its path, and though she'd been fortunate enough to never be caught in the direct path of one, the realization of the immense danger proceeding it was a feeling she'd never forgotten.

She continued to watch the storm gather ground; slowly counting the seconds between lightning flashes until thunder was heard, signaling the distance the storm had yet to travel before it struck. It was a trick her father had taught her when she was a little girl pressed against his work-hardened body while they stood watching a growing storm inch closer. As each flash occurred, her dad would begin to count the seconds aloud until thunder was heard, thus calculating the distance in miles the storm was yet away. When the count was diminished to one, he would take her small hand in his, and tell her it was time they went into the house. Her memory triggered many hair-raising storms throughout her childhood, some bringing severe damage, but she never once doubted her safety as long as she was within the stout walls of her father's redbrick farmhouse.

As she studied the sky, the previous night's sorrow crept back into her stomach, churning it up as much as the blackened clouds she was watching. "Surely there's nothing more to it than just a misunderstanding on my part," she silently thought as anxiety multiplied. Quite some time ago she had learned the lesson of not jumping to conclusions without solid fact to back them up. Yet try as she might those acid feelings of last evening's uncertainty kept eating away. How she wished it to be nothing more than first suspected, for whenever confused or misled about anything she'd always been the first willing to give the benefit of the doubt; more than ever when it concerned Declan and his relationship with her. Lord knows she would expect the same consideration from others, but his age was forever present in her mind, let alone the unsettling situation he was requiring guidance for.

A sudden crack of thunder rattled the windows, announcing the storm's official arrival. Willow had been so lost in thought she hadn't even seen the lightning. "My God!" she exclaimed in stunned surprise, instantly grabbing her stomach. This was going to be a barnburner, causing her to make tracks for the kitchen in order to make coffee before the means to do so was lost. A blinding flash of lightning, accompanied by an ear splitting clap of thunder, sent the coffee canister airborne, and Willow doing her best to retrieve it before it landed. But she missed, and the contents spewed across the vinyl floor, sending her scurrying for the broom. Another crack rattled the house to the point where one would swear the ground was opening. "*Stop!*" she frantically hollered, her eyes filling with fright as she fumbled with the mess upon the floor.

Another rumble shook the house, and along with it a loud banging on the front door. Willow was so submerged in clearing the kitchen mess that she hadn't heard it at first. Thunder again sounded. With aggravation, she thought, "My God when will this ever let up?" The banging grew louder. "What in hell now?" she asked aloud, pulling herself to a standing position and craning her neck around the doorframe to see who was creating the racket. As she made her way toward the front door, wind howled around the back of the house, making her question in acrimonious wonder as to who in hell would be dense enough to be out in this.

"*Who is it?!*" she called loudly, but no answer returned — then again if anyone did reply the wind would have surely snatched it. "*Who is it?!*" she repeated, but still no answer; only loud banging.

She was hesitant to open the door, yet she couldn't just leave whoever it was out there in the storm. Rain pounded the street, challenging the newly-installed storm drains to accept the excess before it flooded the entire area. She was uncertain as to whether she should even try to open the door for fear it be caught by the raging wind and ripped from its moorings. Peering through the lace curtain, she could see a hydro workman trying his best to remain upright on his feet, and she knew she couldn't just leave him out there.

Cracking the door, she inquired, "Yes?" while holding fast to the knob as the door trembled in her hands.

"Ottawa Hydro, are you Willow Crosby?" the workman asked, gripping his clipboard tightly lest it become airborne.

"Yes. Maybe you'd best come inside," she offered, and stepped back for him to enter.

"Thanks, Mrs. Crosby. Sure is a strong wind — lightning's bad too. I'm sure we'll be working overtime today," he announced as he gained his moorings.

"What's this about?" she inquired with interest.

The man shifted his weight from one foot to the other, making it obvious he didn't relish the answer he was about to give, but he finally said, "Well, Mrs. Crosby, I'm here to disconnect your service."

Willow was aware her payments had been staggered since receiving that searing notice, after all how was she suppose to pay when she had nothing to pay with? Yet she realized this was not an acceptable excuse and it was only a matter of time before this would happen. "I sent a payment awhile back, after I got another disconnection notice," she explained. "You should have received it long ago– please - can't you give me a few more days to pay the remainder?" but the sinking feeling in her stomach had already delivered the answer.

"I'm sorry, but I only work for Hydro, you'd have to discuss an extension with head office," he explained. "I was sent to disconnect your service, and I just came to the door to notify you before I did."

"What if I go directly to the office and make payment with my credit card?" she audaciously asked. She had to do something. She couldn't let her service be disconnected and she would try whatever means she could to avoid it, even if it meant using a method that was already stretched beyond its limit. "Please," she pleaded, "don't shut off my hydro. I need it. Just give me a few minutes to get dressed then I'll go directly there."

The workman could see the despondency in her tired eyes. He'd encountered that look many times throughout his career and he hated it, yet he could never understand why people let their accounts slide to the point of disconnection, let alone the embarrassment surrounding the entire issue. "It must be degrading to beg," he thought, though he figured if people were negligent to the point where his service was required then they deserved what they got. It was merely a job to him. Somebody had to do it, so it may as well be him. Still he couldn't ignore the desperation in this woman's eyes. He even found himself wondering when she'd last had something substantial to eat, let alone make payments on a tardy account.

"Mrs. Crosby, I really don't know what to say," he explained, trying his best to hold to rule of thumb and not his growing concern. "It's not my call to give you an extension. Normally the office has already been through all of that by the time they send me."

"*Please*," Willow begged. "Maybe hydro's not as important as heat, but I still require it to cook with - and lights – and …," her voice trailed off before she said *computer*.

Another crack of thunder shook the house as the workman scratched his head, and said, "Well, if you can go right now and pay what owes then I'll not disconnect the service. I've got a few more calls to make and they're over on the west side, so that gives you a little bit of time. As I said earlier, if this storm keeps up I'm going to be called to help the crews that are sent out for that. Just make sure you pay the remainder today and, maybe it wouldn't be a bad idea to have something in your stomach before you go."

Willow wondered at his statement; no doubt her response revealed it. Food was something that had become scarce, though her cupboard still housed a few things.

"That's a rather strange thing to say, wouldn't you think?" she asked, not relishing a reply.

The workman looked at her with sober eyes, and said, "When you've been in this business long enough you get to see all kinds of things, and you get to know the signs of hunger - among other things. I didn't mean to be insulting. I just think you could use a good meal. I'm sorry if I insinuated anything that I shouldn't have."

He was basically a kind man, and Willow soon realized this fact, not merely because he had taken it upon himself to give her an extension, but because it was obvious he cared more for his fellow man than what the position with Ottawa Hydro allowed him.

"Thank you — I really mean that," she said with a faint smile as she held open the door for his departure. "I'll go right away, right after I have something to eat." The wind continued to blow as he fought his way off the steps and to his truck. "Dodged a bullet there," she whispered under her breath, sighing with relief as she watched the truck pull out of the drive.

As relieved as she felt she knew it was only temporary, for sooner or later the remainder of the hydro would have to be paid - and that was for the ones owing - it did nothing for the next ones that would confront her. Tension rose, as she thought, "Hell I can't use my credit card, it's stretched to the max as it is. Maybe I could call Mom. Her letters of late have seemed kinder, she might possibly be able to spare a little — no! I can't do that, I can't ask her. Besides it's not her problem, it's the problem I'm married to. Damn you, Jonas!" She paced the floor, racking her brain for a possible solution when her lawyer suddenly came to mind. "Thought he was suppose to be looking into this," she thought, her mind remembering their last meeting as she further thought, "That was eons ago - in fact it feels like years - especially when each new day is becoming more difficult to survive than the last."

"Timothy Breen's office," the secretary announced in a manicured tone.

"Good morning. This is Willow Crosby. I need to speak with Mr. Breen and it's urgent."

"Mr. Breen is in court this morning."

"Can you tell me when he's expected back?" Willow asked, her anxiety growing with each labored breath.

"Not until early afternoon," the secretary replied with prudence. If Willow didn't know better, she would swear the woman was just being as evasive as she could, and enjoying every second.

In a determined tone, Willow stated, "I'm afraid this can't wait. Is there any possible way he can be reached - better still have him phone?"

"What is this about?"

With annoyance, Willow answered, "I was of the understanding Mr. Breen was to have contacted the utilities to explain the ongoing situation between my husband and me until a settlement can be reached. We had *again* discussed this at my last appointment, and that was *months* ago. The bills are still coming, and I've been trying to keep up with what little I have. This morning a man from Hydro arrived with intention of disconnecting my service, but I managed to stall him. I realize the amount of service I use during the time of our separation still has to be paid, but Mr. Breen said he would try and arrange something."

"You will have to speak with him about that, Mrs. Crosby," the secretary stated in an uncaring manner.

Feeling as if she were talking to the wall, Willow snapped, "I realize that! This is why I *need* to speak with him! This situation has grown dire. If I don't pay the remainder of this existing bill by this afternoon it will be disconnected. Now I'm sick and tired of being given the runaround along with every other excuse in the book! I realize he's in court, but he's not there all day! When can I expect his call?"

There was silence on the line. For a brief moment she wondered if she'd been disconnected. With this thought she emitted a disgusting sigh, shored up by the fact that it wouldn't surprise her, when the secretary suddenly stated, "I'll contact Mr. Breen during court recess at eleven and have him phone you."

"Thank you!" Willow replied bluntly, and hung up the phone.

The storm had greatly subsided. Willow looked out the window for signs of damage and was pleased to see none, as she thought, "Maybe someone is looking out for me after all, and if this is true then it must be Dad," and she sighed, "How I wish you here," while tears formed in her worn eyes as she thought of him. "I don't know how it got like this, Dad. Everything has gone *so* wrong, and I don't know which way to turn anymore. I miss you so much. I know if you were here you'd know exactly what to do. You always looked after me — all of us — you never turned your back when the going got rough or things didn't turn out the way you'd planned. I don't think Mom has ever realized how truly blessed she was to have had a man like you to care for her - most of all love her. Daddy, I love you so much. I'd give anything if you could hold me against you, just for a little while." Tears ran freely as she spoke, but as much as she missed her father she knew he was forever within her, and within her children; all she could do was cling to the strength that knowledge provided.

The morning dragged on. It seemed like eleven would never arrive. Willow busied herself with laundry and the menial tasks that are always taken for granted. She even had to chuckle when she thought about the assorted tasks she did for clients and how important it made her feel at the time, but when it all boiled down to basics it was still menial tasks. The only bit of importance about it was the fact that she received payment for doing them. Her mind, as always, drifted to her young man abroad as she wondered what he was doing, how he might be feeling, and if he was thinking of her. Oh how she'd come to adore him. He filled her life with warmth, the likes of which she never thought she'd feel again. She could never repay him for what he had given her. When her thoughts turned to him in this manner they completely obliterated the upsetting conversation with those girls, and regardless of what they said she had no reason to disbelieve him, or think for one fleeting moment that he would deceive her in any way. Their special relationship was setting like fast-drying cement, and the more time spent together found the cement solidifying into a consistency she thought unbreakable.

Declan's face loomed within Willow's mind. How handsome it was, so young, and vibrant with an air about it that would melt the coldest heart in an instant. She loved the photographs he'd sent which now numbered many, and she cherished each as much as the first. A few weeks prior she had finally conjured up enough nerve to send him some of hers, and as she thought about that a silly giggle escaped her throat. The thought of the giggle even made her laugh, and she couldn't help but think she'd digressed to an adolescent schoolgirl whose hormones had just begun to kick in. But it was how he made her feel. It had been so long since a feeling like that had touched her she'd almost forgotten how it actually felt, let alone how to handle it, but he had rekindled so many dormant feelings within her that she felt anything was possible, as long as she had him in her life. Maybe that was why the conversation with that girl bothered her in the way in which it had - at the very least had a lot to do with it - after all no one likes to be made a fool, nor have anyone think of them in that way. Heaven only knows there were times when Jonas made her feel like that. At least he tried his best. Whether he was successful was anybody's guess, but the way he had treated her for months on end certainly qualified her in that category.

It was well past eleven when she glanced at the clock. "Figures," she thought with annoyance, "I bet Sally Secretary never even bothered to call him – huh - so much for trying to stand up for myself." Her mind shifted into overdrive, wondering what on earth she could possibly do to hurry it up, it was nearing noon, and time was running out, as she thought, "This must be how it feels to await an execution." She'd already tried throwing herself at the mercy of the workman that morning, and if he came back to the knowledge she never even ventured out then a repeat performance would be a total waste. "Come on!" she snapped just as the phone rang. She practically tripped getting to it. "Hello?" she inquired, clutching the receiver in a death-grip.

"Mrs. Crosby?" Mr. Breen questioned, and in annoyance, Willow thought, "Well who in hell else would it be?" but she simply replied, "Yes."

"I received word that you needed to speak with me."

"Yes I do. I was wondering if you've been in touch with the Utility Commission concerning my difficulty to keep up with payment," she explained, finding it hard to conceal the stress in her voice.

"I sent a letter the beginning of the week. They should have received it by now." In disbelief, Willow thought, "What! We discussed this matter *months* ago and you just sent a letter a few *days* ago?" Taking a deep breath to steady her nerves, she said, "A service man was sent this morning to disconnect my hydro. Obviously they haven't received any letter."

"I'm sorry to hear that."

"Well, Mr. Breen, I'm afraid *sorry* doesn't help the situation nor does it prevent me from losing my service. I have done everything short of *starving* myself in order to stretch what money I earn far enough to cover everything. You told me you would do what you could to help me - after all my son is damn well paying you enough - and I am not going to ask him to continue to cover my ass in order to keep my head above water! That is what he pays *you* for!"

"Mrs. Crosby," Breen stated in a serious tone, "please calm down. Getting upset with me is not helping matters. But if it's any consolation I do sympathize with the way you feel." Willow, totally repulsed with the entire situation, sarcastically thought, "Well la de da," but said, "I'm sorry, but feeling remorse for my situation is doing little to help it! I managed to jolly the workman out of it this morning by promising to pay the remainder of the arrears with my credit card, but even that is maxed to the limit and I've got *them* on my back. Mr. Breen, stuff has to be paid somehow! It's gotten to the point where I literally jump out of my skin every time the phone rings because it's always somebody after me about payment for something I can't keep up with, much less *cope* with! I feel like a rubber band stretched totally beyond its capacity to hold! Everywhere I turn is a dead end!"

"Mrs. Crosby —" Breen tried interceding, but she cut him off, as she roared, *"What am I suppose to do when the workman returns this afternoon? Huh?!* Not only that, but what about everything else? I may just as well walk out my front door, step in front of the first *fucking* bus going past, and let the damn bank sell my house for whatever it's worth — *maybe there'll be enough left over to satisfy the hounds from hell!"*

"Mrs. Crosby!" Breen snapped. "Get a-hold of yourself! I will call Hydro's head office immediately and speak with accounts."

The sharpness of Breen's voice brought Willow to a sudden halt. Maybe its abruptness had been required, for she was fast-losing what bit of control she had managed to cling to. It wasn't the lawyer's fault, she realized this, and she had to trust him if she was ever to find a way out of this living hell.

Taking a deep breath, she said, "I'm sorry, Mr. Breen. I really didn't mean to lose it like that, but this has become totally impossible to cope with."

"I understand," Breen relayed in a voice full of sincerity. "I do realize how drawn-out these situations can be, as well as how slow the court system moves, but I do expect our hearing to be scheduled upon the docket within the immediate future. Hopefully this situation can be settled soon."

"If only," Willow thought with want, and taking a breath, replied, "I hope so, the sooner the better. But how will I know if you were successful with Hydro?" she asked, needing reassurance for she could not cope with an encore of the morning's performance.

Trying his best to set her mind at ease, Breen replied, "I'll have my secretary contact you. I'm due back in court early this afternoon, but I'll phone them directly. I still can't promise anything, please be aware of this fact. Companies, such as Hydro, require payment for their service, even in marital situations such as yours. But hopefully they will understand. Also, I trust in the fact that you have been trying to make payment in some ongoing form will be taken into consideration. I'll do my best, and I'll let you know."

"I truly hope so, Mr. Breen. I'll be waiting for her call."

As Willow hung up the phone she swallowed hard, thinking there just may be a ray of sunshine hidden somewhere within the stubborn clouds overhead, but she would wait to rejoice when she actually saw it.

Chapter 22

TESTAMENT TO DETERMINATION

The bold announcement of Matilda Prichard's post-lunch return to the classroom proved evident when the door slammed behind her. She delved deep into the brown leather pouch that was dangling from her arm, retrieved a thick history book, and with a look of distaste upon her face, tossed it in an uncaring manner upon her desk, pulled back her chair, and plopped down. As she settled within it the chair let out a tiny squeak, somewhat like a frightened mouse would do when being stalked by a curious cat. Finally positioning herself to her liking, she peered over her horn-rim glasses toward the timid young man before her, and began the afternoon instruction.

"Master Declan, please open your history book to page two hundred and five. There you will discover a fresh paper containing questions from your earlier exam, now accompanied with additional ones. You are to retrieve the paper, and then close the book until you have completed all questions." The serious tone in her voice grew more intense, as she continued, "Since you failed this same exam this morning - which would not have happened had you, in the very least, applied yourself, instead of nodding off to fairyland or wherever it is your mind has been flitting to these days - this enchanted moment we now find ourselves immersed within need not be happening. So, we are going to give this yet another go. Hopefully this time you will find success, and my additional efforts will not be completely lost, as they seem to be of late."

Her young charge, on the completion of each word she had spoken, felt as if he'd been immersed into a frigid bath, as he annoyingly thought, "I'm not a complete moron you know," while his eyes shot a menacing look her way. It was instantly returned; causing his spine to stiffen as he nervously thumbed the pages of his book. He finally arrived at the designated one but paused for a second as a thought had come to mind.

Releasing an agitated sigh, Prichard asked, "What appears to be the hold up?"

"Nothing," Declan answered bluntly. He knew this would not win him points but he didn't care; he didn't wish to be there in the first place.

In a no nonsense manner, Prichard replied, "Then carry on so this assignment can finally be completed and filed away."

Questions loomed before the young student, taunting him, mocking him, almost as if they knew their correct answers would surely elude him. He read then re-read the words within each one. A few of them presented themselves rather easily, and he lost no time in scribbling the answers. For a brief moment there appeared a beacon at the far side of this raging sea. He even found himself smiling, and confidence rose within him, but it was quickly lost when a series of questions reared their ugly head to suck him to the depth from which they'd come. To top it off the lead broke in his pencil.

He gingerly inquired, "Miss Prichard?" and before he could stop himself, shot his hand into the air with fingers snapping loudly.

"Yes?" she inquired, but the annoying sound continued. "*Stop that insolent gesture at once!*" she bellowed, slamming shut the cover upon her textbook. The annoyance ceased instantly, and her huge-eyed pupil shrunk in his seat. Frightening him had not been her intention, even though she felt at the end of her wits. "Master Declan," she gently said, "I do apologize for raising my voice, but that impudent habit is not only annoying, it is beneath a fine student such as yourself. If you wish to inquire something then simply ask. After all, my dear, that is what I am here for. Now, I believe you have a question?" and in dismay, the boy suddenly thought, "How in hell can I explain my feelings?" His fingers instantly began fidgeting, as his thoughts continued, "She'll never understand anyway," but he answered, "Well my pencil needs sharpening — but —but ...,"

"But what?" Prichard inquired, again hovering on the edge of annoyance, her piercing stare seeming to bore straight through the boy.

Declan's body shriveled further, as he meekly answered, "Well, I-I was really going to ask the importance of this exam," and with this revelation, braced himself for the sharp retort that was sure to follow. But instead of a vigorous reply his tutor said nothing. He thought this rather odd; for in all the years she'd taught him the two things she was never without were her remarkable wit, and her uncanny ability with words. He quickly found himself wondering if she could be testing him, further wondering if her silence might even be prompting a further remark, one she never thought him capable of making, and before he realized what was happening, he nervously stated, "Quite frankly I find this exam a total waste of my time, as well as yours. I mean, it's not like I *need* to know who discovered what way back when, or the date something burned, or sank – you know, insignificant stuff like that. The present is all that's important, and it's all that I care about."

For a moment the stunned tutor said nothing. It was obvious she wasn't sure *what* to say, and if the wrong reply was chosen then she may as well open the door and tell him to go, as she thought, "How could he differ so from his brothers?" Yet when she let her thoughts digress, she had to admit to never experiencing anything too difficult from any of them. Oh sure they liked to tease her, but that was something a teacher came to expect from her student. She even found herself wondering that if a student didn't push an issue, in the very least test the water from time to time, then they were not receiving the best she could give. But Declan was an entirely different story. He had always been in a league of his own, and the normal issues that had intrigued his brothers held no interest for him whatsoever.

He sat quiet, contemplating her answer, yet giving the impression he could care less, while she sat studying him, realizing any rebuttal she may choose would more than likely be lost; but she had to try.

Summoning an understanding tone, she said, "Master Declan, it is as plain as the clock on the wall that you have become rather distant of late, especially when it involves your studies. And I realize it may be difficult for you to comprehend at this, shall we say, disconcerted time, the importance of the studies of which you refer to as *a waste of time*, though, my dear, they are anything but. If you are uninformed of what has gone before then how can you choose the correct direction in which to proceed? You may find history a complete bore, yet if it were not recorded then how would one know the pitfalls to avoid in the future? We learn from what has gone before. This is the reason why history is taught in the first place. It is the reason why *any* subject is taught, and the formative years are the most impressionable time to learn these immeasurable values." In a taunting manner, Declan thought, "Yeah-yeah," as he yawned, drawing a huge breath into his lungs while in further disgust, thought, "Who needs the lecture? My future's already sewn up. Who the hell wants to run a boring distillery anyway? Suppose it's got its benefits, free alcohol and the like — hey, never thought of it that way! Still it's not what I want to do with my life. *Huh*, that doesn't seem to matter because it's only what Ma and Prichard decide. Willow wouldn't do that. She never talks down to me, she cares about me. *Mmm*, I wonder if she'll ever fall in love with me. Oh yeah, that'd be great. I wonder how often she looks at those pictures I sent or, thinks about me or, whether she even does," and he stared dreamily into space while holding to these thoughts.

Trying her best to control her growing agitation, Prichard questioned, "Have you heard one word I've spoken?" The clock ticked away as her charge said nothing. He remained fixated upon his thoughts as she waited for an answer. "Now where in blue-blazes are you?" she silently questioned, and with growing disgust, thought, "Obviously anywhere but here," as she stood, and approached him. "Master Declan, are you alright?" she questioned, and as she spoke her hand lightly nudged his shoulder.

It startled him, and he jumped up, heavily shoving her backward, as he shouted, *"What the hell are you trying to do?!"*

"Saints preserve us!" she exclaimed in shocked surprise, grasping an adjacent desk to break her impending fall.

The young man could hardly believe what he'd done. Jumping to her aid, he exclaimed, "Miss Prichard! Oh, I'm so sorry! I don't mean any harm I-I would never hit a woman or willingly harm one in any way — especially you! Please! I beg your forgiveness!"

After such a violent outburst the size of Prichard's already enlarged eyes further increased for she was not completely sure he could be trusted. "Master Declan," she gasped, groping for support as he eased her upon the desk chair, "I really must insist you explain yourself this instant!"

"You startled me," he explained, and with quivering emotion, continued, "I truly didn't mean to harm you. Are - are you alright?" He was obviously as shaken as she, and fighting to hold his frazzled nerves in check, inquired, "Can I get you anything – water perhaps?"

Straightening herself upon the chair, she replied, "No doubt a dash of cold water would refresh us both."

He was back in a flash, balancing two glasses and a box of tissue within his fingers. "Here you go!" he proclaimed. "Good and cold, just the way you like it," but as he offered her a glass the tissue box fell to the floor. "*Damn!*" he snapped, but the curtness in his tone caused her to recoil in fear. "Don't be afraid, Miss Prichard, please. I'm just annoyed with this stupid tissue box. I thought you might need a few, so I grabbed the box when I left the cooler. Here you go," and he extended the floral-patterned container.

"Thank you, my dear, but I really should take hold of myself instead of carrying on like a frightened ninny. I do accept your apology, though in a number of ways must admit to it not being totally warranted. I could plainly see when I approached that you were heavily consumed in thought," she relayed before taking a sip of water. Declan remained quiet, sipping the contents of his glass, as she resumed, "I had hoped my words were somewhat finding passage. You appeared to be listening, which is why I found it totally overwhelming when you reacted as you did just now." At this point she chose to stop her explanation to take another sip of water.

"I am sorry about that," Declan cried, "I tried to listen - I *was* listening - but somehow your explanation became as boring as—" He suddenly stopped, obviously realizing what he must sound like. In disbelief, he immediately thought, *"Boring,* what kind of idiotic adjective was that to have chosen about her words?" A rush of heat consumed him, and he swore he must have turned beet red. Embarrassment is never an easy emotion for anyone to deal with, and Declan Quinn was no different; in fact with him it was ten times worse.

"Well, Master Declan," she announced candidly, "I must admit there has been the odd occasion - as said by those attending - where my deductions have been a bit over the top, sometimes lengthy, sometimes on the nose, but I must say that in all my years of teaching I've yet to be considered *boring.* However I do admire honesty."

"Well I thank you for that, but it still does not excuse my actions," Declan replied in a reprehensible manner. "I might have been preoccupied, but I shouldn't have reacted like I did and, I shouldn't be excused for it." He bowed his head, feeling the need to look away. He was truly sorry, but his temper seemed to get the better of him, just like in the past, and always producing the same outcome.

"I remain adamant with my apology, Master Declan," Prichard stated firmly, "however I will admit to the importance of controlling your temper. In that respect you have always been prone to ill-nature, and far too quick to respond with your fists, rather than your brain. It has gotten you into trouble more times than it is worth, but at least you've come to realize this fact. Now you must continue thriving to control this demon, instead of letting it control you."

Resuming his seat, Declan replied, "That's easier said than done I'm afraid."

As he finished this statement Prichard felt the time ripe to delve deeper, and she said, "My dear, from the time of primer grade you have been a virtual sponge for knowledge. It kept me on my toes more times than not trying to keep your lessons stimulating enough to satisfy your growing interests. This is why I find it so exasperating to see these desires fall by the way. It seems not to matter in the slightest how riveting a topic is presented, for it is completely lost within your ability to grasp - why you don't even try to acknowledge it - let alone grab *hold* and press it firmly to your memory for all eternity!"

The clock struck 2 p.m. Declan instantly rose, showing intent to leave. He appeared oblivious to his tutor's words just spoken, leaving her in utter dismay, wondering why she even bothered, as she thought, "Oh, my dear, I'm afraid that boarding school appears inevitable," and as she watched him her heart was seized with pain at the sheer notion of his impending absence. "How will we ever inform him?" she thought, the bothersome question seeming to echo within her brain, but there appeared no recourse, and the inevitable decision greatly troubled her. She had been his nanny from birth to the present, and his tutor from the beginning of his formal education. She had spent countless hours trying to guide, as well as nurture him along, yet in the end it would be his mother's place to tell him for it was her decision to make. The two women had endured countless discussions on this delicate topic, each presenting the pros and cons along with the impact this decision might present for Declan himself. But a final decision would have to be made, for it was totally obvious the importance of his education had become the furthest thing from his mind.

The completed exam lay exposed upon the desk, awaiting Prichard's astute eyes, as Declan made his way toward the door with thoughts filling his head as to whether Willow might be checking the chat before leaving for work, if that was the case, he was going to miss her if he didn't get the lead out. In his mind he envisioned her latest photograph, and with growing exasperation, thought, "I hope she waits, she has to wait!" A quick glance toward the clock quickened his pace, and he hastily reached for the glass knob. The door began to open, just as Prichard called, "Master Declan, come here!" With anger, he annoyingly thought, "Oh come on what the fuck now?!"

Prichard could feel the anger rising in her young charge, yet she would chance another outburst for this situation could not be casually dismissed. She must get through to him. The only way she knew how was to challenge him head-on. "Take your seat, if you will," she ordered, pointing in an authoritative manner toward his desk.

"Mm, Miss Prichard," he nervously replied, "I finished my paper and handed it in just the way you always demand. I … well I already know I failed … I-I d-don't need to hang around to be reprimanded about stuff I don't care about — I-I already told you that and, well … I … I haven't changed my mind even though you're trying your best to make me."

"My dear boy," Prichard replied with concern, "I'm doing nothing of the sort. But I am extremely worried about your welfare, and what is to become of you if you do not listen to what I have been trying to explain."

Tears welled in the boy's tired eyes, as he cried, "You're not even trying to understand the way I feel or the reasons I feel that way – neither you nor Ma. You each treat me like a little child that's not minding properly and, I'm not a boy any longer, Miss Prichard, I'm a *man*, and I feel the *needs* of a man, not the needs of a boy! You're trying your best to teach me, I know this fact, and I do not wish to disrespect you in any way, but why can you not *try* to understand, instead of making me feel like a ruddy failure should I choose to take another road other than the one you and Ma choose for me? Why can you not just understand me and what I want?" Tears now came in full force, rushing down his cheeks while his head drooped into his hands the instant he plunked his elbows upon the desk.

The grandfather clock chimed four times, announcing in a melodic manner the afternoon's position. The tone in the classroom remained as it had all day, but it was now tea time, and class was over - at least on a normal school day it would have been - but this had ceased to be an ordinary day by way of measure hours before. Instead it could be compared to a Mexican standoff, with the teacher sitting sternly at her desk, and the student in a slumped position at his. Neither appeared ready to give in, for both remained unyielding in their quest to drive their point home. Prichard could not help but feel remorse toward her young charge, yet she also realized the seriousness of the issue at hand, and knew she could not compromise regardless of how severely he was pulling her heartstrings. Declan felt as though his breath had been condensed to a monitored schedule, whose release was tightly held within the grip of his mother, and Miss Prichard.

The minutes ticked away, each as impending as the next, each moving them closer toward their goal or further from it. Declan glanced up with reddened eyes from newly shed tears with hope his tutor would relent. If he only knew how much she wanted to do exactly that, yet he was as intelligent as she'd always applauded him of being, and deep down knew how she felt toward him. He also realized her reason for holding fast. She had taught him so much, brought him so far, and he adored her for all of it regardless of the fact that he resented her stand on an issue he foreseen as minimal.

The clock had just chimed the quarter hour when a knock sounded on the door. Glancing up from her papers Prichard inquired who it was.

"It be Bridget, Matilda, and I be wondering if yurself and the young master be taking tea with the Mrs. or be wishing me to bring it here?" the housekeeper answered in her zealous way.

"Do come in, Bridget," Prichard stated cordially, and readied herself for Donnigan's entrance.

Declan, hoping to avert the prying eyes of the often inquisitive housekeeper, immediately went to the back of the room and took up residence by the water cooler with his back toward the door. Upon her entry, he swiftly secured a book, and pretended to read.

In a roundabout manner, Donnigan said, "I was beginning to wonder if ye had forgotten the time, Matilda. I surmised something be weighing heavy on yur mind considering the way ye left the kitchen after lunch, but I not be one to pry - ye knows me? But when ye not be appearing for tea as usual I thought I be taking a wee look for meself to see what ye may be needing."

"Well that is most considerate of you, Bridget," Prichard replied gaily while arranging the loose papers upon her desk into a neat pile before her. "Master Declan and I were just completing our final lesson of the day when you knocked," she explained, and swept her hand forward in a mock gesture of befuddlement as she carried on her joyful pretense. "We were so lost in the depth of thought and discussion that we apparently lost track of the time!" Glancing toward the back wall, she called, "Master Declan! It's time to put the book away, even though I know it is difficult for you to tear yourself from," then casting a self-etched smile in the direction of the housekeeper, announced, "This young man is such a slave to knowledge, 'tis a wonder I can even keep up with him. But you know yourself, Bridget, what a delight he's always been during one of his romps about your kitchen on a quest for your scrumptious sweets and, he's fully as delightful in my classroom!" Turning to her charge, she held her arm in the air and motioned to him, as she cheerfully said, "Tea is waiting, Master Declan, do come along!"

The threesome walked in silence along the corridor toward the stairs. Declan was the first to descend, and as he did, Donnigan joyfully said, "Whoa, young snapper, don't be getting too far ahead of us auld gals! Ye always were one to run wild whenever there be sweets to be sampled. But ye best be on yur grandest behavior when ye get before yur mother, for she not be in the best of humor this afternoon."

Declan's pace had slowed at the mention of his mother's name, but at the mention of her mood it ceased entirely, as he anxiously inquired, "What's wrong, Mrs. Donnigan, did she say what's bothering her?"

Shaking her head, the housekeeper replied, "I not be knowing, and I not be asking. Ye be finding out directly." As in afterthought, she looked at Prichard, and asked, "Matilda, do ye happen to have the young master's exam results? The Mrs. had asked me to be inquiring it when I got to the classroom, but it completely slipped me mind." With a chuckle, she added, "*Ha-ha* must be the sign of auld age approaching for sure."

A smile crossed Prichard's lips at the housekeeper's droll remark but it was replaced with a grimace at the thought of the exam results, for she too was dreading the appearance before Cailen, as she said, "Actually I don't have it with me, Bridget, but I'll go back and retrieve it. It will only take a moment. You and Master Declan go along to the drawing room and inform Mrs. Quinn I shall be there directly."

Chapter 23

IRON CLAD WILL

Morning transformed to afternoon and for Willow uneasiness to anxiety. The phone had not rung. Under normal circumstances that would have been a good sign for it meant no creditor was harassing her - which in itself was reason to celebrate - however this time she was afraid its absence meant the lawyer had failed in his attempt to avail, which in turn meant the hydro worker's return and disconnection of service. This time he would not be averted regardless of how much she pleaded. In anguish, she thought, "What am I going to do now?" Staring at the clock with discontent, she wrung her hands, while fighting back tears. "Just calm down, girl," she muttered to herself, realizing that worrying wasn't getting her anywhere. Nervously watching the movement of the second hand, she found herself thinking that there could be a dozen reasons why the phone hadn't rung, and upon further consideration, realized that there hadn't been too many recent calls and she was certain it was working. With discern creeping up her spine, she went to check. The dial tone was happily humming its placid tune, which enticed a sigh of relief to escape her throat, but it wasn't long before her worried mind returned to its present quandary.

Before she knew it three o'clock had arrived but still no word from Timothy Breen's office. With apprehension toward the advancing time, she thought, "Surely he made that call. He knows how important it is. Maybe I should try calling *him*." Her anxiety level had now reached an all-time high. She was beside herself with worry, wondering when the hammer would fall, and fall it surely would if the pattern of late did not change. She wondered if there were any hidden avenues yet to discover, but finding one seemed impossible. She felt the need to talk with Declan, for he appeared to be the only one who held her feet on solid ground, yet if she went online it meant tying up the phone. But her nerves needed calming, and he was the best medicine for that. The computer sprang to life and she lost no time in firing off a message to Galway. To further ease her mind she decided to take a quick trip to the chat with hopes he might be there.

As usual it was abuzz with familiar names, including *Sweet Sue*, along with the same redundant insults flying back and forth. In-fact a considerable amount of time flew past before Willow's presence was even acknowledged. She scanned the lineup, hoping with all her might to see *Dream Come True*, but the name was not there. As tears filled her eyes, a long, disappointed groan escaped her throat. She briefly thought about inquiring his absence but to save argument decided against it. She was just about to leave when a message from *Sweet Sue* shot across the main screen for everyone's eyes to read. *Well well wud ya all luk whos here! tha OL HO... un we all know who she's here lukin ta fuck but shes outta luck taday LMFAO!!!!! he ain't here HAG! even if he wuz hed b LAUFIN along wit US cuz he thinks ur a laf a minute! he's havin a good ole time playin wit ya — he don't care about ya at all SO GIT LOST YA OL PERV - LOL!!!!!*

If that wasn't enough, *Banana-Anna* signed in, and instantly took up the cause. If Willow didn't know better she could swear it was planned, although in all honesty she could hardly see how they would both know she'd be there at that exact time, unless that too was planned — *HOLA!!! IT'S THE COUGER!!!! Anna* fired off in total caps, trying her best to drive her insolent message home. *PACK UP THA YUN GUYZ N HIDES EM CHICKAROONIES! LOL! YO SUE ANCHA GOIN TA B SEEIN DECLAN LATER TONIGHT?!*

Sweet Sue: *sho is g/f wez gunna b plaayin lik niver befo. hez soooo gud ta mez. hez in luvz wit little ole mez + i bez in luvz wit tha fine boy 2 cuz he b SUM fine layyyy.*

Willow instantly bristled, though she couldn't help wondering if this laughable performance was merely playing out to piss her off enough that she'd run with her tail between her legs, or if what they were saying was somehow actuality. But she had news for them, as she typed, *you girls may as well save your breath - or in this case fingers - because your dumb performance lacks about as much intelligence as either of you apparently possess. It's not working this time, so save it for somebody that's hard up for a laugh and possibly interested enough to listen to your mindless prattle!*

Willow had typed with as much venom as these girls had hoped to inject into her. Furthermore she wasn't waiting around to argue with what she considered two wise-cracking bimbos whose hormones were locked in overdrive. But as much as she hated to admit it, she could relate to how they felt, for her own hormones where working overtime, but in the department of confusion. She believed what Declan told her, she had no reason not to; furthermore she had no intention in trying to prove it by stooping to the level of those two girls. Before they could fire-off another volley she signed out and returned to her mailbox to see if there might possibly be a reply to her letter. The box partly opened, but the cursor stopped, and refused to move. It appeared to be stuck, and no amount of frantic clicking seemed to free it. It was apparent the computer had frozen. She'd recently been experiencing problems with it doing just that, but it would just have to wait for repair, like everything else of late. She fiddled, fumed, and cussed, but nothing was happening. It totally refused to connect to the Internet. She finally decided to check the lines in case something had become dislodged, but on thorough inspection found all cables tightly connected. "What the hell's going on here," she thought in disgust as she sat, pondering what to do. "It's got to be something with the phone," she announced to herself, and jammed the receiver against her ear. There was no dial tone! She could not believe it! It was completely dead! "What the hell is this?" she questioned aloud, and tore down the stairs to the kitchen phone. She lifted the blue receiver to her ear, only to find the same problem. She silently cussed. The rest of the phones enticed the same reaction as did their counterparts, reducing their owner to a state of frenzy. A quick trip to the basement proved no help whatsoever for all wires appeared intact, though in all fairness she had to admit to not even knowing what she was looking for. "There has to be a logical reason," she thought in puzzlement, and decided to run next door to see if her neighbor was experiencing the same problem.

"Hey there, Miss Willow, haven't seen you in a dog's age. How's everything going?" Shawn Martin inquired, and happily motioned her inside, as Willow thought, "I really don't think you want to know, Shawn," but answered, "Well I'm a bit peeved at the moment, but otherwise fine."

"What's the matter?" he asked with concern, and pulled out a chair for her to sit down.

Declining his offer, she quickly asked, "Do you have phone service?"

"As far as I know, let me check," he replied, and went to his phone. "Yep, dial tone's there. Is your phone not working?"

"No. I don't know what the problem is. None of them are working. I was online when I first noticed it. The cursor wouldn't move but, you know the state of my computer lately so I just thought it'd froze again — and before you say anything, I know, I should have Wi-Fi, but I can't afford it, besides the method I'm using is fine – that is until now. Never thought it might be the phone itself, so I checked them all, even went into the basement and looked at the lines - as though I know what I'm looking at when it comes to stuff like that – but I figured what the heck, I'd look anyway," she explained in an agitated manner.

With a look of confusion, he asked, "Didn't Jonas have a look? He's usually great at fixing things," to which Willow abruptly stated, "No. But I hardly think he could fix this."

"Well you're welcome to use my phone and report the problem," Shawn cheerfully offered, and swiftly handed her the directory.

The business day was almost over, prompting Willow to glance toward the clock in hope someone would still be in the office. The phone rang a number of times, giving the impression no one was there, which resulted in another heated adjective escaping her grimacing lips. She was just about to hang up, when a woman's voice answered, "Ottawa Direct, how may I help you?"

"Hello. This is Willow Crosby. Sorry to call so late in the day but I'm experiencing problems with my home phone. I'm reporting it from my next door neighbor's. I have no dial tone on any of my phones. I don't know whether the problem is in the lines, or in the phones themselves, and I'd like someone to come and have a look, today if at all possible," and she quickly gave her address and phone number.

There was no response, prompting Willow to inquire the absence of voice.

"Yes, Mrs. Crosby, I'm here. I was just trying to pull up your file but I can't seem to find your name in the computer. In what name is the phone registered under?"

"It's under my husband's, why?"

"Would that be one, Jonas Crosby?"

"Yes. Is there a problem?"

"Well, I have a note here stating that Mr. Crosby came into the office mid afternoon today to say he no longer required service at this number, and requested it disconnected. He settled the account, and his request was immediately carried out."

Willow was thunderstruck, and vehemently shouted, *"I don't believe this! Just what the hell does he think he's trying to pull now!? He can't do that!"*

"I'm sorry, Mrs. Crosby, but he can. The phone was registered in his name so he has the authority to do just that. If you wish the service reinstated in *your* name you will have to come into the office tomorrow and have it taken care of. There will be an eighty-five dollar reconnection fee, payable in advance," the representative explained coldly, giving Willow the impression she could care less one way or the other.

This was beyond reproach. Willow's anger consumed her, sending any hope of kind demeanor out the window, yet in a way her present conduct made her feel rather sheepish. She knew it wasn't the representative's fault, after all she was only doing her job and under normal circumstances Willow would have instantly apologized for her outburst, but regardless of this knowledge, the rage she presently felt was far too strong to stand on protocol. She slammed down the receiver without any consideration for the person on the other end, *or* the fact that her neighbor was watching every move she made with obvious concern toward her erratic actions. Extending his hand to her, Shawn asked, "What's going on?"

With total frustration, Willow snapped, "Jonas had the damn phone disconnected! That's what's going on!"

"What?" Shawn questioned in astonishment, obviously taken aback that his neighbor would do such a thing, and fully as confused with the reason as to why.

Willow knew there was no further use in trying to cover up, and said, "Jonas and I aren't together, Shawn, we've been separated since last fall. Things hadn't been great for a long time leading up to that, but they just got totally impossible to cope with, and he left. I've been trying to maintain ever since but, he's making it as difficult as he can. He wants the house sold, I don't. Therefore he's using every tactic in the book to force me out."

Shawn stood before her, shaking his head in a sorry manner while doing the best he could to absorb what he'd just heard. For as long as they had been neighbors he and Jonas had gotten along well, sharing many a beer on each others' porch, helping each other out, doing all the things that all good neighbors do for each other, so Willow's sudden proclamation was entirely coming out of left field.

Taking a breath, he said, "Come to think of it I haven't seen his truck around in a hell of a long time, but I figured he was just working a lot of overtime; either that or I was just looking at the wrong time. This is rather hard to absorb, Willow. I don't mean to pry, but is there anything I can do?"

WILLOW'S WALK

Doing her best to hold control, Willow replied, "Thank you for offering, but no. There isn't anything anyone can do. It's amazing how fast things can escalate out of control and you don't even see it coming until it's too late. You've always been a good neighbor, Shawn, and I hope I can continue to call you that. But the way things are going I don't know how much longer I can hold on." The more she spoke the more heated her anger became, until she stomped toward the door, shouting, *"But this time he's gone too fucking far and he's going to pay for it! I'm going to his place to have it out!"*

Fearing what might happen if she was let go in this state, Shawn rapidly exclaimed, "You'd best calm down before you get behind the wheel — let alone confront Jonas! You're in no condition to do either!"

Willow whirled to face her neighbor. With growing despair, she said, "I thank you for your concern. I really do. But as far as I'm concerned today's underhanded dealing is the icing on the cake! He knows damn well the state everything's in — he's gone out of his way to make them that way — now this! Well he's not getting away with it! I'm not cowering any longer, Shawn, and he's going to find that out right now!" and before he could stop her she stormed out the door.

The surroundings were a blur as she stomped down the steps toward her house, but as she neared her walk she was confronted with yet another ordeal. The workman from Ottawa Hydro had returned and was waiting at her front door with the familiar clipboard in hand. She suddenly felt as if an unseen fist had slammed her stomach, knocking the wind totally out of her, yet she carried on, ascending the steps as the workman turned to face her, but before he could utter a sound, she said, "I already know why you're here."

A sullen look engulfed the workman's face, as he said, "Guess you didn't get things taken of, eh?"

"Sadly, no," she replied, shaking her head. "The lawyer told me he would contact head office to explain my situation but, either he didn't make the call, or was unsuccessful if he did." Her misty eyes wore a look of vexation, as she explained, "He was to have his secretary call to let me know, but she hasn't." With that a sarcastic laugh escaped her throat with the realization of what she had just said, but she continued, "Guess I'll never know if she did or not. My phone was disconnected earlier this afternoon."

The workman's sad expression intensified, as he said, "Hey I'm really sorry you're having such a hard time."

"Why?" Willow replied. "It's not your fault." She immediately surmised what he was about to say, but beat him to it, stating, "I thank you for your concern, but I know you have no choice in the matter so you may as well do what you have to and get it over with. Where do I sign?"

"I am sorry, Mrs. Crosby," the workman repeated in an apologetic manner, and extended the clipboard for her signature. His face held a look of remorse that told her he was honestly regretting every second, but it was inevitable, and they both knew it. With pen in hand she begrudgingly applied her signature upon the dotted line, wishing with each scratch of the pen it was her nails upon her husband's face. The workman said nothing, for nothing *could* be said. He had done his job, regardless of how he may feel about it, and as he turned to leave he was met by a concerned Shawn Martin waiting by the work truck.

Willow didn't care, and she no sooner stepped inside the house when the first tears slid down her cheeks. There was no further use in holding them in, no more than there was in fighting a battle she couldn't win. What's done is done, and no amount of wishing could change the fact of the way things were. If anything it was a wakeup call to the way things would be from here on in, especially if Jonas had anything to do with it. But she refused to crawl. This was not the way her parents had raised her, and she'd be damned if she would let these embarrassing issues get the better of her. "Heads are going to roll," she thought in anger as defiance rose within her, "someone is going to damn-well pay!"

The lawyer was the first to come to mind, but Willow realized the congestion within the courts as well as the main reason her case was taking so long to be heard. Her children were no longer minors in need of support, the entire situation would have been far different if they had been, furthermore she was able to work, regardless of the ineffective amount she made, or the declining condition of her health. She felt defeated, even more so when she realized she was just another number lost between the cracks in the system's floor. How easy it would be to simply give into the overwhelming burden crushing her shoulders, but she would not. She stood at the door, clicking the powerless switch of the foyer's light, her clouded eyes staring at its inability to work as a bitter taste formed in her mouth. She felt totally chastised, with a need to cry until she died from dehydration, but that wouldn't get her anywhere, nor would it solve the problem at hand. Forceful determination was the only thing that would, yet how could that be realized when she could no longer function? Her mind wandered back to childhood when everything was solid, peaceful, never a care in the world. They were glory days, though she never felt that way at the time, but the more she dwelled on this simple fact the more she realized how wrong she had been to visualize them in any other way, but how was she to know what the future had in store? Now she wished to be back there, just once more, instead of trapped in this agonizing existence. Her rational mind realized that anxiety was getting the best of her. She also realized that things always appeared worse when one lets their fears engulf them. Still, try as she might, she could not seem to avert them.

Evening had arrived, and though daylight hung in, it would not be long before light would be required. Willow knew she'd best gather candles, and not just for light, the heat provided by them would surely help in warding off the nighttime's ensuing dampness. As she went about her task, thoughts of Declan came to mind, along with his handsome face and radiant smile. How she wished she could chat with him, tell him what had happened, and share her burden. Somehow she knew he would help - if he could - but it was only wishful thinking for the computer's life had been lost along with the hydro. And even had she known his number it would be useless, for the phone was as dead as the computer.

Chapter 24

TO RELENT IS TO BE WEAK

The warmth of the late afternoon sun cast an amber glow through the lace sheers as Declan entered the drawing room. His mother sat rigid upon an armless chair with her back toward the entry, but she knew he was there. Maybe she'd been tipped off by the creak of a floor-board, a fleeting shadow across the wall, or possibly the colorful adjective emitting from her boy's lips when his foot slid beneath the carpet edge, hurling him head-long toward the stone fireplace located on the far side of the room.

"Declan, I not be needing to hear such language! Ye sound like ye belong on the docks with the rest of the foul-tongued Divils! Straighten yurself this instant, and be setting yurself before me," Cailen ordered in a tone well-known to her son.

The housekeeper, who also recognized this tone, moved slowly into the room. "Mrs. Quinn," she said gingerly, "I be serving the tea directly. Matilda will be joining yurself and the young master momentarily."

"Where is she to be, Bridget?" Cailen questioned in an amused air. "It be well past the hour. It not be like her to be late."

"Aye," Bridget answered, "'tis true, to be sure, I not be known anyone more punctual. But when I trekked to the classroom to fetch herself and the young whippersnapper I found them deep in thought. It appeared they be unaware of the time, for it took a few rousing knocks on the solid oak to arouse their attention."

Bridget Donnigan adored young Declan fully as much as Matilda Prichard did. She also held great respect for Prichard of who would go to great lengths to protect both herself and her young charge, even if it meant stretching the truth further than it actually was. Cailen, if at all in-tune with what her housekeeper was hoping to achieve, appeared to let the last line ride, for she turned to her son, and inquired the exam results.

Declan swallowed hard and opened his mouth to speak but nothing was coming out. He already knew what her reaction would be, and he'd give anything if the floor would just open and swallow him whole. "Oh, God, how bad will it be?" he nervously thought, just as his tutor entered the room. A groan escaped her throat as she pulled-back a chair from the table, and eased herself down beside her young charge. They quickly exchanged glances, relaying more within those few fleeting moments than any amount of words could say. The boy knew he'd be in for it the moment his mother viewed the results, but having his teacher at his side allowed a new-found strength to surge through him.

"Oh it does my feet wonders to be off them for awhile," Prichard sighed. "I must say, Mrs. Quinn, that today I truly feel my advancing years. Then again one does not go backward in time, only forward, regardless of one's body complaints along the way," and as she spoke her hands massaged her thighs in a circular motion.

Staring in her son's direction, Cailen replied, "I be sorry yur day's been so long, Matilda, and by the look upon me boy's face his was fully as trying."

Declan sat erect, shuffling his feet, a nervous habit he'd had since childhood. "Christ this is torture. Get on with it," he anxiously thought as despair tried its utmost to seize him. The more intense his mother's stare, the faster his feet shuffled, and by the look in her eye there would be no let up soon, as he thought, "Oh, God, she already knows! She has to! Oh please stop staring at me like I've committed murder, it's only a stupid exam!"

"Here be the tea," Donnigan announced, setting a well laden tray upon the lace covered table, and as she began removing the china, she said, "and be minding yurselves for it be hotter than the fires below," then glancing warmly at Declan, added, "I be bringing ye some of those darling sweets ye be loving so much."

"Thank you, Mrs. Donnigan," he replied in kind, "but I'm not really hungry at the moment. I know Ma is wishing to discuss class matters with Miss Prichard and myself, and we'd best get on with it. I'll have some tea though - if you don't mind pouring it for me - I'm sure to make a mess if I try."

Donnigan smiled in a knowing manner, and cheerfully said, "It be no trouble a-tall, darling one. There ye go! Now I be off to the kitchen to busy meself."

Declan's eyes increased in size when Prichard laid the exam results upon his mother's outstretched hand. Time became eternity as she carefully studied the contents while he sat fidgeting; tapping his fingers upon the table in a nervous manner until his tutor calmly reached over and gently laid her hand upon them. "Geez, Ma, do you have to look at every fucking syllable," he thought in anguish as the walls appeared to close in, bringing a nauseous feeling with them, as his thoughts continued, "I failed! That's all there is to it. It's there in black and white to see!"

At that moment his mother glanced up. "Well, me boy," she said in a denouncing way, "ye appear troubled. Could the disheartening results of this paper possibly be the reason for yur turmoil?"

"M-ma, I-I ...," Declan stammered, appearing unable to continue.

Taking up the cause, Prichard said, "As you can see, Mrs. Quinn, the results, along with their outcome is as plain as the look on your face. Master Declan failed. There is no other term to use or delicate way of softening the blow. I am fully aware of what we discussed should this unfortunate incident occur, but in all fairness I carry as much blame as the young master here for I, more than anyone, am aware that he has been somewhat troubled of late, and I, more than anyone, should have stepped back instead of pushing harder."

Taking a deep breath, Cailen replied, "I be respecting yur views, Matilda, but it be totally irrelevant to the outcome. Regardless of the way ye feel about it he already be known what was expected of him this term. He and I be discussing it enough! But when it comes to expressing the seriousness of the situation I too must admit to guilt. I be too lenient, Matlida. Ye be pointing that out on countless occasions, but I never be to listen the way I should and, now I see where 'tis gotten me." The paper lay askew as she tightly clasped her hands together, and directed her attention solely upon her trembling son. "Declan," she said apprehensively, "I be finding this more difficult than first thought. For some time now Miss Prichard and meself have discussed, in depth I might add, yur attention span as well as yur tardiness in getting to class, not to mention falling asleep during because of the late hours ye be keeping on yur computer, doing what ere it is ye be doing. I have spoken to ye about that problem time and time again, but according to the embarrassing results of this *important* exam, me words have fallen on deaf ears." She stopped for a moment to take a sip of tea, possibly gather her thoughts.

As if in a deliberate attempt to avert the inevitable, Prichard said, "Mrs. Quinn, might I suggest the possibility of the assistance of an extra tutor. It certainly would not hurt the cause, and I'll most definitely rally round my young charge in the face of adversity."

For a moment Cailen said nothing, instead studied the exasperation upon Prichard's face. Finally, she replied, "Matilda, as much as that might help in regard to his study load, it be doing nothing for much other at this point, and that be fully as important as the knowledge he be needing to learn."

The conversation carried-on for a few more hours with the two women bantering back and forth as though they were the only ones in the room. At any given time that might be fine, but this was not just *any* time or *any* situation, yet they appeared to have forgotten one small detail, and unfortunately it burst upon them in a way neither where prepared for.

Slamming his fist upon the table, Declan snapped, "It's *my* future you're discussing as though I've no right to say anything that goes on in it!" His temper grew with each word spoken, and before he knew it he'd lost control. "Why can't you ever listen to me? You go behind my back and spin your webs in hope I'll be caught in the middle! You never discuss *anything* with me — *you're doing it right now!* You're *both* talking in front of me like I'm not even here — *Fuck this! I'm out-a here!*" and he pushed his cup forward with such force it smashed against the teapot, shattering both into pieces.

The women were totally shocked! Who would have ever imagined this meek, shy boy - whom under most circumstances was a bundle of nerves - would explode in such a way? Prichard was at a loss as to what to do when her mind suddenly recalled the anger he'd shown earlier in the classroom, but even that paled considerably to what was now happening. Tea flowed toward the table's edge as if a flashflood had occurred, carrying tiny fragments of china within it. Swiftly grabbing a few napkins, the frazzled teacher cried out for the housekeeper's help, while doing her best to endure.

Scurrying into the room, searching about for the hurried need, Donnigan inquired, "What in be-jibbers be the matter, Matilda? Ye sound as if the auld-horned Divil himself be after ye!" But when she viewed the mess upon the table she lost no time in swooping to the rescue.

Doing her best to cover for her young charge, Prichard exclaimed, "It appears as if we've been presented with a bit of a quandary, Bridget! I'm afraid your teapot was so hot it got away from me!" But she had lied.

Scooping the entire mess upon the tray with her apron, the portly housekeeper replied, "Oh 'tis nothing to be upset about, Matilda, I be having it cleared away in two shakes of a lamb's tail!" With a quick glance toward her employer, she said, "Not to worry, Mrs. Quinn, there be several sets in the back cupboard, ye needn't be fretting 'bout the loss of this one. After all 'tis nothing but simple Delph, ye have much finer ones, and I know this not be your favorite. So cheer yurself. I be off to brew another pot!"

Declan, showing neither remorse for his outburst or appreciation for the lie his teacher had spoken in her attempt to protect him, remained in a standing position while the mess was cleared away. Cailen, who had been taken aback at her son's outlandish display, gathered her composure and motioned him to take a seat, as she said, "Be sitting yurself down, and be minding yur tongue. There be no need speaking to Miss Prichard *or* meself in the unacceptable manner in which ye have. I not be having it — none of it! Do ye understand?" she questioned, her glare holding him captive.

"Yes," he groaned, but ignored his mother's directions and turned to go. He almost made it to the door when she blatantly made her intentions known. "Who be giving ye permission to go gallivanting away after I told ye to sit?" she snapped in disgust. "We are not yet done. Sit down!"

Tension rose in every corner of the room as Declan eased himself down the back of his chair until his bottom came to rest upon the seat. With each passing moment he fought his growing anger, actually fearing the outcome should it escape. For weeks they had played this tedious game, and regardless of how hard they tried they were still no closer to the conclusion. If only she knew how he hated it. He wanted to please her, fully as much as he did his teacher and make them smile like he had when he was a child. He was the first to admit he had always been a bit factious and ready for a good fight. Maybe it was because he was the youngest of the family, always feeling the need to prove his worth to them - anybody for that matter - yet nothing he said or did brought him any closer to the understanding he so badly craved.

A freshly-steeped pot of tea was delivered to the table, along with three fresh cup and saucer sets.

"Thank ye kindly, Bridget," Cailen said in a softer tone, "it certainly be welcomed Ye never cease to be tending the needs of this family, and I not be telling ye that enough, nor do I be telling ye how much it be appreciated, as well as yurself."

"Awe, get out with ye," Donnigan stated in appreciation, her hand slapping the air in mock dismissal toward her employer's sentiment, "ye needn't be telling me something I already be knowing. But the song be a joyous one to me ears just the same. Now I be off to tend to supper, and hope it be to yur liking." Turning to Declan, she winked, as she added, "And ye may very well find a wee surprise in the pot tonight."

As the housekeeper took her leave, Prichard grasp the teapot's handle and filled their cups with the pungent liquid, as she said,

"It is a fine pot Bridget just delivered, and we should all partake of the pacification it offers. I think we could all benefit from that about now."

Lifting the freshly-filled cup to her lips, Cailen replied, "Sure in ye be right about that, Matlida. Nerves can be an unforgiving master, if ye let them get a foothold."

The pot's last drops fell into Declan's cup and he lost no time in swallowing them. Then as he laid the napkin upon the table, he cleared his throat, and said, "I would like to tell you both how very sorry I am for what I said, and the way in which I said it. I tried explaining my feelings to Miss Prichard earlier but, it was a futile attempt. It's not that I try to be difficult, but I can't seem to concentrate on the things you both seem to feel are so important and, because of that, you think I don't understand, and am trying to be difficult on purpose."

For a moment Cailen studied her son's face like she had when he was a wee lad caught with his hand in the cookie jar. As she did it brought a twinge of sadness to her heart, for he was now looking at her with that same expression. With a gentle tone, she said, "I not be saying that ye are being difficult, Declan, and I be sorry ye feel that way. But ye have to understand our concern. Ye pay us no mind a-tall when ere we speak about yur studies. Yur temper flares with the slightest mention of it, and I be even finding yur temper short with yur brothers. There be no reason for it. Every time I discuss an issue - let alone yur education - ye speak to me as if I not be known what I be talking about. Ye have become extremely rude and condescending toward both Miss Prichard and me. Ye lack any form of motivation, except for the tremendous amount of time spent on yur computer. Ye are late for meals. Ye never see to yur chores, and ye are never to be helping yur brothers at the distillery when ere they request it. A few months ago ye seemed to take at least *some* interest in the family business, as well as other things within the family. Yur da would be proud of ye for that - I certainly was - but now I not be known what to do with ye."

Declan had remained quiet throughout his mother's well-delivered speech, because to him that's exactly what it sounded like. Part of it may have been right; he gave her that much, though he sat before her reserved and sullen. Prichard sat sipping her cold tea, yet she didn't care, for her attention was certainly not on the temperature of her beverage. She held fast to the words being spoken, and as each one was uttered she couldn't help but brace herself for the response it might trigger.

In a reserved manner, Declan said, "I don't know why you're putting such importance on what I've been doing with my time, Ma. I'm certainly not wasting it."

"I beg to differ!" she snapped. "If ye were putting it to proper use by applying yurself in the way ye should then we not be having this trying conversation!"

In a flip manner, Declan announced, "Well, Mother, since you seem to be such an expert on the topic you may as well go ahead and tell me how I should be applying myself!"

"To begin with ye can drop the arrogant tone!" Cailen snapped, relaying the fact that she had reached the end of her patience, leaving him glaring at her, wishing with all his might to be anywhere other than his present location.

Finally the tedious afternoon gave-way to evening, and with it Declan to a bundle of nerves. As he sat listening to his mother's continued reprimand, his tortured mind cried, "Please stop, Ma. I'm sorry if I let you down but I can't take anymore of this." But Cailen Quinn was not one to let anything get beyond her - least of all her son's growing ineptness and nonchalant attitude toward the future – for both had to change. The disturbing confrontation now happening had been festering for quite some time; they were both aware of this and no doubt hoped it wouldn't reach this point, but it had. She'd been far too lenient with him. Maybe these shortcomings could be attributed to the fact he was the youngest, requiring direction from her in ways his older brothers had not, yet it could have simply been the fact that he so reminded her of his deceased father that she didn't have the heart to be firm. It was plain as the nose on her face that the rebellious pride that Derek had once possessed was alive and kicking within their youngest, and it frightened her beyond reason, especially when she remembered what had happened to him on that fateful day so long ago.

"What do you want me to do, Ma?" Declan asked, wiping the moisture from his cheeks with the back of his hand.

"Oh, son," Cailen relayed in an exasperated tone, "it be not what *I* want, but rather what be best for ye now, and for yur future. Ye seem to be having this wild notion that life be no more than a grand party, where the fun be overflowing from one day to the next with no care in the world – least of all taking responsibility for yur actions, or caring how well ye do in yur lessons and the finality of them. It's obvious ye not care one iota about that — none of it. If ye did this paper would reflect it, and it does not! Ye not care at all, boy! I cannot be helping but think ye find it a grand joke to see how bad ye can actually do, or possibly ye take enjoyment in showing just how much ye can disrespect me — more importantly Miss Prichard — especially when it comes to all the hard work and effort she be giving all these years!"

"Ma, stop — please! I already told you how sorry I am, but you don't listen! It's almost like you purposely close your ears to what I say. *Neither* of you listen to me anymore. You haven't for a long time now! Willow's the only one that actually cares about me — least she listens!" Declan cried, rising to his feet.

"Willow?" Cailen questioned inquisitively. "Who are ye to be talking about?"

Without hesitation, Declan answered, "She's my friend — my special friend. She doesn't talk down to me, doesn't judge me. She cares what I say and, more importantly she treats me like the man I am! She makes me feel alive!"

Cailen's face looked as if it had just been slapped, as she said, "What in blazes are ye talking about?"

"Willow, Ma," Declan cried. "I've wanted to tell you about her. I'm trying to tell you about her now. The way she treats me, the way she makes me feel, not like some scared kid who's afraid of his own shadow!"

Reacting as though she could hardly believe her ears, Cailen snapped, "And I suppose this *Willow* be the reason ye be on yur computer 'till all hours of the night! Could she possibly be the reason for yur lack of attention toward yur studies as well? A woman ye be talking to on the computer no less, filling yur childish head with foolish ideas. Ye still be a *boy*. Stop talking nonsense! Now, as much as it pains me to say, I have decided to send ye to private boarding school in England."

"You can't do that!"

"I most certainly can."

"*No!*"

"Ye leave me no alternative, son. I have been speaking with the head master there —" She was abruptly cut off as Declan again screamed his defiance, but standing her ground, Cailen firmly stated, "Ye may as well stop this right now for it be getting ye nowhere! I have made the decision and I be standing firm!"

"*No, Ma, I won't go!*" he shouted in rage, instantly jumping up. As he did, the entire room spun violently, and he knew what was about to happen.

"Just calm down," Cailen replied in the softest tone she could muster, all the while motioning for Prichard's reassuring aid. "Ye be getting yurself into a state and by the look in yur eyes yur're about to have one of yur spells."

"Master Declan, you must take hold," Prichard injected in a grief-stricken tone. "You are much too distraught at the moment to speak rationally about this issue! Trust me, my dear, we have only your best interest at heart, really we do." She could hardly bear it, and tears welled in her eyes as she looked at him.

Declan felt as if he were falling, but refused to give into the overpowering weakness pressing him down. His hands shot forward, landing heavily upon the table's surface. *"Leave me alone!"* he hollered, giving his clouded head a shake. *"I'm no longer a helpless child — even if you think I am! I don't need your help, and I fucking refuse to be dismissed because you don't know what to do with me! I told you I will not be sent away and I won't! Why can't you be more like Willow? You don't care about me! All you care about is what everything looks like! If you cared half as much as you profess then the thought to send me away wouldn't even cross your mind!"*

He pulled himself erect; all the while the room continued to swim. With dizziness engulfing him, he stood defiant, every nerve now raw. He needed Willow. He needed her now! Not giving them further chance to speak he whirled and stumbled out the door en route to the nearest telephone. Regardless of his ongoing phobia he had to hear her voice. He would not be deterred no matter how difficult the task, and anyone intent on stopping him was damned if they tried. Reaching the front hall, his hurried stare fell upon the huge marble-topped table with the infamous telephone resting in the middle. He stopped dead in his tracks, chest heaving, and breath coming in jagged bursts while he wondered how he would ever manage, but the dire need within him drove his left hand forward until it reluctantly grasped the ivory receiver. His hand shook violently, the receiver fighting to stay within it, but his grip held fast as his fingers did his biding upon the keys. They continued to slip off the numbers as minute perspiration formed upon them. For a moment his bowels felt loose, making him wonder if he'd have to abort the mission in order to dash to the lavatory, yet he knew it was only nerves.

On entering the foyer, Cailen softly questioned, "Just what in the name of Heaven do ye think ye be doing now?"

Trying her best to lend aid to the tense situation, Prichard encouragingly said, "Master Declan, lay the receiver upon the table and come back to the drawing room. We shall send for tea and cakes directly, and then we can all have a jolly old gab like we used to."

The boy eyed each of them as he firmly pressed the receiver to his ear. He surmised they were up to something; their previous attempts to control him had failed miserably so it wasn't surprising they were exploring a different angle. The number was finally ringing. As it did he felt the floor trembling beneath his feet - yet it couldn't be - if it was the women holding vigil before him wouldn't be standing as still as they were. "Oh, God, this is worse than I ever imagined," he thought in desperation as the ladies inched closer. He stubbornly held fast, stepping backward as they closed in. The third ring began but was cut short when the recorded voice of the operator began informing him that the number he was dialing was not in service.

"What?" he uttered softly, certain he had heard wrong. "That can't be. No, no I need to speak with her. It-it can't be out of service - she'd never do that to me!" he cried in anguish, dropping the receiver upon the table while he fought to remain standing.

"What do ye think ye be doing?" Cailen asked, quickly rounding the table en route to him.

Declan cast an imploring glance toward Prichard, but a rather sarcastic one toward his mother as he steadied himself. "What does it look like?" he asked. "I'd think even *you* would know what this is — though you rarely answer it yourself!"

"Master Declan!" Prichard snapped with annoyance.

Cailen's expression toward the tutor relayed the gratitude she felt. After all getting into further confrontation would not help the situation in the least; all it would accomplish would be to make it worse. Prichard had always had a way with her young charge, and it didn't fail her this time, for he instantly apologized for his remark.

Stepping toward her son, Cailen inquired, "Would ye care to be explaining what ye be doing, and who ye be ringing?"

"I'm trying to call Willow," he replied. "But a voice keeps telling me the number is no longer in service. I don't understand, Ma. She wouldn't give me a number that wasn't working. She gave it to me back in the spring – I-I just don't understand what's going on."

Sighing as she shook her head, Cailen said, "To begin with, ye not be truly knowing this woman, and ye have no way of knowing if the number she gave be an actual one. Honestly, Declan, I do not understand how ye can be so trusting about someone ye have yet to meet. She may have simply said that to have fun with ye for her own unscrupulous needs, or simply to pacify ye. Ye simply have no way of knowing."

Declan bristled, and snapped, "No, Ma, she's not like that! She wouldn't do that to me!" His anxiety strangely heightened, enticing him to wonder if it was because of his mother's ill-placed statement, or the possibility that she just may be correct in her assumption.

"I must agree with your mother on this issue," Prichard stated. "After all you've yet to mention this name – with the exception of speaking it in your sleep. Really, Master Declan, you haven't the slightest inkling of this woman's intentions, even if they should be honorable. You just don't know. When you sum it up, how can you be certain she's even who she claims to be? You've met her on the Internet no less and you know as well as I how that can be taken, with a grain of salt as far as I'm concerned. Personally I wouldn't believe one word a person relayed about them self when it comes from a non-reliant source like that, especially when there is no solid proof to back it up."

Declan glared defiantly at the two women, his face a brilliant crimson as he picked up the fallen receiver and slammed it upon the cradle. *"You don't know anything about her!"* he screamed. "How *dare* you imply she is anything but honest? She's come to mean the world to me in ways that neither of you could *possibly* understand!"

Cailen continued to study her son, uncertain of what words to choose that would not elicit further reaction of the kind they were experiencing. Holding firmly against his stare, she said, "Me boy, we only be saying what we have because we both care about yur welfare. Why have ye become so defensive, especially if what ye believe to be true about this woman is in fact the truth?"

The standoff continued as Prichard watched with pain ripping her heart. It was obvious any further amount of cross-examination would result in nothing less than total disaster all around. She felt the need to do something, yet so far every attempt had failed, making it clear he was determined to have his way come hell or high water, still she had to try. Summoning strength, she said, "Master Declan, please understand that we have only your best interests at heart. We are not trying to purposely upset you, but I dearly wish you would give at least *some* consideration to what we have stated, before you blindly leap into a dark abyss from which the return may be virtually impossible."

Inwardly Declan knew there must be a sensible explanation to this entire dilemma, but he was not about to stand and fight about it. In a confused manner, he stated, "I'm going out for awhile and I don't know when I'll be home."

Shaking her head, Cailen, replied, "I not be agreeing with ye going anywhere feeling as ye are. Furthermore we've not yet concluded our discussion concerning yur new school."

The boy was unsteady and it showed as he weaved from side to side. The ladies looked at him with concern toward his present condition, but as they stepped toward him he backed away, stating he would listen no more, and before they knew it the foyer's huge oak door had slammed, leaving them reeling in its thunderous wake. On the other side a ravenous temper had grown to an all time high as its bewildered victim staggered toward his car, daring anyone to step in his way. He was determined to not be sent away, but more importantly he refused to be kept from pursuing his dreams as he settled behind the wheel, rammed the shifter into gear, and tore down the drive.

Chapter 25

THE PLOT THICKENS

Willow, blinded by anger, arrived at the brownstone where Jonas rented a room. Slamming the car's transmission into park, she threw open the door, and stormed up the steps only to be met by Jonas on his way down. They abruptly stopped the magnitude of animosity so intense a pin could be heard dropping; the silence so loud it was deafening as they stood staring into each other's eyes with such intensity, it was as if they were gazing into a dark abyss threatening to swallow them both. As each second passed, the intensity of Willow's anger grew stronger while questions consumed her mind as to how in hell she could ever hope to settle the issue she'd come about if she could not hold her temper in check.

"What do you want?!" Jonas inquired in a sharp manner, doing his best to hurry the issue along. For all intent and purpose he didn't require an answer - he'd already surmised what it would be - yet he found himself anticipating what she would actually say.

Grappling to remain calm, Willow retorted, "You know damn well what I'm here about, you heartless son-of-a-bitch!"

Not relaxing his stance in the least, Jonas replied, "Well I thank you for the compliment with regard to the knowledge I possess, but I'm sure I don't know what you're on about."

Willow could feel a scream pushing up her throat. It would only be a matter of time before it escaped and all hell would break loose, but she held control, as she said, "What I'm *on about* is the phone service – or lack thereof!"

"Hmm, the phone, you say?" he inquired in a flip manner. "I don't recall anything wrong with it - worked the last time I used it – but then that was quite some time ago, wasn't it?"

Ignoring the blatant dig, Willow took a deep breath, and said, "I suppose you're going to feign memory loss now, is that it?"

A cocky grin consumed Jonas' face, as he answered, "You never know, sweetheart, I just might," and if Willow didn't know better she'd swear he was trying his best to entice a riot.

Time ticked away as they stood bickering, each hateful remark fully as asinine as the previous, but neither of them getting anywhere regardless of what was said, or the way in which it was said. Jonas, who had been expecting this visit, knew full-well it was because of his recently having had the phone disconnected. He also knew how much she relied on her computer - no doubt the rest of the family would have clued him in to the ridiculous amount of time it took to contact her via the phone – plus it wouldn't have taken a Philadelphia lawyer to figure out that the loss of the Internet was the reason for this tumultuous visit.

Letting her hands smack his chest, Willow snapped, "I need my phone, Jonas!"

Intently staring at her, he replied, "Somehow I don't think you need the phone nearly as much as the connection it provides to the Net, and whoever the hell it is you've been hanging out with on there."

Unbeknownst to Willow, Jonas was not as unaware of her online activities as she might have hoped. After-all he knew she wouldn't be this frantic if it was simply the loss of the phone - severed connection to clients or not - so it had to be for the person of whom the connection so obviously provided.

"What's his name?" Jonas questioned his voice serious.

Realizing her husband surmised something; Willow swallowed hard, and said, "What is whose name? Really, Jonas, I don't know what you're talking about." There was no need for an accurate answer for the stunned dear-in-the-headlight-look on her face had already confirmed his question.

"Ah-huh," Jonas scoffed, and turned on his heel to leave.

When it came to confrontations, Willow was never one to be left out in the cold, and she stiffened, as she yelled, *"What the hell did you expect me do?! You won't help me! All you seem intent on doing is driving me completely insane with all the nonsense you keep throwing my way! ... Look at me!"*

Jonas stopped in mid-stride, whirled-around, and snapped, "Drop it! You know as well as I that in order to settle things the house has to be sold. Yet you'll hear none of it! Nor will you listen to reason regardless of what I say *or* do. You're hell-bent on having your way — just like always! I gave you your precious space when you required that, and I tried my best to understand what you were going through. But like I told you awhile back, you'd never let me close enough to even touch you, let alone comfort you – the comfort you now say you needed so much – craved! You drove me fucking crazy at the time and you're still doing it with your holier-than-thou attitude. It doesn't seem to matter what I propose. You throw it right back in my face, all the goddamn while screaming and carrying on about what I refuse to do for you when you couldn't give two hoots-in-hell about me, let alone try and work out our problems or come to some kind of agreement so we can settle this enormous debt we're in! All you care about is your precious house – it's only four walls and a roof for Christ sakes, Willow - I know you've got some *dick* on the Net somewhere. What line's he feeding you anyway? Is he telling you he's going to make it alright — your night in shinning armor perhaps? Shit, you'd be gullible enough to believe every word he fed you ... What? You finally have something to say?"

Willow found her husband's rant rather startling, and she wasn't sure how to react to the accusations concerning her *Net connection*, for that was the one area she had tried her damndest to keep secret. She had come a long way from her fickle-minded youth where the attentions of a sought-after male constantly filled her every-waking moment, or had she? Jaded laughter filled her mind when she let her thoughts dwell on just that fact, along with the denial of it; for she *was* acting that way, and the worst of it all was that it had succeeded in consuming her life. Her young Irish consort had taken over not only her life, but her better judgment, still she could not let this be known to Jonas. She had to somehow find a way around her phlegmatic husband and get him to reinstate the phone service.

Conjuring a fake smile, she said, "I really can't disagree with you. I realize the way I acted - still act and yeah - it must be confusing. But as I told you before I can't help how I feel, anymore than the confusing way I'm trying to explain it now. I know my problems were the main reason for our breakup. But how am I supposed to cope with something when I'm not sure what that something is?"

Shifting his weight, Jonas coldly answered, "I've tried my best to come to terms with the health issues – even the refusal to sell the house - but that's not what I asked."

Tension soared, but Willow would not give into his taunting, as she arrogantly said, "I already told you I don't know who you're talking about, or has your hearing become affected?" yet she could feel the noose tightening.

"Nothing's wrong with my hearing, babe - for that matter any part of me - and maybe you should have tried a little harder to get some professional help. I sure as hell didn't stand in your way —"

Totally cutting him off, Willow snapped, "That's a joke if ever I heard one! You couldn't spare the time; much less tolerate the amount of *money* it would have taken. So what was I to do?"

Jonas stood fidgeting, looking as if he were an ant stuck on a hot griddle not knowing which way to hop. It was obvious his wife's words were hitting home, jostling nerves best left untouched. It is said that whatever you put out in life comes back three-fold, and the nastier the intent, the more intense the return. Yet in all fairness the same could be said of Willow, for she was not as innocent as she was feigning.

"Well this is getting us absolutely nowhere," he moaned, proceeding to push past her.

Grabbing his arm, she sniped, "That's it! Run away, just like always! You're a master at that! You're always throwing it in my face about how much I demand my way, but you're no different — in fact you act more like a spoiled brat every day because I won't give in to your damn demands. Go on then – walk away – see if I care! I don't need *you!*"

The pressure was building more than either knew how to handle. It had always been like that whenever they fought; no doubt it always is when one has a temper fully as intense as the other, and these two were a prime example. Jonas, stopping dead in his tracks, swung fully around, encompassed his ruffled wife within his arms, and kissed her brutally. His lips pressed fully upon hers, his arms pinning hers solidly against her sides as his kiss intensified. She fought to pull back, yet he held her firmly against him while his tongue spread her lips wide, snaking deeper into her mouth, sucking her tongue while his voice moaned his distraught emotions. One could not be sure if it was intense anger being unleashed toward a situation he felt now totally out of control, or whether he was again feeling desire for the woman he once held such passion for that the heat actually seared him whenever he was close to her.

Willow fought to free herself, yet as hard as she tried she could not break free. She was held captive by her husband's strong arms and so enraptured by his compassionate touch she could no longer stand erect, and her knees buckled. In an instant Jonas scooped her into his arms and returned to his room. She had become as putty in his arms, letting him mold her into any shape he so desired. With passion building, he stretched her fully upon the bed and began to remove her lower clothing. She was helpless to avert this, yet she somehow didn't want to, even though her boggled mind was telling her to stop, halt his aggression, and reel him in. But his touch stimulated her senses to the point where she allowed full penetration, his dripping erection parting her, gliding deep within her, thrusting, moaning, his strokes growing faster – deeper - his penis throbbing with such intensity that he could barely keep from exploding within her. He suddenly pulled out but left his mouth fully upon hers, manipulating her lips as if they were made of rubber. As if by habit his finger began stimulating her clit, teasing her, enticing her, bringing her dangerously close to orgasm. She cried out for him - wanting him – needing him – while he frantically massaged her, building her moisture to the point it was seeping down her inner thighs. She was ripe for the taking, and he took her, fully, plowing his throbbing manhood deeply into her red-hot chasm, moving swiftly - jamming hard with intense rhythm - desire building, compressed love exploding to the surface with each enormous stroke.

This was not supposed to happen, yet it was. Willow, as much as she had fought against it, now totally resigned her body to her husband's familiar touch, his abandoned touch now returned, and she wanted more. She found it hard to believe. After all she was in love with Declan, wasn't she? Her mind even tried envisioning his face, but it was totally gone, and she actually had to admit she wasn't sorry. Confusion engulfed her as she returned her husband's kiss and readied herself for the orgasm she felt building. This was incredible, regardless of any misgivings surrounding the entire scenario. Pressure was building. She could feel the pace of her husband's rigid member slowing, trying its damndest not to erupt within her, but he was coming - she was coming – and it felt as if the weight of the world had finally been lifted as fevered climax exploded, ending this unintended venture, and leaving them in a spent, sweat-laden heap.

They lay together, breathing deeply, trying to catch their breath and wondering what in hell to say to each other. They hadn't planned this. Even had they, it could never have been realized in the sumptuous way it just was, nor could the raw emotion throughout be conjured in such a conscious manner. Jonas actually felt the love he had tried so hard to suppress, and Willow, no longer certain of anything, felt caught in a catch twenty two.

Chapter 26

HAVING ONE'S WAY

The jazzy red sports car flew down the highway toward Galway at top speed; its wide-set tires screeching their reluctance to hold to the payment each time they rounded a bend. As they did, the driver, still dwelling on the conspiracy being plotted against him, spit obscenities as if they were going out of style. It mattered not in the least what he said - or what he did - even his blatant reaction - as he had stood in defiance of a mother who was determined to have her way regardless of the outcome. But he would show her. He would show them all!

The downtown core of Galway was alive with sound, especially in the bar where Declan liked to hang his hat. He was always welcomed there, no doubt because of the amount of coin dropped on each visit, for it was certain to be a good night's tally whenever he, for that matter any of the Quinn boys, dropped in.

"Look who be here, 'tis himself, to be sure!" Pat the bar-keep exclaimed as he diligently dried a beer mug. "What be yur taste tonight, young fella?"

"Hello, Pat," Declan said, plopping himself upon a bar stool, "how's it going? I'll have a pint of the usual."

"Oh will ye now?" the bar-keep stated in amusement, applying just the right amount of pressure to the draft handle as to prevent an unwanted foam overflow in the glass he was pouring. "And what be bringing ye here at this hour? Best not be letting that razor-tongued mother of yurs be knowing yur whereabouts, or she's likely to thrash ye within an inch of yur life – not to mention me!"

"Na, Pat," Declan remarked as he readied himself for indulgence, "she doesn't know where I am - no concern of hers for that matter – and you needn't tell her either should she come in here tomorrow asking."

As he wiped the froth from a newly poured glass of draft, Pat replied, "Not to worry, mate, I don't intend to butt heads with that one anytime soon. I well remember the last time, and I be in no hurry for a repeat!"

Laughing, Declan replied, "Can't say as I blame you. She can be a bit much. The worst of it is she never knows when to quit, even if her intentions *are* in the right place. She just keeps going on and on and well, I don't need to tell you, and I shouldn't even be speaking like this. I really don't mean her disrespect; I just wish she would listen more to what I'm trying to say, if she did, maybe we wouldn't get into it like we did tonight."

As Declan sat chewing the fat with the bar-keep, a young woman sat nursing a glass of wine at a table located across the room before the fireplace. The way in which she kept glancing at the young man at the bar made it obvious she knew him, and aside from a dry cough, and continuous whipping of her reddened nose, she didn't appear anxious in any way, in fact it was almost as if she knew how long it would take him to notice her. An hour went by as the bar-keep wrangled lightheartedly with his young patron. He really did enjoy the boy's company, even took pride in knowing that his words might help ease yet another unsettling situation.

"Well, Pat, I think I'll have one more before I go, but I need to make a pit-stop so don't pour too soon," Declan said, rising from his stool and turning around. As he did the young woman awaiting this movement set down her glass, and with a broad smile upon her ruby lips, motioned him to join her.

Declan, giving the illusion of being taken aback, stopped dead in his tracks. "Well if it isn't Galway's esteemed whore," he announced in a curt manner. "What brings you here, couldn't find any gobshites elsewhere?"

"Well now," the young woman replied as she casually patted the adjacent chair beside her, "that's not a very nice greeting for someone whom you always loved to f... Well, I suppose I could say 'someone you liked to spend *quality* time with.'"

Shaking his head in an objective manner, Declan coldly stated, "Really? ... Well I don't intend to sit there or anywhere near you. I don't even know why you bother, Aednat. I don't care about you anymore, *especially* after what you caused me to do last year."

"Is that right? I don't recall pouring those pills down your throat."

"Maybe not, but you were the reason I did, so you may as well have held the bottle in your fingers. Now you've got the gall to sit there and nonchalantly suggest I join you for a drink or, could it possibly be for your nightly ride? What sorry plonker's giving it to you these days?"

"You really don't expect me to answer that, do you?"

"I don't care whether you do or not. No more than I care what bushwhacker's shoved-up your cunt, making it wider than it already was when I last had you. Got the picture?"

One could feel the room rising in heat, but not the kind that emits when lovers unite. Declan was in the act of leaving when the miffed young Aednat quickly wiped her nose, and said, "Speaking of gaping holes, have you managed to cyber the old hag yet?"

Young Quinn's temper instantly erupted. "Shut your fucking gob!" he snapped, and stormed toward the men's room.

Watching him go, the now-vexed Aednat called, "Aw, Puss Face, don't go away pissed! I'm sure she's not as dried up as we think! She might even give a bogey like you a good shag yet!" before proceeding to blow her dripping nose into a red silk hankie.

"Is there no let up to people's lame remarks?" Declan thought as he veered away from his prior destination and stomped out the door to his car. The motor roared to life, and he was instantly on the road toward home with Aednat's illicit words chewing at his brain. "She's a fine one to talk. Who gives her the right to judge anyone?" Declan thought with animosity, but it hurt, and as much as he tried denying her bawdy suggestion, he had to admit to the basic truth of it, for it was exactly what he wanted to do to Willow, he just never had the nerve to ask.

Nervously hoping to slip into the foyer unnoticed, Declan quietly opened the mansion's huge front door, and stepped inside.

"Where have ye been?" Cailen questioned as she entered the foyer carrying a beaker of tea.

As much as Declan had hoped an admittance free of confrontation he soon realized that was not about to happen. He veered straight for the stairs, but was strategically deterred when his mother informed him she needed to speak with him. "Oh please don't start again," he thought with growing animosity and braced for a new round, but he was delightfully surprised when the expected hassle did not materialize.

Sweeping her hand toward a foyer chair, Cailen said, "Sit ye down and pay attention to what I be saying. Now I be thinking long and hard about our situation, and I feel what I have decided will be of greater benefit than me previous intention. Instead of the London Business School, I have decided to send ye to the School of Business at Carleton University in Ottawa. Miss Prichard and I have been researching it ever since ye bolted out the door, and we find it to be exactly what is required for yur future training in regard to the running of the family business, much more so than at London Business. Miss Prichard has managed to contact Carleton's Dean. It took a bit of convincing, but she managed to assure him that even though ye are below the required average ye will still excel with yur present one – embarrassing as it is - and I have secured an apartment – at phenomenal cost I might add - within walking distance of the campus. The summer semester has only been in session a short while, so ye will not be far behind. Ye are to begin classes on Monday morning. I have booked an early Friday morning flight to Pearson International in Toronto, where ye will arrive mid-afternoon. From there ye will board an airbus to Ottawa International which will get ye to yur destination by late afternoon. It will allow ye the better part of the weekend to settle in. This is a done deal, Declan, and there will be no back talk or nonsense in the slightest. As much as Miss Prichard and I wish differently - and will miss ye immensely - ye have left us no choice. Now it is late, and ye are to go straight to yur room. I will see ye at breakfast, and I will expect ye to be on yur best behavior. I now be bidding ye a fine goodnight."

"Did I just hear right?" Declan wondered with excitement, hardly believing the words to be true, but somehow knew they were. "Ottawa! Willow's city! I can actually be with her, hold her, kiss her and, make love to her!" There would be no back-talk this time, for as much as his mother might have thought she was having her intended way, he was getting exactly what he wanted, and he could not wait.

Chapter 27

RETURN TO REALITY

Willow opened the front door of her house and stepped inside her solitude. The only sound heard was that of the battery clock upon the mantle, diligently ticking away the time. Thoughts consumed her, thoughts of what lay ahead, the problems that continued to plague her, and what she could do – if anything - to avert them, still regardless of these all-consuming thoughts, her strongest centered on Jonas, and what had recently happened between them. "How I could have done that, let alone allowed it is beyond me," she thought, chastising herself for her behavior, her lack of judgment, as well as conduct. She thought about what had been going on for so long, the wretched arguments they had endured, and the horrid words they had spoken to each other. Yet in those few, lust-filled moments together, all of that ceased to be as if their rift had never happened. Jonas had made love to her - she had *let* him make love to her - which in turn allowed her to feel wanted, enraptured, needed by him in the way she had once felt. For Jonas it might possibly have come about because of anger, frustration, or his inability to cope with a woman whom he could no-longer control, but if he had felt that way, it had soon given way to passion, the passion he once felt for her. She could not deny what she had felt during their recent copulation; in fact she savored it, let her mind devour it, and now found the remembrance of it embedded in her soul.

The stillness beckoned her. She moved about the room, looking at the blue damask walls and to the pictures lining the mantle. She did this often. It brought her comfort to do so, but not only comfort; it steeled her wool, shored up her weakened damn, and allowed her to regroup. But the illicit moments recently spent with Jonas did not diminish the present problems between them. If anything it made them worse, for here she was, supposedly in love with a man so ridiculously young that even *that* was inconceivable entirely on its own, almost unlawful — my God if he was one year younger he would be jail-bait, prison time — if she were caught. Now she'd gone and complicated that with re-awakened feelings for her estranged husband. Then there was the ever present debt situation that seemed to grow larger with each passing day. When it came to Willow's walk, there didn't appear to be any let-up to the absurdity surrounding it. She had always been a bit on the facetious side, always at the ready to defend her latest venture regardless of how inconceivably outrageous it might be, but now she found herself at a loss for direction, at least a sensible one.

The silence of her recollections was interrupted by the dropping shut of the mailbox lid. In fact it was so loud it echoed upon contact with the rest of the metal box, almost as if it was meant to summon urgency as to what had been dropped inside. Willow actually felt a sinister twinge creep up her spine as she moved toward it, causing her to approach with caution. As she opened the lid, her eyes instantly fell upon the latest correspondence from the gas company, which in turn summoned a question as to its contents, yet how stupid could she be? No answer was required to such an idiotic question; she already knew the jest of its contents. Retrieving it, her fingers tore it open to reveal the final notice with regard to arrears before the service would be discontinued. There was no cause to fret nor oppose it. She knew she might just as well wait for the workman's arrival, and be ready with pen in hand. With this realization she actually breathed a sigh of relief, for there was no way she could possibly pay another dime, let alone arrears, as she thought, "It's summer, I don't need heat, and whatever cooking is required can be done over the fire pit – hell - there may even be some leftover fuel in the bar-b. For bathing and laundry I can always draw water from the backyard well, and it will also provide endless refreshment to quench my thirst — what luck!"

It was simply the way life had become for Willow and she knew it. It was never going to be any different. Maybe her stubborn streak had finally done her in, depleted what backbone she had managed to reserve, but she refused to shed one more tear because of it. She had cried enough to fill the Rideau, and not a single tear had made one speck of difference in the end. She was alone, stripped of all pride, and broken. There was nothing more she could do, nothing more she could give. As she strolled past the dining table the notice dropped from her hand, landing upon the pile of previous ones now grown to monstrous size. They no longer mattered. They had simply taken their place among the things she could do nothing about.

Reclining upon her bed, she let her thoughts drift to Jonas and the recent happening they had experienced. It brought her a strange yet comforting sensation to think about it, relive it in her mind, every sensuous moment. But as her thoughts returned to a normal state she couldn't help but wonder if Jonas, in a covetous way, had been right all along. A smug smile creased her lips as she thought; "I'm a fool to fight him. I cannot win, and all of this has brought nothing but heartache for both of us. Declan is no better. He told me he'd be there for me—" That thought caused her to burst out laughing, for she knew how utterly inane the entire relationship was; had been from the very beginning. Why it was almost cynical. "I can't even tell him, let alone cut it off," she thought, struggling with the need to find some form of normalcy in her life. She clung to the well-worn adage that time heals everything, brings clarity to the forefront, and peace to the tortured mind. But she had waited so long for that to happen that she had finally given up all hope.

A loud knock sounded upon the back door, startling her to her feet. "Who could that be," she thought with annoyance as she made her way through the house. Reaching the door, and gazing through its window, she could see it was her next door neighbor Shawn. His face held a somber expression, which seemed to project the fact that whatever he was there for was going to be unsettling for her.

"Hey, Willow," he said as she opened the door, "sorry to disturb you, but I have a message with regard to your client Winifred Brown. I … I really don't know how to tell you except … well, to simply deliver the message. Her niece Magdalene just phoned. She couldn't get you on your phone and knew my number was your back up." His stare instantly cast downward, as though it could no longer hold connection with hers, as he continued, "She asked me to come over and tell you that … that her aunt passed away. I'm really sorry, and I thought that maybe you'd like to come over and use the phone."

Willow was dumbstruck, not believing what she was hearing, as she thought, "That can't be true, not Winnie! Not that dear, wonderful soul — she can't be!" She fought to hold composure while grief clawed her heart. Winifred Brown had been so much more than a favorite client; she had become Willow's treasured friend, a confidant who had been there in whatever capacity she could be throughout Willow's entire ordeal.

"She was so full of life, Shawn," Willow stated, tears streaming down her cheeks as she spoke, "I ... I was just with her the other day; she was fine, nothing appeared wrong – *ah-ha* why? She ... *ah-ha* ... she can't be gone!"

Shawn's arms quickly encircled Willow's shoulders as he helped her to a kitchen chair and then swiftly fetched a glass of water. "Here," he said, holding the vessel outward, "sip some of this."

Taking the glass within her hand, she said, "Thanks, I'll be alright. It's just a shock to hear, I mean, it's something I never expected — especially like this. I realize she was aged, but she was always so vibrant, cheerful, and so strong with a wonderful zest for life regardless of what it threw her way. I've never known anyone like her, Shawn. It's just not going to be the same without her."

It was obvious Shawn felt uncomfortable. In times like this, words, at least the proper ones, are difficult to summon, that is if you can find any to voice at all, yet he knew he should say something. Leaning against the counter, he gently said, "It's not an easy time when you lose someone that means a lot to you. I didn't know her, but I remember hearing you talk about her many times over the years. I knew you were fond of her. I've never worked in a situation like that, but I do know that friendship can certainly develop between those who do, let alone an employee and their employer."

"Yes," Willow replied, nodding in agreement while dabbing her eyes with a tea towel, "that much is true. She and I were fortunate that way." Rising to her feet, she continued, "There was just something about her that was special. She was genuine, always open and honest regardless of the situation - and kind – so very kind and gentle. My heart goes out to her niece and, I also hope her animals manage to find a good home. They will be lost, especially her little dog Jeeves. The poor little fellow won't know which way to turn."

Walking to the door, Shawn said, "The niece might take him, maybe all the animals."

Finding a breath, Willow replied, "Possibly. Winnie always spoke of Magdalene's love for animals. I'll come over in a few minutes and put through a call to her, in fact I think I'll drive out there. Might lend some comfort to her; least it will for me to be in Winnie's home among her things. Thanks, Shawn. I realize it's not easy to be the bearer of bad news, but I appreciate your help, in all matters right now. I'll talk to you later."

Chapter 28

GOODBYE DEAR FRIEND

Magdalene Harris opened the back door of her aunt's gingerbread-gabled house with a look upon her face that revealed how thankful she was to receive the person standing before her. For a few elongated moments they stood silent, a disparaging look within their eyes. There was no need for words; their thoughts were already locked in the same place, on the same woman, and the ways in which she had impacted their lives. Willow, only knowing Magdalene in a social manner, could only imagine how Winifred's exceptional outlook toward life must have enriched her personal life. And it showed, for Magdalene was every bit as robust and outgoing as her aunt had been, with the same values and respect for those around her. Now that Winifred was gone things would never be the same, and both women realized this fact when they finally embraced.

"I'm glad you came," Magdalene said, patting Willow's back in a loving manner, "Auntie Win was lucky to have had you as a friend."

Embracing the young woman tightly, Willow replied, "I'm the lucky one, believe me. Ever since receiving this upsetting news,

I couldn't help but think about the years your aunt and I spent together, so many wonderful times, and so many entertaining conversations. You know, I think we actually set a record for consumed lunches at the local diner. We even had a specific table, which I'm sure everyone knew about because it always seemed to be empty upon our arrival." The two women somewhat chuckled at this lighthearted remark, but it was through innocent gestures such as this one that grief could be dealt with, at least managed, if not totally resolved. Willow didn't make friends easily. When she did she cemented them into her life, and she knew the loss of this one was a void that would never be filled. She was certain that Magdalene felt the same. How could she not? Winifred was one of the few who had what it takes to forever remain in someone's heart, let alone memory, and along with this fact were the irreplaceable memories from years spent together.

"What happened?" Willow questioned, releasing the young woman from the tight embrace she had her locked into. "I realize it must be difficult to talk about, but I need to know. She was fine the last time I saw her, and that was only a few days ago. There was absolutely no sign of anything out of the ordinary. She was excited about you coming, and we made sure to have everything ready for you. I just can't believe this, it's such a shock."

Taking a deep breath, Magdalene replied, "Yes, it is difficult to discuss, but regardless it doesn't change the facts, and because of your close connection with her you have a right to know. You probably knew her better than most. It happened last night about eleven. She said she felt as if she had bad indigestion that wouldn't go away. We'd had Chinese for diner – you know how much Auntie loved that kind of stuff and often had it delivered from the take out down in the village - well a few of the dishes were rather spicy, but as you know that was the way she liked them regardless of my suggestion she watch her diet. That might have been a contributing factor to the indigestion she was experiencing, I don't know, but when it wasn't subsiding I suggested I take her to the Emergency. But you know how independent she was. She said she'd just take some bicarbonate and she'd be fine. She admitted to having had that problem before, said it was becoming more frequent, but she wasn't overly concerned about it and told me not to worry. I had gone up to bed and she was still puttering around down here. I was reading when she called up to me, said she couldn't breathe properly. I got her into the car and sped to the hospital. They took her right in, but ...." Her explanation trailed off, and it was plain to see she was reliving her words, but taking a deep breath, she continued, "There was nothing they could do. Auntie's heart simply stopped. They tried over and over to restart it but, she was gone. At least it was quick. The doctor said she wasn't aware of anything, she just went to sleep, *aha* ... she didn't feel it, I'm ... *aha* ... I'm so glad she didn't suffer. If ... if Auntie had to go then I'm glad it was the way it was and, swift as it was."

Willow's feelings of distress heightened. She knew Winifred's passing was not her fault, yet she couldn't help wondering that had she not been so wrapped up in her own thoughts she might have clued into something out of the norm, but she hadn't, and her old friend seemed like she always had. Now all that could be done was to cope with the aftermath, as she asked, "Where is she now?"

Wiping her eyes, Magdalene replied, "At the hospital. They were keeping her until I notified the funeral director this morning. Auntie is to be cremated, and he was making arrangements for that to be carried out early this afternoon."

Willow's heart beat fast as her ears absorbed the words being spoken. She had asked, though now wished she hadn't, but she needed to know. Nothing would bring back her friend, regardless of the words said or the actions taken, but she still felt the need to reach out, as she said, "Doesn't seem like much, my dear, but if you need any assistance planning the service, don't hesitate to ask."

"Thank you, Willow," Magdalene replied in kind, "but Auntie Win already had everything taken care of. It was almost as if she knew. All I have to do is make arrangements for the memorial at the Twilight Room down in the village."

With a half-sigh, Willow replied, "Somehow that doesn't surprise me. I never knew anyone as organized as your sweet aunt. Still I wish there was something I could do. It might help to somehow absorb the loss – if anything will – but I would like to honor her memory in whatever way I can."

"That's kind of you, Willow. I'm sure there is something you can do."

"I truly meant what I said."

"I know you did. How about having some tea and we'll discuss it. I noticed a rather large assortment in the cupboard," Magdalene commented as she moved toward the kettle.

Seeing to the cups and saucers, Willow replied, "I'm sure you did. Your aunt not only seen to my needs, she saw to my wants as well. She knew I liked tea, and she always kept a large variety on hand. I never told her, but I do hope she knew how appreciative I was." She stopped briefly, as if to gather her thoughts, then arranging the tea things on a black enamel tray, continued, "I think that is one of the biggest regrets one experiences when it comes to coping with the loss of someone. There's always something left unsaid – undone - and I wish I could have told her things that at the time might have been considered rather menial, or possibly unimportant. I just hope she knew."

The afternoon progressed into evening, and after a few pots of tea Willow rose to go. "Thank you so much, Magdalene. It means a lot to simply sit at this table and chat. I think it's done us both a world of good – I know it has me. I find it comforting to be here, and I'll be back tomorrow to make sure the house is spotless for people's return after the memorial on Thursday — by the way, I'm so relieved to know you'll be taking Winnie's animals. Jeeves is such a loving little dog. He'll be loyal to you. It's his way."

"Thank you, Willow," Magdalene replied. "I look forward to having him; the kitties as well. I'm also happy that we had this chat, and when the memorial happens I would appreciate it if you would stand with me and greet people. I'm sure there will be many and, some I won't know that you possibly will."

Smiling, Willow replied, "Yes, I could say the same, and don't give it a second thought, I would be pleased to stand with you."

The day of Winifred's memorial was proving to be a hot one, not helped in the least by the fact that the Twilight Room's air conditioning had, on this day, chose to break down. Somehow Willow's thoughts centered on this fact, and how her old friend would be getting a kick out of the rising temperature now producing additional beads of sweat upon the brows of those whom considered themselves above such human response. In-fact there were a few – had they known - with whom Winifred would have loved to have had the last disparaging word, but even had she, she was far too gracious to have voiced it. As Willow looked about the enormous room she could almost swear that the afore mentioned *few* were giving themselves away, for their eyes shifted from one to the next, as if hesitant to remain upon any one person lest their hypocritical thoughts be revealed.

But is this not often the way when people gather to bid farewell to someone they know, a family member, fellow worker, friend, least of all an occasional acquaintance? There's something austere about the finality of a funeral - or memorial – for both is for the purpose of paying your last respects, and saying goodbye. And whether that goodbye is actually meant in an honest, regretful way, it makes one realize that that particular life has come to an end, and cannot return. As people moved about the room partaking in chit-chat, sampling plates of tempting treats, or enjoying a beverage of choice, Willow couldn't help but dwell on the reason why the majority, with the exception of her and a few others, were even there. A lot of those present would not have been considered a close friend by any means, yet even they had the right to say goodbye. "How do *I* say goodbye?" Willow thought as her eyes misted. She could feel the dam of tears trying their best to break free and reveal to every single person there how this death had affected her. But she held them in, just as she had with her father's death, the demise of her first marriage, and the death of her second. They were a private part of her that was for her only, to be revealed when she could let them flow free without the need to explain why. It was simply the way she was, and she could never seem to change. In those few moments Willow could again hear her mother's voice telling her to 'hold it in, do not be weak, and carry on as best you can'.

A sterling-framed photograph of Winifred sat upon a lace-draped table accompanied by a huge vase of colorful summer flowers. It seemed appropriate, for colorful was exactly the way Winifred viewed life. It was a wonderful way to envision things that might otherwise prove too harsh, or distorted by dull shades of grey. But for Willow, the friend she was there to honor, and their time spent together, would always remain alive within her memory, forever present, forever smiling. As Winifred's picture smiled back, Willow raised a glass of raspberry cordial, and with a single tear sliding down her right cheek, whispered, "Good bye, dear friend."

Chapter 29

CALCULATED DELUSION

It was late Friday afternoon when Declan Quinn's plane touched-down upon the heat-scorched runway of Ottawa International Airport. The entire day had been hot – in fact it was the latest in a growing line hell-bent on setting a record this early in the summer season - but at least the temperature would lessen once the sun set. Maybe the rise in temp was in keeping with the young man's well-fueled intention to secure Willow Crosby's affection once and for all. Had she actually known this fact, she might have been well advised to pact up and leave. Yet victims in any given scenario are always the last to know.

The blue taxi, concluding the relatively short trip from the airport, pulled up before a fairly new, three-story condominium complex to let the excited young Irishman out. Opening the main entrance doors to the dignified residence, Declan sauntered in, his designer carry-on draped casually over his shoulder, giving the illusion of a rich tourist's arrival to a posh, well sought-after retreat, while wondering if his luggage, which had been sent earlier, was waiting in his apartment. His excitement grew as he rode the elevator to the top floor where his hastily acquired digs awaited his grand arrival. Unbeknownst to him it had been recently decked out with two florist-wired vases of assorted summer flowers, one from his mother; the other from Matilda Prichard. What a welcoming sentiment they would have made - had they been noticed – but their recipient had other things on his mind as he entered his totally furnished pad. He eased the heavy carry-on to the floor and lost no time in yanking a map from his side pocket. His eyes scrutinized the layout upon the paper that of which contained a very in-depth layout of Ottawa, in-fact it was so precise that the city's drinking fountains were marked at their exact location, as he thought, "Not a bad idea in this heat," and instantly upped the central air. He returned to the map and continued his study, taking note of the street patterns, how they aligned, and where a certain address was located. Delving deep into the pocket of his khakis, he retrieved a small piece of paper containing a single phone number of which he had scribbled some time earlier. Quickly locating the phone, he swallowed hard, and moved toward it while suppressed fear shot to the forefront. His trembling hand reached for the black receiver but stopped just slight of it. Beads of sweat formed upon his forehead as a familiar dread churned deep within his gut, taunting him, daring him to pick it up and chance the dreaded clown leaping forth. In his mind the macabre face of *Peepers the Clown* forever remained hidden, dwelling within the receiver of a phone which also contained the screeching threats spoken in the ominous tone in which they had once been.

The hastily secured phone continued signaling the intended recipient, but no one was picking up. Finally, on the fourth ring, a voice was heard. Declan's heart almost leapt through his chest while he instantly began stuttering Willow's name - that is until he realized it wasn't her at all but instead a recorded voice telling him that particular number was no longer in service. This had happened the last time he had tried phoning her, but he had chocked it up to temporary disruption caused by any number of things, but never once did he give one measure of thought to the fact that the reason could have been beyond her control. "She lied," he thought, yet he was so certain that the woman who had stolen his heart would never do that to him, or lead him on, or drop him like a lead weight. He could not understand it, nor did he ever once consider anything but the convoluted picture of things he'd concocted in his mind. "It just can't be," he thought in anguish, still holding the now-dead receiver to his ear. "Maybe the clown *should* leap out and grab me, rip my head off … kill me," he lamented, for that was exactly how he felt. "I believed her I … I really believed her," he cried. "She told me she *cared*, told me how much she wished we could be together - but she lied — she fucking lied!" he snapped, anger bubbling to the surface. "Ma was right! She tried to tell me — so did Prichard! Oh, Miss High and Mighty Willow. Well, now we'll see, won't we?" he stated in a plotting manner. "I'm getting sick and tired of being used by women then tossed aside when the amusement wears off. We'll see, miss. Yes, we will. Nobody takes advantage of a Quinn, and you're going to find that out!" His aggravation continued to grow as he intently studied the map. "This looks about right," he announced as if he were addressing an audience, "there's her street, right there!" and he flipped-open his laptop. The screen instantly came to life, the Wi Fi's green signal flashing quickly, and he lost no time in commanding his favorite search engine to bring up the street view of Willow's address. "Huh," he grunted, seemingly amused at the sight of her unpretentious house, "don't know why she's fighting so hard to hold on to *that*. Certainly nothing to boast about — *huff* — nothing like what *I'm* used to anyway, but I suppose it suits her common needs."

    Retrieving his mostly inanimate cell from his pocket, he quickly snapped a picture of the location then stood to stretch. The heat in the room was lessening. He hoped that his exasperation would lessen as well, and even though he felt his feelings warranted, he still could not help but feel somewhat sheepish, after all if he honestly felt love toward Willow, why then would he become disillusioned so quickly, or disgusted over a simple phone call, or lack thereof? As these thoughts pummeled his brain he roamed about the room, gazing at the still-life paintings on the wall accompanied with rural landscapes of the surrounding countryside. These rustic images tweaked his interest. "Yes," he thought, newly conjured ideas taking root, "when I see her I'll be sure to entice her into it. How could she not be interested, worse still turn me down? She's still a country girl at heart; no doubt would adore the chance to sit in a meadow with me. How could she not?" With these thoughts fresh in his mind he hurriedly began scribbling his newly devised plan on a crumpled piece of paper.

Daylight had faded by the time he'd finished, but he couldn't help reveling at the boldness of it all, as well as the romantic sentiment behind it. In his mind Willow couldn't help but be impressed when he whisked her to the countryside in the brand new convertible he intended to purchase come Monday. Maybe his mother would be content in thinking him diligently working away in class, but he had other plans, and what she didn't know wouldn't hurt her. He had no intention in letting her know either, and if she checked he would simply summon an excuse as to why he wasn't in class. There could be a multitude of reasons - some legitimate - but regardless of whether they were or not he was not going to worry about it. He had other things on his mind, more pressing issues, and not a lot of time in which to carry them out.

But Declan had no way of knowing what was happening with Willow, or how recent events had begun to affect her. Whether he would understand was anybody's guess, but the nineteen-year-old native of Galway was nobody's fool. He usually got his way in anything he set his mind to, and was convinced this would be no different. In all of the time since he and Willow had been conversing he had never once doubted his hold on the inside track. He never once gave thought to the fact that her estranged husband might re-enter the picture, or in any way cause the woman he'd set his cap for to turn her face away, let alone her heart. He had spent months convincing her that he was not only worthy of her attention, but her heart, and that he was the man who could set her worries free. He knew he was the one. He had thoroughly convinced himself of it; more importantly he was certain he had convinced Willow Crosby of it too.

Chapter 30

BITTERSWEET REMINISCE

The old air conditioner chugged away in Jonas Crosby's room like a laboring old engine on its last legs, as he sat on the bed, staring at a vacant portion of the mattress aside him. His eyes held a dreamy look, as if they visualized something that might remain transparent to others, yet he stared as if something was actually there. Moving closer, he laid his hand upon the bedspread, lightly swirling the bedraggled fabric while a faint smile creased his lips. He remained quiet, yet there was something within his silence which spoke volumes, and the more he stared, the wider his smile broadened. Rising to his feet, he sauntered to a bar fridge tucked neatly in an alcove beneath the air conditioners window, located in a kitchenette at the far side of the dingy room. The fridge door opened to reveal an ample supply of beer, a box containing two-day-old pizza, and a container of dried-out French fries, all sitting upon the top rack. Selecting his choice of brew, he removed the cap, and took a long drink before roughly seizing the pizza box.

As he consumed his cold dinner an assortment of memories needled his mind, memories of time gone, associations long past, and the recent happening with Willow. He found it as well as she occupying his mind constantly, and regardless of what he did he couldn't seem to clear those thoughts. He wondered if she might be experiencing the same, possibly savoring each unexpected moment of it as much as he, yet he somehow didn't think so, as he thought, "Why would she? All she cares about is holding the house in a death-grip, the damn computer, and trying her best to blow me off." In all honesty he couldn't blame her. He'd not been the kindest toward her in a very long time, and even though the wretched words that had passed between them were embedded in his mind, he could not help feeling the love that was still present within it, as well as within his heart. Obviously it must be; otherwise he would have never touched her in the way in which he had, let alone be overcome with such passion that he'd let it get the best of him. Now it once again consumed him.

In his mind he pictured his wife's soft skin, the tautness that time had not stolen, and the way she had moved beneath him. It was like they were young again; enrapturing one another within the lust they felt, the desire to become one, the exhilarating climax of a passion so hot that the mere thought of it brought his blood to a boil, accompanied by a trophy-winning erection in his jeans. But she had met someone – though she refused to talk about it – but he knew another man existed. This thought caused jealousy to erupt within him. He needed to know more, and though it might mean total annihilation of any possible reconciliation – even should she consent - he had to find out who the guy was, plus his intention.

Images of the sexual encounter with his estranged wife continued to consume Jonas' mind. They tortured him, laughed at him, and even taunted him until he could barely stand it a moment longer. He realized the way he had been treating her, as well as the heartless actions he had taken. It settled around him like a fog engulfing a standing pond on a sultry evening. "What's done is done," he thought, though he knew that anything can be fixed if one truly cared enough to try. But in all honesty he realized the extent of the actions he had taken, and even though Willow was a forgiving person, how could he expect forgiveness for the blatant anguish he had caused her?

Continuing his meal, Jonas let his memories travel back to their early years, how she had made him feel, and the way she stood by his side whenever trouble faced them down. She truly had been a good wife, in many ways a much better wife to him than he as a husband to her. Maybe he should have tried harder, tried harder to understand what was going through her mind, her changing body, and the way it was affecting her mind. Isn't it a husband's place to know these things, find answers to questions that elude him, in the very least support his wife until he could? But he hadn't. He had turned his back when she needed him most. The hardest part to accept was the fact that he had chosen ignorance instead of what he should have been doing, and blast the cost. He could have found a way – *should* have found a way and carried through - but he hadn't, and now he was paying the price.

He got to his feet, and strolled to the window, the frigid air pummeling the bare skin of his still-trim waist as his hand stroked his enlarged member. It brought him excitement to do so, more importantly it brought him escape, escape to the place he wanted to be, buried deep within his estranged wife, enjoying her, letting her enjoy him. His rigid penis quivered with the rapid action of his hand engulfing it, stroking it hard, enticing it to come until the pent-up content sprang freely, filling his hand with sticky, warm release. Night had settled over Ottawa providing a beautiful setting in which to ponder. The canal outlined in lights, the parliament buildings in the foreground, and the time displayed upon the Peace Tower's clock like a welcoming beacon in the night. Jonas let his eyes drink deep of it while drying his hands before the window. "Lovely evening," he thought as he swallowed the latest mouthful of brew. "Wonder what she's doing, where she is? Wonder if she ever thinks about that day? Damn it was fine! Couldn't have been better had we planned it - oh how I love her – but how do I tell her – how do I make it up to her for everything I've done, all that's happened? I do love her; she needs to know this, at least take it into consideration before she chooses to—" He stopped himself before he said 'divorce me, leave me for good'.

The more he thought about it the more his desire for Willow grew. He could not stand by and let further damage be done. "There has to be a way," he thought, doing his best to rack his mind as to how he could change things, explain himself, and get her to listen. In the distance the Peace Tower's clock rang nine times. It wasn't late, but Jonas was not yet ready to face Willow. He wanted to speak with her – needed to speak with her – but it must wait until he was totally equipped with the correct words that would be needed to convince her of his feelings, his intentions, and above all that they were genuine. If he failed in any one of these aspects then any connection was as much as down the drain, along with him. The first step would be the reinstatement of utilities at their house as soon as time allowed it, and regardless if it meant that the phone would be back in service - which in turn meant the return of the Internet - it was certain to cheer her, and because of that, provide an opening for his return. He could not fail in his efforts, and he'd be dammed if he would.

Chapter 31

A DEAL WELL EXECUTED

The morning dawned on what appeared to be another scorcher. Storm clouds could be seen gathering in the west, but whether they would result in a cooling rain was yet to be seen. Hopefully the stifling heat of the last few days would soon break, for it was beginning to create problems for those who did not have the benefit of air conditioning. Willow Crosby was one. Air conditioners require hydro in order to work, and hers was long-gone; she could not even use the ceiling fans, but she could fan herself via the aid of an old magazine that she'd lost no time in grabbing. Maybe she was limited in regard to working amenities, but it did not require electricity to move her hand as fast as she could muster. Leaning on her bedroom windowsill, she breathed deep of what coolness still remained in the fast-warming air, while the temperature in her body increased.

Across town, newly risen Declan Quinn was stepping out of the shower, his rock-hard manhood looking up at him as if to beg release of its contents. But its master paid it no mind, no more than he had each morning since reaching adolescence. It would eventually wither - it always did – that is if he didn't have someone with him that could suck it dry in record time. Reaching down and giving it one gigantic stroke, he envisioned Willow's lips encircling it, taking it deep within her mouth, pulling on it, sucking it hard with full intent on bringing it to climax before she laid him on his back and fucked him until he came within her – *deep* within her – until she could hold no more. Oh how it made him feel, and before he knew it he had ejaculated all over his stomach. His eyes lit with excitement the more he relived his latest vision. He wasn't fooling around any longer, but he realized Willow might not be as anxious - at least to the extent he was - yet nothing gained if nothing ventured, and he quickly removed the spent semen from his skin.

Morning classes would soon be convening, but not for Declan. In his mind he could envision endless rows of students, none of which in his view had minds of their own, dutifully moving toward their designated classes like a group of risen zombies. But he had a far different destination in mind, and he'd be dammed if he would be swept along with them to a musty classroom where his eyes would be required within the pages of a well-read book. "Good luck with that," he thought in defiance, and carried on dressing. It was obvious that his intention to purchase a high-quality vehicle was imminent, as the address of the foreign dealership he had chosen lay scribbled on a notepad adjacent the phone. He was used to the best, and this purchase would be no different. Before long the same blue cab that had dropped him off at the university gates was depositing him before the parking lot of *Ottawa Foreign Import*.

In the window of the grand showroom lit to the nines in brilliant light as if it were a renowned celebrity posing upon the red carpet, sat a white, two seat hardtop convertible. It was grand, and it instantly caught the eye of the young Irishman. "My, what a fantastic set of wheels, no doubt as fast as my car back home," Declan thought with excitement as he envisioned the wind in his hair while studying its sleek lines. The fact that it was a striking white made it that much more desirable, for what better way to signify the arrival of a knight in shining armor - that of which he pictured himself - than to arrive in a stunning ride like the one before his gleaming eyes. It was certain to blow Willow's mind, if not her G-spot when he went down on her in the back seat of it. He had to have it.

Upon entering the showroom, the boy was met by an astute salesman who had already noticed the interest upon the young man's face, not to mention the tantalizing way in which his eyes were seducing the showroom's main attraction.

"She's a beaut!" the salesman exclaimed in faux excitement, straightening the vest of his Italian suit before extending his hand. "I can see by the look on your face that you agree."

"That she is," Declan replied as he vigorously clasp-hold the man's outstretched hand. "But I don't see a price, how much?"

Seemingly to ignore the question, the salesman went straight into his well-rehearsed pitch of what a good buy it was at any price, before revealing what that price was, adding that it was worth every penny, and ending with, "Would you like to take her for a spin?"

Declan couldn't help wondering what his mother would think if he actually bought the car, for it was a bit over the top, even for his bank account, but he wanted it, as he thought, "Everyone should be frivolous once in awhile, and it is a good buy." But still the price was iffy, and he knew it, as he replied, "I might, but first I'd like to discuss terms of sale. If I pay you by an express draft drawn on my bank in Galway would it make a difference in the asking price — I mean, would you drop it somewhat?"

The salesman, looking the boy over, didn't appear to be buying into this auspicious offer, as he said, "That is not our policy, young man. You don't appear to have a trade-in, though with cars of this caliber we don't usually accept trades, unless they are of the same make of course."

Declan didn't flinch, as he replied, "I already own a car in this price range. Unfortunately it's back home in Galway. I'm a first-year student of business here at Carleton University on a summer make-up semester, just arrived actually, and I need a car. This beauty is in the range of what I'm used to, doesn't make sense to keep looking, and I'd really like to have it. Surely a direct draft makes a difference as opposed to slower methods of payment?"

The salesman remained hesitant, and it showed. It was obvious he felt this kid nothing more than a mere university frosher sent on a hazing rite by some overly-zealous sophomores, but he was not going to be fooled, and he was certainly not going to bite, as he asked, "What makes you think I'm going to take you seriously?"

The Quinn family was not used to rejection in any form whatsoever. The salesman's confusing remark was no different, enticing Declan to question it.

The salesman, straightening his tie, answered, "Well I'm sure this is a prank; has to be. After all a kid your age couldn't have much coin, especially the kind it takes to buy a car like this."

"Don't be too quick to judge."

"Come on now, you can't be serious."

"Try me."

The dubious salesman was on the verge of scoffing, for all intent and purpose this kid couldn't be serious, could he? How could a young guy like this have money, especially the amount it would take to blow on a car that was way beyond the normal Joe's ability to even gaze at, let alone purchase, that is without first going into massive debt?

In a serious tone, Declan said, "I can arrange payment within the hour."

Deciding to play along, the salesman asked, "What bank did you say you deal with?"

"The Bank of Galway, main branch on Shanahan Boulevard in City Center. I can give you the phone number, besides it's right here on my cheque. You can put in an overseas call and speak directly with the manager Darcy MacLauchlan. He personally knows me as his bank is the one that backs all of my family's business needs. He's known me since I was a wee lad. I know he would set your mind at ease with regard to my purchase of this car, by the way you can add the cost of the call to the price of the car."

Upon handing the salesman his cheque, Declan followed him to the office, and nonchalantly settled into the client's chair while the required verification was being carried out. He knew his bank manager would vouch for him, possibly suppress a gasp at the enormous amount being discussed, but knew the deal was as good as done.

Time seemed to drag. It always does when one is anxious about the outcome of something, but the boy sat quiet, biding his time while the interested salesman chatted away, stopping periodically when the voice on the other end must have been having its say. Finally the conversation ended, with the salesman stating, "I've enjoyed their brew for years, but I never once thought young Quinn here was part of *that* family. I guess it goes to show that one shouldn't be too quick to judge. It was a pleasure speaking with you, Mr. MacLauchlan, very enlightening indeed. I shall await the transfer of funds into our account; in the meantime I shall take care of the necessary papers finalizing the sale. Your client has just bought himself a very handsome ride. Take care now." Setting the receiver upon the cradle in a business-like fashion, he gazed at Declan, and said, "Well, young man, looks like you've got yourself a car."

"Never doubted I would," Declan replied in what appeared a confident manner, before shifting himself into a more comfortable position. Though unbeknownst to the salesman, it had briefly occurred to Declan that MacLauchlan might have thought differently, which in turn had caused a touch of anxiety within his stomach, but he was not going to show it. Leaning forward, he stated, "I'm ready to fill out the papers if you are."

Before long the documents were complete, insurance intact, and the expedited payment in the dealership's account. Declan watched as the fully licensed car was carefully removed from the showroom, gassed up, and left waiting for him to take command. Everything was falling into place as planned, and before he knew it he was streaking toward the designated address of Willow Sutherland-Crosby.

Chapter 32

SURPRISE!

The morning's heat was fast encompassing the house as Willow tended to chores, all the while fanning her face with what remained of the bedraggled magazine. The battery clock read 11:00 a.m. as she pushed on, one hand revving the paper remnants as fast as it could, while the other continued wiping her sweat-laden face with an already-drenched cloth. "This has to be the hottest day yet," she thought as she pushed on toward the conclusion of her chores. "Well, Willow," she announced aloud, "that's got to do it. These days there's only so much one can do without hydro. Even if I had any I'd be throwing in the towel." Setting down her duster, she made her way to the kitchen where she seized-hold the cup awaiting duty within a pail of freshly drawn water from the backyard well. "I've forgotten how good well water actually tastes," she said as if doing a well-rehearsed commercial, and then looking around as to see if someone might be watching, refilled the cup, leaned over the sink, and poured it over the nap of her neck. She repeated this twice before deciding to pour a few cups over her sweat-drenched head. It felt heavenly, and it instantly reduced the heat within her body while her hand fumbled for the towel hanging aside the sink. Wrapping it loosely around her head, she began patting dry her hair when a knock sounded upon the front door.

"Great!" she fumed, vigorously rubbing her head before fashioning the towel into a turban. The knock again sounded, prompting her to hasten in step, but as she made her way past the living room window her eye was drawn to a gleaming white glow seemingly directly beneath it. Looking through the sheers, she was intrigued to find a luxurious sports car parked proudly in the drive. "Wow," she thought, wondering who on earth it belonged to. No one in her crowd could as much as dream of owning such an extravagant vehicle, let alone actually acquire one. Another knock - somewhat shy of pounding - sounded, enticing her to sprint for the door, and open it a crack.

Declan Quinn, immediately assuming the pose of an excited game show host when announcing a contestant's win, exclaimed, "Surprise!"

Willow was immediately thrown into a quandary as to who in hell this was supposed to be. "Excuse me?" she said in question, not certain whether to open the door further, or shut it entirely.

Declan was taken aback, and it showed, as he thought, "Surely she knows me." But the response he was receiving was far from the one expected. Trying his best to assert his accent, he exclaimed, "'Tis me!" before resuming his previous pose, and stating, "I've cum ta whisk ye ta the cuntryside in me *brand new car!*"

Willow was not in the mood for nonsense, and even though this smallish man appeared pleasant enough, he held an uncanny resemblance to an overbearing salesman who had been recently making the rounds, trying his best to obtain signatures upon yet another energy contract, and though the hands of this present kid remained free of the all-annoying clipboard, she was not about to be sucked into any new fan-dangled utility program when she didn't even have any, let alone any other fast-paced deal.

"Look," she said in the most aversive tone she could muster, "I'm not interested in anything you've got to sell. So you may as well get back into your fancy car and be on your way."

"Don't you know me?" Declan inquired in his natural elocution, certain she was simply having fun with him. He could hardly believe she was standing before him, and even though her bedraggled appearance was not quite what he had expected, she did resemble her pictures.

Willow had no idea who this was, as she said, "I'm afraid you have me at a disadvantage. Am I *supposed* to know you?"

"Well," Declan said, his excitement somewhat easing, "I would think you'd at least recognize me ... apparently not."

"I'm sorry, but I don't. Who are you?"

"Declan Eamon Quinn at your service, miss!"

The floor felt as if it had suddenly let out from beneath her, as she thought, "Declan ... what would you be doing here and ... and you look nothing like your photographs!" She couldn't believe the striking difference; he was barely as tall as she, and though he was dressed to the nines in designer wear, he was nothing like the tall, well-muscled, desirable hunk he had lead her to believe he was, but instead a mere waif of a boy hardly shed of short britches. "Declan? I-I would have never known it was you had you not told me," she stated, her speech slightly faltering. "When ... I-I mean how ... Excuse me, but what are you doing here?" she asked in confusion, still trying to take it all in.

The young man could not believe the treatment he was receiving; it was certainly not what he had expected, as he thought, "Why is she not throwing herself upon me in unbridled ecstasy? Why, she's acting completely indifferent, as though I were a mere commoner, not a member of the esteemed Quinn family of Galway. This is unbelievable. Why does she not display the affection she typed on countless occasions?" As the elusive answers to these questions encompassed his mind, his mother's condescending words on just this subject immediately jumped to the forefront, again reminding him that she just may have been right in her assumption. But she was not here to support him, nor was Prichard, whose opinion mattered more than she realized, yet he had to find out for himself. Hoping Willow might clue-in, he stated, "I'm Declan Quinn from Galway Ireland. We've been corresponding via the Net for eons I … I find it hard to believe you don't know me."

Willow, certain the guy was simply trying to pull a fast one, said, "Well I find it hard to fathom what you're telling me. You may speak with somewhat of an Irish accent, but you look nothing like your photographs, so how can I be sure you are whom you say?"

The young man swiftly shoved his hand into the back pocket of his jeans. Retrieving his wallet, he reached inside, pulled out a laminated card, and in a trembling manner held it out, as he said, "I haven't, as yet anyway, obtained a Canadian driver's license; this is my license from home. It contains my address, and my current picture. Hopefully this is proof enough that I am who I say."

Taking it gingerly from his outstretched fingers; Willow cast her eyes upon it. Sure enough, it was him, as she silently questioned, "Why would he have sent the photos he did if they weren't him? He certainly has nothing to worry about in the looks department." Emotions quickly seized her, causing her to feel compassion for him but at the same time *used*, as she thought, "What has been so secretive that he couldn't be honest at the beginning of our friendship? All the things we've since said, emotions I expressed, thoughts – my most inner thoughts of which I openly divulged as if

I were offering the contents of my soul for redemption. If he could carry through with deception like that, knowing full well my fragile state of mind - let alone the condition of my heart - then how can I believe one word he will say from here on?"

Her reaction not only saddened Declan, it angered him. He couldn't help thinking that if she had been the kind-hearted, open-minded person who had typed what she had for all the months leading up to this meeting, why then would she doubt him simply because he didn't resemble the man in the infamous photos? His mind quickly swept over those images, as well as the reason he had sent them. His hope had been that she would find the dashing images attractive enough to become ensnared, and then accompanied by his own stimulating personality, figured she would be totally enraptured. After all if he had sent his actual picture she would have never given him the time of day. But she had experienced his titillating wit, the arousing charisma within the words and expressions of which he had typed countless times, so why now could she not be enthralled with him just because he wasn't the man in those images?

"How in hell do I consistently get myself into these messes?" Willow thought, but immediately knew the answer without need of clarification, while she stared at the young man, and let her mind remember the wonderful words that had passed between them. Finally, she said, "Would you like to come in?" and pressed her body against the doorjamb to allow him entry.

He lost no time in moving forward, deliberately, and forwardly brushing his entire front against her as he passed; pausing briefly to be sure that she felt his huge erection.

Willow may have been lacking in conduct of late, but she was not a total idiot when it came to the assorted ways in which a man chooses to seduce a woman.

"Back off!" she snapped, shoving him backward. "Who do you think you are coming in here like this thinking you can do as you please and try the likes of that?!"

It took Declan by surprise, and he snapped, "You owe it to me!" and shoved her against the doorframe with enough force the secured turban came unraveled, and dropped to the floor.

"Oh you think?!" she retorted, swiftly sliding to the side. Running her fingers through her damp hair, she snapped, "You've got some nerve, kid! You lied to me from the very beginning. Why? Did it make you feel more a man to play those sick games — especially with someone whose heart you already knew was broken? Or was I simply someone you thought an easy mark in which to play-out your perverted fantasies?"

"No! No, it wasn't like that," the young man declared in a rattled manner while the look on his face revealed remorse. "I never meant to hurt you or … or lead you on, I mean, you would have never paid me the least amount of attention had I shown you what I really look like. No one takes me seriously. Everyone thinks I'm still a boy and treats me as such. It wasn't until I met you on line that I started feeling the way I wanted others to make me feel. You didn't appear to mind! You never seemed to doubt me. You believed in me, everything I said. I suppose it *was* a challenge to see if I could make you feel the way I wanted you to, toward me, for me and, well, that was why I sent those pictures. I figured if you thought I looked like that you'd be taken with me. Could you honestly say that you would have found me desirable if you'd actually known what I look like?"

The young man stood before the irritated woman, his huge eyes pleading, begging her to believe his words, and forgive his actions. He had tried his best to explain, but he figured that in her mind his words were simply that, words, not actual feelings. He turned toward the door and started to leave, but before he made it all the way through, Willow reached out, and touched his arm. "Wait," she said, the tone of her voice softening, "you don't have to leave. It's obvious you've gone to a lot of trouble to be here, so the least I can do is invite you in and offer you a cold drink or something, how about it?"

Realizing that he hadn't been tossed out on his ear, Declan, inexperienced in matters such as this, decided to make the most of what he thought was being offered. Turning to her in a nonchalant manner, he answered, "Sure, whatever you've got to offer."

Chapter 33

YOU DON'T LOVE HIM YOU LOVE ME!

A noise resembling that of a loud thud sounded in the living room, while in the master bedroom Willow sat upright in bed, her inquisitive stare catching the nightstand's battery clock whose bold red letters displayed 11 pm. She couldn't help wondering what had caused the recent sound, and sweeping back the cool satin, proceeded to investigate. Securing a green silk robe around her bare body, she cautiously ventured down the darkened hall to peer around the doorframe into the living room, where she discovered a disheveled Declan Quinn, sitting upon the floor in an upright position beside the sofa. He had landed in the familiar puddle of light cast through the window by the security light in the adjacent parking lot. It was obvious to Willow that he had fallen off the sofa, as the bedding was rumpled, the top sheet still wound around his bare body. He seemed disoriented, and she lost no time in assuring him that all was fine, while at the same time inquiring what had happened.

Gazing up in a confused manner, he answered, "I'm - I'm not quite sure. I was dreaming — I think, and went to roll over. Guess

I thought I was in my *spacious* bed at home instead of a confined area like this. Sorry if I disturbed you. What time is it anyway?"

Overlooking the adjective description of his own bed, Willow answered, "Just past eleven. Sorry about the cramped quarters, but since you've misplaced your dorm key it's really all I can offer, at least for tonight, come morning though you'll have to be on your way. I'm glad to see all's well out here. I'm going back to bed now, you should as well. Can I get you anything before you settle back down?"

Giving his head a shake as he climbed upon the sofa, he replied, "I don't need anything, though I'd really like to talk some more I … I mean we didn't discuss much earlier, except how I come to be in Ottawa as opposed to where I was originally going to be sent. Glad that didn't happen; if it had I wouldn't have *actually* met you and I have a confession to make. I, well I didn't lose my dorm key because; you see I don't live in residence but rather a high-scale condo not far off campus. You really don't think someone of my standing would be living in a *dorm*, or cheap hovel somewhere because of a limited amount of funds, do you? I had to tell you something to get you to let me stay. But I really am grateful that you did. It's certainly not late, and it would be nice to talk about *other* things — by the way you look lovely, just the way I envisioned you when we exchanged descriptions of each other. I knew you would look as you do, so sure of yourself, and beguiling. I've imagined your touch … *mm* … dreamt about your lips …*ah* … the depth in your eyes as you teach me ways I've yet to experience. Why don't you sit here," and as he spoke his hand patted the area aside him in a coaxing manner.

Willow was still uncertain about the reason he was even there - or about him in general – but she was still drawn to him, she couldn't deny that, yet she could not get past the fact that he had purposely lied to her; further more had chosen to continue the ridiculous masquerade as if he was that person in the photos he'd sent. He didn't seem to accept the fact that he had been caught in his lie; further confusing the issue by demanding she conduct herself like the emblazoned woman he had fantasized about for months. It was just one of the many ways in which he needed to grow up; if not acquire a reality check along the way.

Standing before him, she said, "I think I'll refrain from sitting there or anywhere at the moment; however I do agree that we need to talk, but it should wait until morning. Things always appear much clearer in the daylight, instead of trying to mull them over in the dark. Declan, I want you to understand why I asked you not to leave, I just don't want you to *misunderstand* it, okay?"

The boy said not a word, but the expression on his face revealed a sorrow that Willow could see, even in the defused light. This hurt her - even though he had brought it on himself - but the ways in which he had made her feel throughout the grueling months she had endured could not be dismissed lightly, let alone forgotten as though it had never happened. This was the same young man who had deeply touched her, extended kindness and assurance when she needed it the most, so how could she now turn her back as if he'd never entered her life? She stood pondering this, wondering what to say, or if she should say anything. She remembered telling him months ago that what they shared could be nothing more than a special friendship, the kind that two people whom had endured heartache and upset could feel; at least understand, but certainly not a sexual one. She also realized that she, as the elder, must do what she could to explain the entire scenario in the way it truly was, even if it meant breaking his heart in the process. She took a deep breath, and settled beside him.

"Thought you didn't want to sit down, even be near me," he relayed in a reserved manner.

Smoothing the housecoat's glossy fabric upon her lap, she replied, "Well I need to clarify things, and I really need you to listen. I realize the way things between us have gotten to be - at least in your mind - no doubt your heart - and I must admit that I did feel *affection* for you. But I'm afraid that's *all* it was. When I encountered you I was at a very low point in my life. I really did think my life was over; I had nowhere to go *or* turn least of all have someone in my life that cared about me in the ways in which a woman needs a man to care. Then I met you. You were so sweet and kind to me. You truly made me smile again, made me feel like getting up in the morning when I couldn't see any reason to even try. But as much as I felt that way, even to the extent where I was experiencing fondness for you, I tried my best to keep it grounded and in check. I realize the meaning of the words I said, and I feel that I meant them - at the time - but I also knew it was wrong, and could never be the way that you had hoped. I was out of line to have said *any* of the things I did, or make you think in any way there could be a future for us other than friendship. Nothing is like you think it is, Declan, and I don't want to hurt you, truly I don't but, you have to understand why our relationship can be nothing more than friendship from here on in. There's been a change in my relationship with Jonas –" She had stopped for the boy was staring at her as if he were awaiting his execution. But as sympathetic as he looked the information she was divulging needed to be voiced, so she continued, "It was something I don't think either of us expected, least of all me. And I really don't understand how I could feel this way about him, especially after the difficult way it's been between us. Maybe neither of us has ever stopped loving one another. I don't know, but I saw him awhile back. It was right after he'd had my phone cut off and I'd gone to have it out with him. We began to have words about all the disconnections and what he'd been doing and, well, things just got out of control and we ..." Again her voice tapered off before she divulged what had happened. She knew how it would sound. She also realized how much it would hurt, especially if his feelings for her were genuine, but he had to know, so she continued, "I wanted to tell you, *needed* to tell you because it's very important, and you've a right to know. Honesty is the most important part of any relationship – even friendship – but I couldn't. First of all I had no way of letting you know, and I didn't want to call from my neighbor's or use his computer because I didn't want to upset you but, in all honesty I didn't want anything getting back to Jonas. I mean, we've got a ton of issues to work through, but I'm ... I'm still in love with him." She shifted about in a nervous way, knowing full-well what she was about to say was not going to be taken lightly, still it had to be voiced. Taking a deep breath, she said, "There's no other way to go about this than to simply tell you. Jonas and I made love. It might have initially come about from the heated words being exchanged, but when it happened it felt *so* right. I'm sorry, but you need to know this."

Declan looked at her as though she had slapped him straight across his face. He couldn't phantom how much he had misread her, but he still felt that he had not been mistaken in his assumption that she loved him. The words she had written to him were genuine, they had to have been. Surely he was not such a novice in the ways of love that he could have misread her words, or the feelings that had enticed her to express them in the first place.

Turning to her, he awkwardly said, "I ... I don't understand any of this. I believed in you, Willow. I believed the words you told me, the feelings you said you felt for me — I realize how young I am, as well as the enormous age difference between us, but if two people really love each other nothing else should matter; nothing should stand in the way. I *was* honest with you in the words that I wrote I

... I just wish I could have trusted you enough to have been honest in other ways, you know, my appearance."

"Declan," Willow swiftly injected, "there is nothing wrong with your appearance. You are a very pleasant looking young man, even hands —"

"Don't say something you don't believe to be so!" he snapped with vehemence while positioning his body front and center to hers. "You were going to say *handsome!* But you don't honestly believe that. If you did you wouldn't have carried on about the fact that I was not the person in those lame pictures, and you sure as hell wouldn't have done the *thing* you said you did with your husband. You would have accepted me for who I am - how I look - especially how I feel! But you didn't! You scolded me like my mother does! She was right, you know? So was Prichard! They both had you pegged for what you are!" His temper escalated, and he exclaimed, "You're nothing more than a tease, you know that!? *You're a goddamn fucking slut!* You have a lot of nerve sitting there in your luscious gown, blatantly telling me you let your estranged husband fuck you! After all he's done to you! *Put you through!* Then because he spouts words that turn you on, you end up on your back with him inside you all the while knowing how *I* feel about you and you - *yes you* - doing your best all that time to convince me that you wanted *me* - would do whatever you could to assist me - even going so far as lying to me, *making me believe you loved me!* Well, nobody cheats a Quinn, sweetheart! You want to know what happens when somebody messes with one of us?!"

Before the startled woman could answer, he drove his doubled fist straight across her left cheek, driving her backward and into a stupefied state. In one frantic moment he was on her, but quickly stopped! He looked around, as if to scope-out the area for he had no way of knowing the layout of the house. He assumed the door off the living room led to a hallway, which in turn led to the bedrooms – Willow's bedroom – the bedroom she had described as her den of iniquity. He scooped her into his arms and lunged straight for it. Reaching her bed, he dropped her upon it and proceeded to plunder her robe. She moaned, doing her best to hold to consciousness as she lay before him, totally nude while his hands fondled her breasts, his fingers doing their best to tweak her nipples to attention. She tried pushing him backward, but he was too strong for her. Suddenly his lips were engulfing her nipples, sucking them, pulling hard as his index finger pummeled her clit. Her awareness had totally returned. She screamed! His hand cupped her mouth, totally stifling any further sound she might make. He continued to hold pressure upon her mouth - upon her body - but she fought back. Struggling upward, she managed to push him off her, and climb toward the edge of the bed. She almost made it, but he seized her, and with one mighty shove, hurled her upon her back! She viciously spit into his face, screaming at him to stop while trying her utmost to avoid his disgusting intention.

His anger exploded, and he hollered, *"You don't mess with a Quinn, baby!"* and his fist again encountered her jaw - *hard* - this time knocking her completely senseless. He had lost all coherence. All he could think about was the hurtful words she had spoken, the despicable way she had treated him, and how she had made a fool of him. Now she would pay, and pay dearly. He flipped her upon her stomach, unbuckled his belt and ripped it from his waistband! Securing it like a dog collar around her throat, he pulled the excess leather back and let it hang loose with the intention of using it like a leash. Instead he noticed an assortment of macramé belts dangling from a hook on the closet door. He instantly secured her arms, pulled them behind her back and hastily wrapped the knotted wool around her wrists, securing it tightly. He performed this same procedure to her knees and ankles until he had trussed her securely. Lifting her lower body, he proceeded to arrange her legs beneath her so her buttock lay fully exposed. He swiftly pulled out his cell and proceeded to snap away while he inserted his index finger deeply up her anus, pummeling it, jeering with a childlike expression of meanness as air let forth, followed by a small amount of excrement. He found it amusing to think the uppity woman before him was actually soiling herself before his very eyes, and he laughed as he thought it appropriate for the occasion. Somehow the picture before him enticed his penis to rise, and he straddled her, driving his rock-hard manhood deeply into her, thrusting twice until he realized where his endowment lie. He quickly retracted, and resumed a standing position. He then proceeded to balance her on her right side by firmly holding the *leashes* in one hand, and planting his foot on her buttock. He secured her rigidly while he snapped a few pics and planed his next move. All the while he was not so consumed in his plight that he over-looked the fact that she might wake, but if she did he would swiftly take care of that with a well executed jab to the jaw – Irish style. He had not won all those donnybrooks by fist inaccuracy, or drive. She would come to regret what she had enticed, and he vowed he would not leave until he had received payment in full.

    She moaned softly, but to his ears it sounded as if she was purring, begging him to go down on her. He removed her bondage, and eased her backward until she was positioned on her back. Before climbing aboard he noticed a pitcher of water sitting on the nightstand. Grasping it, he poured a generous amount over her pubic hair to ensure moisture would be present for easy movement. Positioning her legs together and arms at her side, he straddled her, and with cell-cam at the ready, held himself slightly above her, bent down, and began tickling her clit with his tongue, flicking its tip, wildly licking, and finally shoving it fully into her newly moistened lips. He giggled loudly, his pleasure showing fully while he thought about the humiliation he was inflicting. Her moaning grew louder, consciousness was returning, but he was not yet finished and this could not be let happen! He swiftly drove his fist across the tip of her jaw! She lay still, and he smiled triumphantly, knowing he again remained supreme. He continued upon his playground until his erection demanded attention, action, and full release. He spread her legs, and drove his rock-hard penis deep within her chasm, pumping fast, driving in and out, *hard*, faster – *faster* – envisioning the unconscious woman actually smiling up at him, encouraging his moves, enticing each thrust he made. But the longer he rode her limp body the more his temper grew. "How could she humiliate me like that?" he thought, her elicit confession of late consuming his senses, while he continued ramming his rigid endowment into her as if it were a jackhammer pounding concrete, as he hissed, "You don't love *him* you love *me!*"

He finally came; firing his wad deep within her, filling her to capacity while he panted above like a ravenous dog. As his shriveled manhood was retracted, excess semen followed, oozing from her battered vagina in the same fashion molten lava travels down a mountainside. He viewed the body before him, somewhat like a discarded Cupi-doll is viewed upon the floor at the circus, broken, and tossed away after having provided fun for some ungrateful child. He could see deposits of blood upon her thighs which instantly caused him to wonder if he may have gone too far. In his mind he realized what he'd done, but he could not take it back; even if he could it would not wipe away the humiliation he had endured listening to her nauseating confession, how she still loved her husband, and that she had let him fuck her. He knew he must leave before she came to. He could not face her, and he would not. In a feeble attempt to lend a measure of redemption for his covetousness act, he straightened her body, grasp the pink satin sheet that had lain beside her throughout her taking, and spread it smoothly over her.

Bruises were already visible on her face. Declan realized he could not remove them, but he did search the bathroom medicine cabinet where he located a remedy used for such purpose. Shards of daylight were creeping through the window as he applied the solution to the discolored areas. To help cover them he used makeup, that of which he'd found on her dressing table, and after expertly applying it, finished with glossy red lipstick, that of which he had pulled from his pocket, as he thought, "Good thing I have this, it's most befitting for a *brasser* like you." Again the cell's camera captured the happening before it. Willow did not stir, but instead lay still as a corpse. "My God, what if she really is," he thought, placing his fingers against her neck. She was so still, almost rigid, feeling cool to the touch. This increased his fear, but it was laid to rest when a pulse was found. "The saints be praised," he thought with gratitude, yet figured it would only be a matter of time before she regained consciousness. Then there would be hell to pay. But she had been out a long time; bringing thought to his mind if an ambulance should be summoned. "Maybe I should take her to the emergency myself," he thought, but along with this thought wondered how he would explain how she got this way. Furthermore whoever examined her would find out what had happened, and the bruising would confirm how it came about. "She's alright," he thought as he backed out the door. He felt wrong in leaving, yet knew he must; he also knew he must summon his mother for she always got him out of trouble - regardless of what it was - and this would be no different.

He dressed, and then slipped quietly out the front door to his awaiting beast in the driveway. The engine sprang to life, and the car began easing out of the drive. The first rays of sunshine were visible on the eastern horizon and morning traffic had begun, making it difficult to leave, but he waited for an opening, revving the engine in anticipation of bolting forward the second a slot opened. As he waited, he thought, "She'll be far too embarrassed to say anything. Even if she does who will believe her, a woman of her age, involved with a man thirty-five years her junior? She'll become a laughing stock, and rightfully so. I'm home Scott-free."

But unbeknownst to the arrogant coward awaiting his getaway, Shawn Martin, always an early riser, was standing on his front porch, sipping his morning coffee, and watching the sports car's every move. He was not only a concerned neighbor, but an astute one, who lost no time jotting down the illuminated plate number before the car finally crept onto the street, and headed west.

Chapter 34

HOW DOES ONE TURN BACK TIME

Jonas Crosby, both thankful of the old air conditioners ability to clear the day's excessive heat from his room, while totally oblivious to what would later happen at his old address this night, sat at his kitchen table, consuming yet another brew, while penciling his intended plans upon a yellowed tablet. His mind had been made up, and there would be no turning back. He should have done this long ago, had he, maybe the situation between he and Willow would have never reached the extent of which it had, yet if it hadn't, they would have never experienced those delectable moments of the other day. "Am I reading more into that encounter than I should?" he wondered, hoping he was reading not only his own reaction to it in the way he'd anticipated, but if it could have possibly become embedded within his wife's mind in the same manner.

He closed his eyes, while in his mind he saw her, felt her, relived every single moment of that wonderful encounter. He could smell her, taste her cum still reminiscent in his mind, the tartness trickling down his throat as he drank all she could produce, while his tongue enticed the orgasm she was experiencing. It affected him to think this way, affected every part of him, and again he rose to the occasion, begging release of what his newly risen erection held within. Oh what he wouldn't do to Willow, if allowed. He would finger her clit until she was rigid with excitement. He would go down on her, bring her to the verge of explosion, and then suck her into an orgasmic haze until her uterus was totally emptied. Then, just as she was slipping into sleep, he would fuck her into total exhaustion. As she slept he would gently cleanse her, tenderly kiss every part of her body before covering her with the pink satin she so loved. It would highlight her every feature, every tilt, every angle. He would lie beside her. She would be perfect. They would both be perfect, just the way they had been the first night they had ever made love. These visions made him smile until his entire face was engulfed in the wonder of it all. Yet he also realized that he was only experiencing *his* wants and desires. Willow may have a far different take on the entire matter; that is if she was to have any take at all. But he could hope, and he was not giving up on his plans. Most of all he wanted to make things right between them, and try his best to make up for the wrong he'd done, as well as the hurt he'd caused.

As he scribbled away, his thoughts turned to his wife's mystery lover. "Who could it be? Where was he from? What were his plans? Surely she'll use common sense," Jonas thought, but he also knew his wife's impetuosity with regard to her past encounters, not to mention the inept way in which she often handled herself. Willow was a young woman when they had met, one who wore her heart on her sleeve, and unfortunately gave it away far too quickly to whomever said a kind word, or the right words. For all intent and purpose he could put himself into this category, as he remembered long-ago conversations with old buddies whom had remarked on the speed of his involvement with her, how quickly their relationship was growing, and the time-frame surrounding the marriage. It really had been a whirlwind courtship, and Shay Sutherland's untimely death hadn't helped matters. Jonas knew how much Willow adored her father, how extremely close they were, leaving him to ponder the possibility that he just might have been a surrogate for Shay. After all there had been times when Willow had put him in that position, yet he knew her strength, fully as much as her weakness. He had loved her, everything about her, so the speed in which he married her was something that he had never questioned, even if others did.

He continued scribbling upon the tablet while he swallowed the latest mouthful of beer. Before he realized it midnight had come and gone, but work never waits, and when morning rolls around it does not accept the flimsy excuse that one is too tired to do their job. He stood, stretched, and then stripped down for bed with thoughts of the soon-to-be reinstated utilities occupying his mind. Hopefully his wife would see that he had finally realized the error of his ways, and was trying his utmost to rectify them, even if it might be arriving a tad too late.

The next morning found an anxious Jonas at his job but his mind anywhere but. This lack of attention could be dangerous on any job, but for one who works with moving parts that could quickly remove a hand or an entire arm faster than you can say your name, it was a horrific accident just waiting to happen. But Jonas was fully as seasoned in his line of work as he was experienced in life. An accident like that was not in the cards for today, or any other if he could help it, but he knew that if he didn't keep his mind on the mission before him, then he just may find things playing out in an entirely different way, so he shut off his machine, and left before nine with the excuse he had personal business to take care of, but upon completion, would return to work.

He couldn't help but feel redemption growing in leaps and bounds as he walked into Ottawa Gas to request reinstatement of the now defunct service at his old house. After settling the account and paying the reconnection fee, he was informed the service would be engaged no later than three that afternoon, as he apprehensively thought, "I would think it could be done a bit sooner than that," but didn't question it, instead bid the receptionist good day and strolled to his pickup. Next stop was Ottawa Hydro where the same procedure was carried out; however this service was guaranteed reconnection no later than ten that morning. Last stop was the one he actually dreaded, the phone, which was slated for reconnection no later than ten thirty that morning. He realized that along with this service came the Internet, but so be it, he would chance it and the rest be damned, as he thought, "Surely Willow understands the difference between an actual person voicing words in person, as opposed to a faceless one on the other side of a screen merely typing them."

These thoughts pummeled his head as he kept mulling them over. Each time through angered him more, causing jealousy to grip his heart, yet in all honesty he could not fault her if she *had* turned to someone else, God knows she had every reason, but still he could not stand the thought of another man mowing his grass. "I can't let that happen," he thought, true to his convictions as he decided right then and there that he was not going to let that materialize.

Chapter 35

YOU CAN FOOL SOME PEOPLE SOME OF THE TIME, BUT YOU CAN'T FOOL MOM

Early afternoon had arrived in Galway, but an agitated Cailen, who had spent the prior night tossing and turning because of her bank manager's call the prior day, could not rid herself of the anxiety she felt. "How extravagant can the boy be?" she questioned in silence, her motherly intuition assuring her that she was not far off the mark with her present assumption, and she announced, "Ye never miss the water 'till the well runs dry. He must be daft!" Springing to her feet with the dire need to discuss the latest development with Prichard, she lost no time traveling the few carpeted steps to Prichard's room. Rapping firmly upon the door, she called, "Matilda! Are ye to be available? I be needing to speak with ye about Declan!"

Prichard had not enjoyed much rest the prior night either, for she had been the one who had answered the bank manager's midafternoon call. She wondered what it had been about, for the tone of the man's voice was stern, more so than usual for him, and she had taken his calls enough to know. "Yes, Mrs. Quinn, do come in," she replied, and readied herself for a conversation she felt certain would be upsetting.

The door only opened a crack but enough for Cailen to shove in her head, and ask, "Are ye to be sure? I realize ye may be busy, but I do need to chat. I be just trying to grab a wee nap with hope of replacing the sleep I be losing during the night. 'Tis a wonder ye not be doing the same, for I be hearing ye pacing in the night as well."

Prichard motioned her in and toward a heather-toned wing chair before the fireplace, as she replied, "Yes, I have to admit to a restless night, and it might be nice to chat over tea. I shall ring the kitchen and see if Bridget could fetch up a right-ole pot."

Smiling at Prichard's good-intentions, Cailen replied, "Aye that would be welcomed indeed. It might also help in calming the nerves. I know how mine be presently feeling, and I've not a doubt ye are experiencing a bit of the same, if not totally."

It wasn't long before the housekeeper arrived at the door, her well-rounded arms struggling to support the heavily-laden tray held within them.

"I be having tea for two!" Donnigan called loudly while asserting her hold on the sagging tray lest it crash to the floor.

Upon opening the door, a surprised Prichard quickly seized one side of the dipping tray, as she exclaimed, "My-my, Bridget! Why do you load yourself down in such a manner, especially when you know you've a ways to travel, not to mention stairs?" Not waiting for an answer she continued to assist the ruffled housekeeper in sliding the tray onto a lace-draped table before the window.

The grateful housekeeper lost no time in praising the much-acquired help, as she joyfully stated, "Oh but ye are to be thanked a million times, Matilda! Ye helped avert a catastrophe in the making! I not be knowing why I load the tray as I do ... suppose it be habit, after-all I've been loading them for years, *ha-ha!* Let me arrange these things before I be pouring for yurself and the Mrs. And be sure to be enjoying these scones - fresh out the oven they are – and the crabapple jelly be from last year's harvest – good and tart it be! Ring me when yur're ready for the tray's removal, and I'll be here in a flash to snatch it. Now enjoy!"

After the housekeeper had closed the door Prichard mentioned to her employer that an elevator would certainly be welcomed, especially in knowing that none of the manor's female population was growing any younger.

The suggestion did not fall on deaf ears, as Cailen replied, "Aye, that not be a bad idea. I had given it thought awhile back, but never acted on it. I really must, for I cannot be expecting Bridget to continue in the manner we just witnessed." Taking a large sip of tea, somewhat as if to steady her frazzled nerves, she then dabbed her mouth with a linen napkin, and continued, "I shall ring the carpenter today, but first I need to discuss the reason for MacLauchlan's call."

Prichard, sipping her own tea, braced for the latest development. She remained quiet, though in her mind envisioned Declan abroad and couldn't help wondering what he'd gotten himself into this time, as Cailen rose to her feet, and paced about the room. After a few minutes she returned to the fireplace where she stopped, and began gazing at the aligned pictures of her sons upon the mantle. Letting her eyes fall upon her youngest, she sighed, "I believe he be lost to us."

Looking up from her tea, Prichard questioned, "Why would you say that? I do not believe for one moment that Master Declan is yet finished with our influence, much less our input. He is still young and inexperienced in many ways, but he is not a bad boy, Mrs. Quinn, and he is certainly not lost."

With tears welling in her eyes, Cailen replied, "Love can cause one to do inconceivable things, wretched things; things that can only bring heartache in the end." Pacing the room while wringing her hands in a nervous fashion, she took a deep breath, and continued, "MacLauchlan rang to inform me of an outrageous purchase Declan made yesterday - a car - a very expensive one at that. He arranged a direct draft for payment. MacLauchlan looked after it personally as he often does for Declan and the money be in his account, of course, it's not *that* I mind - it certainly is not going to bankrupt us by any means - but it be why he did it, Matilda. I'm certain 'tis because of that woman — Willow – was that not the name he be mentioning awhile back?"

Taking a quick sip of tea, Prichard cleared her throat, and replied, "Yes, I believe it was. You don't suppose she lives in Ottawa, do you?"

"Aye," Cailen answered the tone in her voice somber and the look in her eyes intense, "I'm beginning to think just that. Afterall, Matilda, look at how eager he be to go to that city after having fought us every step of the way when he thought he be going to London."

Getting to her feet, Prichard went to Cailen's side, and said, "Do not upset yourself or jump to conclusions, Mrs. Quinn. We have no way of knowing where she lives, Ottawa, or otherwise. This may all be simply coincidence. He's only been in residence two days, and you know how he is when it comes to his independence, especially having to depend on public transit to get about *and* in a strange city. He's always been used to his own automobile from the time he was old enough to drive, so I'm sure that is all it is."

Retrieving Declan's picture from the mantle, Cailen replied, "'Tis my hope that be all it is, but I somehow feel 'tis not. I wish I was there to see for meself. I realize how I am when it comes to me Declan, and I also realize how protective, maybe too much so for me own good but I cannot help it. I have never forgotten the problems he be having over the years and how they be affecting him. Why it was only a wee year ago that he … well, ye remembers just as well as I, and how we sat at his side all that time after he'd … I prayed so hard that he would open his eyes and not be taken from me like his da. Now he be in an entirely different place and … and possibly with someone who might hurt him worse than ever before."

Prichard well remembered, as she envisioned Declan upon his bed, fighting for his life after having ingested a full bottle of sedatives, and all over the loss of a girl who had consumed him. Now he could very well be heading for the same outcome, but without herself or Cailen there to stop it – or in the very least help – it could prove disastrous. Standing erect at her employer's side, she said, "Do not freight so, Mrs. Quinn, we must be strong. We must not borrow trouble where there may be none in the making. We must trust in the teachings we've administered, and hope those teachings will be first and foremost in his mind."

Sighing long and hard, Cailen replied, "I realize what ye say is true, Matilda. Ye have always been strong, always so assertive and sustained. This be not only with me boys but with me too, and I thank ye more than ye realize. But I must somehow find out what be going on. I'd like to ring his cell, but 'tis early morning in Ottawa, so I shall ring again shortly and catch him before he leaves for class. I'll let you know as soon I get him on the line – that is if he even answers - but I know ye will wish to have a few words as well."

Chapter 36

CONFUSION ABOUNDS

The mid-morning sun sizzled in the sky, turning the day into another scorcher. This was turning out to be the hottest summer that Ottawa and the surrounding district had experienced in a very long time. Storm clouds were again spiking, but that was nothing new for that had been happening daily of late, yet they never carried through with their threats. Crops were suffering in the surrounding countryside, especially around Smith Falls where a few farms had already lost everything, their once lush bounty now brown and shriveled. So far Mary Sutherland's clover crops had been managing to escape the drought but that, as her hired man pointed out, was only because the enormous irrigation pond, that of which Shay Sutherland had implemented forty years earlier, had not dried up, but unless there was rain, and soon it was only a matter of time.

This threat was forever constant on Mary's mind, for upon her husband's death the management of the diary farm had fallen squarely on her shoulders, but being the strong-willed person she was, carried on the best she could. The unforgiving heat and crop problems were not the only ones monopolizing her mind, for she had not heard from her daughter in quite some time. Mary was aware of the Crosby's marital problems, though her daughter managed to downplay the seriousness of it every time they had spoken on the phone, having told her mother she was managing alright, and that things were beginning to look up. But Mary had no way of knowing what an accomplished liar her daughter had become, further more had no reason to doubt what she was being told. Her call to Ben Sutherland did little to shine light on the matter because he was as much in the dark as was she, so was his half brother Shay, both men stating they had recently spoken with their dad, and they had also spoken with their mother - awhile back - quite some time in fact – but she had not told them anything different than what their grandmother already knew. None of the family knew what was going on with Willow any more than what she let them know. But a mother's intuition should never be taken lightly, for Mary surmised something was definitely out of the ordinary, and she was not about to let that submission ride, as she thought, "Willow can sugar-coat everything as much as she likes, but something is just not right."

Opening her address book, the aged Mary dialed her son-in-law's new phone number. It rang several times; finally the call-answer picked up. A recording device was the last thing she wanted to deal with, yet she figured she had better. "Hello, Jonas, this is your mother-in-law. I'm calling with regard to Willow. I know the two of you have issues at the moment, but I've not heard from her in quite some time, at least two months - possibly more - and I must admit I'm concerned, worried actually. She's never been one to call all that often, as you well know, but I have this feeling that something's not right. Could you please check on her, and call me with your findings. Thank you, Jonas. Goodbye."

How Mary wished she could have actuality conversed with her son-in-law in, but at least he would get her message. Maybe he and her daughter were on the outs, but she figured he would never hurt her, at least in a physical sense, but the more she thought about it the more anxious she became. With that, an idea sprung to mind, and she lost no time in phoning Will Sutherland. Again the phone rang continuously, or so it seemed when it was finally picked up.

"Whazzz up?" Will Sutherland stated in a bold manner.

"Is that you, William?" Mary questioned, the tone of her voice most indignant.

Realizing who it was, Will shockingly exclaimed, "Aunt Mary! *Um*, is that you?"

"Yes," Mary answered with annoyance, "and I might ask what kind of greeting that was supposed to be? Do you always answer your phone like an imbecile? In my day we conducted ourselves responsibly, even with something as trivial as answering the telephone."

Will swore he felt the sting of her rebuttal reach through the receiver like the tentacles of an Octopus after its intended meal, and he meekly answered, "Sorry, Aunt Mary, I don't have call display and I thought you might be this guy whose call I've been waiting on forever. I never once thought it could be you."

"Obviously," she stated coldly, "or else I would hope you would have been a bit more sensible with your greeting."

Will, judging from the amount of non-existing calls from his aunt, figured this was not a social one, prompting him to inquire the reason for this one, the point of which she lost no time in getting to, as she asked, "Have you spoken with Willow lately?"

It had been a long time since Will had heard from his favorite cousin, and in realizing this fact, couldn't help but feel remorseful because he hadn't bothered to contact *her*. He had always made a point of never letting too much time lapse in between their conversations, but life has a way of consuming a person to the point where they disappear entirely, much like Willow it seemed.

"I haven't spoken with Low in quite some time now, Aunt Mary," he answered sheepishly. "The last time I did she was a bit down ... I ... well I suppose you know that she and Jonas had a parting of the ways."

"Yes," Mary replied in a reserved manner, "I knew."

It was difficult for Will to speak with his aunt because he knew exactly how the situation between she and his cousin had always been. Maybe this time was no different, and she was simply trying to acquire details about Willow's life in order to validate the ongoing void. Will had always felt protective of his cousin and this time was no different, still he would not be impertinent, as he said, "The last time I saw her was, oh, half a year ago, maybe less. At the time I knew things were not great between she and Jonas, and she did talk in depth about it but, she did so in confidence, Aunt Mary, and I'm not at liberty to divulge what that was. You see I'm not only Low's cousin; I'm her best friend — along with Meg that is. Have you tried her? I hardly think she'd discuss Low either, besides she's no longer around these parts but I do know they still keep in touch, least they were the last time I *spoke* with Low. However with regard to what was discussed I have to ask that you please not put me in an awkward position by asking me about it."

"I wouldn't dream of doing such a thing, William, but I'm concerned about my daughter. No-one has seen nor heard from her in quite some time. I realize that she and I have our differences, but at least she would phone occasionally."

"Have you tried phoning her?"

"Yes, I finally broke down and put through a call the other day, but a recording informed me the number is no longer in service. Most strange, after all you would think she would have somehow informed me of the phone's loss, or fill me in as to what is going on."

"Have you tried calling Jonas?"

"Yes, but all I got was his answering device. He's yet to return my call."

"What about the boys?"

"Neither has spoken with their mother in quite some time. That is not like her."

"No," Will replied with concern, "it's not. But I don't want to intrude; she'd ream me out if I interfered, Aunt Mary, but I'll stop by work. Maybe Jonas knows what's going on."

In a nervous tone, Mary said, "If you find out ... *anything* ... will you please call?"

Will was certain he could detect a quiver in his aunt's voice, somewhat as if she were doing her best to keep from crying, as he answered, "Don't worry, Aunt Mary, I'm sure everything is fine. You know how Low can be. I realize that's not much consolation, but I happen to know that she loves you very much, regardless of how things have always been between you. I will call you if I find out anything. Either way, please stay in touch."

With trembling breath, Mary replied, "I will, dear, and thank you."

Chapter 37

AFTERMATH OF MISJUDGMENT

The ceiling fan above Willow's bed, having not been turned off before the hydro had been lost, rotated in its normal manner, sending a welcoming breeze to the occupant below. It was late morning, but the bit of coolness that had been in the room was quickly fading; even the fan's speed could not halt the rise in temperature. The noise from the street carried through the open window along with the chirping of a few zealous birds. Their song was cheerful, picking up in volume as if in effort to entertain the sleeping woman on the bed, or possibly rouse her.

The outside activity continued as Willow opened her eyes. For a moment she lay still, gazing about in wonderment of where she was. Finally she moved, but it was a painful effort to do so, so she settled back as the ache in her body worsened. "What on earth?" she thought, trying her best to remember. She hurt. Every muscle in her body cried out, demanding to know what had happened, and why they felt so wretched. Finally, pushing aside the sheet, she managed to sit upright and let her legs dangle over the side of the bed until the stalled circulation began to move. She rubbed them, and as she did she noticed dried remnants of blood on both her inner thighs. "What in hell?" she voiced aloud, wincing with the pain the movement brought about. Fear gripped her insides as to how the blood had gotten there while she racked her brain, desperately trying to remember what had happened. Her left cheek hurt; her lower jaw ached unmercifully, it was an effort to even open her mouth and she demanded answers, but first she needed to get to the bathroom. Stumbling as she stood, her body fell against the wall and as it did her hand landed upon the light switch, forcing it upward. Light instantly flooded the room. It actually startled her, for it was the last thing she had expected. "What's going on?" she wondered, gazing about in total confusion.

The journey to the adjacent bathroom seemed an eternity to make, each step feeling as if she were carrying an enormous weight upon her back, crushing her down, demanding she give way beneath its ensuing pressure. This encumbrance was not the only area requiring ratification, for in the next instant she was leaning over the toilet bowl with an overwhelming need to throw up. Half digested stomach contents hurled into the bowl with such fervor that water exploded upward, dousing the front of her legs in her own vomit while urine trickled down her thighs, removing a portion of dried blood as it ran. Suddenly her entire insides felt as if they were giving way, tumbling downward in a frenzied need to flush away what had happened. Her legs gave way; she slid to the floor, head hovering above the bowl in a total daze. The standing air in the room was pungent, the rising heat making the odor ten times worse than it otherwise might have been. Her jaw felt as if it too had become unhinged and had fallen into the toilet along with her stomach contents - she knew this was impossible - yet checked to be sure. Fragments of what had earlier taken place flashed in her mind along with wonder as to how Declan could have done that. "That son-of-a-bitch raped me," she thought, folding her arms across her belly as if to somehow shield it from unseen eyes lest they judge her idiocy, mocking her, applauding what she had brought upon herself. "How could I have been so stupid as to get mixed up with someone like that?" she silently questioned, just as the phone rang. She could hardly believe her ears, but she knew what she had heard. Thoughts swiftly filled her head, the majority of which questioned her sanity - or loss thereof - for she found it hard to believe that the lights were working, and the phone was back in order which meant the utilities had been reinstated, but when, and by whom?

The phone's signal continued, as she wiped her mouth, and lurched toward the hallway. Finally reaching the phone, she could see Will Sutherland's name displayed in the caller identification and she quickly snatched up the receiver, only to be met by the dial tone.

"*Willy!?*" she cried, hoping she might possibly catch him. Realizing she hadn't, she lost no time in returning the call.

"Hey there, Low!" Will stated in total surprise. "I thought you weren't home. I haven't heard from you in eons, how have you been? You know your mom has been trying to reach you. She even called *me* wondering about things, and asking if I'd heard from you. It might possibly have been to gain access to what you're up to these days, possibly not but, she did seem overly concerned, cousin dear. You really should call her."

Doing her best to steady not only her body, but her voice, Willow replied, "Hey there, cousin, good to hear from you, too. I really must call Mother, I know. When it comes to correspondence I'm terrible. You, more than anyone should know that, but …" Her voice trailed off before she could divulge the reason why no one had heard a word from her, as she thought, "Should I tell him? There's nothing he can do anyway; no sense upsetting him," before she continued, "Sorry to be so out of the loop with everyone. You know that Jonas and me have been having issues for quite awhile …" She again stopped, her eyes gazing about as she absorbed the obvious fact that Jonas must be responsible for the freshly engaged utilities. "Must have had a change of heart," she mumbled to herself, but her intent of speech had not gone unheard by her cousin, for in a hurried fashion, he asked, "What's that you say?"

Willow, realizing he must have overheard, replied, "Oh I was just thinking aloud, nothing to be concerned about. How's your grandson these days?"

Will Sutherland was nobody's fool, and when it came to his favorite cousin he was even more in tune, as he answered, "Fine, thanks, he's here today, playing with his toys at the moment. You were talking about a change of heart. Whose heart might you be referring to, Jonas', or your own?"

Knowing full-well he could read her like a book, Willow replied, "I wasn't referring to anyone in particular. It was just a figure of speech."

Will would not be put off; besides he sensed something off within her voice, as he said, "This is me you're doing your best to fool, Low, and it isn't working. Something is going on. What's the matter?"

The conversation had become more intense than Willow had planned. She didn't want to drag her cousin into something that she herself must bear the brunt of. It was her problem, whether she had asked for the extent of which had come from it or not, but she must be the one to deal with it, however that might be. The remaining contents within her stomach begged release, but she paid them no mind. Taking a deep breath, she replied, "Nothing is wrong, really I … I think I might have caught a cold – as odd as that sounds with the outrageous temps of late – but you know how that can affect you, especially if the heat already has you tired out. I'm just going to go back and lay down – in fact that's where I was when you called – took me awhile to get to the phone. Anyway, things are looking up between Jonas and me and, I'll be sure to give Mom a call, but right now I'm ...."

She had to stop for she had become so lightheaded she could no longer stand. Suddenly she felt a warm sensation moving down her inner thighs making her think she must have wet herself, but upon gazing down, discovered blood trickling toward her knees. Before she could utter another word she felt herself falling. The receiver remained in her hand, and as she collapsed the base of the phone went with her. She lay on the floor, whimpering, unable to move.

Will couldn't help but hear the commotion. He instantly called into the receiver, but no answer was returning. "Low, what's going on? I heard a loud noise. Are you there? Can you answer me? *Willow!*"

Willow opened her mouth to answer but had no strength to call-out. Will again fired his concern into the phone, but to no avail. He knew something was terribly wrong, and he lost no time in putting through a call to Jonas Crosby.

Chapter 38

CONFESSIONS OF THE HEART DON'T ALWAYS FREE THE SOUL

Afternoon in Galway was swiftly moving along as the huge grandfather clock in the foyer of Quinn Manor began tolling the hour, signifying not only the time of day, but the daily serving of tea in the dining room. The mistress of the manor, who had been working in her office all afternoon, did not require notification via the clock for the immense rumbling in her stomach had already informed her. It had been a long go since the tea and scones from earlier and Cailen could not wait to see what Bridget Donnigan would be serving. She also realized that Prichard would be arriving shortly, and she could not wait to continue their earlier conversation, but before joining her, would again try ringing Declan. This would be the third try, and she was fast losing patience, but she would give it another go and hopefully this time find success.

The ringing continued as she rapidly tapped her fingers upon the top of the mahogany desk, wondering where on earth her son could possibly be, and if by some miracle would even answer the call.

It was eleven o'clock in Ottawa; classes would have been in session for quite some time, so expecting an answer was almost impossible. Shaking her head in disgust she rose to begin the lengthy journey to the dining room. As she moved along the exquisite down stair corridor her attention was anywhere but on her present location. She suddenly stopped, having almost run smack-bang into Matlida Prichard who was hurriedly exiting the drawing room with her head down as if she were a linebacker preventing further yardage on the field.

"Mrs. Quinn!" Prichard exclaimed in utter surprise. "I believe we almost had a right-ole-run-in!" Catching her breath, while smoothing her Herringbone suit, she continued, "I really must apologize for not watching where I was going, but instead bolting out the door like a bull out of a chute. Do forgive me."

"Oh not to be worrying, Matilda," Cailen replied inattentively as she gathered her scattered wits. "If we had collided it would have been as much my fault as yurs. I suppose we both have our minds elsewhere, instead of what is presently before us. I was just on me way to the dining room. I be sure that is where ye be heading as well."

Patting her stomach, Prichard replied, "Yes, my tummy informs me it is that time. But in all honesty I must say that my mind was occupied within the pages of the latest whodunit. My, but I do admire the tactic of the cunning sleuth. Oh to be that daring and bold but, what can I say? I am but a simple teacher – one - I might add that has been set adrift of late." Suddenly reining herself in while dabbing her left eye with a tissue, she continued, "Oh but I do miss Master Declan. You know how fond of him I am, and I knew I would miss him, however I did not realize how much. But now that he is not about, challenging my every word, I find the hours in my day quite stagnate. I suppose that is why I've resorted to sleuthing, *ha-ha!*"

Smiling as she shook her head receptively, Cailen replied, "When it comes to entertaining yurself, Matlida, ye are never at a loss. Aye but I do know what ye mean with regard to me Declan. Still I be realizing that he has to stand on his own two feet at some point. I be not knowing a better way to go about it then to have done as we have. Yet I cannot help but wonder if we have possibly jumped the gun. In fact I have been second-guessing our decision all morning - and I still cannot reach him on the phone."

Speaking in a decisive manner, Prichard asked, "Not as yet? Well it is possible that he had an early class, and should his cell go off, could not have it disrupting the silence, so he turned it off. With regard to our decision, Mrs. Quinn, I do not think we acted in haste. The young master may be wild in many ways, but no more so than any of his brothers at that age - though there is that temper - not to mention the swiftness of it."

"Aye," Cailen replied in agreement, "but I just wish he would check in with me. He's not done so since his arrival there. I'm sure he believes he's pulled a fast one with the purchase of that lavish vehicle. He would never think that MacLauchlan would ring me, I'm sure of it, but I cannot help but wonder what he be up to, let alone how I be coping should it be another of his escapades gone array. At this point all I can say on the matter is if God sends ye down a stony path, may He give ye strong shoes."

The table looked inviting. As always Bridget had gone that extra mile in making sure everything was just perfect. She had always been that way, meticulous to a fault, which had endeared her to the Quinn family possibly more than it otherwise might have. Standing aside the generous spread, Bridget joyfully announced, "Tea be served, Mrs. Quinn, and I really must be insisting that ye both be filling yur cargo holds to capacity," and taking note of the hour, continued, "By the looks of Father time here I should be off to the kitchen to whip-up me pudding. Now don't be the shy ones, I want to be hearing those forks in action as I close the door behind me."

Both ladies lost no time in digging in. Swallowing her first mouthful, Cailen whipped her mouth, glanced at Prichard, and said, "She never fails to please me, or ye by the looks of it."

"That is precisely so!" Prichard exclaimed as she smacked her lips upon the tartness of the homemade dressing adorning the fruit salad. "Bridget's creations never cease to astound me. Master Declan could never get enough of her delights. Why two days before his departure I remember him carrying on about a sweet she had made, how it —" The phone had suddenly rung, severing Prichard's statement, and taking both ladies by surprise. Prichard was the first to reach it, snatching the receiver from its cradle, and announcing, "Quinn residence, Matilda Prichard here!"

"Miss Prichard, it's Declan, I really need to speak to Ma!"

There was urgency in his tone, alerting her to the fact that something was wrong. She realized he had asked for his mother, but she thought that he just might confide in her, like he often did, so she inquired the reason for his call.

He quickly answered, "I don't mean to be impertinent, Miss Prichard, and I know you must be thinking just that, but I really need to speak to Ma."

Feeling rather devalued, Prichard replied, "All right, I shall fetch her."

Cailen flew to the phone as if her feet had suddenly sprouted wings. He had called! She could hardly believe it! With no time to spare, she exclaimed, "Son, it be so grand to hear yur sweet voice! I have been trying to ring ye all day but ye not pick up. How be everything?"

"Ma ..."

The boy sounded as if he were crying. Cailen knew her son like the back of her hand; this was no different, and she asked, "What be wrong, lad?"

"Ma ... Oh, Ma, you were right, you ... you tried to tell me but I wouldn't listen ... I ... I was so sure ... I thought I loved her ... I thought ... *ah-h* ... I was convinced she felt the same about me ... she told me ... *she did!* ... Ma, I didn't mean it ... didn't mean to ..."

"Declan, what be going on? Ye must calm down and tell me."

"Oh, Ma, I didn't mean to hurt her ... I would never purposely hurt her ... but I ..."

Despair had drenched Cailen, coming over her as if she had actually been standing beneath a huge wave at the ocean side.

"Declan," she said, trying to sooth him, "ye must be calming down and tell me what has happened. I cannot help ye if ye don't divulge what ere it is."

Prichard had been reverently standing aside Cailen in hopes her presence might somehow lend support, that of which was obviously needed. Reaching out in a helpless manner, Cailen grabbed hold of the woman's outstretched hand, and cautiously asked her son what he had done.

The boy could feel his mother's anguish permeating the line, and it bothered him that much more to know that she was thousands of miles away, unable to wrap her arms around him like she always did with assurance that all would be well, regardless of what it was. How could he tell her what he had done? He could barely believe it himself.

Taking a deep breath while his muddled head swam, he moaned, "I attacked her."

In a frenzied manner, Cailen asked, "Ye did what ... to whom?!"

Struggling to express himself, the boy cried, "I ... I attacked Willow she ... oh, Ma, she belittled me so - told me things about her husband - what they did - how she still feels for him. *She let him fuck her!* How could she do that, Ma? How could she tell me she cared for me then carry on like that with *him*, especially after he used her so shamelessly?"

"Ye must be full of Blarney! What in B-Jasus are ye to be telling me?" Cailen inquired, hardly believing what she was hearing. She suddenly weakened, her knees practically buckling while she struggled to stand erect. Prichard grabbed a chair, and helped ease her down, her grip assuring the usually strong matriarch that she was right beside her come what may. Nodding thankfully toward Prichard, Cailen instructed, "Declan, just take a deep breath if ye can, and try and explain."

Somewhat settling himself, the upset boy replied, "I need your help, Ma. I-I can't face her. I can't stay here a moment longer - I didn't mean to I ... I didn't want to harm her but she told me things, things she should have kept to herself. Before I knew what was happening I - I hit her - punched her – *hard* across her jaw. Then I carried her to her bed and I ..." His nerves were unraveling, his breath jagged, but he pushed on. "She came to then tried pushing me away — shoving me — *me! A Quinn!* She asked for what she got, Ma! Nobody talks to one of us like that! They can't be let away with it - you've told me that yourself - *many times!* She wouldn't lay still so I ... I knocked her cold. She just lay there. I couldn't stop myself! I ... I did things I ..." He was losing control of his breathing, beginning to hyperventilate, as he screamed, "Ma, I ... I *raped her!*"

Chapter 39

SURVIVAL IS AT HAND, BUT WHOSE?

The receiver trembled in the Quinn matron's hand, threatening to spring from her grasp and plummet to the floor, prompting Prichard to act quickly, lest her employer collapse entirely. Cailen was a strong-willed woman, one who had endured countless tribulations, but everyone has their breaking point, and with this latest declaration she felt she might have finally reached hers. Prichard felt useless, no-longer able to hold herself erect in the stiff fashion of which she'd become accustomed. The sound of Declan's voice when she'd answered the phone had alerted her to the fact that something dire was afoot, but he had refused to confide in her as he once did; still that did not diminish her need to support him however she could, nor did it avert her away from her employer's obvious need of the same.

As the two women tried coping, Declan's hysterical voice could be heard pouring from the receiver. *"Ma, did you hear what I said?!"*

"Aye, but I cannot believe it!" Cailen gasped as she secured Prichard's arm around her waist in a desperate attempt to hold herself together. She took a moment to gather her thoughts, while her son's agonized voice kept screaming, *"What will I do, Ma?!"*

But she could not answer for she was too busy trying to catch her breath. *"Ma, please answer me! ... I ... I can't stay here ... but I don't know what to do ... what will happen to me when Willow realizes what I did?!"*

The usually resilient matriarch was finding it beyond her ability to summon an answer, though she realized something must be said, yet all she could muster was an agonizing moan.

Picking up the fallen gauntlet, Prichard seized-hold the receiver, and snapped, "Master Declan, your mother needs a moment to gather her composure. You need to be patient. I do not know what you have just relayed, but judging from her reaction it must be extremely serious. I have never seen her react to anything in the manner of what I just witnessed." Calming her nerves, she summoned a deep breath, and continued, "Will you please confide in me? You have always been able to do so, regardless of how difficult the subject. Your mother is most distraught, please; can you not tell me what is going on?" The sound of crying could be heard emitting from the receiver as if it were foam oozing from the top of an over-worked shaving dispenser, rising in volume then fading back. "Master Declan," Prichard instructed in a firm manner, "you *must* take hold. After all nothing can be solved carrying on like this. Just take a deep breath, gather yourself, and tell me what is wrong."

"I can't!"

"Yes, you can. Just take your time."

"I can't tell you, Miss Prichard, I'm sorry, but this is too personal. I *need* Ma!"

"How I can help me boy when I cannot even speak without losing composure," Cailen thought, realizing she must get her act together if there was to be any hope whatsoever. Swallowing hard, she summoned the receiver from Prichard's hand, and said,

"Declan, 'tis Mother. Now, ye must calm down and speak with a clear head."

"But, Ma," he cried, "I can't calm down ... *I can't!* What if she calls the police?"

"Oh, God," Cailen swiftly thought, nerves totally unraveling, but she replied, "Ye must take things one at a time, me boy. Was she aware of things when ye left her?"

"No!" he snapped. "I stayed for awhile – I ... I even did what I could to help her, but I was scared and ... well, ashamed of what I'd done — I didn't mean it, didn't mean to do what I did but I just couldn't help myself!"

The boy was fast losing what sanity he had managed to cling to but Cailen already surmised this. Oh how well she knew what he was like. He had always been this way, and it totally escalated whenever he had done something wrong. She must control him, like always, but it was going to be next to impossible with her in Galway and him where he was. Looking imploringly toward Prichard, she said, "Declan, ye must stay where ye are and sit tight. Miss Prichard and I will be on the first flight we can secure out of Galway. I'll ring ye back as soon as I have made arrangements. In the meantime ye just sit tight, do not answer the door, and try yur best to remain calm, do ye hear?" He did not respond, making her concern heighten, as she asked, "Are ye there?" but again no response. "Matilda, he not be answering!" she remarked, jumping to her feet in anguish. Starring toward the English nanny, while holding the phone tightly to her ear, she snapped, "What do ye suppose is going on? I can hear sounds, somewhat like air rushing ... *Declan, are ye there, boy?!*"

Taking the receiver from her employer's trembling hand, Prichard repeated the same question, but no response was returning.

In his well air-conditioned condo, sprawled upon the floor, lay Declan, his breathing sporadic, pulse racing. His cell lay where it had slid from his opened hand. He had heard his mother's instructions, even Prichard's addition, but he could not answer. In his mind he had envisioned the recent happening and what he had done. He may have become a bundle of nerves ready to unravel at any second, but he remained rational enough to realize it was only a matter of time before he was found out. He could not let that happen. He was a Quinn, the youngest member of the wealthiest family in Galway who were above redemption, never did they faultier in side-stepping the law, regardless of the seriousness of the charge. This would be no different. He had heard his mother say that she and Prichard would board the first plane out of Galway. "That should not take long," he thought, and calculating the five hour flight, border nonsense, and cab time, they should arrive in the early hours of the morning. He could hold out until then. He would do as instructed, lie still, and be quiet. His mother had been right, just like always, and if he did as he was told no-one would know he was there. He would be home free, they would arrive, gather him, and before long he really would be free, back home where he belonged. As he lay there the cell signaled an incoming call. "Should I answer?" he thought, while visions of the infamous clown taunted him, daring him to go for it.

Chapter 40

ANXIETY WITHOUT CERTAINTY

A sweat-laden Jonas, fresh in from work, walked straight to the fridge with two things at the forefront of his mind: a nice cold beer to quench his enormous thirst, and Willow's anticipated reaction to the newly activated utilities, as he thought, "She must be over the moon by now, not to mention plopped before the damn computer, pounding out an answer to the latest come-on declaration from the dick on the other side of the screen." The very idea made him seethe with anger, and the newly-opened brewski disappeared quickly, as he thought, "Damn him to hell and back. If I ever get my hands on the motherfucker I'll rip his balls off!" This thought escalated as it summoned images of what might be going on, and regardless of how he tried disbursing them, they would not leave his mind's eye. Abruptly standing, he stomped en route toward the fridge when his eye was caught by the phone's flashing red light signaling an awaiting message.

Twisting the cap from a newly acquired beer and tossing it into the sink, his finger finally landed upon the message retrieve and Mary Crosby's voice began speaking her concern. Jonas listened then immediately listened again. There was something in the anxious tone of her voice that told him something dire might be threatening, but he wasn't about to discuss things that could not be changed, and he certainly wasn't about to reveal anything pertaining to he and Willow's recent copulation - especially to her mother - but he still had to return the call.

The phone began to ring and with it a rush of uncertainty up his spine. Mary had always treated him with what could only be described as reluctance, she certainly had not opened her arms to him in any welcoming manner, but he also realized it was her way, with most anyone, yet he always felt that had it been left up to her his marriage to Willow would have never taken place. It had always been a black mark between them, that, and his knowledge of the ongoing reservations between she and her daughter. As he pondered these recollections, Mary, whom obviously did not have caller identification, came on the line, inquiring who was calling. Taking a deep breath, he replied, "It's Jonas Crosby, Mrs. Sutherland. I just got your message. It sounded rather urgent. Is there anything wrong?"

Mary immediately stated her concern of which she had earlier rung about, ending with, "I don't know what to make of things, Jonas. I just feel that something is terribly wrong."

The sheer abruptness of Willow's visit the day he'd had her phone disconnected, accompanied by her outright haughtiness of the lost connection to her latest flame, prompted Jonas to answer, "I'm not sure what to say, Mrs. Sutherland. The relationship between your daughter and me has been strained of late, as you must be aware, although we have recently managed to somewhat bury the hatchet – without securing it in each other's head I might add, *ha-ha!*"

Mary bristled at his light-hearted pun, prompting her to snap, "I do not find this situation laughable in the least! I realize that you and I have never been close, by any means, but I find it totally reprehensible that you can simply brush my concerns aside so easily!"

Realizing his stab at humor was totally misplaced, Jonas apologetically said, "I'm sorry, Mrs. Sutherland, really I am, please forgive me. I realize your concern is valid, and I will drive by the house and check on Willow. Don't worry; I'm sure all is fine, and I will tell her to get the lead out and call you as soon as she can."

"Thank you, Jonas," Mary replied, "I would appreciate that and, I'm sorry I snapped at you. Should you happen to be out this way please drop by for a visit."

"Well thank you, Mrs. Sutherland, I just might do that," Jonas replied, thinking it rather nice that she appeared to be extending kindness toward him.

After hanging up the receiver, Jonas thought it best to shower before venturing over to Willow's. He was not sure how he would be received, hopefully the reinstated utilities would allow a jovial greeting, if not an overly-exited one, which in turn might prompt another passionate encounter, but he could hope, and hope was better than despair. This made him smile as he made his way toward the bathroom.

A few minutes passed before a rejuvenated Jonas returned to his living room, lower half wrapped in a yellow towel, and beads of moisture still embracing his chest. "Man that felt great!" he exclaimed to himself as he stood before the mirror, running his fingers through his thick graying hair. Late afternoon was fast closing in while he dressed, but rubbing his new whisker growth, thought it best he shave before venturing out the door. After all a smooth face is always best when making out with a lady as opposed to rough stubble irritating her skin. "Willow never liked that," Jonas thought as he again envisioned their last encounter, and the way her inner thighs moved against his face while he helped himself to her delectable nectar. "Nope, can't have stubble interfering," he thought, but before he reached the bathroom door the phone rang.

The caller ID displayed Will Sutherland's name, and Jonas, in a hurried fashion, exclaimed, "Yo, bro, what's up?!"

"Hey, Jonas, I think something could be wrong over at Low's! I've been trying to track you down all day! I just tried again but your line's been tied up!" Will exclaimed.

"Yeah," Jonas answered, "I had running around to do today; managed to get back to work mid-afternoon. I see your name on the caller's list here, but no message. I was just on the phone with Mary. She'd called earlier but I didn't get her message until about a half an hour ago, so I called her back and she told me she was concerned. I told her I'd swing by Willow's and check on things. Just got out of the shower actually, and was soon heading out the door."

In a frenzied tone, Will replied, "I was talking with Low awhile ago, mid-morning or so; she sounded odd before there was a loud racket and … and then nothing. I wanted to go right over – should have gone - but my grandson was here with me and I had no-one to stay with him. I didn't think it wise to take him with me but my neighbor is finally home and I've taken him over there. I'm leaving now for Low's. God I hope everything is okay. Meet me there, *and hurry!*"

Jonas felt a sudden twinge of dread, as he thought, "Jesus no! Please don't let anything have happened to her." Sweeping his eyes around the room in dread, he secured his hat, grabbed his keys, and raced out the door.

The drive across Ottawa's east side was busy, even though rush-hour had finished a hour earlier, but still vehicles moved like snails, the odd one pulled part-way off the street with steam rising above its opened hood, and adding to the congestion was an impending storm, for the sky to the west had become as black as coal. But Jonas pushed on, doing his best to snake around the over-heated vehicles without one thought to help. Any other time he would have been the first to lend a hand, but at the moment he had much more pressing issues to tend to. Finally his old address came into view, and he swung into the drive with Will Sutherland's car directly on his tail.

Chapter 41

F1 - POSSIBLY HIGHER

The two men jumped out of their respective vehicle, smacked their right hand together as men often do when meeting, and raced to the front steps. The look on their face conveyed their growing concern without need of verbal confirmation, as they sprint-up the steps to the front door. Jonas knocked loudly, calling out to Willow as he did. When no answer came, he called again this time supported by Will Sutherland's voice, but still no reply to either of them. As they again tried, a jagged shard of lightning ripped the sky, accompanied with a tremendous clap of thunder. The ground actually shook, causing the men to hasten in their plight.

"*Willow!*" they called in unison, their fists pounding the door.

Their actions continued as another bolt of lightning sheared the sky, the thunder again shaking the house and everything around it. Suddenly all went quiet, as if a radio's blaring volume had been instantly switched off. The remaining blue in the sky had turned an eerie green, while the smell of the air held a rancid odor.

"Good Lord," Will groaned in an apprehensive manner, his eyes studying the sky, "we'd best get a move on."

Taking a quick look about, Jonas replied, "No shit, this is not good!" and with that took a step back before kicking the door as hard as he could, but the solid wood held fast, not yielding in the least. He repeated his kick. This time the sound of wood splintering could be heard, and they could see a noticeable movement within the doorframe.

Sounding as if he should have stated this fact before the door was totally destroyed, Will exclaimed, "Why don't you just smash the fucking glass!"

A determined Jonas, hell-bent on taking the door completely out, exclaimed, "Goddamn it!" just as his boot slammed directly into the door's lower portion, sending it flying inward with glass shattering everywhere! The men raced into the foyer, but they were not alone.

Shawn Martin, having moments before stepped out on his porch to survey the impending storm, took notice when he heard the commotion taking place on his neighbor's porch. From his own porch he could only see the mouth of Willow's driveway; he had no-way of knowing it was his absent neighbor come with a friend as opposed to a couple of guys busting in. He never once thought about the possible danger to himself, and there hadn't been time to call the police. Besides his neighbor might be in danger, he had to know, so he had come right over.

"What the hell's going on here?!" he boldly questioned, stomping in behind the two who had just entered.

Swinging around with a doubled fist at the ready, Jonas yelled, *"Get the fuck out!"* but when he realized who the intruder was, he immediately calmed down, and stated, "Shawn, it's you! Sorry about that, man! Will and I are here to see Willow," but before Jonas had a chance to further explain Will's excited voice summoned him to come as quickly as he could.

The two men rushed into the bedroom hallway to find Will hovering over his nude cousin, who lay on her right side, with the phone receiver in her limp hand. She was partly conscious, but incoherent. Will was beside himself with concern, as he knelt beside her, gently rubbing her back as if this action would somehow make everything okay. Jonas, completely anxiety stricken, fell to his knees, hardly able to absorb the sight before him, while Shawn Martin tried his best to comprehend what had happened. The phone's dial tone, long diminished, was now emitting an annoying busy signal as the receiver was gently taken from Willow's hand, her limp fingers slipping off of it one by one as it was removed. Will, intending to bring her some form of dignity, had gone to the bedroom and returned with a sheet in which to cover her. Unfortunately the one he'd brought was the one Declan had covered her with, now soiled with blood and spent cum.

An enormous clash of thunder shook the house and with it a noise resembling that of an oncoming train bearing down on a crossing. Upon hearing this unsettling noise, Shawn Martin had bolted to the front porch, only to be met with what he had surmised. He tore back into the house, voicing his find, as he yelled, *"To the basement, everyone! Fast moving funnel out of the west and it looks to be coming straight for us!"*

Jonas, not believing what was taking place, moaned, "My God, this can't be happening. Look at her. Who the hell did this?! She needs a doctor – Christ she needs an ambulance!"

"There isn't time, Jonas!" Shawn hollered. *"I don't know how much of it we've got but it isn't much! Come on! Lift her as gently as you can and get her to the basement!"*

Will, returning from his own check, stated, "He's right, Jonas, it's coming fast! Here, wrap the sheet around her! I'll help you. Take her legs ... gently ... I'll lift under her arms, go easy now!"

Shawn had gone ahead to clear the way as the two men carried their bundle as carefully as they could, taking great pains to not jostle her while they descended the basement stairs. Willow moaned softly, as if in a dream, and it was a help for the men to know she was as far out of it as she was for nothing could be done for her at the moment; in the meantime the cellar would provide safety. Hopefully the house would be spared, at which time they could summon help, but until then they must remain where they were until the danger passed. Time can be punishing, each second a signal to possible doom and ruin; but it can also be a friend by way of holding destruction at bay until danger had passed and all was again well.

High wind could be heard screeching above as heavy thuds sounded against outside walls. Windows - those of which were still closed upon the tornado's arrival - lost their glass in outward bursts, the pent up pressure so strong nothing could withstand it. Darkness had encompassed everything as the outside noise carried inward. The four in the basement held vigil beneath Jonas' solid oak workbench, certain to uphold the heaviest ceiling beams should they come crashing down, that is if the twister didn't first suck them up. Jonas, knowing his wife required proper medical attention, not just what he had learned in his first aid course, had tried treating her as best he could, but was now cuddling her in his arms, no longer caring whether she could withstand it or not. The dire straits continued as Jonas and Will gently laid her upon an old discarded blanket, shielding her with their bodies in hope they could somehow save her should the worst present itself and the house be removed above them.

The storm's intensity felt as if it would go on forever, but in actuality took only a few minutes to pass. When a tornado happens everything feels as if it is happening in slow-motion; then again the duration of anything horrific feels like an eternity has passed before it ends. Finally daylight returned, though twilight now in the day's duration, and darkness would soon settle in. The men knew they must seek immediate help, yet couldn't help wondering if the phone still had service, or if an ambulance could find its way unscathed to the house if they did manage to summon one. They even wondered if the house remained unscathed. It stood - at least the majority of it - that much they could see for the floorboards directly above them remained intact. Venturing from beneath the safety of the workbench, Shawn carefully made his way up the stairs, followed closely behind by Will. As much as Shawn was concerned for his neighbor's welfare, he was fully as concerned for his own, as well as that of his home.

"Let me know if there's anything I can do," he relayed to Jonas, "anything at all – well would you look at this! Believe it or not the street lights are coming on, wonders never cease I guess. I wouldn't have thought they'd even be standing, let alone lighting, obviously the hydro hasn't been lost, and look here, the kitchen fan is rotating as though nothing has happened. I'm sure the phone is active as well. Can I call the ambulance for you?"

Jonas, again accompanied by Will, had carried the semi-conscious Willow back upstairs and down the hall to her bedroom, all the while casting a glance about to determine the extent of damage, and with the exception of two broken windows, and some garbage blown in through the gapping front door, everything appeared fine. Arriving at Willow's bedroom, Jonas looked about the room and sighed in an apprehensive manner, but what he was thinking was as plain as the look on his face, as he said, "Yes, Shawn, the sooner you can get the ambulance here the better. She's breathing easier, but I'm concerned about her overall condition." Casting his glance toward Will, he questioned, "Do you have any idea who might have done this?"

The bewildered cousin shook his head in denial for he was as much in the dark as everyone else, as he replied, "No, Jonas, I don't. You have no idea how much I wish I did. I'd make the sorry bastard wish he'd never been born." He was visibly shaken and lost no time grasping the half-filled pitcher of water from the nightstand. Pouring a good amount into tissues, he knelt by his cousin, and proceeded to wipe her face with coolness.

Standing with the receiver in his hand, Shawn said, "I've called the paramedics. They'll be here directly and, about what the two of you are discussing, I might have a clue for you to follow up on."

With a hopeful expression engulfing his face, Jonas said, "Tell me, please, whatever it is."

As though he couldn't wait to divulge what he'd seen, Shawn replied, "Very early this morning, I suppose five thirty - possibly six - I saw a brand new white sport convertible pulling out of your drive and heading west. Daylight had just broken over the horizon, and as you know I'm a very early riser, so I was out there with my coffee and I saw it. I don't know who it was, I mean, I don't know who Willow's friends are these days, with the exception of a few that I haven't seen in awhile, like Will here. I can't say who it was because I don't know, but I jotted down the plate number. I don't know why, possibly thought it might be of some importance. I'll bring it over as soon as I check on my house."

Shawn immediately sped out Willow's non-existent front door toward his own. One would never know by the calm, subtle evening now presenting itself that there had even been a storm, let alone tornado, for with the exception of a few uprooted trees, hundreds of torn shingles now dotting the landscape, assorted windows free of glass, flattened flowerbeds, and an unusual amount of garbage strewn about, things appeared fine. Shawn's house had but a few broken windows, which would have certainly numbered more had he remembered to close the front door on departure. Thankful for small mercies, he grabbed the track pants he'd been wearing that morning and retrieved the paper containing the plate number from a side pocket. Tearing back to his neighbor's, he handed it to Jonas, just as the ambulance pulled up in front.

Will greeted the medical team, who were apologizing for taking as long as they had, and proceeded to lead them to Willow's bedroom where they found Jonas sitting beside her, stroking her hair. "Please help her," he said anxiously, grappling to his feet to make way for them.

"Are you next of kin?" the one paramedic asked, settling beside the unconscious woman and opening his medical kit.

"Yes," Jonas said, "I'm her husband … well, estranged husband, we've been separated for months."

The second attendant, who remained standing, jotted down Jonas' words, but asked, "Mr. Crosby, do you know what might have happened here - by the way - if you and Mrs. Crosby are separated, what are you doing here?"

Jonas instantly bristled, for he considered the question a blatant insinuation that he was responsible for his wife's condition. He did have to admit - though only to himself - that he was responsible, but only for the wretched actions and words that had passed between them, certainly not this, as he replied, "I didn't do this to my wife, if in fact that is what you're implying."

"No," the attendant said, "I'm not implying anything of the kind. I'm simply asking a question. Do you have any idea who might have?"

Jonas instantly pictured Willow's over-the-top performance the day she had come to confront him about the phone disconnection, and he knew right then and there it was because of the lost connection to whoever had come into her life, in whatever form that might have been, and he suddenly thought, "I wonder if that son-of-a-bitch showed up here, done this ... raped her!"

He lost no time in pulling the recorded plate number from his pocket, that of which enticed him to scoff as he read the personalized inscription MiT*Quin. Turning to the attendant, he said, "I have a feeling the guy's name is Quinn, either his first or last name, but I'll find that out when I have the cops run the plate. How's my wife doing?"

The attending paramedic looked up, and replied, "Well she's pretty banged up, but she's holding her own, though she needs to be taken to hospital for tests, possibly X-rays to be sure nothing's broken and, no-doubt suctioned. Actually I'm more concerned about the blood loss, as she appears to have suffered some mild hemorrhaging, possibly a few hours ago or more, judging from the color of the blood on her thighs. She's still unresponsive, pupils dilated, and she's dehydrated. I've just connected her to a heart monitor and started a Saline drip. She's ready for transfer; will you be following us to hospital?"

"Yes," Jonas and Will replied in unison, stepping back in order for the attendants to place their patient upon the awaiting stretcher.

The attendant who had been recording the action upon his clipboard, stated, "That was some storm. The radio is saying it was a tornado, F1 - possibly higher. There's a fair amount of damage around, the usual, uprooted trees, missing shingles, that sort of thing, but nothing to stop people from getting around. But there will be some major clean up. The route to hospital is clear, so we should be there in fifteen. Be sure to give your wife's particulars at the Emerge, and I'm sure you'll be able to go in as soon as they check her over. She will be admitted."

With gratitude, Jonas said, "Thank you, thank you both. I really appreciate you coming as fast as you could under the circumstances. I wanted to take her there myself, well me and her cousin Will here, but the storm sort of changed our plans. We'll be right along."

Will followed closely along as the attendants wheeled Willow to the ambulance and placed her inside. Jonas again studied the name on the personalized plate, thinking to himself that it would only be a matter of time before the punk is revealed and caught. With this thought in mind, he put through a call to the police, but inwardly vowed he would see to things personally, and whoever this Quinn is, he will come to rue the day he ever laid eyes on Willow Crosby, let alone his hands *or* his dick.

Chapter 42

DEMANDS ARE NOT ALWAYS MET

A number of inquires had been made over the course of the late afternoon and early evening, but none had brought the required results which Cailen Quinn had hoped to achieve. Even her demands, which were normally met with immediate execution, had run into a dead end. Nothing was working, and try as she might she could not arrange an immediate flight for herself and Matilda Prichard. Obviously miffed, she openly scoffed, before stating, "Are ye certain ye cannot bend the rules at least somewhat?! After all we have certainly spent enough at this airport over the years to expect a bit more consideration than I appear to be receiving!" The person on the other end of the line must not have been co-operating, for Cailen loudly snapped, "This be total nonsense! I not be asking for the moon here, simply two first class accommodations on a direct flight to Ottawa Canada — what be that?"

Prichard sat quietly, not expressing her thoughts but that did not deter her from thinking them, nor feeling their bite, for the sordid details of Cailen's conversation with Declan had yet to be divulged to her, and she couldn't help but feel dejected, as well as shutout. But regardless of these feelings she would remain stalwart, as always, knowing if all went as it usually did she would be needed in whatever capacity that might be.

It was plain to see the telephone conversation was fast heating up, as a disgusted Cailen snarled, "Aye! We *must* get there as soon as possible ... What be that ye say? ... Life and death, aye, ye wretched woman, *'tis* a matter of life and death to be sure! Me son could well be in tremendous danger, I need to be there with him. What be that? Aye, if that is all ye *have* then reserve two seats in economy! Blast it, woman, ye have me credit numbers on file; all ye have to do is look! Cailen Quinn and Matilda Prichard ... aye that be correct, the same credit number to be applied for both! We will arrive within the hour; have the boarding passes at the ready!" With total exasperation, she slammed the receiver upon the cradle before turning toward Prichard, exclaiming, "Really, the stupidity of some! I have never to be experiencing such incompetence in *anyone* as the brainless twit at that airline just now! Over the years I be spending money enough in which to construct a new airport! I hope ye not mind the fact we be flying economy; according to Miss Fancy Pants there be not one available seat in first class, but we must get there as soon as we can. Do ye think I should call ahead to secure a cab - possibly reserve hotel accommodations? We can hardly stay at Declan's cramped condo – there be only one bedroom - and I did notice some lovely hotels close to the university when I was researching the area."

Nodding her head in compliance, Prichard replied, "That would be an excellent idea, Mrs. Quinn. It would alleviate that bothersome worry upon arrival. The accommodations matter not to me, after-all we shan't be there long."

"Well then," Cailen stated reprehensively, "if we must fly *economy* then our Ottawa accommodations shall be nothing short of five star, I can assure ye of that!" then checking the time, added, "I will try ringing Declan again, hopefully he will answer this time, then again ..."

Her voice had trailed off as she put through the call. It rang a number of times, until Declan nervously answered, "Hello. Is that you, Ma?" Judging by the uncertain tone in his voice she could tell he was doing his best to keep his nerves from unraveling entirely.

"Aye, lad, it be me," Cailen answered with as much assurance as she could muster, "how are ye to feel now?"

He hurriedly answered, "I'm managing to hold it together. There haven't been any inquires since I got back here, so I suppose that's a good sign. Did you get your flight arrangements made?"

How she wished to be able to tell him she could be there within the hour, instead of simply arriving at the Galway terminal at that time, but at least they would soon be on their way. With confidence, she replied, "The arrangements be made, though we could not secure a flight as soon as we had hoped. But I managed to reserve two seats on an economy flight leaving at eight our time. That should put us in Ottawa at eight yur time, pending no problems of course. We shall come directly to yur condo, so keep a watchful eye. I be seeing to the hotel accommodations as soon as I hang up the phone. Miss Prichard and meself will be picking ye up and taking ye directly to our hotel, so be having yur bags ready so we not be losing precious time. I will be arranging our return flight when I arrive at the airport tonight." She could hear him sighing heavily and knew this news must be the best he'd received in a long while. It settled her nerves as well, as long as he stayed put. With this hurried thought, she said, "Ye just remember what I told ye earlier, and all will be fine."

"I will, Ma," he replied, "and please thank Miss Prichard for me. She was, as usual trying her best to be supportive, and I know I must have sounded rude. I don't want her to feel as if she's no longer important, or included in my life and, the way I must have sounded when she answered might possibly make her feel that way."

Cailen had to smile at her son's compassionate gesture, and she quickly relayed his feelings to the intended source. It was immediately accepted in the way in which the boy had meant, for the look on Prichard's face relayed the fact that she never once doubted Declan's intentions toward her, even if she at times questioned his mother's.

Chapter 43

ONE WELL KEPT SECRET

The evening progressed and with it soaring heat. One would think the recent storm's intensity would have brought cooler temps, but that didn't appear to be the case. Jonas sat by his wife's side in the hospital's emergency, waiting for her to open her eyes, while Will held vigil beside the pop-cooler located in the waiting room. The attending physician, following Willow's latest examination, had left for the night, but before departing, had discussed her condition with Jonas, explaining the procedures that had been applied. She had been through X-ray and Ultrasound, both of which revealed extensive vaginal tissue damage, confirming the fact that his patient had not only been abused, but raped, prompting him to take extra precaution in assuring no pregnancy by performing a vacuum aspiration prior to repairing the battered uterus and severely torn cervix. Her jaw had been dislocated, but had been maneuvered back into place without wiring. She had also required a blood transfusion and finally, to ease the emotional distress of the entire scenario, had been placed under sedation, of which she still remained.

Jonas breathed a sigh of relief as he thought about the doctor's encouraging words, for they had brought assurance that his wife, after a few days of much-needed rest, should be fine. He sat quiet, thinking how thankful he was for small mercies, as well as for central air, yet the cool breeze circulating the room did little for him at the moment, for the sweat continued to permeate his rugged face. He realized the excessive sweating was caused by nerves, how could it not be after the trying events of which he'd recently endured? But try as he might he could not rid his mind of the tremendous guilt he felt. Gazing at his sleeping wife, he couldn't help but remember the better times between them, and he silently vowed their return regardless of the tumultuous months now gone. But first things first, he must notify the family.

"Hello?" Mary Sutherland inquired, having snatched up the receiver on its second signal.

"It's Jonas, Mrs. Sutherland, I'm calling from the hospital." Suddenly thinking the situation best kept as minimal as possible, he continued, "Nothing to be alarmed about, everything's all right. I just wanted to let you know what's going on with Willow, as I know how worried you've been, and I told you I would let you know as soon as I had news. You know how dreadfully hot it's been of late? Well, apparently she's been coping with excessive heat exhaustion for awhile now. Earlier tonight it got the better of her and she was overcome. As a precautionary measure she was brought by ambulance to the hospital, checked over, and has been admitted for a few days."

"What!" Mary exclaimed, certain there was more to this than what she was being told. "What is going on, Jonas?" He was well-aware of his mother-in-law's uncanny ability to seek out the truth, and he swallowed hard, as she further inquired, "What are you *not* trying to tell me? I have never heard of a body having to be hospitalized for becoming overheated. Are you certain you don't mean heat stroke?"

Jonas was not in the mood to argue the political correctness of a medical situation or bat about a medical diagnosis; besides he could not very well divulge what had actually happened, and since the doctor had confirmed a complete recovery, he found no need to upset her by going into detail about something she could do nothing about. With this thought in mind, he replied, "The doctor didn't say. He just commented on the excessive heat of late, and that she was dehydrated and needing a few days rest in hospital." He hadn't actually lied, she was dehydrated and in need of rest, he just hadn't given the total report.

With this, Mary questioned, "Is she able to come on the phone?"

"No," Jonas replied, "I'm not in her room at the moment, I'm calling from the nurse's station."

"Do you think I should have the hired hand drive me in? I assume she's in Ottawa General?"

"Yes, but she's only going to be in a couple of days and there's really no need to drive all that distance. Her phone is back in service, so I'll have her call you when she gets home."

One could tell by Mary's elongated pause that she was not overly amused, and she carried on the intended silence in order to emphasize it. She was certain her son-in-law was again sidestepping an important issue, and doing so intentionally, but she was not going to press it. The absence of her daughter had been explained. She was fine, according to what was being told, so she would wait to hear from her daughter, but before Jonas got off the line, she said, "I'll inform the boys of their mother's whereabouts and the reason for her hospitalization. They will want to know, after all they've been kept as much in the dark as have I. Now you be sure to have Willow phone, and give her my love when you next see her."

Silently emitting a sigh of relief, Jonas replied, "I will, Mrs. Sutherland. By the way, Will is here with me. He was concerned about Willow and arrived at the house at the same time as me. We had both just managed to beat that horrific storm actually. Is everything all right at the farm?"

"Yes, we faired not badly," Mary reported confidently. "The funnel touched down about a mile from here, tore up a few trees, and removed the roof from that derelict barn just down the road, making it appear more unsightly than ever, but we didn't suffer any damage here. We were lucky. I just wish this heat would subside. It appeared to, immediately following the storm that is, but it's hotter than ever now. Oh well, the electric fans will just have to work harder, and the cows will have to stay beneath that row of shade trees lining the west side of the back pasture."

Though Mary could not see it, Jonas nod his head in agreement, as he replied, "That's for sure. Let's hope this heat breaks without need of another storm," but before he could continue, Mary cut in, inquiring if Willow's house had suffered damage, to which he replied, "A bit, mostly broken window glass that blew out from the pressure in the house, but nothing that isn't fixable. I'll get on it as soon as I can. Now I really have to get going. I want to spend a few more minutes with Willow before they give me the boot. I'll talk with you soon, and I'll call the boys and catch them up on the goings on — by the way, with all that's happened did you manage to find out if they suffered any damage. They live on the opposite side of town which was far from the tornado's path, but the wind would still have been strong. Not to worry though, I'll find out when I call."

"Yes, you do that," Mary said. "Tell them I'm thinking of them, and will ring them in the morning. But I will be here should they decide to call before then."

Mary's conversation remained fresh in his mind as Jonas returned to his wife's bedside, causing him to wonder if he should have told her everything, after all she had a right to know, yet it wasn't his place to divulge what Willow would consider secret. She had always been that way when it came to anything she considered fuel for the misunderstandings between she and her mother, and he couldn't see the latest happening being any different. Besides it was up to her to fill in her mother, he just wanted what would be best in that respect, but it was a totally different story with regard to who had attacked Willow, and he would not rest until justice was served.

Chapter 44

A WHOPPER YOU SAY?

The next morning Jonas arrived early at the hospital to find Willow safely secured in a ward on the fourth floor. Sunshine-embedded heat streamed through the window, determined to set yet another record, but the women in the room paid it no mind for the conditioned air circulating throughout was keeping everyone cool and comfortable. He could see the horrendous bruises upon his wife's face, causing his own to wince in regard to the ferocity in which they must have been delivered, and he swore he would avenge each and every mark procured upon her body. She stirred as he approached the bed, and opened her eyes, staring at him as if she could hardly believe he was there. Yet her eyes held a look of shame, as if she had been caught in a seductive dance, the kind that had landed her where she now was. Her stare could not hold with his and reluctantly fell away. He stepped closer, cautiously reaching out to touch her hand, as he said, "There's no need to feel that way with me. I'm just thankful you weren't hurt worse."

Willow's eyes traveled to the destination of her husband's intended touch and she briefly considered retracting her hand, but changed her mind, and let it accept the comforting feel of his hand.

She knew what had happened was not his fault, she alone must bear the brunt of that tiding, and she would accept her guilt in the portion she had enticed, but she'd be damned if she would accept total blame. That sullied portion belonged to Declan Quinn. She realized she had reached the end of that road, but the experience of her journey upon it was one that would forever remain embedded within her mind. She knew he could not be let away with what he had done, yet how could she bring about his atonement when she shared so much of the enticement which had caused it? All that time, days, weeks, months in which they had danced to the made-up melody within their minds, regardless of her constant reminders of how far their relationship could be let grow. How many times had she told him that they could be nothing more than friends? Yet she had not held to her own volition, nor had she held *him* to the rules within the game they were playing. "Was it a game?" she thought, her mind sweeping back over the entire farce, making her guilt even more impossible to cope with. But her want of valediction did little to ease her mind, nor did it remove the pain in her body caused by his vicious attack, the brutal tearing of her cervix, or the embarrassment she must now cope with because of it. How could she explain this to her family, let alone to Jonas? Her mind flashed to that unexpected, yet delectable encounter between them; she still savored it, she forever would, but Declan's unexpected attack had only brought pain, compounded by fear of ever being touched again by any man.

Looking up at her husband in a sheepish manner, she replied, "Yes, I suppose I should be thankful for small mercies. Thank you for coming. I think Will was here awhile ago, I'm not really sure, the pain medication they keep feeding me make things hard to clarify, but I'm pretty sure he was. Have you let the boys know? Please don't tell them what happened, I mean … It's … well, so damn embarrassing,

I mean, how clumsy can I be? It's been incredibly hot, unbearably so and I was upstairs checking on the opened windows. I apparently became light-headed while coming down the stairs. When I came to I realized I'd fallen, must have banged my face pretty good on impact. On top of that Will called, and I tried getting to the phone maybe quicker than I should and lost my balance and, well ... I've had a bit of problem with spotting lately. When I tried getting down the hall to the bathroom I collapsed - but you don't need to hear about that - female stuff and all, I mean we've certainly had our arguments about that, haven't we? I should be home in a few days, and I can speak with the boys then - oh yes and Mom."

Jonas wondered at this odd reaction, not to mention this ridiculous synopsis of what she claimed had happened, she'd even forgotten to mention the tornado in the yarn, though had she, maybe her warped account of things might have had her sucked up into it, stripped of all clothing, and then deposited on the hall floor where she'd been discovered. "Why not?" he thought, "couldn't be any further from the actual truth; furthermore it was a feat in itself that she would think me gullible enough to believe such a whopper," but he would play along, for now, and would not press the issue, or for the rapist's name.

Clearing his throat, he said, "We don't have to revisit there, that's water under the bridge, and besides I think we've both traveled a ways since then, hopefully toward each another."

He could see it was difficult for her to smile, but she managed as well as she could, as she said, "That would be nice, Jonas. What's that old saying? 'You always hurt the ones you love, the ones you shouldn't hurt at all.' Maybe those words are from an old song, I'm not sure, but I tend to believe they apply to us."

"I suppose they do," he replied. "We've certainly put them to the test enough. But I want you to know that I'm truly sorry for everything, each and every anger-filled word, every wrong doing — all of it. If I could take it all back I would, please know I would."

"It's okay," she said softly. "I, more than anyone know how things can escalate out of control, and before you know it you yourself are out of control. It gets to the point where you can't stop, let alone stay on course, or move toward what you hope to achieve. I know how hard-headed I am, let alone stubborn. Now I see where it's truly gotten me."

Tears filled her eyes as she spoke, causing Jonas to bend down with intention of kissing her. She instantly pulled back as if his lips held poison. Realizing her reaction could be chocked up to the recent attack, he quickly said, "It's okay, Willow, I'm sorry. I should have realized how that might be taken out of context; I won't press you."

She was not long in apologizing, for she did understand the way in which it had been meant. She knew she would not only have to come to terms with the rape, but more importantly the obvious fact that her husband truly did mean what he said, and with time and patience would be the one to lead her to a far better place than where she now found herself.

As they quietly spoke, Will Sutherland sauntered into the room carrying a huge potted fern of which he awkwardly placed on the table adjacent Willow's bed. "Hey there, cuz," he cheerfully stated, "you're looking pretty good — in fact you're beginning to look like your lovely self again. And I see my old buddy is keeping you company. How's it going, guys?"

Extending his hand, Jonas replied, "I think she's looking pretty fine too, Will."

Grabbing his friend's arm, Will exclaimed, "Well you can't keep a Sutherland down! Not for long anyway! But if you would kindly excuse us, Low, I need to pull Crosby away long enough to discuss something, okay?"

Smiling at her cousin's well-intentioned antics, Willow replied, "That's alright, just don't keep him too long," then proceeded to admire her newly acquired mini palm as the two men stepped into the corridor.

Gazing around as if to be sure no-one could overhear, Will said, "I was just at the police station to see if they've any updates, and by their reaction they've obviously run the plate, but me not being next of kin they wouldn't divulge anything. You'd best get on over there as soon as you can, before the son-of-a-bitch disappears."

Nodding his head in compliance, Jonas replied, "I was in touch with them this morning before I came to the hospital, but they hadn't as yet any news. I'll go in and tell Willow I have to meet with the insurance adjuster about the storm damage to the house. You know I don't think she even knows there was a storm, let alone a tornado, but I'll come up with an excuse, even if it's telling her I have to check into work for a bit. Don't worry, I've got it covered. I've had the same feeling as you, and that fucker isn't getting anywhere if I have anything to do with it. Can you spend a bit of time with Willow after I leave?"

"Sure can," Will replied. "Grandson is at the sitter's, and I've taken the day off. If you need me, I'm there. Now let's get the ball bouncing!"

Chapter 45

ESCAPE GOES ARRAY

The flight carrying Cailen Quinn and Matilda Prichard touched down at the Ottawa Airport at its scheduled time, and the ladies lost no time in arriving at Declan's condo, only to find him in the throes of hysterics. He had convinced himself that it was only a matter of time before the entire Ottawa police force would come kicking down his door, secure him in cuffs, and haul him off to solitaire confinement. He couldn't embrace the women tight enough, all the while screaming his need to board the first flight heading for Ireland. He would not be pacified, regardless of what they said, which left Cailen no choice but to suggest Prichard administer a heavy dose of his nighttime medication. But the state in which he was now in told them the meds in their normal form would not likely work swift enough, so to ensure not only rapid results, but prolonged, Prichard opened her medication valise and secured a vile of Hypnovel.

The following morning found the scorching Ottawa sunshine filtering through the mini blinds into Declan's bedroom, as Cailen and Prichard sat chatting, sipping freshly delivered coffee while Declan lay asleep before them. They had no way of knowing the outcome of the boy's untimely visit to Willow, nor did they know that it would only be a matter of time before his biggest fear would materialize, yet if their thoughts had been directed in the proper way they would already expect what would rightfully come, but Cailen Quinn was as determined as ever, and like always, would contend with it in the manner in which she always did. Her first intention, as earlier relayed to Prichard, had been to gather her son as quickly as possible and head straight for Galway, yet a peculiar feeling of which she could not explain told her to wait.

"How long do you intend on staying, Mrs. Quinn?" Prichard inquired as she set her empty cup upon the glass-topped nightstand.

The Quinn matriarch sat rigid, not answering; instead drawing short sips from her cup while studying her sleeping boy. Her thoughts remained upon his welfare, regardless of whether he was in the right or not, but even should he have done what he claimed, she would not desert him. She found it difficult to fathom, and though her son had always been impetuous, she couldn't help but lay the blame where she was convinced it rightfully lay, right in the lap of Willow Crosby. But that would be fully as difficult to prove as would be Declan raping her, even though he had admitted to having done so, as she silently thought, "He admitted that to *me*, no one else knows, and I be certain the tramp would be far too embarrassed to admit she had enticed a boy of Declan's age, seducing him via the Internet, therefore both encouraging and enticing him to come to her — and me, like a bloody Eegit, decides to play right into her focking hands by sending him to a school not far from her blasted door."

Cailen's mood could be seen as plainly as the sunbeams streaming through the mini blinds, causing Prichard to inquire if there was anything she could do.

"Not at the moment, Matilda," Cailen answered. "But I be thanking ye for the generous offer. I realize I be not the best company, but I need to gather me thoughts in order to decide what is to be done."

Prichard's mood was certainly not one of the finest she'd ever experienced, and it certainly didn't help to be constantly kept in the dark about issues she might otherwise be able to assist with - at the very least - be a sounding board that could very well lend support. She knew that one solitary person cannot shoulder the weight of the world, nor can they continue to deny a situation that may be too intense to handle alone. Still the strong Irish matron sitting across from her was determined to do just that, and it showed through the defiant look upon her face.

Going to check on Declan, Prichard said, "He should be rousing by now. That injection should have worn off long ago, yet he sleeps as if it were just administered. Mrs. Quinn, would you hand me my medical kit from the table? I want to check his breathing. His pulse is a bit erratic, judging by the secondhand movement on my wristwatch - definitely faster than it should be - and his pupils are still dilated. That should not be happening. Their size should have diminished long ago along with the sedation, unless there is another substance in his system that we are unaware of."

With immediate concern, Cailen asked, "Is it to be serious?"

Continuing her examination, Prichard replied, "I cannot be certain, Mrs. Quinn, but it might not be a bad idea to have him checked by a doctor."

When it came to Matilda Prichard's observations, Cailen was the first to not doubt them, and this was no different, as she secured the phone and punched in 911. Before long the ambulance arrived, and the same paramedic team that had attended Willow Crosby the prior night, came swiftly through Declan's opened door with stretcher in tow. Prichard quickly filled them in as to the injection she had administered, being sure to inform them of the boy's medical condition to date, while his mother answered the many questions bombarding her. A few of them appeared rather scathing, but she answered to her best ability. She was certain the medical team must think her and Prichard irresponsible, or possibly drug addicts that had blatantly overdosed young Quinn, but before either knew what was happening, the unconscious boy had been ventilated, connected to IV, and strapped upon his transportation.

The concerned women followed close behind the moving stretcher as the paramedics directed it toward the back of the waiting ambulance. Prichard, fighting to hold composure, did her utmost to steady a very nervous Cailen whose demeanor was now bordering hysterics. Holding vigil, while the stretcher was secured inside, they couldn't help but remember this exact procedure being carried out a year earlier, but that had turned out fine, hopefully this would as well. Cailen, desperately holding to sanity, climbed in beside her son, while Prichard rode shotgun up front. A few curious onlookers had gathered, but not recognizing the occupants inside the vehicle, quickly dispersed to other areas of interest. Without need of siren but red lights flashing, the big white ambulance pulled away from the curb, and proceeded in the direction of Ottawa General.

Chapter 46

THE TYPICAL RUNAROUND

The main doors of the Ottawa police station closed behind Jonas Crosby in an authoritative manner; somewhat giving the illusion that once you entered you weren't soon getting out, but he gave it little thought as he quickly approached the front desk to inquire with whom he needed to speak with in regard to the matter he'd come about.

"That would be Detective Levi Mann," informed the attending clerk efficiently. "He's been assigned the case," and he quickly punched in the required extension number. "Yes, Detective," he stated, "Jonas Crosby is here at the front desk … Yes, I'll let him through," and he motioned Jonas through the turnstile located in the middle of a wooden barrier running from the right corner of the desk to the outside wall.

As he stepped through the go-round, Jonas was greeted by a fairly tall young man, dressed in casual attire, looking no more than thirty years old at the most. "Mr. Crosby," the young man cordially stated while extending his hand, "I'm Levi Mann. How is your wife doing?"

With a sober look, Jonas answered, "Let's put it this way, Detective, she's seen better days."

Nodding his head in compliance, Mann replied, "No doubt. Please follow me to my office; there are a few things I'd like to discuss. I've run that plate number, and I have some news I think you'll find enlightening."

"I don't find any of this shit enlightening," Jonas stated seriously. "The thug that plate is registered to doesn't deserve any notoriety, other than to become known for the sadistic bastard he is. I've no doubt the smug asshole beat my wife then raped her, and I want justice served as soon as possible."

The detective glanced up from the report he was holding. He could well see the irate husband before him was determined in his cause, and if the plate owner was guilty of the assumed crime then the man had every right to feel the anger he was experiencing, but first it had to be proven. The detective's mind traveled back to a few similar cases, some of which the perpetrators were never tried, let alone found, but he must try his best to be sure the same didn't happen in this case, as he said, "I can't blame you one bit, Mr. Crosby. This can't be easy for you."

"You got that right, Detective; let's just say the son-of-a-bitch is fortunate I'm going through the proper channels."

Realizing to what Jonas was referring; Mann casually laid the report on his desk, and said, "You do realize this is a police case, Mr. Crosby, not a personal vendetta to be carried out however you can."

Nodding his head, Jonas replied, "I do. But I also know the speed in which a case like this is often dealt with. Regardless of that, it does nothing to comfort my wife, or remove the pain inflicted upon her, *nor* does it remove the physiological damage she will no doubt live with for the rest of her life."

Knowing there was little to be said by way of word; Detective Mann simply nodded in compliance, and opened the report. He motioned Jonas to sit in the chair in front of the desk while he settled in his own. He studied the report, carefully checking a couple of notes at the bottom of the page, while Jonas did his best to remain calm, that of which was becoming more difficult with each passing second.

Scratching his chin in an uncouth manner, Mann said, "The plate is registered to a nineteen year-old man by the name of Declan Eamon Quinn living at this address," and proceeded to show it to Jonas, who amusingly remarked, "Hmm … Sloan. I know that area well; the Farmer's Market is on that street."

The detective had already surmised by Jonas' blatant demeanor that there might possibly be a problem, not that Mann could blame him, but he could not be let take matters into his own hands, as he said, "Mr. Crosby, I do realize how you must feel - I have a wife too - but you must leave this up to the police. We'll take care of it, and Quinn will be apprehended and held for questioning."

Jonas scoffed, as he snapped, "Questioning?! Do you really think that zit-faced dickhead is going to confess?"

Mann swiftly replied, "I realize how that sounds, but Quinn first has to be brought in. It's often the case in matters such as this that the body language reveals much more than the suspect openly admits. If he raped your wife, we'll nail him."

Jonas rose to his feet while shaking his head in an unrelenting manner. He allowed himself a few moments contemplation, then said, "Somehow I find that hard to swallow. I know how I must sound - you can hardly blame me - but these assholes are let walk far too often instead of made pay the price for what they do. Of course he's going to deny it - that is if you can even find him - and he's sure-as-hell not going to hang around waiting to see if you come after him, now is he?"

"I'm sorry, Mr. Crosby," the detective said in a reprehensible tone, "but you must leave this to us and not go rogue trying to deliverer your own brand of justice."

Half-laughing, Jonas replied, "*Ha*, that's a good one. Try telling my battered wife that, and while you're at it try asking yourself if you'd be this calm if it was *your* wife. However I do respect your position, but one way or the other Quinn is going to pay for this, either by your hand, or mine."

"I'm warning you, Mr. Crosby, do not go after this guy. Give me your word that you won't."

"I'm not planning to go after him, but I'm not promising I won't either. Look, this is why I brought the plate number to you in the first place, so it could be run, and this skank found! So far all I'm hearing is the usual *we'll look after it*, but this attack took place the night before last, and I brought you that number along with my official complaint last evening. What have you done about it, other than run the plate and obtain a name?"

"Mr. Crosby, these things take time."

"That's what I expected you to say. Yet it didn't take much *time* to abuse and rape my wife! If you don't get out there and find the fucker you never will! He ain't sticking around, and I'm *not* letting him get away!"

"Mr. Crosby, I don't need to remind you that should you interfere in this case you will be charged with obstruction. You cannot go around attacking people and be let away with that, regardless of the issue, or what this suspect has or has not done. Do I make myself clear?"

"My answer to that, Detective, is just find the fucker!"

With that, Jonas left the office and headed straight for the parking lot. He was boiling mad, yet as much as he hated to admit it the detective was right, but as he drove toward the hospital he couldn't help thinking about the days of vigilantes and their brand of justice. They may have carried things too far in many cases, yet in some they could not be blamed, especially when those responsible for committing horrific crimes had managed to manipulate the system and get off, as he thought, "How is that justice for the victims, as well as for others bereaved? I guess the only comfort one can take from something like that is in knowing that Karma truly does exist, it visits each and every one of us, and yours is about to happen, Quinn."

Chapter 47

WHEN TOLD TO JUMP NOT EVERYONE ASKS HOW HIGH

The ambulance arrived in the emergency, and Declan Quinn was quickly wheeled into a treatment room, followed closely behind by his mother and Matilda Prichard — that is until the attending physician stepped into their path, stating that they must remain in the waiting area, and he would report to them as soon as he had news. A miffed Cailen, not used to treatment of this kind, was most indignant, but Prichard stepped up to the plate, boldly stating what she surmised might have happened, and also what she had administered during the boy's anxiety attack the prior evening. This not only lessened Cailen's stress level, but the doctor, rethinking his decision, let them both remain in the treatment area provided they stayed out of the way.

The next morning found young Quinn still unresponsive but his stats normal. This was most encouraging as the doctor, having run several tests, had determined his current condition to be that of consuming Prozac at some point prior to receiving the Hypnovel, but any danger he might have faced had now passed, and he should soon be waking. To assure proper recovery, the medical team had taken the necessary precautions to assure all went as expected, as the doctor directed the concerned ladies to the adjacent waiting room with assurance they would be notified the instant he was settled in a room.

The exhausted ladies had taken up residence upon one of the waiting room's vinyl beige sofas, each sipping lukewarm coffee from a convenient beverage dispenser, and quietly chatting. Their conversation consisted of small talk as both openly did their best to avoid the current dilemma.

"From what I've seen thus far, Ottawa certainly has a fine medical facility," Prichard stated confidently before taking another sip of her dishwater Java.

"Aye," Cailen replied, quickly emptying her cup, "everyone appears quite efficient."

"I would have to agree," Prichard stated in acknowledgment, "but the coffee leaves a lot to be desired."

In an outright scoff, Cailen replied, *"Aye! To be sure!* I have never to swallow anything so vile, 'tis certainly not Bridget's!"

"Ah-no," Prichard stated, shaking her head in compliance, "that it is not. But I suppose it is better than nothing at all; least it wets the whistle."

The mundane conversation continued as each kept watch on the clock. Finally the doctor came into the waiting area to inform them that Declan had been moved to a room on the fourth floor, but he was obviously not amused when questioned as to whether or not the room was private with its own nursing staff, and the resounding answer he gave made it perfectly clear that Cailen would accept what was offered, and be thankful for it. The Irish matriarch stiffened while defiance rose to the forefront, but it was soon suppressed when Prichard's hand settled upon her forearm. A swift glance at the English nanny's expression reminded her that they were not at home, and the usual tactics were totally out of line here. With her self-absorbed intention curtailed, Cailen apologized before suggesting they adjourn to her son's room.

They arrived to find him sitting up in bed, somewhat dazed, but aware enough that he greeted them upon entry.

"It makes me spirit soar to see ye too, me boy" Cailen stated happily as she engulfed him tightly. As she embraced him, Prichard patiently waited her turn, making use of the time to gather her thoughts. In her mind, she continued to believe that his obsession for the woman whom he could not refrain from contacting was the reason for this recent turmoil, not debauchery. She and Cailen had discussed Willow Crosby many times and each knew their feelings in regard to the woman, but without knowing the details of the present situation it was impossible for Prichard to properly comment, and it showed in the way she addressed the young man.

Encasing him in her arms, she compassionately cried, "Master Declan, you poor, poor boy. Please know that I am here for you however I can be throughout this entire ordeal. I do hope you understand what I mean."

Pulling back, Declan immediately stated, "Then you know what I've done."

Prichard looked imploringly into his eyes, and said, "Well, I do know your obsession for the woman you consistently pursued has brought this unfortunate situation upon you - if that is to what you are referring."

The boy suddenly realized that Prichard did not know the entire facts; if she did she wouldn't have stated her concern in the way she just had. He couldn't see how she would ever condone rape, let alone abuse. Glancing toward his mother as if he might be sorry for his answer, he said, "Well, not quite, Miss Prichard, you see —"

"Declan, me boy," Cailen abruptly stated, cutting him off, "Miss Prichard does not be needing an untimely burden placed upon her. That be not her position in this family. Do ye understand what I mean?"

He knew only too well what she meant, but as he quietly thought about it he really could use Prichard's remarkable understanding, and unyielding friendship. She had always stood by him, more than his mother in many ways, but he realized that even her remarkable strength could not aid him, and he couldn't help but feel remorse for having realized this sobering fact. Maybe nothing could help him this time, not even the Quinn wealth.

The three carried on conversing when out in the corridor came the sound of Jonas Crosby's voice, complying to that of Will Sutherland's calling out to him from the room directly across the hall. "Hey, Crosby, glad you're finally back! Do you realize how hard it is to keep your wife from talking, especially when she knows she's not supposed to?"

With a half-laugh, Jonas answered, "*Ha*, you don't need to tell me, Will, I know only too well what Willow is like."

The men's jovial conversation could not avoid traveling across the corridor, and upon hearing Willow's name, Declan's heart felt as if it had suddenly stopped. He couldn't have been mistaken with what had heard, after all how many people have that unusual name, so he listened, hoping to hear more while his mother and Prichard sat chatting between themselves.

A fit of coughing preceded the now familiar voice as it reached Declan's ears. It was raspy, rattling with mucus, but it was undeniably Willow's, as it said, "It's not like I can help it, guys. Do you honestly think I like lying here, twiddling my thumbs all day hoping the pain medication continues to keep this discomfort under control?"

"Sorry, Willow," Jonas' voice was heard stating, "we don't mean to tease; we're only trying to help you feel better."

"Yeah," Will was heard adding, "it can't be much fun having to stay put and remain quiet. Can you forgive us?"

"I'll have to think about that," Willow was heard replying in a choking manner. A few moments passed while she cleared her throat. Finally her voice resumed, stating, "Well, I've thought about it, and I do. Besides the nurse who was here earlier said she'd be back to change the intravenous bags and give me something for pain."

Declan strained to hear every syllable Willow spoke, making him wonder as to whether he should inform his mother of his discovery, but there was no need, for the lighthearted conversation filling his ears had already made its way into Cailen and Prichard's, and they both vowed to take a little trip across the hall as soon as the chance to do so presented itself.

Chapter 48

INCHING EVER CLOSER

Late afternoon had arrived and with it another storm. Lightning seared the sky, accompanied with horrendous cracks of thunder, bringing the recent tornado to mind, and jostling everyone's nerves in wonderment of whether it might be shaping up for a repeat performance. Wind could be heard outside the closed windows, as treetops bent to its will whenever a strong gust hit them in just the right way, but so far the storm remained just that, a storm. Willow lay sound asleep, the result of the latest injection, shored up by a newly installed intravenous bag now sending its soothing medication on down the line. Jonas and Will had left for a much deserved dinner but had vowed to return to spend the evening, while across the hall, Declan, taking advantage of the downtime before dinner would arrive, was catching a nap.

Cailen and Prichard realized the hour, but they also realized the time was ripe to take a look at the infamous woman across the hall. They looked at each other in a precarious manner then proceeded on their journey. To anyone passing in the corridor their plight might appear innocent, simply two ladies on their way to visit a sick friend and possibly lend support in time of need. But to anyone who might be wise to the entire scenario it was two women who had a score to settle. A loud clap of thunder rattled the window, but the sleeping woman did not stir, and it appeared a welcomed relief to the two women who now stood viewing her.

Cailen's eyes held a menacing look. Prichard's simply scanned the woman on the bed before her. But it wasn't long before the Irish matriarch took the initiative, and stepped to the foot of the bed where the medical chart hung in full display. Grasping it in her hand, she began thumbing the pages, three in all, containing the recent history, stats, and medication of the patient's name it carried. After having viewed the rape description, Cailen decided to check it out for herself, and before Prichard could stop her, she had removed the sheet to reveal the patient laid-out before her, now clad in a skimpy blue hospital gown which barely came to the knees.

"Mrs. Quinn," Prichard stated in a subdued but serious tone, "what do you think you're doing?"

Not taking her eyes from her mission, Cailen replied, "I be having a look for meself."

Totally shocked, Prichard said, "I do not think that wise in the least. You do not have the authority to examine her, and a nurse may step in at any moment," but the determined head of the Quinn clan paid her no mind, as she nonchalantly lift the gown to survey the damage.

The two women could not overlook the excessive amount of stitching along each side of the clitoris, now drenched in scarlet disinfectant, and further scan revealed the bruising now appearing in numerous areas on the body, the worst being the chin and left cheek. The closed left eye was surrounded in a ghastly hue of purplish black which showed no sign of fading anytime soon.

"So this be the *cunt* that enticed me boy," Cailen announced in an amused tone as she replaced the sheet.

Giving the impression that she wished to be anywhere but her present location, Prichard replied, "Apparently so. But it still does not give you the right to invade her privacy as you just did, Mrs. Quinn, and I will not be a party to it any longer."

With that statement she turned to leave, but Cailen was not long reminding her that her precious charge was a victim fully as much as the colorfully bruised woman before them, and if she cared for him half as much as she claimed, she would continue to support the vendetta which had to be carried out.

"I've recorded her address in me mind, Matilda," Cailen stated in an ominous tone as she moved around the bed, "and I be calling on her when she returns to it. 'Tis the least I can do under the circumstances. Meanwhile we shall take up residence at the Capital Elite where suites be already reserved."

With surprise, Prichard asked, "When did you do that?"

"Awhile ago, while ye were taking a rest," Cailen touted as if Prichard should have already known this. Moving toward the door, she continued, "We shall check in this evening, as soon as Declan has finished his evening meal."

The ladies no sooner left Willow's room when the first of the dinner trays began arriving. As they stepped back into Declan's room they found him sitting like a king awaiting his dinner, stating he was ravenous, and couldn't wait to sink his pearly whites into whatever fare was being offered. Cailen quickly filled him in to her intentions for the evening, making sure he had the suite numbers at Capital Elite.

"Now are ye to be certain ye be understanding everything?" she asked while swinging the over-bed table across his lap to accommodate the newly delivered tray.

"Yes, Ma, but I hope you and Miss Prichard are not leaving already."

"Not just yet, me darling one, but we must soon adjourn for dinner. It has been a rather long day for us, as ye can well imagine. Now enjoy this lovely meal - such as it is - and we shall be back first thing in the morning."

As the ladies started toward the elevators they noticed two men stepping out of the opened doors and proceeding in their direction. The men politely nodded while passing, but continued down the corridor until they came to the room opposite Declan's. They appeared to converse briefly, and then entered the room. Cailen, realizing who they must be, looked with astonishment toward Prichard, who said nothing, but the look on her face revealed plenty. How she wished to be home in Ireland - better still England - as she endearingly thought, "Maybe I should have never left."

Chapter 49

WHEN SHIT HITS THE FAN
IT DOES NOT SMELL SWEET

Willow lay asleep, unaware of the brash intrusion not long before, as her husband, accompanied by her cousin Will, plopped themselves into chairs beneath the window. A dinner tray, awaiting consumption, sat on the swing table adjacent the bed as the two quietly conversed about Jonas' visit to the police.

In a tone that already surmised what the answer would be, Will asked, "Have they come up with anything?"

"What do you think?"

"Well I would hope they've done *something*, put out a bulletin, that sort of thing."

"I spoke with a Detective Mann, a young guy who looks to be barely out of Police College - mind you looks can be deceiving - and he seemed genuinely concerned. He ran the plate. It's registered to a Declan Quinn in the new condo high-rise over on Sloan - and get this - he's nineteen, according to the info. Makes you wonder what in hell Willow was thinking … then again if I had been acting sensibly maybe she wouldn't have paid him no mind, regardless of his age. But thirty five years is a bit much, wouldn't you say?"

Totally surprised, Will replied, "Well, yeah!"

"I know," Jonas stated openly, "it's absurd. But I still share the blame."

As the two conversed, a shriek of laughter was heard emitting from across the hall, but it was silenced as quickly as it happened, as if the person emitting the noise suddenly clued-in to the establishment they were in.

"What the hell was that?" Will questioned, rising to his feet then sauntering toward the opened door.

"See anything?" Jonas asked, getting to his feet as well.

Straining to look, Will answered, "Nope, can't say that I do, but it's obvious someone's moving around for I can detect shadows on the wall."

A muffled laugh was heard along with a woman's voice, stating, "Mr. Quinn, you must behave yourself, and get back into that bed before someone finds out. I'm really putting my hatband on the line by what I'm doing, not to mention what might happen should you fall from trying to get me into bed with you. Really now, you have to stop!"

"Did that woman just say what I thought she did?" Jonas questioned as though he could hardly believe his ears.

In amusement, Will replied, "Yeah, she said Quinn, I'm sure she did. How many people with that name do you think are around these parts?" and he glanced back at his friend as if no answer was needed.

"Only one," Jonas growled, and proceeded to move toward the door.

"Wait," Will cautioned, "that nurse is still in there. By the sound of it the asshole's coming onto her too. What a fucking dick!"

Stepping slightly backward, Jonas replied, "Well she can't stay in there forever. We'll just keep an eye peeled for when she leaves."

The evening wore on. The dinner tray, long cold, had been removed from Willow's room, and visiting hours were fast drawing to a close. The room across the hall showed no further sign of activity as the young nurse, certain she had not been detected, had slipped out on her way to other duties. Jonas, realizing the nurse had gone, as well as the fact that he must soon leave for the night, approached the room with caution, while Will Sutherland took up position at his flank. As the two men stepped into the room, Declan Quinn peered up from the magazine he was reading, and asked, "Who the hell are you two?" and immediately secured the call buzzer in his hand.

"Don't really know if you'll much like who I am, and I wouldn't push that button if I were you," Jonas replied, and proceeded closer to the bed.

Will Sutherland fought the urge to pound the kid until there was nothing left but a grease spot, yet he knew better, and remained still.

"Am I supposed to know you?" Declan inquired, the tone of his voice revealing nerves moving about in his stomach. He suddenly wished his mother and Prichard's decision to not return that evening had not been made.

Slowly shaking his head, Jonas answered, "Na, you don't know *me*, but you sure as hell know my wife."

The boy sat quiet, studying the man before him while at the same time keeping tab on the one bringing up the rear. His gut told him these two were there for something he would not relish, but he would not be intimidated, after-all he was a Quinn, and they had experienced this kind of confrontation many times. They had always reigned supreme, and this would be no different, as he said, "Know your wife, you say. How do you figure — I mean, who is she?"

Drawing a deep breath, Jonas replied, "You not only know her, but you *beat* the hell out of her before you *raped* her."

The shit had hit the fan, and it did not smell sweet. The young Irishman knew he had been found out, but regardless of that he would not appear guilty, and he'd be damned if he would cower. Holding himself erect with his finger posed on the buzzer, he replied, "I don't know what you're on about, dude. You've obviously got the wrong guy, I mean, why on earth would I be guilty of something like that? I don't even know you, let alone your *wife* — shit you're an old man — your wife must be fully as ancient, so why in hell would I be fecking a cunt that old?"

Jonas was beside himself with anger, not to mention disgust toward the obnoxious attitude he was receiving, and he lunged at the kid. Will, fully as angered but keeping a clear head, grabbed his friend's arm, and pulled him back. Jonas fought to free himself, but Will held on, dragging him backward, as he snapped, "Don't! We'll call Detective Mann and get him down here."

Declan could hear this, and boldly stated, "Go ahead and call whomever you like. You can't prove anything — *I* didn't do anything to anyone — let alone your dried-up old prune of a wife! Who do you think you're speaking to anyway? Don't you recognize my surname?"

Jonas could not believe the boy's pretention, as he snapped, "I don't give two hoots in hell what your family name is! I know *what* you are, and you're damn well going to pay for what you did to Willow."

Young Quinn's temper went off like a firecracker, and he screamed, *"Don't you threaten me! I can buy and sell you in a second!"*

"Is that supposed to impress me?" Jonas questioned, not believing the extent of the kid's arrogance. "You can shove it squarely up your ass! My neighbor got your plate number when you were slithering out of the driveway like the cowardly *snake* you are!"

Staring his confronter down, Declan yelled, *"I don't know why you're trying to pin something on me when you've no-one to blame but yourself! If you were able to keep up with your woman she'd have no reason to go looking elsewhere! So stop your sick insinuations and quit trying to hang the blame on the first guy you can! Now get out of my sight before I have you removed!"*

Jonas' anger had reached its limit, and he snapped, "Willow has refused to say what happened or who attacked her! But I *know* it was *you*, you cocky little bastard, and if you step one foot toward her again you will be sorry!"

Will, no longer trying to hold his friend at bay, growled, "Don't think for one minute that you're getting away with it, money or no money, Quinn. You did it! You're as guilty as sin and all your bragging about who you are, and what you can do will not help you one iota! I *saw* what you did to my cousin!"

Young Quinn's quick-witted, self-absorbed nature kicked in quicker than he might have liked, for even though Will had meant his words in an entirely different way, Declan openly revealed his guilt, when he snapped, "You didn't see a thing because no one was there!"

"So you admit it!" Jonas exclaimed, hastily shoving his doubled fists into his pockets before he could smash them into the jeering mug before him.

In outright retort, Declan snapped, "I did nothing of the sort, and you two can leave right now!"

The overly-heated confrontation had alerted security, and two uniformed hospital guards, accompanied with the familiar nurse, rushed into the room, demanding an explanation of what was going on; ending by telling the two disgruntled men they must leave immediately.

Declan, taking advantage of the situation, feigned sudden illness, demanding the nurse sedate him before summoning his mother from Capital Elite.

Jonas could hardly believe how well the kid could act, but he also realized it would do he and Will no good to retaliate. Holding his arms in the air, he said, "I'm leaving, no need to press the issue here, but I want Quinn to know that this is not finished, and I will be engaging both the police, and my lawyer."

Will, who also held his arms in an upward position, said, "Hey, guys, we didn't come in here to cause trouble. Mr. Quinn started that when he began screaming like the spoiled brat he is, but my friend and I are leaving peacefully."

It was plain to see that Declan felt he was home-free as the guards escorted the two men out the door, leaving the young nurse to attend her duties.

"Do you still wish me to phone your mother and sedate you?" she inquired while she plumped the pillow behind his head.

Smiling in a provocative manner, Declan replied, "No, it's not necessary, but I would love a soothing backrub and, possibly *something* to help me sleep." He stretched his arms in the air, but before turning to his stomach, said, "I hardly think anyone will bother me again tonight, so how about stretching out beside me for a little while. Surely you could do that for a young man in need ... a young man that's ... well, been upset by a couple of fossils doing their best to show they're still men by flexing their sagging muscles however they can ... but, they don't begin to flex a certain muscle like *I* can. So, miss, what do you say? Do you wish to - pardon my boldness – climb aboard?"

Jonas and Will had left the hospital en route to their respective vehicles, but the anger within each had not subsided. They knew they had Quinn dead to rights. They also realized how crafty he was, and they must be careful how they played it out. But one thing was as certain as the sun rising in the morning, they would play it out, and he would not like the final outcome.

Chapter 50

THE PAST ALWAYS HAS A WAY OF FINDING THE PRESENT

The following morning found Prichard preparing breakfast in Declan's condo kitchen, while a determined Cailen rummaged through her son's things as if she were at a bargain basement clearance sale, all the while conversing on her cell to an undisclosed source in Ireland. The Quinn matriarch had spent a sleepless night worrying about the latest predicament, the extent of her son's involvement in it, and how she would deal with it all. She knew she must remain strong, but the ability in which to do so was becoming more difficult each day. Being the mother of four strong-willed sons had not been an easy task. She had lost count of the times she had been called upon to deal with an issue that one of them had laid at her feet, but her youngest had always brought the highest count, and the most difficult in which to solve. It had become a habit with him, and his outlook toward the end result of anything was always the same, *his money*. He had always viewed the Quinn fortune as if it had been provided for his personal disposal, and regardless of his elder's teaching to the contrary he continued to believe it.

"Mrs. Quinn, breakfast is ready," Prichard announced as she poured boiling water into the two mugs already containing their measure of instant coffee.

"I be there directly, Matilda," Cailen replied while she hurriedly closed the lid on her son's travel trunk.

Settling herself before her plate of toast, curry, and applesauce, Prichard remarked, "It's another beautiful day – though hot - I didn't realize Canada had this kind of heat," and she immediately began sipping her morning stimulant.

Prichard's remark enticed Cailen to check the thermostat before sitting down to her morning fare. Having done so, she replied, "Aye, 'tis set cool enough to be sure, but it greatly depends on the outside temperature and, by the current feel of this apartment, 'tis going to be another scorcher," then realizing the sparse offering before her, continued, "Maybe we should have ordered room service before we left the hotel. Does Declan not have anything other than these unappetizing tidbits?"

Sighing, Prichard replied, "I'm afraid not, in fact I was lucky to have found this lot."

Setting her coffee mug upon the table, Cailen said, "Well it be alright this time, but we shan't be repeating it. As soon as we have finished we shall be off to hospital. I really feel we should have returned last evening instead of going straight to our suites. But we both needed time to ourselves, do ye not agree?"

Nodding her head in an amiable manner, Prichard replied, "Yes, we certainly did, but we did not come all this way for a holiday. Master Declan is sufficiently gaining ground, and there is really no plausible reason for him to stay in hospital. After all I'm here, and I am fully qualified to take care of him so, do you have any idea when we shall be leaving for home?"

Rising to her feet, Cailen answered, "I not yet be given it serious thought. But judging from what we witnessed yesterday I feel the time will soon be upon us to do just that. I be checking the flight schedule on our return to the Elite."

Cailen had no sooner left the table en route to her previous exploration when Declan's discarded cell signaled an incoming call. Moving quickly, she snatched it from the nightstand before the sound of the annoying ringtone could have another play. She couldn't help but emit a groan when the name Aednat appeared on the screen, accompanied with her latest photograph of which left nothing to the imagination whatsoever.

Noticing her employer's reaction to the call, Prichard asked, "Who is it, Mrs. Quinn?"

Clearing her throat, Cailen replied, "It be that damn gold-digger from last year."

In an indignant tone, Prichard inquired, "What could *she* possibly want after all this time? And why would she still be in his address book? I suppose she's blazed-through the outrageous settlement you gave to hold her at bay. Too bad you hadn't pressed charges. That ridiculous low-life is certainly deserving of whatever prison time could have been rendered. I still say she got off easy, and you should have pressed the issue, after-all look what she caused."

Having silenced the ring, Cailen stood quiet, contemplating the reason for a call from someone who had been told never to contact the Quinn family again. Her thoughts continued, along with the not forgotten images resulting from her son's ill-fated dalliance with this woman. Continued thoughts triggered the need to investigate further in hope of finding clues to the present contact attempt. Like many of her generation, Cailen was not thoroughly versed in the area of computerized gadgets, but she fumbled along, doing her best to open any message or indication that might possibly explain the girl's reason for calling. Suddenly her finger hit upon a key that opened the cell's photo gallery. There, displayed before her enlarged eyes, were assorted pictures of a woman in the nude with her wrists bound behind her back, legs trust-up like a turkey awaiting the roaster, lying upon what appeared to be a bed covered in pink satin. Cailen's eyes were consumed by the X-rated material before them. It was all there, in glorious color, each and every image providing solid evidence of what her son had admitted to having done to Willow Crosby.

"Saints preserve us!" she exclaimed, encompassing the cell within her trembling hands.

Coming to her aid, Prichard took the device and began her own pornographic trek. Her usually intense jaw suddenly fell as if the bones had become unhinged, while she did her best to stifle the need to openly gasp her abhorrence. "This cannot be happening," she thought, her eyes scanning the vivid images now in slide-show mode. As much as she found it disgusting, she could not pull her eyes away, all she could do was look, and utter the odd moan.

Suddenly Cailen snatched the devise from Prichard's hands and shoved it into her pocket. She wasn't sure what she would do with it, but it could not be left unattended. Should the police obtain a search warrant, it would allow them to check every nook and cranny of the condo, thus locate the cell and its incriminating evidence. But if it remained in her possession it was as if it never existed. Casting an imploring glance toward Prichard, she said, "Do not say one word about our unfortunate discovery. No one needs to know, and it would serve no purpose other than to send me boy to prison." A strange look came over her, as if she suddenly remembered something. Grabbing Prichard's arm, she exclaimed, "Declan be only nineteen, not twenty one ... he be a minor here ... a minor cannot be charged!"

It was obvious Prichard had been taken aback. Usually it was she who made excuses for Declan, but something told her that he would not escape retribution this time, regardless of his age or excuse rendered. Staring over the top of her horn-rimmed spectacles, she said, "Mrs. Quinn, the legal age in Canada is nineteen, and this is where it unfortunately took place. It is obvious he raped that poor woman. Why else would he have pictures of it? I am utterly mortified! Master Declan has never done anything of this nature before — not that we know about — but after finding this, who is to say?" The Irish matron was about to interrupt, when Prichard continued, "We cannot uphold him in this, Mrs. Quinn. Surely you cannot stand there and defend what he's done, especially with the evidence so plain within those vulgar images."

Not waiting to think about it, Cailen snapped, "They can be done away with! We must, Matilda! I cannot run the risk of them being seen by anyone! Ye must show me how 'tis done."

"Pictures or not," Prichard rebuked, "it will not help him should he decide to come clean – confess his crime - and that might be his only chance, especially should Mrs. Crosby press charges - or her husband. He is determined, judging by the words we overheard him say last evening. He is not going to let this go, Mrs. Quinn, and you had better think fast and hard. I feel we must return Master Declan to Galway immediately, or send for your solicitor as soon as we can."

The grieved look upon Cailen's face revealed the indelible fear she felt, made worse by the logical procedure she knew must be followed. Prichard was right, and the Irish matron knew it. Grasping her own cell tightly, she began to put-in an overseas call when a loud knock sounded upon the door, accompanied by the stern voice of a man, announcing, "Police! Open up!"

Chapter 51

ONE BAD TURN OFTEN SIGNALS ANOTHER

Thunder again rumbled in the west, but by now everyone considered it to be part of the morning, like the sun rising or the bird's singing. The recent tornado was yesterday's news; no-one gave further thought to a recurrence, but should another strike they would take it in stride, like they took everything, and Willow Crosby was no exception when it came to accepting what couldn't be changed.

A tired Jonas had arrived to escort her home for she no longer required hospitalization and what healing was yet to take place could be done in her own bed. Willow not only agreed with this summation, she couldn't wait to return to her comfortable abode. But Jonas was beginning to feel like a rubber band stretched to the limit, for eight hours of the day was spent at his job, a few hours before and after work overseeing repairs at the house, and the remainder spent at his wife's bedside until visitation for the day was over. Whenever the time allowed he would check in with Detective Mann to see how the case was progressing, but so far all he was being told was the same old 'you have to be patient we're doing the best we can' routine, ending with the redundant interference warning. Mann said nothing regarding a police visit to Declan's condo; possibly if he had Jonas could have directed him to the intended source hold-up in the bed across the hall, but he was behaving himself, tending his own business while letting the authorities tend to theirs.

Stepping into his wife's room, Jonas asked, "Are you about ready? Sorry I couldn't be here sooner but I've been kept busy at the house."

"Good morning, Jonas, thank you for coming to bring me home," Willow replied with a smile. Suddenly, as if in afterthought, she asked, "What were you doing at the house?"

Thinking her totally incoherent of recent conversations between them, he answered, "I've been trying to get the tornado damage repaired."

She quickly looked at him as if she thought him two bricks short of a load, and exclaimed, "Tornado! What tornado?"

Shaking his head in an appeasing manner, he explained, "A tornado hit the same day we brought you to the hospital. It was small - well if any tornado is considered minimal - but it still caused damage, burst windows, that sort of thing and I've been overseeing repairs while you've been here. There's yet a few things needing to be done, but overall it's livable." As he completed his explanation thunder again rumbled, causing him to glance out the window as if the recent tornado discussion might have conjured-up another. Realizing the sky was indeed growing darker, he said, "Looks like another storm is coming. Hopefully I can get you home before it arrives."

Glancing in the same direction her husband was looking, Willow replied, "We've certainly been getting our share recently, but I still don't recall this tornado you're talking about. Maybe it's just as well I missed it," and as she snapped shut her suitcase the rumble of thunder was again heard, just as the nurse arrived pushing a wheelchair.

"Here you go, Mrs. Crosby, the latest model, fresh off the assembly line," the nurse stated in kind, and immediately began helping her patient aboard.

The trio had no sooner started down the corridor when Cailen Quinn, accompanied with a suitcase-toting Prichard, stepped out of the elevator and began their short jaunt to young Quinn's room. While passing, both women took notice of Willow, as well as Jonas, but at this point knew better than to utter a word. The couples, having never met, did not recognize each other, therefore passed in silence, but had the Crosby's glanced behind them they would have noticed the room in which the two women entered, but they hadn't, instead carried-on their conversation with the nurse while awaiting the elevator's arrival.

Declan, intently watching the storm gather ground, was seated in a chair by the window, his back to the door, when the two women silently entered his room. Unaware of their presence, he was totally startled by his mother's voice, as it snapped, "Hurry, me boy! We must make haste to the airport!" As she spoke Prichard riffled-open the suitcase and hurriedly removed a navy suit, its accessories, as well as a pair of highly polished black shoes, all of which she quickly laid out upon the bed.

Turning in astonishment, the startled boy gasped, "Ma! I didn't hear you come in! What is this? Why are the two of you in such frenzy?"

Not wasting a second, his mother replied, "The law be after ye! They be at yur apartment this very morning! We managed to sidestep their insatiable questioning by telling them ye were not present upon our arrival, and we not be knowing yur whereabouts.

But I be thinking them not convinced by our lies. They not be having a search warrant, so they could not be entering to look about, but I feel they will soon be returning with one. Time be of the essence, boy! We must be on our way as soon as ye can get dressed."

The young man looked at the two before him as though he could not believe one word being spoken. After all this wasn't the first time they had approached him in this fashion, or with this same over-the-top effort in which to make him do their bidding, but arrogance had not yet consumed him to the point where he had forgotten about the police. In all intent and purpose he couldn't understand why they hadn't showed up at the hospital, but by some unexplained reason they hadn't. So far he was still a step ahead, but he knew each day found that distance lessening. Looking at his mother, he said, "Have you made flight arrangements?"

"Aye," she answered rapidly, "there be a flight leaving in three hours. It allows just enough time to get there. Now be moving about, instead of pondering on thought!"

The boy was unsure as to how to explain the way he presently felt, or the insurmountable need to make Willow further pay for the humiliation she had dealt him. He realized the position in which he was about to insert his mother, but he also hoped she would understand the need to do so. Even if she didn't, he was certain Prichard would.

"I really don't feel the need to run, Ma," he stated. "It appears the police don't know where I am. If they did they would have hauled me off long ago but, Ma, I'm not yet finished with that Crosby bitch. She needs to pay for what she did to me."

The two women could not believe what they were hearing, and Cailen, totally taken aback, thought; "Surely ye've not become so full of yurself that ye would risk prison in order to settle a vendetta." She would not allow such stupidity, and she snapped, "Have ye completely rounded the bend!? Do ye not understand the seriousness of what ye did - let alone what ye face should ye be caught? We saw the pictures on yur cell - mind ye it was by mistake - but we saw them nonetheless! Ye *did* rape that woman, not to mention beat the Divel out of her! Ye cannot be found out, Declan. I not be allowing it! Now, Miss Prichard and meself will step out in the hall so ye can get dressed. Be quick about it!"

The boy could see he had hit a wall. Somehow he was not surprised but he was not giving up. All he could think of was the humiliation Willow had caused him, as he thought, "That calculating whore needs to pay more. She got off easy last time, and if she thinks she experienced pain then it's nothing compared to what she's going to feel. Hell, if I could get away with it, I'd knock her off," as he grabbed his clothing, and began dressing.

The cab ride to Capital Elite was made in silence, but the thoughts screaming inside each of the patrons' head was deafening. Prichard's instinct to protect her young charge was ever-present, and it showed as she gently held his hand within her own, as if this gesture could somehow wipe-away what had happened, but try as she might she could not get past what he had done. Surely her teachings throughout the years had lent some form of guidance and structure, yet if they had those despicable thoughts would have never entered his mind, let alone the way in which he'd dealt with them. But regardless of Prichard's wonted thoughts, Cailen knew how vengeful her son could be, after-all he came to it naturally, assisted by some very bad examples along the way, but that did not excuse the present trouble, and even though he had brought the majority of it upon himself, she could not throw him to the wolves, and she'd be damned if she'd let him be caught. She would bide her time and hide him. When all was finished it would be as though he had never set foot in Ottawa. As she rode along she silently planned the course she would take, and aside from one initial step already executed, her second would be straight to Willow Crosby's door.

Chapter 52

HOME SWEET HOME

The buttercup yellow of the newly installed front door welcomed Willow as she stepped through, thankful to be home. With the exception of a continual ache inside her cervix, accompanied by tenderness in her jaw each time she spoke, she didn't feel too bad. Her biggest problem was keeping uneasy thoughts in check, for knowing what had taken place within these walls was something that brought an intense uneasiness, and she wasn't referring to the tornado's visit. But as always she would accept the change, still that mindset did not make it easy, for each glance in the mirror was a constant reminder of what had happened. The house, through no fault of its own, brought the most uneasiness. This is where it happened, each blow to the jaw, every tear of the cervix, thrust to the uterus, and every pain-encompassed movement thereafter. But she had survived. Somehow she had hung on. This thought always summoned gratitude to the powers that be above. Without them she might have perished. As it was she was left with the insurmountable impact of living after having been raped, abused, belittled, and forever diminished in self respect.

Walking just slightly behind her, Jonas inquired, "What do you think of the new changes?" Without outwardly admitting it he already surmised how she felt, and as he spoke he took-up position aside her in a forward attempt to lend support.

Willow silently ruminated on his question but took a few minutes before answering. She liked what she saw, so far, but more so the fact that her husband had been generous enough to have replaced what he had. Yet it was simply replacement of material objects, not the self-worth that had been lost to her. She further wondered how he could ever accept what had happened - what she had *enticed* to happen - and regardless of the sincerity in his words, or the way in which he delivered them, how could he ever be expected to treat her like he had before? She was now damaged goods, just as sure as if she had been a newly acquired purchase that had arrived soiled, spoiled, or torn. He would not be expected to accept that without complaint, and he certainly would not be expected to pay for it. Maybe she was splitting hairs with an assumption such as this, after-all she was not a material object, but just the same they were questions needing answers, and the answers were painfully important.

Walking through the house, scanning the newly refurbished areas, she said, "Whoever you got to do the repairs have done a fine job; everything looks great but …. Well … it must have been costly."

"That's what insurance is for, Willow," Jonas said with assurance. "And I have to admit to not feeling one bit guilty about making the claim. After-all how many premiums have we paid over the years? The cost covered by them is a mere drop in the bucket compared to what we've dumped into their bank account, so don't give it a second thought."

Willow, carrying on her inspection as she moved toward her bedroom, replied, "I can't help it, old habits die hard I guess …

I mean … I've done without for so long it's become a way of life. Unpaid bills have reached an all time high, it's a wonder I haven't been hauled off to jail, or sued by every utility in the city, so I guess it's not surprising that my first thought would be about cost."

Jonas reached for her arm, but she hurriedly shunned it as if his touch would somehow burn her flesh. The look on his face revealed this concern. He had meant her no harm, but he also realized how this action might be taken out of context, regardless of the innocence behind the intention. He also realized why, as well as the reason behind that. He waited a moment then tried again. "Don't be worrying about the cost, or anything else," he softly said but made certain to watch where his hand was. "Your present concern should be to get well, and you're not going to accomplish that by discussing things that upset you, so how about taking a rest for awhile before I fix us some lunch."

Realizing he was skirting her action, she said, "That sounds like a good idea, Jonas. I think I will, for a little while anyway, hopefully it won't bother me to lie …" She stopped talking, but that hadn't stopped her unspoken words from being heard.

Jonas had always had an uncanny knack of knowing what his wife was going to say before she even knew, at least in most cases; this was no different, for he had instinctively clued in to the reason she had hesitated. He couldn't blame her. He could only imagine the way she must feel, and even if he could experience what she had endured he would still not feel it in the same way, for everyone experiences things differently.

"Why don't you have a lie-down in the boy's old room," he suggested, hoping his idea would help alleviate her anxiety.

Staring at the perfectly made bed before her, she replied, "That might not be a bad idea, but it doesn't help me to overcome my present hesitation, or the reason I feel it in the first place."

"Maybe not," he said, "but it might help take your mind off what it's presently thinking."

Willow, acknowledging her husband's well-paced suggestion, softly replied, "Hmm, that's true," and began the short journey down the hallway.

As soon as she entered her sons' room her mind was flooded with memories near and dear to her heart. The room appeared like it always had, enticing her eyes to both mist and smile when they fell upon assorted posters of her boy's favorite bands making the rounds during their teen years, each a reminder of the many conversations she had endured with them as they discussed *and* argued the fashions of the time, and why they could not become carbon copies of their musical idols. But they were unique in their own right, and she never missed an opportunity to tell them just that. She so adored them, and the stalwart, successful men they had become. How she wished time could be turned-back, if not totally frozen where she wanted it, never to be altered in any form. But life does not allow its rules to be changed by anyone, and so this desire must remain captured through memory.

"Willow," Jonas called softly, "I've made some lunch. Are you ready to have some?"

"Oh hi, Jonas," she replied in a sleepy tone, opening her eyes to his voice, "I must have dozed off. I'd forgotten how comfortable these beds are." For a few moments she lie quiet, before answering, "Yes, I am a bit hungry, but I don't expect you to wait on me, I'll come to the table."

"I don't mind," he replied in a sheepish manner, "maybe I should have done this a long time ago – if I had maybe we would have never reached the fork in the road that we did, but better late than never I guess."

Pulling herself into a sitting position, Willow remarked, "Maybe, but we both contributed to that fork. Funny isn't it? I mean, sometimes it takes what we've gone through to realize what we did to each other or, how important we actually are to one another."

Nodding in agreement, Jonas replied, "I know what you mean. All the shit between us that was going down and, well the anger we were feeling was blinding us to what we really feel." He moved closer and sat down on the side of the bed, but as he did she moved back. For a moment he said nothing, but his intended movement did not rattle her like the previous gesture. She knew her husband better than she knew herself – she also knew his gestures, as well as the motivation behind them – most of the time – but she would not be forced. Finally his eyes met hers, as he softly said, "I love you, Willow. I always have, always will. I hope you know this and, I hope it still means something to you."

Not hesitating, she cried, "It does, Jonas, I ... I love you too, I do, but it's ... well, all that's happened recently ... I just hope you know how ashamed I am, I mean ... I should have never let that kid get to me ... should have never listened to a word he said but I ... I was just so depleted, so hurt and dejected by you that I let the first compliment turn my head, even if it was a bold-faced lie, which it was, all of his shit! You hurt me so bad ... you basically abandoned me and I wanted to hurt you too, hand you back some of what you were dishing out but, that was wrong, it was stupid; it was so ... so ... oh I want so much to apologize to you. I should have been more understanding instead of the demanding bitch that I was. I've always been hard-headed; always had to have my own way regardless of the path I was barreling down – full speed ahead – no brakes no hesitation never listening or, God forbid putting anyone else's needs ahead of my own."

Jonas' arms instantly engulfed her quivering body, as he said, "Don't. Don't do this, don't punish yourself like this. No one knows how they will react to anything until they are presented with it. We can only do the best we can with the hand we're dealt. You're no different. And regardless of the way you presently feel, or what you say in regard to your actions, you have never put your needs ahead of the kids, so don't go on like this. It's not doing you one bit of good."

But Willow disagreed. She couldn't help but feel the need to purge, cleanse her soul of the way her soiled body presently felt toward the abuse she had invited, and regardless of how much Jonas tried comforting her, she would not be consoled.

Chapter 53

QUEST FOR JUSTICE TURNS YET ANOTHER PAGE

The afternoon was far busier than the morning had been, as Detective Mann polished-off his latest cup of coffee, while studying the contents of a slender manila-hued folder with the name Quinn stamped slightly askew on the cover. The young cop mused silently, as if this summoned gesture better assisted his waning concentration. This was not the only case he had been recently assigned. Heaven knows there were other issues requiring his attention, but there was something about this one that kept eating away at him. The information was sparse, not much more to go on than a plate number, registration, and ownership of an extremely expensive sports car. Mann instantly felt envious of such extravagance, certainly something that any man would desire, yet only affordable by society's elite. He could not afford such eccentricities on his salary, and a deficient sigh escaped his lips the more he dwelled on it. The sigh further increased when he thought about the last time he had enjoyed a raise, let alone any luxury that might come along with it.

Thunder still rumbled about, but so far that was all it did. Everyone, including Detective Mann, wished it would either morph into a storm, or move on. In their mind the sound had become annoying, like a pesky mosquito hovering around your head the minute the lights are shut off, or that of a growling stomach demanding it be filled. But none of these comparisons did anything to lessen the bothersome heat that would not leave the area. Rising to his feet, Mann turned with the intent of refilling his cup, but was instead greeted by a disgruntled Will Sutherland standing just outside the office door.

"Can I be of assistance?" Mann inquired with growing interest, but he remained still.

With ill-amusement, Will replied, "I would hope so. Detective Mann, I presume?"

"Yep, that's me. What can I do for you?"

"The officer at the front desk said I could come back and see you. I'm Will Sutherland, first cousin to Willow Crosby — rape victim — remember her? I was wondering how the case against Declan Quinn is progressing."

"I'm afraid I'm not at liberty to discuss that with you, Mr. Sutherland."

"Well," Will grunted in a dishearten tone, "you don't appear to be discussing it with anyone, least of all Jonas Crosby who brought you the plate number of the bastard's car. You see, Willow is much more than my cousin, she's my best friend, and I *hate* what has happened to her. I also hate the idea of the perpetrator getting away with it so, what has been done to find him? Have you even searched for his car?"

Mann pointed to the chair in front of his desk then returned to his own. He realized how the situation might appear to an outsider, but there were guidelines to be followed, and in that respect this case was no different than any other. Still he could appreciate the family's concern.

"I realize it must seem as if nothing's being done," Mann relayed, settling further into his chair, "but we are on the case."

Will, shifting himself within the chair he'd been directed to, snapped, "He was hospitalized! Right across the frigging corridor from my cousin! If you'd bothered to check out the hospitals you would have found him! Jonas and I spoke with the smug asshole and guess what? He as much as admitted raping my cousin! We wanted to pound the little fucker right on the spot —"

"You cannot do that!" Mann exclaimed loudly, jumping to his feet as he spoke. "People cannot go around taking the law in their own hands *pounding* someone they think did something they might or might not have!"

Will abruptly retorted, "Don't fret it we kept our hands to ourselves! The way you blatantly *insisted* we do! But you never once set foot in there to look for him; he would have been discharged by now! It's been a few days since the attack; surely you've tried locating him! He can't have disappeared entirely — that is unless he's managed to sneak out of the country. Have you checked the recent flight manifests to Ireland, anywhere for that matter?!"

Holding his hands in the air, Mann replied, "Mr. Sutherland, please calm down. Now as I stated when you first came in, I'm not at liberty to discuss this case with anyone other than the victim and her husband."

As if trying to make excuses, Will explained, "Jonas has been tied up trying to get their house back in shape following the recent tornado, and Willow just got out of hospital today. I wanted to find out if there's been any progress. I'm just trying to help where I can. It's so damn frustrating, but I will tell them what you said."

Rising to his feet, Mann stated, "Have your cousin come in as soon as she can. Her statement is essential in order to proceed further."

Giving the detective's outstretched hand a quick shake, Will replied, "I will. I'm going over there right now. Please do whatever you can. I realize this is not your only case, but you did not see my cousin after he got through with her. If you had, you might have a better understanding as to why this can't be let ride."

"Good enough, Mr. Sutherland," Mann stated in an appeasing manner, "tell your cousin what I said, and thanks for coming in."

The door no sooner closed behind his visitor than Mann was on the phone. There had been an urgent tone in Sutherland's voice, something which alerted him to the possibility that young Quinn just may have flown the coop, somehow managing to stay below the radar in doing so, and if this was the case it would be almost impossible to track him. Ireland was known for protecting their citizens from extradition, especially if it was simply for investigation, and he had not been officially charged with anything. The rape victim must come forth in order for charges to be laid.

"Hey, Jim, Levi here, have the Chief call me as soon as he gets back from lunch. We have got to get this rape case on the go," he instructed as he starred at the sparse info on the desk before him.

This was the first rape case Mann had been assigned; he realized that for him it would be like walking barefoot on crushed glass, and no doubt unsurpassed embarrassment for Willow Crosby, but if charges were to be laid she had to reveal what had happened, as well as any possible guilt she may share in the attack upon her person. It would not be easy for either of them, but he was not one to turn away from a challenge, and he hoped she wasn't either. She must soon come in and speak with him, time was of the essence, and every lost second was one more strike against her; not only that, it allowed Quinn to distance himself from the issue, and if enough time went by justice would slip further away, making it impossible to be levied. As it was the courts were filled with cases pending solutions, judges rendering decisions, all that must be done to exercise the letter of the law to its fullest extent.

An hour had gone by before a knock sounded upon Mann's door, followed by a deep-throated voice requesting entry, and to be quick about it. The detective, already knowing who it was, looked up from the papers before him, and without hesitation, stated, "Come in, Chief. Take a seat. I need to discuss a case that seems to be dead in the water."

"I'm sure you're referring to that supposed rape case you've been assigned?"

"That's the one. I've had my feelers out on this one since I received what info I have, but so far nothing's coming back. The victim's cousin was in here earlier raising hell — not that I blame him — but I don't need amateurs getting in the way. Do you have any idea how we can proceed with what little we have?"

The Chief suddenly inserted his right pinkie finger into his ear, and proceeded to quiver it about as quickly as he could in an attempt to put an end to what appeared to be an annoying itch. While doing so, he lowered his abundant behind into the chair before Mann's desk. This was not as easy as first thought, and it made him silently wish that all the chairs within the prescient were as generous as his, however this one was proving rather pliable and should release him when required. Finally settled, he began scrutinizing the file before him. He was no novice in cases such as this, having solved many throughout his career, but he too had to admit to the strangeness surrounding this particular one. It was as if that sports car had totally vanished. No-one in their observant circle had seen it anywhere, and they had left no area undisturbed or clue overlooked. Still it had to be somewhere.

"I'll call out the K-9 unit if I have to," Mann said in a tone nothing less than determined, for the entire scenario had become both disgusting, and embarrassing.

Struggling upward from his confinement, the Chief belched, and then growled, "Do whatever you have to, but before you do much more get that Crosby woman in here for questioning. Truth be known, she probably enticed the young buck in the first place, but you never know. Some of these whippersnappers I see coming through here leave a lot to be desired, but the ones with a few bucks to their name are by far the worst. This Quinn character obviously has money or access to it in order to pick up a set of wheels like he did. But keep on it, sooner or later something is bound to turn up."

The detective thought about what the portly Chief had said long after he had ambled out the door. There was a lot to be said in the words he'd spoken, as well as the reason he spoke them. All Mann could do was build upon it, and follow his instincts. He was a smart cookie, certainly worthy of the position he held within the local law enforcement, but he did not realize what he was up against. If he had he might have requested instant dismissal from the case, or at the very least assigned assistance, for he was soon to encounter the Quinn matriarch, and her special brand of justice.

Chapter 54

WHEN YOU ENCOUNTER RAPIDS IN THE RIVER A WATERFALL IS NOT FAR AHEAD

Two weeks past, and Cailen, having followed her lawyer's advice, had kept a low profile during the time since contacting him in regard to the present quandary. She'd even gone so far as to use an alias at the Capital Elite's front desk. Strange how cash makes a difference, but it was required in order to pull off her plan, and her credit cards carried her name, or that of her company, so she thought it best to refrain from using them. She'd even gone so far as to prohibit Prichard from using hers, but instead cash, sent by the Quinn's lawyer via direct payments through Western Union. She was following his instructions to the letter, which would be required if she was to successfully carry through her vendetta against Willow Crosby.

She had kept Declan under wraps since his discharge from hospital, prohibiting any activity outside his condo, even going so far as screening incoming and outgoing calls on his cell. She had even reregistered his condo title to that of her lawyer's private holdings. Anything that could be traced by the police was kept at a minimal.

Cailen was a smart woman, she didn't require instruction as to how to conduct herself in dealings such as this, but she did realize the necessity of practicing prudence, and making sure everything that possibly could be covered or altered was done in order to make it virtually impossible for anyone to discover their continued existence in Ottawa. As far as she was concerned there would be no further reason for a police visit, they had been there, seemed satisfied with what they had been told, and left. All seemed to be falling into place as planned.

All this time Prichard felt remorseful. This was not what she had signed on for so many years prior. Those years had been good ones, filled with both accomplishment and encouragement. Derek Quinn had personally sought her out, and welcomed her into his family as if she had been a dear relative returning home after an extended hiatus. His children always treated her with respect; she felt they even loved her, and she dearly loved them. Her immense pride in their accomplishments shone daily, and it still filled her with pride to know that she had helped pave the way for the heights they had reached. But her thoughts soon settled on Declan, and with them, a torrent of feelings ranging from admiration to vile. She regretted the latter emotion, it was something she never once thought would surface in regard to this young man to whom she had given so much, a stellar education, endless encouragement, and unsurpassed love. Yet when all was said and done where had it gotten her? She had long wondered about her relationship with the Quinn matriarch, and though she knew the woman respected her teaching abilities - possibly admired her Ivy League education - when it came to friendship, especially the kind which two people working in close encounters form over the course of many years, she couldn't help feeling like a stranger who continues to be disallowed entry inside.

This latest development was just one more chapter to be written into Prichard's growing book of adversity. How was she to cope when she could not be confided in - worse still - treated like a second class citizen who is given no more consideration than that of what a slave receives? She felt trapped, without the freedom to speak her mind, or act on her impulse to simply leave. Yet that would not help Declan, and even though she did not uphold his recent actions in any way, she once again swallowed her pride, and carried on her duties in the fashion of which she always had.

Dinner had been completed, and she was just finishing the dishes when Cailen entered the kitchen. Prichard knew the woman's moods inside and out and whether she needed to discuss something; this time did not differ, and she proceeded to inquire her employer's obvious need of enlightenment.

Sitting upon a chrome chair, Cailen said, "Aye, ye knows me so well, Matilda," then reaching for the teapot sitting in the center of the table, proceeded to pour herself a cup while offering to refill her employee's in the process.

Prichard thought it most kind, especially after her recent thoughts, and she replied, "That would be lovely, thank you. These days it seems like we use more dishes with every meal consumed."

"Aye," Cailen stated as she nodded her head, "I be sure it must feel that way, but all ye need to do is ask for my assistance — better still Declan's. Would not hurt him in the least to do some down to earth chores, in fact it be doing him a world of good - show him how the other half lives - those who have to do everything for themselves, not have it done for them. I often be wondering if that might have attributed to his Divel-may-care-attitude toward things. What be yur take on this, Matilda?"

Prichard couldn't help but smile when she thought about what she was being asked, her opinion on something, something other than the duties for which her expertise had been engaged. Laying down the dishtowel, and picking up her freshly filled cup, she replied, "Would not hurt him in the least. I'm sure he's had to do his own chores since arriving here, though he was not here that long before …"

Prichard stopped before she finished her sentence, but she was not the only one who understood moods, voiced opinions, or the lack thereof, as Cailen said, "I know to what ye are referring. No need to feel as if ye cannot speak openly. I suppose I have made that rather difficult lately and … well, I be sorry for that, Matilda. I know how ye feels about me boy, and I also know what ye have given him in so many ways. I get wrapped up in me thoughts and emotions, and if it seems as if I not be listening, or taking yur views into consideration then I be apologizing for that. I *will* try to do better."

Prichard hardly knew what to say. Maybe she had been mistaken, or possibly reading recent actions in a way she hoped to, which in turn would validate her recent take on things, but regardless of her mixed emotions, or ill-placed loyalty, she was glad to hear these present words. Relinquishing a smile, she said, "I thank you for that, Mrs. Quinn. I must say that I had begun to feel chastised, but in hindsight I may have jumped to conclusions. Wouldn't be the first time, so with regard to our present scenario, I shall try also."

Declan had been resting in his bedroom since dinner and paying the ladies no mind. He was miffed to think his freedom to do as he liked had been diminished to the point in which it had. He felt as if he'd been placed under house arrest by his own mother, and it was not sitting well. Flouncing to the kitchen, he announced, "I'm going out for a walk!"

His mother, not believing what she was hearing, looked up from her tea cup, and said, "Ye'll be doing nothing of the like!"

Prichard said not a word, even though the boy's eyes had summoned her attention with hope she would somehow intervene, when she didn't, he immediately bristled. Once again his temper flared, and he exclaimed, "And what are you going to do about it, *Mother!?* If I want to go out then I shall! This is ridiculous, keeping me locked up as though I'm a prisoner in my own home!"

Showing no sign of upset whatsoever, his mother calmly replied, "Under the circumstances that is exactly what ye are."

"I am nothing of the sort!" he snapped, and proceeded to move toward the door.

In a serious tone, she asked, "Then tell me this. How do ye expect to keep from being locked up for real if ye are spotted, or possibly identified by someone following recent police cases? There are such people about ye know."

Holding his body in a self-important stance, he sarcastically remarked, "If the police were sure it was me they would have returned by now. They haven't! So they've either thrown out the case, or have a new boy on the hook. With that whore it could have been anyone, so —"

"Stop right there!" Cailen snapped, pointing to the chair adjacent her. "Sit ye down right now!"

"Oh my," he audaciously thought, "now I'm really going to catch it!" It was obvious his mother was about to lower the boom but as far as he was concerned she could go right ahead. He'd had enough of this tiresome lockdown and was ready to carry out his own brand of justice.

But his mother had something else in mind, as she said, "Ye will be going nowhere, young man, the only activity ye will be doing is schoolwork. I've had Miss Prichard, through me lawyer of course, contact the Dean at Carlton, and a new issue of summer work was delivered via courier while ye were sleeping. Ye will begin it as soon as ye finish the remaining dishes —"

"*What!*" he yelled. "*You can't be serious! Me?! Doing menial chores?! I'll be doing nothing of the sort, dishes* or *homework!*"

"That is enough!" Cailen retorted, making it obvious she had reached her limit. "I will not allow anymore outbursts! Ye have some nerve to speak to me in that tone and it ends now! Ye gave up yur freedom when ye raped that woman, and even though the like of such is appalling - not to mention the fact that it was carried out by me own flesh and blood - I will not turn me back. But ye will toe the line, do as ye are told, and without backtalk! Now, while ye were in hospital a message came to yur cell from that goddamn extortionist Aednat Mulkearns, demanding ye ring her back. Have ye? And what did she have to say for herself?"

The boy reacted as if someone had punched him square in his gut. This girl had messaged him alright, but nothing she ever said could be believed so he had dismissed it, as he thought, "I never once thought Ma would know she called, then again I never thought she would see those pics while I …." His thoughts stopped. He could not go there; if he did he was totally sunk. But he didn't have to worry about that for his attention had been rapidly secured when his mother again demanded to know what the girl had said.

Taking a deep breath, he replied, "She hasn't been feeling well lately. I run into her at the pub awhile back. She didn't look the best, always seemed to be wiping her nose, so I figured she'd caught a cold, but with her anything is possible; anyway apparently it wasn't going away so she went to the doctor to see about it. He ran some tests. According to her they revealed an internal virus, and she thought it best to tell me in case I might want to get checked out, but there's no need for that." He ceased talking because the expression upon the ladies faces looked as if he had just slapped them. He instantly knew what they must be thinking, and to avoid further interrogation, quickly added, "You needn't look as you do. I never had sex with her."

The two women sitting before him could not believe what they were hearing, both thinking it could not be so, and that they must have taken his words out of context. But as far as Cailen was concerned it could simply be another extortion plot being set into motion, yet she stared at Prichard with a questioning look that implored any other plausible answer.

Hardly believing what she was hearing, Prichard immediately tried setting her employer's mind at ease. "Well I shall ring the hospital and speak with Master Declan's attending physician," she said. "There would have been blood taken for testing. If there is any infection it will show. Try not to borrow trouble, Mrs. Quinn; it is always there to be found if you entice it. It will work out fine, just like the other existing problem."

The words Prichard spoke were meant to hold anxiety at bay, but she wasn't fooling anyone, least of all Cailen, and as their eyes met, each could see tears welling within.

Chapter 55

BRIDGING A LONG AWAITED GAP

Willow was entering her third week at home. Each new day found her wishing her spirits would rise with the sun, but so far they hadn't. Her want of absolution finally drove her to the newly installed computer, now on the main floor, but this time it was not in search of someone to relate to, but rather articles on the rape victim, and the expected follow-up of such. She had an idea of what to expect, but every person is different in the way they perceive things, the way they heal, and also the way in which their mind reacts to it all. She had spent countless moments reliving what she could remember of that horrid experience, as well as coming to terms with the aftermath. The hardest part was coping with her reluctance to let Jonas touch her, anywhere, for as much as she loved him she could not rid her mind of Quinn's attack. Thoughts of this made her skin crawl, virtually, as if dozens of insects had somehow managed to burrow beneath the surface, ravaging cells, sucking her life, and each time she envisioned their movements, it was as if it were Quinn's hands plying her skin, or his disgusting penis doing its best to degrade her, humiliate her to the point where she wished he had outright killed her, instead of diminishing her to the point where she now found herself. Yet she knew these feelings were all in her head, embedded in her mind; possibly forever.

Noon had just past when the phone rang. As always her mind jumped to conclusions, wondering who it might be how much they would want, or was it simply someone trying to belittle her further? She realized these actions, like her follow-up reactions to the rape, were totally in her mind. She even wondered if she could be in the beginning stages of a major breakdown, as she thought, "Who in hell could blame me?" Yet she continued to move forward, trying her utmost to put the past where it belonged. She still ached; each movement being made with extreme caution, especially when trying to access stairs, so she remained on the main floor.

The phone was on its fifth ring by the time she finally answered.

"Hello, Willow. I thought I would have heard from you by now – in fact *long* before now," Mary Sutherland stated in her usual no nonsense manner. "Why I hear from David oftener than I ever hear from *you*."

Willow had planned on ringing her mother as well as her sibling a couple of days after her return home, but those well-intended plans had gone array, like a lot of her best laid plans seemed to. Gathering her wits, she said, "Good morning, Mom. Thanks for calling. I did plan on phoning, but you know how it is."

"Yes, I do," Mary answered, "especially with you. How are you feeling?"

"I feel just capital, Mother," Willow sarcastically thought, but said, "I'm getting there. Each day is a bit of a struggle, but better than the previous, so I guess I shouldn't complain. You taught me better than that, remember?"

"Yes, but I also taught you not to lie," Mary said, driving home her well intentioned point.

Gathering her defenses, Willow replied, "I'm not. What makes you say something like that?"

"Willow," Mary said in a knowing tone, "I saw you in hospital. I had my hired hand drive me in the day after you were admitted. No one was in the room at the time. You didn't know I was there, you were unconscious - or heavily sedated - but I saw your face. I couldn't believe the bruising. It appeared as if someone's doubled fist had punched it, more than once I might add." No sound emitted from Willow's end of the line. For a moment Mary thought she had gone, discreetly hung up the phone without a sound, so she inquired her daughter.

A few moments passed, before Willow said, "I'm here, I … well … I don't know what to say to that, other than I simply tripped and fell, I —"

"Don't lie to me!" Mary snapped. "I read your chart. I know what happened, so do not try sidestepping this issue with a half-baked story from your vivid imagination. I want to know what happened, the entire story."

"I wasn't intending to lie. I just wanted to spare you further embarrassment of having to speak to a daughter who had been raped. I didn't ask for that - well - at least to the extent that I received. It took me awhile to admit it, and it certainly wasn't easy, but I finally went into the police station and spoke with a Detective Mann, as well as the Chief of Police. I must admit it was the most embarrassing thing I've ever had to do, and they certainly didn't make it easy. By the way I was treated one would think me the criminal instead of the victim - I mean the questions they asked - and the way in which they asked them, well it appeared as if they were doing their best to trip me up, or get me to admit I enticed what happened and I didn't! It was nothing like that. I know how that must sound, Mom, but I don't know how else to explain it — and please don't tell the kids. It's not been easy to talk about – with anyone - and it's even more difficult to discuss with you. It's always been that way, about anything, but certainly not the likes of this."

In a much softer tone, Mary said, "I don't understand what you mean. Why would you think that you could not speak to me?"

Willow's stalwart defense suddenly came crashing down around her, as she thought, "How am I ever to explain myself without showing weakness. She won't stand for it, never has in the past, so why would she now?"

But her mother was not letting it pass, as she said, "Please speak to me, Willow. If you'd like I'll have the hired hand drive me to your place. It might be easier to speak in person than on the phone, that's rather impersonal, especially with something this important. What do you think?"

The sudden realization that her mother would sit face to face with her discussing something as personal as her rape sent Willow into a tailspin. She couldn't do it, yet she somehow felt the need to unload, clear her conscience, and sweep the rancid happening from her mind as quickly as blood lets from slit wrists. She had even entertained the thought of doing *that*, but she was as much a coward as she was squeamish. She could never stay conscious long enough to break the skin, let alone cut through her arteries. But she was desperate. The many weeks since it had happened had not brought comfort, as she thought, "So much for time and distance," before asking, "Are you really sure you want to discuss it?"

Mary instantly replied, "Yes. Something like this cannot be left to fester. It's very much the same as an open wound left unattended without care, most importantly a mother's care for her daughter when she is in such need of it. Please consider my coming."

Moisture had consumed Willow's eyes. At that moment she felt like a little girl needing the comfort only a mother can bring. Yet in Willow's case that comfort had always come at a price, that is if it came at all.

"Mom," she cried, doing her best to hold it together, "I truly want to speak with you, but I'm not sure you will understand or even listen - really listen to me. You ... you would never listen to me before when I tried talking to you, or try to explain something that was important to me, you, you always cut me off, belittled me, made me feel inept, like I didn't have a brain in my head. Maybe ... maybe you didn't mean to, but it hurt, Momma, it always hurt so much when you turned away from me or called me down for whatever I did that you thought was wrong, or dumb, or whatever you yourself might have been taken to task for as a child. I know your childhood wasn't easy, maybe that's what hardened you against me or, possibly the way Daddy was with me. I know he spoiled me and I took advantage of that, so many times but, Momma, he would listen to me about anything I needed to talk about. You wouldn't ... you always found fault with me. Oh, Momma ... *aha* ... I have to say this and, please don't be mad at me ... but I always wondered why you even had me because you always treated me like someone you wished would go just away and not bother you. Did ... *aha* ... did you *ever* love me? Do you love me now?"

She had to stop; she had become so overwrought she couldn't go on. Her sobbing could be heard permeating the phone line. She didn't know it, but her mother was sobbing harder than she. It wouldn't be easy to hear the words just spoken, whether they were in fact accurate, or simply a fabrication of something that had been left to time, growing so out of proportion that it came rushing forth like a burst damn when it did come. Regardless, the words were painful for Willow to say, and agonizing for Mary to hear.

The line had been left empty. Neither woman emitted a single word for they were both sobbing with the need to embrace the other in a way they could not do on the phone.

Mary, the strong-willed woman she was, finally said, "Willow, you need to take hold. This isn't getting us anywhere. I want to see you. I feel the need to assure you of things that you obviously are not aware of. I shall try and be there within the hour."

Reeling herself in, Willow replied, "Alright, Mom, that will be fine. I'll expect you soon. Travel safe."

Before she could hang up the receiver, she heard her mother say, "I love you."

Maybe it was the sudden shock of those words being spoken, or the overwhelming need to hear them spoken, but Willow cried, "I love you too, Momma. So very much, always know that. Please come soon."

She heard the click of her mother's receiver followed by the dial tone's happy hum. She somehow felt relived, yet nervous. This would be a first, but she was ready. She had waited all her life to hear her mother say those three little words. She still found it hard to believe she had heard them being spoken from her mother's lips, but she was not mistaken in what she had heard. How she savored them, and she couldn't wait to hear them again.

Before long a knock sounded upon the front door. Willow knew it couldn't be her mother, there hadn't been time. Even if the hired hand drove at breakneck speed there wouldn't have been time. She wiped her eyes, and smoothed her robe before venturing to the door where she noticed a rather tall, immaculately attired woman, whom she judged to be in her late fifties, standing in wait on the porch. She didn't recognize the woman, but still opened the door to greet her.

She was stunned, when the woman in a thick Irish accent, stated, "Willow Crosby, I presume?"

Nodding her head, Willow replied, "Yes, and you are?"

"I be yur worst nightmare come true," the woman replied while maintaining a self-important stance.

Willow wasn't sure what to make of this woman who appeared to favor mind games, something that she despised, but she would not be intimidated, as she said, "Well nightmare or not, who are you?"

Without hesitation, the woman boldly announced, "I be Cailen O'Brian Quinn – Declan's mother – and we be needing to talk."

Chapter 56

GOOD AS GONE – OR IS IT?

Across town, the long trying morning, that of which had engulfed Detective Levi Mann, had not lessened throughout the lunch hour. The Crosby/Quinn case was not making much headway, not even with Willow Crosby's statement. Mann supposed he and the Chief had been hard on her, that was their job; after all one does not make detective and Chief respectively by being soft, or showing compassion, even if one felt it, but the Chief's words had hit their mark, not to mention the lack of concern in which they had been delivered. Mann couldn't help but think that that is what happens to any cop if they have been on the force as long as the Chief, especially tending to cases which disallowed room for any form of sentiment. Maybe if feelings were let to the forefront it would hinder the outcome of the case and Mann had done his best to harden to this one.

A knock suddenly sounded upon Mann's door, accompanied with the excited voice of the young officer who had been assigned to assist with the case.

"Get in here!" Mann exclaimed as he stared at the door while running his fingers through his rapidly thinning brown hair.

The young officer burst in, it was all he could do to stay quiet long enough to sit down.

Staring at the rookie, Mann said, "You got something for me?"

"Right on, Detective!" the young officer exclaimed with an air of pride. "A couple of buddies and me were partying at the mouth of the canal last night and —"

"Weren't you supposed to be on duty last night?" Mann questioned in a serious tone, pulling himself more upright in his chair.

Looking a tad sheepish, the young officer replied, "Yeah, I was supposed to be, but I wasn't feeling the best so I got Officer Brown to fill in for me - he owes me a shift - anyway along about nine or so my buds stopped by and asked if I'd like to hang on the ferry landing below The Hill, so I said yes."

"Get on with it, I haven't got all day!"

"No, I suppose you don't, but I think we found it!"

Again Mann's lack of excitement showed, as he asked, "And what would that be? With you clowns *it* could be anything."

Getting to his feet, the officer replied, "I'm talking about the car you've been searching for belonging to that Irish kid!"

Mann could hardly believe what he was hearing. The police had looked everywhere for that car but it had simply vanished. With boredom now erased, Mann inquired, "Where did you say you saw it?"

Flipping open his cell to display a recent picture, the young officer replied, "South shore of the river, just west of the mouth of the canal. The ass end of it was showing, and I got the plate number, see? It's the same number you're looking for, right? We saw the cruise ship coming up our side of the river, and as it passed the huge wake came ashore. As it did the ass end of the car rose. It also looked to be stuck on a submerged tree trunk, or huge branch. Best get a crew down there before it breaks free and either sinks again, or travels on."

"I'm on it!" Mann exclaimed, and as if in afterthought, said, "Don't go away. You'll be needed to go with the team," and he immediately put through a call to the Chief.

By early afternoon a salvage crew had been dispatched to retrieve the small sports car. It was located exactly where the young officer had said, entangled in the limbs of a large maple which had fallen into the river due to the swift current eroding the shoreline. There was no way of knowing for sure, but all conjecture pointed toward the car being driven to a sharp point at Major's Hill Park, then pushed off the roadway into the river. Not the wisest move on the part of the guilty party, for the chartered cruise lines used this route daily for their public excursions; it would have only been a matter of time before the car surfaced.

"I wonder who in blazes the kid got to trash it," Mann queried aloud as he rubbed his chin, lending the impression he was deep in thought. In actually he was amused a kid of that age would have the gumption to think up such a caper, much less pull it off, but he obviously did, and if it hadn't been for the young assistant's irresponsible work ethics, Quinn might well have been successful. At this point it was still speculation with no way of proving any of it, but at least they had the car. Now all they had to do was find its owner, who had vanished like the car, but if the car could be found, so too could he.

With amusement, Mann openly said, "You would think if he had the brains to dump the car like this he'd first have the smarts to pull the plates. Strange that, maybe he was on the move or, possibly didn't get the chance or, maybe he just never thought of it. It's fairly secluded down here, not much traffic, especially at night, though it is quite popular with lovers."

The Chief had arrived and had been listening to Mann's summation, thinking it quite brilliant, that is until he got to the part about the lovers. Clearing his throat, he said, "You must be speaking from experience with your child bride, Mann, or could it possibly be wishful thinking on your part? I thought this location was only popular with my generation. I would think it too quiet and mundane for those who are more into the Ottawa nightlife - what's that called, 'making the scene'?"

With a look that could only be described as playful, Mann replied, "I wouldn't know about that, Chief, though it is kind of cool to know where you and your better half used to get it on."

Bristling, the Chief growled, "That'll be enough of that, Levi. We're down here for a much more important issue than where I got lucky, or didn't. Have that car hauled to the police yard and tagged. We already know who it's registered to so there's no need for DNA testing." Turning his eyes upward, as if to summon help from above, he continued, "I would really like to know where that young son of a bitch is. I spoke to the salesman over at Ottawa Foreign Import who apparently sold Quinn the car, and all he remembers – according to what he says anyway – is that the kid was rather short; slight in build; said he had fairly dark hair, and a wise-cracking mouth. He also said he was quick with responses, and seemed to know how to manipulate, but as far as physical description that was about all he could give me."

Nodding his head in agreement, Mann replied, "Well he's got to be somewhere. I took an officer and went to the address that the plate was registered to but he was nowhere to be seen, however I did speak with a woman there – come to think of it she spoke with a thick Irish accent – but that could have been coincidence as she said she was the cleaning lady, and that she'd been hired by Quinn that same day to come once a week. When I pressed her she said she'd never met the kid but was told to arrive specifically at eight and the door would be unlocked. According to her the kid had left her pay on the kitchen table along with a key, and having no search warrant, I couldn't enter to have a look. She said if she saw him she'd have him contact us, but of course we know that's never happened, and when I went back there the woman was nowhere to be found. It's like she vanished along with the kid. At this point it's hard to say whether he's still in the country, but I've got this feeling that he is."

"I hope you're right," the Chief replied as he and Mann walked toward their vehicles. "It'll be next to impossible to nail him if he's back on Irish soil." Stopping just slight of his ride, he turned to Mann, and said, "I don't think it would be a bad idea to return to that address with a search warrant."

As he opened his car door, Mann replied, "That's a good idea, Chief, it sure wouldn't hurt to have another look." Starting the engine, and letting the car role slightly forward, he continued, "I'll let you know how it goes," and then sped along the narrow blacktop that meandered below Parliament Hill.

The Chief, having his own agenda, had decided to recheck a few things as well; one of them being a few incomplete answers given by Willow Crosby. He felt that if she would further co-operate then more light could be centered on the issue, and if so then Quinn just might be found. After all most criminals return to the scene of the crime at some point, and he somehow felt that Mann had been right in assuming Quinn was still in Ottawa. He would let his detective check out his own theory, and he would check his. Starting his car, he set off toward Willow Crosby's eastside address.

Chapter 57

CONTINUED HEAT, TABLETOP DALLIANCE, AND AN OPAQUE OMEN

Jonas Crosby was fast at work at the machine shop that employed him, trying to endure the suffocating heat - that of which was now a staple - while doing his best to keep his mind on the inept machine before him and not on the recent happenings in his personal life. Neither was an easy task, but regardless of this, he felt happy whenever he thought about how his and Willow's relationship had grown ever since their splendid copulation weeks earlier. But the rape had brought any further physical encounter to an abrupt halt. He understood this, he even found himself experiencing guilt every time he as much as thought about touching her. In his mind he hoped that time itself would be the healing factor, and possibly with enough time, they could return to the bliss they once shared.

Lunch break had come and gone. The machine in which Jonas was operating had been having problems and he could not stop for lunch at the designated time. On top of that the temperature inside the plant made him wonder if he could manage to hold out until the end of his shift. He no longer enjoyed the stamina he'd had in his youth, but he had not lost his taste for money, and this job paid well, he could not afford to lose it and he would endure whatever he had to in order to avoid that. Besides the work day was a slow one by way of required production, and a late lunch could be enjoyed beneath the shade of a few mighty oaks whose age dated back to the founding of Ottawa. Each one provided shade enough for the assorted picnic tables scattered beneath them, where one took their life into their very hands trying to nab one, especially during the normal lunch hour, but they were now vacant, and he settled himself upon one at the far end of the property. It was not only cooler there, it was quiet, something he relished immensely.

He hadn't as yet spoken to Willow. He'd been rushed that morning, having overslept, which hardly left enough time in which to shave and shower before racing out the door en route to work. However he did manage to breeze through a local drive through and grab a large cup of his morning stimulant which somewhat made up for his lost breakfast. He was now reduced to a cola from the lunchroom's vending machine in which to wash down his peanut butter sandwich with. It might not have been his first choice, but at least it was wet, and it did quench his thirst. As he sipped his drink, his mind again envisioned his wife's disrobed body beneath him on his bed that day, the way she had reacted to his touch, the warmth of her lips upon his, her hunger for him, and the need to engulf him in the flames of desire they so wanted to experience again. These memories engulfed him to the point where his now erect penis suddenly reminded him of where they were, as well as the assorted eyes that would be upon him should he react to its demands.

Realizing this he looked about in embarrassment; but relief flooded him when he realized the tables were vacant, which meant no unnecessary audience for the hand puppet movement being carried out in his pants. But his relief was quickly replaced with a sinking feeling when he realized his break was over, and he was late. "But do I really want to go back?" he thought, dreading the heat that awaited him, as well as the fact that he still had a few hours to go before his shift was over. Also, he could not rid his gut of a feeling which could only be described as dread. "Is it something to be taken seriously, a possible omen?" he hesitantly wondered. Still, whatever it was, it did not appear to be vacating no matter how much he tried to dismiss it.

Returning to his station, he could not stop thinking about what was causing this present sensation. The feeling continued to chew away until he decided to phone his wife. Hopefully speaking with her would help dispel any present misgivings, as well as lift his spirit the second her voice was heard. Slipping into a private office, he put through the call only to have it ring numerous times without answer, as he thought, "Hmmm, maybe she's gone out somewhere, but she never said anything about doing so today." He waited a few more moments then rang again, only to be met with the same response. He now wished he would have included call answer when he'd had the phone reinstated, at least he could have left a message, but as always he had been thinking about the added cost, as he thought, "I really need to rid myself of that stingy habit, it's not like I can't afford it." He turned to leave, but stopped when the thought entered his mind to call Will Sutherland and see if Willow might possibly be there, or if he might know her whereabouts, like he often did.

The phone rang a few times before Will answered, announcing, "Blast your words my way, mates!!" It was obvious he had forgotten his aunt's indignant take on his phone answering skills.

"Hi, Will, it's Jonas; I was hoping you'd be home. I didn't know what shift you were on and I didn't see you out on the floor."

"I'm on afternoons," Will said, "but if this blasted heat doesn't damn-well subside I'm not coming in. I'm sitting smack dab in front of my AC. Can you believe this fucking heat?"

"It's something alright. Hey, Will, I need to ask if you've by any chance spoken with Willow today."

"Nope, haven't spoken with the girl for a couple of days. Anything wrong, possibly news of Quinn?"

"No, no news. I'm pretty sure the asshole got away; no doubt back in Ireland stalking some other mark. But I plan on swinging by the police station after work and touching base with Mann, other than that I've not heard anything. But I can't get Willow on the phone, and I don't think she was going anywhere, if she was she never told me when we spoke last evening."

"You don't think anything is wrong, do you, Jonas?"

"I don't think so but, well I sort of have this feeling in my gut like, well, it's hard to explain."

Will was nobody's fool, and he replied, "I know what you mean. I've been known to get them too. Whenever I'd be having one Aunt Mary would always tease me and ask if I was experiencing another of my *omens*. It's not funny really, especially when something awful happens and you can remember feeling an unexplained dread not long before it did."

"Well," Jonas said, "I don't think anything's wrong or about to happen, I just wish she would have answered the phone."

Will surmised his friend might require the support of a close buddy, and he said, "How about we meet for some suds. I hardly think you want to sweat it out at the plant for the rest of the day, so how about it?"

Jonas was hesitant. Will's suggestion did sound inviting, and maybe they could indulge in a bit, but he first needed to check on his wife, and he said, "How about you meet me over at Willow's. We can go to the pub afterward; she might even come with us."

"That sounds like a good idea, Jonas. I'll leave right now and I'll see you over there."

"Okay, I'll check out of here as soon as I can. There's not much going on today, production's been great all week and we're ahead of our quota, so I really can't see me knocking off early is going to make any difference."

"I've got my grandson here again today, but I'll drop him off at the sitters a bit earlier than the usual time. The lady that looks after him is a great old doll. She really enjoys having him around. I sometimes wonder if he's too much for her to handle, he's growing so fast and goes like a bat out of hell, but she says he's no problem. Maybe she wouldn't admit it if he was, but he enjoys being with her too. He's got to have female interaction from someone, sure as hell doesn't receive any from his flake of a mother. Too bad Dane took a page out of his old man's book and chose the wrong woman. But don't get me started on that. Hey, time's a wasting, buddy boy. I'll see you at Low's."

"Hey, no prob," Jonas replied, "and thanks again, Sutherland, you're a keeper. I'll see you soon."

Chapter 58

CONVERGENCE

With no time to lose, the Quinn matriarch tried pushing her way into Willow's home without as much as an excuse me, sorry, or may I come in? She was no longer fooling around, time was of the essence, and she had tired of this insipid waiting game. She had spent a ridiculous amount of time contemplating the entire issue, how she would make her move, when to make it, and if it would come off as planned; besides it had grown increasingly harder to control Declan, and as much as she didn't wish to admit it, Prichard appeared to be following in his footsteps. She would no longer wait, it was now or never, as she boldly ordered, "Get out me way, woman, I be coming in!"

Willow was taken aback, but not so bowled-over that she had forgotten how to stand her ground, and her arm instantly blocked the entrance, as she exclaimed, "Stop right there! You are not welcome here and you are *not* coming in!"

"Stand aside, kiddy fiddler!" Cailen blatantly ordered. "Ye might be thinking ye got away with enticing me boy with yur come on fancy ways and female wiles, but I be on to yur game. Playing young boys with yur fetching words, ye do, especially if they be wealthy ones whom can give ye a whirl on the coin ye entice them to spend on yur selfish wants. Well I got news for ye! I be bringing charges against ye for entrapment and extortion. Ye'll now pay the Divel for yur underhanded deeds - plotting yur witchcraft - casting spells on me boy to enter yur den of iniquity. Blast ye, cunt, ye not be getting away with any of it! Me lawyer be drafting the papers as we speak! By the look of ye, ye got just what ye deserved, and if ye try to move against me I be giving ye more!"

Willow found none of this amusing, and even though she realized the woman barking in her face felt it her right to defend her son, regardless of what he had done, she was not about to be accused for enticing him, or maligned for any part she played in it, as she thought, "I wonder if that *son-of-a-bitch* sent her here to do his dirty-work?" and the more she thought about the brass demeanor of the woman, the more she could not help thinking her point-on comparison to that of a female canine was not far off the mark.

The angry matron slammed her hands against Willow's chest, pushing her off balance and against the inside foyer wall. But she had underestimated the frail-looking woman, for she regained her balance and pushed back; slamming the Irish matriarch into the doorframe, while she yelled, "*Get the fuck out of my house now!* You've got some nerve pushing in here and running your mouth with crap! That's all it is, a load of bloody crap! Your cowardly son *raped* me, after he *lied* and took advantage of a situation that anybody with one lick of sense would have known better than to even consider! Goes to show the apple doesn't fall from the tree! If you don't believe me then ask your arrogant, holier-than-thou-son all about it! If he tells you any different then he's *lying*; then again he's a master at that!"

It was as plain as the startled look upon her face that Cailen didn't expect this kind of resistance. She was not used to being rebuked, in any form, let alone receive a dressing-down in this fashion from a woman who was well beneath her in economic standing. Cailen stood tall, exerting power in her stance, but Willow would not be intimidated. Holding her ground, she snapped, "Leave now or I will call the police! They're after him you know, and they *will* catch him, sooner or later, and when they do I will throw the book at the little fucker! Now get the hell out!"

The Irish matron was beside herself with anger, and before she realized what she was doing, she doubled her fist and slammed it straight into Willow's stomach, as she screamed, *"Ye not be threatening me boy with police warrants! Not after ye enticed him to yur cunt, and if he should become ill it will be on yur head! I know yur kind and how ye mind works! Ye now meet* me, *and if ye try and move against me I'll lay yur guts open before ye know what hit ye! Ye not be messing with me boy now, ye be suffering* my *wrath!"*

Willow dropped to her knees, breath coming in spurts while pain encompassed her lower front. She was certain the woman was deranged. What other explanation could there be for someone to carry something this far? But she didn't know the extent in which Cailen would go to protect her son in any situation, and all Cailen could think about was the way in which Willow had maligned her son, and even though she knew his guilt, she would not relinquish her obsessed hold on him.

From out of nowhere, Declan, having arrived by cab mere moments before, burst upon the porch with a frenzied Prichard, having arrived right behind him, trying her best to stop him.

"No disrespect meant, Miss Prichard, but back off!" he exclaimed as he ripped-open the door, yelling, *"I intend to finish the bitch once and for all!"*

The boy could see his mother towering over the fallen Willow. He also knew his mother's wrath, and instantly grabbed her arm before she could drive home another boilermaker. Cailen swung around; ready to face-down whoever was opposing her, and not realizing it was her son, drove her fist toward his jaw! But he was too fast for her and ducked to the side. Cailen's swing had been so intense she swung completely around and almost fell to her knees. She was like a woman possessed, bound and determined to carry through at all costs. She again lunged at the fallen woman, but Declan thwarted her attempt by grabbing her arm and swinging her around! Prichard stood horrified, cemented to the floor.

"Ma!" Declan exclaimed. "I intend on finishing her myself! It's me she done this to, not you!" But his mother paid him no mind; instead assumed a boxer-like stance.

Willow had risen to her knees with the intention of crawling to a nearby chair, but the Irish matron launched another attack, and lunged upon the injured woman, taking her to the floor! Declan wrenched his mother from Willow, and pushed her against a wall all the while threatening to bring his doubled fist across her jaw if she did not stop. Prichard could stand no more, and hurriedly insinuated herself between mother and son, pleading for them to cease their violence, and remember who each were. The staunch nanny would not relent, standing as stiff as a statue while repeating her prior words.

"I'll not be spoken to as if I be an impertinent child, Matilda!" Cailen exclaimed. "Stand back this instant!"

"Mrs. Quinn!" Prichard snapped in an imploring manner. "You must calm down and look at things rationally. Violence is not the answer! From either of you! Please! You *must* take hold of yourselves!"

The Quinn matriarch resumed her prideful stance, as she replied, "Ye not be addressing me in such a disrespectful tone,

Miss Prichard! We be discussing yur insubordinate action later! Declan, ye and this insolent *employee* will be leaving this instant!"

It was obvious Declan had taken offence to his mother's degrading remark toward his tutor, for he snapped, "Do not speak to or about Miss Prichard like that! You should be grateful for all she does for this family, not to mention what she puts up with from you!"

He no sooner got out the words when his mother's hand came firmly across his face! Prichard's unyielding support suddenly snapped, and she immediately brought her hand across Cailen's face, as she cried, "How does it feel, Mrs. Quinn?! How do *you* like it?!"

Willow's composure had returned and she could breathe easier, but she could no longer tolerate the unruly nonsense playing out in her home. She was about to order everyone out, but before she could Declan tore out the front door with Prichard and Cailen directly on his tail. The empty lot adjacent Willow's drive had become a parking lot, accommodating the newly arrived vehicles of Jonas Crosby, Will Sutherland, and Mary Sutherland whose car was being driven by her hired hand. They had all converged at once, but no one had as yet gotten out of their vehicle.

The young Irishman, doing his best to keep in front of the two women whom he now considered his jailors, went racing down Willow's front steps en route to freedom, but in his haste to escape retribution, ran blindly in front of the car driven by the Chief of Police. The startled Chief, who had slowed his vehicle in order to negotiate the turn into Willow's driveway, had been watching his rearview mirror, but by the time he saw young Quinn there was no time to react. The momentum of the impact sent Quinn over the hood and on to the pavement in a horrific thrust! Cailen and Prichard could not believe what had just taken place before their stunned eyes.

"*Declan!*" Cailen screamed, hardly able to breathe as she fell to her knees aside her crumpled son. "*Saints help me boy! Oh my God, Derek, our boy, me darling boy ... NO! ... Ye cannot be taken from me! NO!!*"

Prichard, hardly able to grasp what had happened, knelt beside her fallen charge, sobbing, but holding it together as she did her best to apply her nursing skills.

The Chief was out of his car in a flash, kneeing beside the unconscious boy while punching in numbers on his cell. Unbeknownst to him, Mary's hired hand had already called 911, but he instantly barked orders into his cell then grabbed the hysterical Cailen and eased her to the ground, doing his best to comfort her, while trying to cope with what he had done. "He came out of nowhere," he remarked, his voice sounding as wobbly as his legs felt.

"Help is on the way!" Mary Crosby exclaimed as she made her way toward her daughter who stood on the front steps, clutching a porch column, staring in disbelief at the scene before her.

Jonas and Will had hurriedly gotten out of their vehicles and approached the fallen boy as quickly as they could. "*Somebody get some blankets!*" Jonas yelled, his first-aid training instantly kicking in. As much as he despised this kid, he still had to do whatever could be done until the paramedics arrived.

Prichard remained vigilant, doing her best to sooth her injured charge, and though he was unconscious, she knew he was certain to feel her presence ever strong beside him. The Chief had managed to get Cailen away from the scene and into Shawn Martin's front room. Shawn had heard the screeching tires mere moments before and had raced to see what was happening. Offering his home was the least he could do, and for the moment the ill happening toward his neighbor had ceased.

A crowd had gathered, as is usual in cases such as this. Will Sutherland did his best to provide control, for he felt it was not only required, but his way of helping, and even though he hated the injured boy, he felt obliged to do what he could. A couple of blankets, a kind offering from the neighbor directly across the street, had arrived and one was spread over the injured boy while Prichard fashioned the second into a pillow beneath his head. She continued her vigilance, never faltering in her plight, never allowing weakness to appear in her eyes, but her heart was breaking. This young man, though rebellious in many ways, meant the world to her. She would do anything for him; even give up her life in return that he might keep his.

The paramedics arrived, and began checking their patient to be sure he could be moved without further damage. He was alive, but injured, the extent of which was yet to be determined. They began triage maneuvers, as they always do in cases such as this, but their faces held a somber look throughout their examination. If their minds could be read, the news would not be good, but they said not a word as they went about their duties, though one could tell that time was of the essence, and they lost none as they prepared their patient for transfer. Not certain as to the extent of his injuries, a spine board was laid beside him. Gently rolling him unto it, he was secured, and transported to the ambulance where Prichard climbed in beside him. Cailen, far too upset to sit aside her son, was placed up front with the driver. As the ambulance pulled away with sirens engaged the astounded onlookers watched it go, each wondering if the injured occupant would even make it to the hospital. The concerned Chief of Police, now accompanied by Detective Mann, was efficiently carrying out their duty by questioning those who had witnessed the unfortunate incident.

Each, in turn, gave their statement, but they could only relate what they had witnessed. No one knew what had earlier taken place, or what might have caused the young Irishman to come bolting out the door and into the oncoming path of the Chief's car. It wasn't until Willow's statement was taken that these holes in the story could be filled.

"Mrs. Crosby," the Chief questioned, "what happened prior to Mr. Quinn racing out of your home, which in turn brought him directly into the path of my car?"

Willow, accompanied by her mother, sat on her living room sofa doing her best to answer the question, as she said, "Well, Mrs. Quinn came here earlier to apparently have it out with me in regard to what had happened between her son and me. She was adamant that she was coming in, pushing, shoving against me, and when I stood my ground she became violent and, things escalated from there. Before I knew it, Declan, and their assistant Matilda Prichard, arrived. I heard him scream that he was going to finish me off, but the second he got in the front hall he could see what was happening. He tried to control his mother, who by this time was totally off the meter, still he continued to try, but she was intent on carrying through her vendetta and again attacked me. It was then Miss Prichard interceded as best she could. Mrs. Quinn had a few choice words to say to her of which Declan obviously disagreed with, and he spoke his dissatisfaction to his mother, who then slapped him across the face. Then Miss Prichard slapped *her*. It all came to a head so fast. I was just in the act of ordering them all out when Declan took off out the door with his mom and Miss Prichard behind him, and well, he ..." She ceased her explanation. The Chief could plainly see she was upset; besides at this point he really didn't require any further information.

Before anyone else could speak, Mary Sutherland stated, "I believe my daughter has endured quite enough. She is still convalescing, and does not need this added stress. If you require further information, she can come to the station in a few days to give it."

"No," the Chief said, "she won't be required to do that. We have enough information, and the facts of the actual accident are totally clear. He was all of a sudden *there*. I could not avoid hitting him. I've never experienced anything like that before. But we shall have to wait and see what the report from the hospital entails before we press any charges. You, as a private citizen, may press charges against his mother for forcible entry and assault upon your person. The rape charge is still pending, but it will have to wait until this latest occurrence is cleared away. Mr. Quinn was alive when he was loaded into the ambulance, but he is hurt, possibly broken bones, and head trauma no doubt. I've investigated accidents of this nature many times, but have never been the cause of one."

Glancing up at the Chief, Willow said, "You weren't the cause, Chief. Under the circumstances you could hardly avoid what happened out there. Declan used to tell me about the relationship between he and his mother, even Miss Prichard to a certain extent, so I already knew how much he was trying to distance himself from his life in Ireland, still I'm sorry what has happened to him, regardless of what he did to me."

Scratching his head in a matter-of-fact-way, the Chief replied, "Sounds kind of fishy to me, the uncanny hold on Mr. Quinn by those two that you're talking about. I've heard of overbearing mothers and teachers, but based on what you've described it almost sounds unnatural, sort of mind controlling. I wonder if they used him in any sexual manner."

Willow stared at the Chief as if she could hardly believe what he was hinting at, and she quickly asked, "What do you mean? I … well I hardly think they would conduct themselves in such a fashion. No, I don't think there was anything like that going on. Declan was very open about his life, and never once mentioned anything like that, or even hinted at it, that is if he could be believed, but somehow I think he was truthful. He used to say how controlling his mother was and how much he adored Miss Prichard, though he once said there were times when she made him nervous, but that was all. But he always spoke about his mother and how she forever kept him under her thumb, seemed intent on grooming him to take over the family business, and that according to her, resembled his father who had been killed in a car accident when Declan was a small boy. But she certainly is obsessive about him. Will you let me know how he gets along?"

"Well," the Chief grunted, lifting his large body to his feet, "I would hardly think you'd care. Especially knowing what he did to you. But given the present circumstances I can understand how you must feel. I'll let you know. Thank you for your time." Turning to Jonas, he said, "Thank you for your help as well. Mann or I will be in touch."

A few hours passed as Willow continued to sit on the sofa with her mother at her side. Jonas, though wanting to comfort his wife after such trauma, thought it best she have this time with her mother, and accompanied Will to have the beers they had previously planned on. Willow felt numb. She wanted Declan to pay for what he had done to her, but she never wanted payment this way. In her mind she remembered the kind, caring young man that had befriended her so many months prior and the words of encouragement he had typed, hoping they might lift her be lingered spirit, as well as the pink rose image he had sent to remind her that spring would come, even though the snow continued to pile higher with each difficult day she faced. It wasn't all bad, even though the ending was not that of a fairy tale, but it goes to show how quickly things can change. If she had it in her power she would change it all, but she didn't, and once again she would accept it, just like always.

Chapter 59

FRACTURED DARKNESS

Night had settled over Ottawa. The darkness had become a welcome commodity, for it was then the citizens of Ottawa and the surrounding district could enjoy the summer elements without need of refrigerated air do so. One could actually stroll about, sit in the parks, marvel at the amusements, and truly enjoy all that summer has to offer. Daytime was a totally different ballgame. The stifling heat continued, little, if any rain and no break in sight which made outdoor activities next to impossible, even the traffic upon the Rideau had decreased. It really was a record year for heat, not only the extreme temperature, but the amount of time in which it secured its hold.

The hospital's central air conditioning was working overtime, but at least it was keeping the patients comfortable, as well as those who sat in wait, hoping those they were there for would soon be given a new bill of health, discharged to their homes, and freedom. Many enjoyed this gift, but there were those who languished in their bed, no longer able to function, dependent on machines to keep their heart beating, lungs functioning, and blood coursing through their veins. There were those who required this assistance for a short while, others an extended period of time, and there were those who would never be free of them. Declan Quinn was one. The accident had dealt him a few broken ribs, a fractured wrist, and minor contusions to his face and hands. These would all heal with time, but far worse was the skull fracture his head had received upon impact with the pavement. The doctors had run several tests, including a CT scan, all of which arrived at the same conclusion. Their diagnosis was grim, and Cailen, along with Prichard, sat listening to the dreaded words being spoken. According to the head Neurosurgeon, Declan would remain in a vegetative state for the rest of his life. He may possibly have conscious moments, but it was highly unlikely they would remain for any period of time if they did appear. The most that could be done was to keep him as comfortable as possible.

The Quinn matriarch sat as if entranced, her spine rigid, eyes staring straight ahead. She had heard every word the doctor had spoken, but she would not accept them. In her mind, her boy would be fine, just like always, with the same Devil-may-care attitude which at times drove her to the end of her patience. How she would welcome his challenges now. But when it came to accepting this newest challenge her determination was immoveable. She would arrange to have him flown home where she would secure round the clock care. She would implement a mini hospital if need be, but she would not knuckle under to the adversity now facing them.

Prichard had her own demons to deal with. This latest quagmire was one that would take an inhuman amount of time to not only endure, but to conquer. She knew Cailen's faith was strong, and maybe that was what it was going to take, but Prichard, through her brief medical training, realized this kind of injury was not going to heal, nor go away. "He is lucky to be alive," she thought, "yet in the long run how lucky? Is this any quality of life? Would he want this if he could answer for himself?" Somehow she didn't think so, but she was only his nanny and tutor, she had no say in his life other than in those two areas. But he was a grown man who no longer required a nanny, and his education was now that of the level she could no longer provide. She had done all she could for him, and it was killing her to see what had happened to him. "Could I have prevented this?" she thought, agonizing on the subject, but knew it was impossible to answer regardless of what she might have said or done. She had been with this family for so long, and she was certain whatever she could now lend would be useful, so she would stay for as long as she could endure.

Turning to her employer, she said, "I really do think you should have a lay down, Mrs. Quinn. The arrangements can wait. I can even see to them if you like, but you are still in shock, and really should be resting. There is nothing more you can do here for the moment. Master Declan is resting comfortably, and he will be fine until your return."

The Irish matriarch continued to stare ahead, giving the impression she had not heard one word spoken, but just as Prichard was about to repeat them, she replied, "I be hearing every word ye have said, Matilda, there be no need beating a dead horse. Blast the wretched doctors and their idiotic Glasgow Coma Scale. I not be believing one word of it, and I not be leaving me boy's side this night. Come the morn I will make arrangements to have him taken home, where he belongs, where he should have never been driven from. A lot of this lies squarely on yur shoulders, Matilda, ye will just have to take over his higher education, that be all there is to it. If ye cannot presently do this then ye will have to do what ye can to learn; if not yur service will no longer be required. If ye had been able to teach him what be required he would not be lying here now."

For a moment Prichard was taken aback. "Surely the woman does not mean what she just said," she thought, and quickly dismissed it. Shock can be the cause of many things, some of which are words taken out of context, and thoughts centered in the wrong places. But shock eventually diminishes, yet words said in haste cannot be taken back. These were Prichard's thoughts exactly, and she held to them instead of letting Cailen's words upset her. After all what good would it do? She would simply wait until morning. Everything looks better in the light of day, much clearer than in the mist of the night, or a fog over a river.

"We'll discuss this later, Mrs. Quinn," Prichard said as she rearranged herself in the chair in which she was seated. "But I still think you should rest. I could arrange a bed close by. They will not allow you a bed in here; in fact both of us should not be here at the same time. Hospital rules are all the same in Intensive Care, and I will stay right by his side while you rest."

"I told ye I not be leaving him!" Cailen snapped indignantly.

Realizing she had reached the overwrought woman's limit, let alone her own, Prichard replied, "Then I shall step out for awhile. I could really use the break; in fact I may return to the hotel for a lie-down. If I am to become super woman then I will require all the rest I can secure."

"Ye are leaving?!" Cailen inquired as if Prichard did not have the right.

"Yes," Prichard answered, "until morning. There is nothing I can do here, and Intensive Care does not allow multiple visitors. He is your son, therefore you should stay, even though I feel you should rest, but I understand why you cannot leave. But I am done in, therefore I am going. I'll return first light."

"Then be off with ye," Cailen growled, and getting to her feet, said, "Me boy and me do not be requiring someone who cannot be remaining loyal to the present cause."

Stopping in mid-stride, Prichard replied, "Mrs. Quinn, there is no need to take that tone with me. You, more than *anyone* know how I feel about that boy lying on that bed. How dare you accuse me of disloyalty? I have remained true to your family throughout thick and thin, always at the ready to help and support however I could, I still do. I am here because I want to be here. I could not love that young man any more than if he were my own child, and this is how I have felt for countless years, I still do, I always will! How can you be so heartless toward me? I understand how you feel, how hard this is for you, and regardless of everything, I want to believe all will be well - my God how I wish it - but I am a realist, Cailen, and I must conduct myself as such. I cannot stay here and be treated like this. I will return in the morning, but in the interim I suggest you think about what I have said. Try and get some rest before you collapse. If that should happen - and prey God it doesn't - what earthly good would you be to your son then? Good night."

The Quinn matriarch sat aloof, head held high as to give the illusion she was above redemption of any kind. She was the head of the family, she called the shots, and no one, regardless of what they said, was going to change that.

Prichard arrived to her suite at Capital Elite, totally exhausted, emotionally drained with Cailen's words still echoing in her head. It was all too much, and her heart felt as if it were being wrenched from her chest. Declan Quinn meant the world to her, and to know what lie ahead for him was more than she could bear. Matlida Prichard was a strong woman with a will of steel, but the more she thought about her young charge and what he faced, the more diminished her will became. Her heart was totally broken, and as the Peace Tower's clock signaled the beginning of a new day, she buried her face into the pillow, and cried like she had never done before.

Chapter 60

A TOAST TO EMPATHY

Midnight had arrived to find Jonas Crosby and Will Sutherland seated at a corner table in a well-patronized Sparks Street bar, lifting their latest draught, and conversing about the horrific accident they had witnessed earlier. The empty beer glasses dotting the table revealed how busy the waiters were, as they did their best to keep sales climbing by delivering full glasses as opposed to removing empty ones. The two continued to drink, possibly to quench their thirst brought on by the day's unyielding heat, or to blot-out the day's unsavory happening.

"I hated Quinn's guts, but I never wanted retaliation like this," Jonas declared before downing half of his newly arrived brew.

Nodding his head in agreement, Will replied, "I know what you mean. I would have loved to have thumped him out that day in the hospital when he sat so smug in his trundle bed, running his over-used yap. But seeing him smashed onto that pavement like a sack of wet cement was not satisfying in the least. I'm amazed his brains weren't scattered everywhere. Goes to show he's got a hard head, it's just the insides that are scrambled."

"Mm-hmm," Jonas mused openly, and then lifting his glass, said, "Here's to Karma, and its swift delivery."

Hoisting the remainder of his brew, Will exclaimed, "I'll drink to that!"

They both sat quiet, as if they were contemplating their remarks just said, but each felt appeased that their loved one had been avenged. Yet they also knew that Willow, as much as she had every right to expect redemption for what had been dealt her by that kid, would not be at ease by the way it had come. She was a pacifist, under normal circumstances at least, and no-one could have blamed her had she taken comfort in it. In fact they would have been surprised if she had.

Will looked at Jonas, and said, "Do you think Low will ever get over this?"

Jonas remained quiet, contemplating this question. He knew Willow better than most, he also knew the vindictiveness she had felt toward him; he also felt that she had every right to feel it, yet he had experienced her gentleness many times before their breakup and a few times since they reconciled; then again she had never been raped. Rubbing the whisker growth on his chin, he replied, "If she does it will certainly take awhile. She cringes every time I as much as touch her hand, let alone try and embrace her. She was never like that before, not even if we'd quarreled. This scar runs deep, Will, right to her core, so it's highly unlikely she'll ever be the Willow I knew. It's a crying shame what Quinn not only did to her, but what he *took* from her, and regardless of what has happened to him I will never forgive him for that."

Nodding in compliance, Will said, "Can't blame you one bit. I feel exactly the same. You know I sometimes let my mind go back to when Low and me were kids, the silly nonsense we'd try and pull off, and the laughs we had. She loved to laugh, her eyes smiled as much as her lips did - her eyes don't smile anymore - it's totally gone. It hurts to see that, Jonas. You would have loved her as a kid, just as much as I did; she was special, not just my cousin, but my friend. She's always been there for me. I just wish I could somehow put back what's gone."

"Hopefully time will replace that," Jonas said. "But it's something that can't be forced by any of us." Reaching into his jeans, he pulled out his wallet, took out a few bills, and then shoved it back into his pocket. Holding up two fingers as a signal to the waiter, he continued, "Was actually good to see her mom there with her. Mary seemed almost concerned - well I really shouldn't talk like that, and I am thankful to know she was there for Willow. I don't need to tell you how things have always been between them - I'm sure it was like that long before I came on the scene - but even though it's coming late, it's better late than never I suppose. *Was* it always like that between them?"

Nodding his head in gratitude for the latest brew, Will replied, "Pretty much. Aunt Mary always seemed to be on Low's case about something or other; then again Low could ask for what she got. She knew Aunt Mary well, and she also knew just what buttons to push. I suppose when it comes to our parents we're all guilty of that, but Low and Aunt Mary seemed to go head to head more than any other mother and daughter I knew. I swear if the community would have held confrontation contests, those two would have won hands down, each and every time."

"Really," Jonas said, settling back in his chair, "I only know what's gone on since I met Willow. It was her dad she was close to, maybe too much so, and maybe that was why Mary treated her the way she did. Mind you, I know how Willow can piss a person off, but I also know that her mother's treatment of her always bothered her. I know it still does. I'm sure she would have loved to have been able to confide in her mother about the rape, I don't know, I would think that would be something any daughter would need their mother's support for. I wonder if that was why Mary was there."

Shrugging his shoulders, Will replied, "I don't know, possibly, then again it could have been for any reason. Aunt Mary was extremely perturbed about Low's lack of correspondence; at least by the way she spoke the last time she phoned to ask if I'd heard from her. She was most indignant, but I also realize she was worried. You certainly can't fault her for that. Low developed a bad habit of that, especially these last few months. Maybe had she kept in touch a bit more we might have noticed something off or, possibly gotten wind of Quinn before things got to the point they did."

"Maybe, but whether she would have listened to anyone would have been the next thing," Jonas said, and then finished his beer. Setting the emptied glass upon the table, he continued, "Can't help but feel sorry for the Chief. Imagine, someone running directly in front of you like that. The man couldn't stop *that* fast. Good thing he had slowed down to make the turn, otherwise Quinn would be dead."

Shaking his head in wonderment, Will replied, "Tell me about it. The Chief doesn't show emotion very often, but that had to have been hard to swallow. Besides, it brings the case to a close really because it was the police that hit the kid, and after this I don't think Low will press charges."

"No," Jonas replied, "I don't think she will either. I mean, she's nothing to gain now, he can't very well be brought to justice the way he is, but I still wonder about that mother of his. I realize it would be traumatic to watch your kid mowed down like that, but that dame's got a screw loose, especially after listening to what

Willow had to say about the way in which she was carrying on prior to the accident, not to mention the way she's always been with her boy."

Nodding his head, Will said, "I don't think you're far off the mark with that assumption. Too damn much money and power if you ask me. Sure goes to some people's head. But I'll never have to worry about that."

"Me neither, Will, at least I don't think so," Jonas replied, rising to his feet. "Well I think I'll be off. I wanted to call Willow to see how she's doing but it's gotten late and I'm sure she's gone to bed. I'll wait until morning and call her before I leave for work, you in tomorrow?"

"I'm supposed to be," Will replied. "Guess I'd better punch the clock if I want to continue to get paid. Damn heat, it's getting to me, but I'll see you in the morning."

"Will do, Sutherland, and thanks for all you did today, as well as talking out stuff tonight."

"Hey, that's what friends do."

They each shook each other's extended hand before walking out to their vehicles. As they drove in opposite directions they each felt a surge of relief, yet what relief they felt was somehow overshadowed by the ongoing distress toward Willow's condition. They must somehow find a way to relight the spark in her eyes, replace a smile to her lips, and bring contentment to her soul. But each knew that it would be a task that may never celebrate fulfillment.

Chapter 61

IN RETROSPECT

Two years had passed since the day of convergence, when life seemed to change for everyone. Declan Quinn still remained in a vegetative state, opulently displayed beneath satin as if he were royalty in his private chamber, that of which had become a shrine to what it had once been. His mother, through her unshakeable determination to remain oblivious to what each and every doctor had stated since her son's initial diagnosis, carried on as though nothing out of the ordinary had happened, though she did incorporate a small hospital into her home, providing round the clock care for her son, though she didn't want things to appear as such. The medical staff had been given strict orders as to their conduct and dress just in case their patient should acquire a few lucid moments of consciousness, which had managed to appear from time to time yet never lasted more than a few moments, but Cailen did not want her boy distressed or confused in any way during those moments. Cailen herself had changed, no longer the approachable, down to earth woman who once cared for others in ways which most people of wealth and privilege seldom do, and because of this newly adopted outlook had, with the exception of Prichard, driven away her longtime staff.

Change had not only come to Cailen Quinn, it had also come to Willow Crosby. The last two years found Willow pushing forward, trying her best to overcome the adversity and humiliation suffered at the hands of Declan Quinn. She now realized her share of blame in everything that had happened, and as much as she still despised him for what he had done to her, she could not get the vision of him lying broken on the street out of her mind. She couldn't help thinking that if she had conducted herself properly, or in the very least cautiously, then the appalling end to that drama might not have come about, at least in the way that it had. She still found it difficult to let Jonas touch her, and this bothered her. Though they had managed to find their way back to each other through his return to their home, it wasn't all smooth sailing, yet each day was one more step toward what they hoped to again find. "Was happiness even possible?" Willow often wondered as her mind swept back over everything that had happened. But she was determined to find it. She was also determined to bring happiness to Jonas, for regardless of the way he had treated her during their estrangement, she'd come to realize that even that was not entirely his fault, and if they were ever to find what they again hoped to achieve, it would never come about if they were forever rehashing the past.

She had also returned to her cleaning service, but each day was growing more difficult to get through, for her declining health was always an issue. She realized she was growing older; everyone must face this same fact, but she couldn't help wondering why she felt it more than others her age. It had taken quite some time for her female anatomy to heal; she knew it would never be as it once was but she did her best to cope. The hardest, as always, was the unsavory memories embedded in her mind, and every time she saw a couple on the street her first thought was to what might be going on between them, how they treated each other, and how they would end. She realized this was not a healthy habit, but she could never seem to cease doing it.

Willow was always happy to see favorite clients, namely the McCarthy's, but my how she missed Winifred Brown. She intentionally refused to work the days that would have belonged to Winifred. It was her way of respecting the woman whom she dearly loved and heartbreakingly missed. She even drove past the house from time to time, just for old times' sake, if nothing else. The green-gabled house, having been sold the year before, now housed someone else, and Willow could never inquire who it was, or bring herself to the front door to inquire within. Her memories of that house, the way it appeared inside, as well as the grounds surrounding it must remain in her memory unaltered, undisturbed, and untouched. This was her way of keeping her life before Declan intact. It may have appeared silly to some, but to her it was part of her survival system.

It was now night time in Galway. The evening meal had finished, and like always, Cailen, accompanied by Prichard, took their meal at Declan's bedside. Prichard never thought this proper, but each time she brought it to Cailen's attention she was immediately shot-down. If one was to ask Prichard, she would say she was 'simply put in her place,' yet if Cailen realized what she was doing, she might have chosen a better avenue in which to go down, for the situation within the House of Quinn was growing direr with each new sunrise. Cailen found fault with everyone, regardless of how they strived to satisfy. Prichard felt remorse for each of them, even going so far as assisting in places where she otherwise would have never considered with the old staff. How she missed Bridget Donnigan, her old pal and confidant. She often thought about days long past, when Bridget's jolly laughter and confident outlook helped raise everyone's spirit whenever they were down, or faced with the latest adversity on the calendar. She suddenly thought about the plight of that poor old woman, and how she never got the satisfaction of bringing those laden trays to the upper floors via the lift which was supposed to have been installed for just that purpose. She shook her head, and a disgusted sigh could be heard leaving her throat.

Things were looking up for Will Sutherland. Since coming to Ottawa, Will had never taken the time to get to know the eldest granddaughter of his grandson's sitter, until a recent night when he had been asked to gather the boy while Dane enjoyed a night out with his friends. Will and she had taken notice of each other, but they never spent much time discussing topics of which they each had in common. He was a few years older than she, but nothing that would cause a stir among those assigned judgment of such things, namely his Aunt Mary Sutherland. Since the passing of Will's parents many years earlier, Mary had taken it upon herself to sit in their vacant seat, and in doing so, would voice her opinion rather frequently. This practice had increased, and for Will it clearly brought Willow's tolerance, or lack thereof, to the forefront. He had to admit to not liking it, but remained cool about it, and kept his opinions to himself. For the first time in many years he was truly happy, not just for himself, but for his family, who had been without a woman's guidance far too long. But that might all be about to change, for he had recently received his divorce decree, and had secured a date with his new found interest.

Bedtime had arrived in the Crosby home, and Jonas, freshly shaved and showered, crawled into bed beside an already sleeping Willow. He wondered if he should embrace her, possibly lean over and kiss her lips, but because she was unaware, figured he best just go to sleep. They had managed to gain ground, dearly needed ground, but if he was to shake the tree too hard, it just might fall.

"Be grateful for what you got," Jonas thought while he gazed at his sleeping wife, but he also felt uneasy in knowing that her health continued to decline. He couldn't put his finger on anything per se, but something was definitely off for she was losing weight, not alarmingly so, but enough that was not only noticeable, it was preying on his mind as to what was causing it. He had to be careful how he approached the issue, because he didn't want her thinking the wrong thing, or that he was dissatisfied with the way she looked. In his eyes she was beautiful, still the same, exciting woman he had fallen in love with so long ago, but she should not be losing energy so quickly. He had made certain to keep only nourishing food on hand, a practice he had gotten into during the hiatus from his marriage, and he had to admit he relished it. Thoughts of the empty cupboards in which his wife had faced during their time apart were always front and center in his mind, and he swore that would never happen again. He had found himself swearing to a lot of things over the course of the last two years, each one fully as important as the next, and come what may he would always remain adamant about them. He realized that both he and his wife had been blessed to have found their way back to each other, and he'd be damned if he would ever be parted from her again.

Chapter 62

ONE LAST ATTEMPT

Days turned to weeks. As each one finished, Willow felt finished, as if she were winding down like an old fashioned clock whose time had run out. Fall had arrived, and with it a great change in the air. The clear crispness of it was almost ironic, because the heat of the last two summers, plus the limited amount of rain throughout that time, had been unyielding. It was a miracle any crops survived, and those growing in areas that hadn't been completely whipped-out by the tornado two years earlier, had managed maturity once again only to find death awaiting them within the huge harvesters that now removed them, leaving the soil looking as if they'd never been there.

An annoying cold, that of which Willow had developed a few weeks earlier, appeared to be worsening, and the reddening of her nose caused from the constant blowing was making her nostrils appear as if she'd become a cocaine addict. The nasty virus appeared adamant in bringing her down, but the strong will she'd possessed throughout her life was determined to stand fast, yet it was growing increasingly difficult to do so. She had decided to keep it from Jonas, after all the majority of problems had finally settled between them, and she didn't want to upset the applecart by complaining about another health issue. She couldn't help remembering the earlier grief her complaints had brought her marriage, and she could not gamble a repeat should she mention anything out of the norm.

But she was unaware that Jonas already surmised something, but had never revealed how he felt or what he thought, for he too remembered the way things once were, back when he should have had someone give him a swift kick for the way in which he had reacted to them, complaining because she had to miss another day of work instead of caring about the reason as to why. But when he truly thought about it, he really didn't think her present condition was due to a woman's ailment, not in the way it had once been, the symptoms were not the same, still whatever it was it was certainly doing a number on her health.

Willow had retired from her cleaning service, having done so two weeks earlier, much to the chagrin of the McCarthy's, but she couldn't continue a service which no longer delivered the goods, and after a tearful farewell, had promised to stay in touch. But that was highly unlikely, because with clients of a cleaning service - with the possible exemption like Winifred would have been if she were still alive - it was simply not done, but she would try. In many ways that kind of employment is considered impersonal, certainly something that is not held in high esteem in the world of employment, nor the respect of such, but it was honest work just the same. She would miss some of them, of that she was certain, after all one cannot be a part of another's life and not make some kind of impression, even in the world of cleaning.

The morning dragged on, like so many now seemed to for Willow as she enjoyed the morning coffee of whose brewing Jonas had again taken over. How she savored the taste, almost as if the

Columbian Gods themselves had ground their scared beans into prized nectar to be tasted by the humble servants below, namely her, but regardless of this over-the-top description, she was certainly enjoying every single drop. She laughed with subtlety as she thought about this, but was certainly glad that Jonas was again in charge of it. She was glad that so many things were now settled between them; she just wished her anxiety in the area of intimacy would settle.

These thoughts continued to consume her mind until a knock sounded upon the front door. Upon answering it, she was surprised to find a courier standing on her porch, holding a brown envelope in his hand and a pen at the ready.

As she opened the door, he inquired, "Are you Willow Crosby?"

"Yes."

"Sign here, please," the courier requested.

Willow, not realizing what it was but remembering she had earlier ordered something via courier, took pen in hand, and signed on the dotted line.

Returning the pen to his pocket, the courier said, "You have just been served, have a good day," and he moved down the steps toward his van.

"What the hell?" Willow said with curiosity as she returned to the dining table with the intent of depositing the envelope on the table surface, but as she looked closer, her eyes were mysteriously drawn to the intended person's name, which was her, but the return address was that of one Shamus D. O'Riley, Attorney at Law, Galway, Ireland. "Now what?" she thought with rising contempt as she ripped-open the envelope. "Surely the moronic nonsense of two years ago is not starting again," she thought as her hackles rose, "one would think that obsessed bitch has enough to contend with without starting up her ridiculous vendetta again," and her eyes studied the words displayed in black, which read:

Shamus D. O'Riley
Barrister-Solicitor-Attorney-at-Law
September 22, 2005 A.D.

Dear Willow Crosby,

I am writing to inform you that a legal suit of Entrapment and Extortion is being levied against you by my client, Mrs. Cailen Cathlaine O'Brian-Quinn, CEO of Quinn Distilleries Inc. ® Galway, Ireland. My client, mother of Declan Eamon Quinn, is bringing charges against you with full intent of proving that you willfully, during the course of late winter of 2003 through early summer of 2003, put into play, via the Internet, entrapment measures to ensnare Declan Eamon Quinn to your Ottawa Ontario residence.

My client further states, that throughout mentioned period of time, you purposely beguiled her son to your home with willful intent of committing acts of debauchery upon him, thereby enticing sexual intercourse through plotted measures, resulting in personal injury to Declan Eamon Quinn, as well as demands for enormous monetary compensation for yourself. When he refused, you claimed rape, and secured charges of such to be brought against him. Because of your degenerate act, Declan Eamon Quinn, Cailen O'Brian-Quinn, and the entire Quinn family, have been publically disgraced, and humiliated. My client is seeking punitive damages of IR£ 1.5 ml.

My client further demands a public apology be boldly displayed in the Ottawa Sun, as well as Galway

Independent, claiming your debased actions which has resulted in these charges being levied.

Your immediate response is required no later than October, 3rd, 2005, at which time the Court of Galway will begin proceedings against you. These proceedings may consist of immediate garnishment of your income, seizure of your house and contents, and or incarceration of up to fifteen years. Kindly have your solicitor contact my office in regard to these matters.

Respectfully,
Shamus D. O'Riley,
Attorney-at-Law.

Willow could not believe the words before her eyes. "Why that insolent, self-centered rich bitch," she thought, "my God what will I do?" Her anguish continued to intensify. She was mortified, paralyzed with fear, and she suddenly thought, "How do I tell Jonas? How *can* I tell him? I brought this to our doorstep! I was the one that caused this, but I did *not* entice that conniving young liar!" Thinking about Cailen and her outrageous demands, her thoughts continued, "Now I know where *he* gets his holier-than-thou-because-I'm-rich attitude. They honestly think they can do and say whatever they please without redemption or thought thereof. Well they're not getting away with it! I refuse to be browbeaten any longer!" A sinking feeling encompassed her stomach, as she thought, "My family, I have to protect them against that bitch. I wouldn't put it past her to go after them too! I've managed to keep all of this despicable happening from them. How can I face them ever again if this gets known? *I can't!* I should have pushed through those charges, nailed his sorry ass against the wall — if not his shrunken balls - should have nailed them to a stump and pushed the son-of-bitch backward - and that sorry excuse of a mother of his - what a sanctimonious bitch she truly is! I can't believe I felt remorse for her when he got slammed to the pavement. How stupid could I have been?"

But Willow couldn't help the way she was, or the way in which her heart dealt with things that were totally out of her control. The summons's was issued the day before, but the response time was just over a week! There was no way in hell that she could pay the amount being demanded in that summons, should it carry through, and unless Timothy Breen could do some fast talking there may be no other choice, but she suddenly remembered the speed in which he had moved in regard to the utility crisis, and her stress level heightened. Yet it was short-lived, for during those few impossible moments her husband's shark of a lawyer came to mind, as she openly said, "He is exactly what I need. It's going to take a shark to kill a shark, at least wound it to the extent it will never swim again." She lost no time securing her address book, and quickly punched in Patrick Doyle's number.

Chapter 63

THE ONLY WAY OUT

The more the day lengthened, the more nervous Willow became. She had managed to reach Patrick Doyle's office only to find him away, and not expected to return for the better part of two weeks. He'd gone abroad, according to his secretary, but regardless of how much Willow begged, the woman would not divulge her employer's whereabouts. The imaginary rope in which she felt around her neck continued to tighten. She had to somehow get in touch with the only lawyer she felt capable of not only taking-down Cailen Quinn, but her entire family, lawyer to boot.

Feeling all hope would be lost if she did not get word to Doyle, she hurriedly exclaimed, "But this is urgent! I *must* get in touch with him!"

The secretary instantly replied, "You are not his client, Mrs. Crosby, your husband is, and unless he needs urgent assistance there is nothing I can do. *Does* your husband require assistance?"

"No," Willow cried, "I do."

Sensing the woman's frenzied state, the secretary calmly replied, "This is rather unorthodox, Mrs. Crosby. Usually a lawyer who has represented a husband or wife in a matrimonial action does not take on the representation of the other."

Trying her utmost to remain calm, Willow said, "This doesn't concern our marital action. Jonas and I have managed to work on our problems, and settle pretty much everything that we were going to court for."

Trying to efficiently do her job, the secretary inquired, "What do you need to speak with Mr. Doyle about?"

Willow bluntly replied, "I'm being sued."

"Who is suing you, and what for?"

"I ... I can't ... I, well ..."

"Mrs. Crosby," the secretary stated, sounding determined in her reaction, "you need to get hold of yourself. I haven't time for run-around issues like this."

"It's too embarrassing to divulge to you," Willow cried.

"Then I'm afraid I cannot help you," the secretary replied.

Willow swiftly injected, "Wait..." but it was to no avail, Doyle's gal Friday had left, and all that remained was the dial tone.

Totally vanquished, Willow sauntered to the table where the summons lay in wait, chastising her, mocking her, and daring her to move against it. She could almost hear Declan Quinn and his entire wretched family laughing, celebrating their latest victory. Try as she might, Willow could not see a logical way out. The one route she thought might be her saving grace had proven a dead end, like so many routes she had taken throughout her life. The mantel clock ticked away as she sat, listening to the precise measurement between each delicate click the pendulum made as it moved toward the completion of another hour. "Another hour of my life gone," she thought as the ticking permeated her mind. She grew tired, but she was not sleepy, she was simply tired, tired of fighting tired of living. "I know what I'm thinking is wrong," she thought in apprehension, but she had reached a point where common sense no longer mattered. She was just about to go to the bedroom when the phone rang.

"Hello?" she said in question, not really caring as to whom it might be.

"Hi, Low!" Will Sutherland exclaimed as if he were trying to get her attention from across a crowded room.

"Hey there, Willy," she replied. "What can I do for you?"

In his always lighthearted, loving manner, he said, "Ask not what you can do for me, but what I can do for you. Hey, weren't those words used in a presidential speech at some point, over the course of history or something?"

Quietly laughing, Willow replied, "Well something like that, cousin dear, but I think they were spoken a bit differently, and with a much different meaning."

"I suppose," Will said rather uncaringly, "but you know me when it comes to history, never did listen up all that well in class. *Anyhoo*, Jonas is swamped at his machine, and he wanted me to call and tell you he has to work late tonight — we both do — and he didn't want you worrying when he didn't show up at the normal time."

Again laughing softly, Willow said, "Well I thank you, cousin dear. I might have wondered where he was come dinner time when I'm sitting there alone stabbing at my dried-up old chicken."

Will sensed something a bit off in her voice, the tone of it, or the quiet giggle, as if it where someone else replying to him. He wasn't certain, but she didn't seem herself.

"Low," he said, "is everything alright? You don't sound yourself."

"Well who else would I be?"

"Very funny, girl, but you know what I mean. What's wrong?"

"Nothing is wrong. I'm just tired."

"Well you can include me there. Starting to get a tad old for these long days of overtime, but I should be glad to have it, for that matter even a job, especially one that I like."

"Yes, Jonas would agree. Thanks for calling, and tell him I'll leave his supper warming in the oven."

"Don't go yet, Low!"

"Will, I want you to know how grateful I am for having you as a cousin, every second of it. We've sure had our times over the years, haven't we?"

"That we have!"

"Remember the time above the granary in Grandpa Sutherland's barn when we dared each other as to who could walk the high beam the most without falling? I continued to be cocky and just *had* to outdo you, until I lost my balance, and crashed-down on that old steel fanning mill. The impact shoved my right kneecap off center. You got it back into place, while I screamed bloody murder. I'm sure you felt sorry for me, but I think you were more scared that Mom would find out."

"I do remember that, Low! I *did* feel sorry for you, I knew it hurt terribly, but I had to fix you if I could. But I was scared, more scared than a jack rabbit trying to outrun a starving dog, 'cause if Aunt Mary had ever found out she would have tanned our hides raw — especially mine. I think she always thought me a bit of a troublemaker. Imagine, you talking about that now."

"It just came to mind. I can remember so many things from that time, Will. Never forget them and, don't let too much time slip by before you secure that new stepmom for Dane, okay? Regardless of how old they are, they still need a loving momma."

Will was growing concerned, but his break time was over. "She said she's just tired," he thought, yet he couldn't help but feel something was out of balance. Aside from the ongoing cold that seemed to hold her hostage, he felt she had been gaining ground since all that Quinn nonsense, but he truly wished he could spend more time with her.

"Hey, Low, how about you and Crosby coming to dinner with my sweetie and me say, this Saturday night? We could go to that new restaurant everyone's raving about. You know that new one in Byward Market?"

"That might be nice," she replied. "We'll see. I'll talk it over with Jonas when he gets home tonight. He'll let you know. Talk to you later and, Willy, *I love you.*"

Will definitely knew something was not right. He knew she loved him, he loved her that went without saying, but the way in which she said it bothered him. It was as if she were saying goodbye.

"Willow, talk to me, there is something wrong, I know there is, please talk to me," he pleaded.

"There is nothing *wrong*, Will. I'm just tired, as I said before. This damn cold or whatever it is continues to kick the shit out of me, so I'm going to have an early night. I'll see you soon, okay?"

"Yes, pretty Low, see you soon."

Willow had left the conversation, leaving only the dial tone's placid nuance to entertain her cousin's ear. He did not like the feeling in his gut - another omen perhaps? Hopefully nothing to worry about, but he would mention his concerns to Jonas with hope he might possibly be able to knock-off early and go home. He would feel much better about all of this once he heard from his long-time friend, or saw him at work the next morning.

On the other side of town the phone rang a few times before Catharine Whidbey answered.

"Hello, Catharine. How are you today?"

"Oh hi, Willow. I'm fine, thanks, how are you?"

"I've had better days, but no sense in complaining, I'm tired of doing that. Would Benny be home by any chance?"

"Not yet I'm afraid. Is it important?"

"Not overly so, I was just thinking about him, haven't spoken with him in awhile, nor his brother, who I intend to call after this."

"Well you can catch them at the office. Ben said they both had client presentations this afternoon. Why don't you try them there? It'll be quite awhile before they're home."

"Thank you, Catharine, I'll do that. By the way, give the kids a giant hug for me and, give them my love."

"Will do, you have a good one, Willow. Bye."

"Bye bye, Catharine."

The phone at the design center rang a few times before the receptionist answered. Willow immediately requested to speak with both of her sons. "I'll buzz them in the board room," the young lady said in a pleasant tone of voice. "The meeting has finished, but they're both still in there. Hang on, Mrs. Crosby."

It wasn't long before Ben Whidbey came on the line.

"Hi, Mom!" he exclaimed, obviously happy to know who he was conversing with.

"Hi, Benny," Willow replied with fondness. "I rang the house, but Catharine said both you and Shay were working together today."

"Yeah, that's right; we decided to gang-up on a couple of clients who've been dragging their feet about closing a deal. Nothing like doubling up on effort; hang on; I'll put you on speaker."

"Hello, Mom!" Shay Crosby exclaimed in the same happy tone as his brother had used. "How are you?"

"Fine, now that I get to hear both your voices. For some reason I just needed to hear you both, and get to talk for a few minutes," Willow said as she fought-back tears.

"We don't get to talk enough," Ben said, and Shay added, "I'm with Ben there, Mom. I wish we could have spent more time with you following your ordeal but, well, in this business the demands of work are always calling."

Silently weeping, Willow replied, "Yes, I'm sure they are. But you both knew that when you became design artists. I want you to know how very proud I am of both of you, not just in business, but in your personal lives as well. You chose good women, and you both have beautiful, wonderful children. You've made me very happy. I love all of you so much, but there is something extra special in the love a mother has for her children. It is unconditional, and forever. Always remember that."

"Is something wrong, Mom?" Ben inquired, his voice taking on a serious tone as if he was searching for something that he couldn't quite put his finger on.

Shay suddenly added, "Mom, are you *sure* you're alright? Is Dad there with you?"

With tears dripping down her cheeks, Willow replied, "I'm fine, boys, I just wanted to talk with you both and tell you how I feel. There's nothing wrong with that, and no, your dad is still at work, in fact he's working late tonight. Your cousin Will called awhile ago to tell me that. By the way, Benny, should you be talking to your father anytime soon, give him my best, will you, and tell him I think of him often and, with fondness whenever I do?"

"What is wrong, Mom? You haven't mentioned my father's name in a very long time," Ben commented as he wondered why she would mention a man he barely knew.

She quickly replied, "I'm fine, son, you don't have to worry about me. I was just thinking about Bernie. I haven't seen him in so many years, but that doesn't mean I never think about him and the time we had together, I mean, that time together produced you, and besides I do have fond memories of him. Anyway, I have to go, supper doesn't make itself. I'm sure you both remember all those years of burnt offerings and sometimes not so tasty morsels. But I did try my best, that's the main thing."

Chiming in unison, both boys said, "You did okay, Mom! We'll see you soon!"

"Yes," she softly said, "you will. I love you both. Stay safe, and well — and be happy."

"The same to you too, Mom!" they called-out together.

She had one more call to make, one that was most difficult.

"Hello?" Mary Sutherland inquired.

"Hello, Mom!" Willow exclaimed with faux happiness. "How are you doing?"

"I'm well, dear," Mary replied. "How is that cold that's been plaguing you for so long now? I hope you went to the doctor and got medication for it. Don't wait, something like that can become very nasty if let go unattended. Maybe you should be applying mustard plasters. Have you? I know you know how to make them."

"Whoa, Mom, slow down. I know we've been getting along much better ever since I … well, ever since. The cold is still with me but I don't think it's any worse, I'm just tired. On that note I'm going to go and make an early night of it. I just wanted to call and hear your voice."

"Well that is sweet of you, dear. I too am happy that we've managed to become closer. I'm really looking forward to Christmas this year. You will be coming home to the farm, I hope?"

It was all Willow could do to keep from breaking down entirely, as she replied, "That's a ways off yet, Mom. But I'm sure the family will all be together with you."

"That would be lovely, dear. It's been so long. I don't think that has happened more than a few times since your father passed away."

Willow immediately said, "Do you remember the Christmas' when I was a little girl? I do, they were so nice. You always did your best with what you had to work with in order to provide a good holiday for David and me, and maybe I've never told you enough how much we appreciated it, I certainly did, everything you ever did for me, not just at Christmas, but always. Please know that, and know that regardless of the way it always was between us, I always loved you, and I always will. Could you pass that sentiment along to David too?"

"Oh such a Gloomy Gus today, Willow, so nostalgic. But I must say it's always nice to reminisce, and feel what is always stored in the heart. I love you too, dear."

"I know you do. Now I must go and fix dinner for Jonas. He's working late tonight, but I'll keep his dinner warm in the oven. Thanks, Mom."

"I'll talk to you soon, Willow, and take care of that cold. Bye for now."

"Goodbye, Momma."

Again Willow sat staring at the dreaded papers from Galway, certain there was no alternative but the one she was contemplating. She wondered if she should write the all-so-important-note to Jonas, yet knew if she did it would only add further embarrassment to what he and everyone would already feel, not to mention what they would cope with. Yet they all deserved some form of explanation for her selfish act. "My entire life has been a selfish act," she thought, feeling remorse, and knowing self-pity is the worst way in which to deal with something that had become too much to cope with, but she had reached the end. She felt driven to it, possibly that was the way she was meant to feel.

Acquiring a piece of note paper with the letterhead stating 'From the Desk of Willow Crosby,' she sat down at the dining room table to begin her last words to Jonas.

Jonas, my dearest love;

These are the most difficult words I have ever to write. You and the family do not deserve what I am about to do, or the hurt and embarrassment it will bring to each of you to have to deal with in your own way. It is selfish, I realize this, but the reason is valid as to why I feel the need, because without completing this act, what will come upon this family because of me and what I have done, regardless of any guilt I may carry because of it, is something that I cannot allow. Therefore if I am no longer around, there will be no further need to be targeted or further disgrace brought upon any of you, your names, or your lives.

I made the biggest mistake of my life the day that I encountered Declan Quinn. One has no way of knowing what the future will bring, or what a simple salutation can lead to. However I do feel that had I not been as vulnerable as I was at the time, nothing he would have said would have brought as much as a second glance from me. Still, it is no excuse for what I did, which in turn led to what has since happened. I hope in time you all can forgive me.

The day I met you, Jonas, was a joyous one. I can still remember everything about it. You brought me joy, happiness, and in many ways contentment, much more so than I ever thought I would find throughout all the avenues I went down in search of it.

I spoke with the boys today. It was nice to hear their voices as well as their laughter. I am so proud of them, the men they have become, and the fine women they have chosen to share their life with. Giving birth to each of my boys was the finest accomplishments of my life. I will forever love and cherish them, the same as I will forever love and cherish my grandchildren.

I also spoke with Mom. It was nice, and I'm glad we managed to bridge our gap. Tell her I will forever love her, and David.

Tell Will he has been a great cousin, but most of all, my friend. I love him dearly. Please be sure he knows that, and should he ever hear from Megan, ask him to give her my love, and tell her thanks for everything. The last I heard from her she was in Zurich romancing some rich Swede. (Cousin dear will love that)

WILLOW'S WALK

I'm thinking of my father, as always, and I hope that if a next life exists, I can join him there. I also hope that I will again be with each of you in a life that is kind, people are fair and gentle to each other, and where peace and love take precedence over all.

'I love you, Jonas'. Find peace, as well as happiness. In time you will, and please know through your finding of these, you will have brought them to me also.

I love all of you. I always will.

Willow.

Folding the letter and inserting it inside the matching envelope expressing Jonas' name, she carried it to the bedroom, laid it at the base of the bedside lamp, and then opened the bottom drawer of her nightstand. Securing a small brown prescription bottle of which contained a strong nerve medication prescribed early in her separation, she poured the contents into her quivering hand. Thankful for the bottle of water awaiting its duty, she took a drink, before emptying the contents into her mouth. Swallowing hard, thankful for their minute size, she quickly washed down any left-behind pills with the remaining water.

The clock read 7 pm as Willow, freshly attired in a recently purchased ankle-length, lavender silk nightgown, lay back upon the bed, and readied her mind for what was to come. Time now ticked away, time she wished she still had, time that might change things if that were possible, but she had resigned herself to what no longer could be managed, her life; the life that would soon end. She listened to the sound of the clock, and as it marked each second with moving sound, the seconds became minutes, minutes became hours, as they moved her closer to the end.

Chapter 64

SAVING GRACE

A few hours had lapsed since Will Sutherland's strange conversation with his cousin, but along with the passing minutes, the anxiety he was feeling could no-longer be controlled. He realized the difficulty his cousin had endured throughout her convalescence; each day an agony in itself to maintain some form of decorum. He seemed to feel it in ways Jonas did not. Maybe that could be chocked-up to the closeness he and Willow had always shared from the time of childhood, whereas Jonas could only claim twenty nine years of it. He tried to work, but the peculiar sound of his cousin's voice would not leave his head. It almost sounded lost, like it had when she was a little girl afraid of the dark, or a spider lurking beneath her bed, ready to crawl in beside her, and suck her blood. Thinking of just that, he remembered her speaking about her phobia of them, and the patience her father would always show as he sought them out. Each and every night throughout the entire summer season he would go on the *spider watch*, as she used to call it, and hunt them down. He never once complained. He wanted to keep his little girl safe at all times. Will, having a child of his own, could understand that, but he had also felt the need to protect his cousin whenever something or someone was trying to hurt her, and the way he was feeling now was no different.

Walking up the line of machines, he stopped at the intended one, and called, "Hey, Jonas! I really need to talk to you! Turn off your machine and let's go outside for a few minutes!"

In no time they had settled beneath a huge oak, as Jonas said, "What's going on? Did you manage to call Willow for me?"

Nodding his head, Will replied, "Yeah, but something is off with her. I can't put my finger on any one thing, but she's not herself, Jonas, her voice sounded strange. I have a bad feeling; maybe you'd best leave and go check things out."

"If you think so," Jonas said, "I'll leave right now. But she seemed fine when I left for work this morning, well, outside of that damn cold that won't let go, but other than that she seemed okay."

"Go *now*, Jonas. Call me on my cell later and catch me up."

"Cover for me then okay?"

"Sure will, my friend, and give my best to your beautiful wife," Will said, rising to his feet and strolling toward the shop door.

The factory was located across town from the Crosby residence. On a usual night it took about one half hour to make the commute, that is if the traffic co-operated, and tonight it was. Jonas drove along, thankful for the limited amount of vehicles on the streets which allowed clear cruising. As he pulled into his drive the 10 pm news had just begun on the truck's radio.

The house was dark, the porch lights remained off, which caused a touch of concern to enter his mind, for his wife always had them on to light his return. He let himself in, and proceeded to move into the huge room which served as both living and dining room. He knew the route so well it was as if a blind person lived there, where the furnishings could never be moved after a designated floor plan had been agreed upon. Switching on the burgundy, Deco-styled chandelier hanging above the table, he could see the mail piled in a heap in the middle, and on the very top, fluttering in the movement of air caused by the living room's ceiling fan, was the Shamus O'Riley letter. Picking it up, Jonas read it over, and after emitting a few derogatory words that could turn the air blue, strode off in the direction of the master bedroom.

The room was fairly dark; the only light reaching in was coming down the hall from the dining room as Jonas entered the bedroom. In the limited light provided he could see his wife lying on the bed, the glossy fabric of her nightgown shimmering as if she were attempting to entice her lover to her side. Switching on the nightstand's lamp, his eyes fell upon the envelope addressed to him, but he paid it no mind, for he could see Willow perfectly. She laid on her back, stretched fully out, arms folded across her stomach. At first glance she appeared reminiscent of the literary Lady of Shalott floating in her canoe upon the lazy river bound for Camelot. The only pieces missing were that of the pearl garland around her head, and the white Lilly clutched within her hands.

Jonas was well aware of his wife's flair for drama, and how she often staged this kind of effect to help immerse her into a sexual fantasy she had planned for them both. But ever since she had been raped, the only kind of reaction that could be counted upon was that of disgust, and fear. Yet there was something about this that did not seem right. She was breathing, but Jonas soon realized it was not in a normal way. He shook her to elicit a response, but received none. He called her name, but to no answer. On the floor beside the bed, lying where it had fallen was the prescription bottle. Snatching it up, he studied the label, but not knowing what it was, least of all how to pronounce it, quickly realized its emptied contents lay inside his wife's stomach. For a brief moment he panicked, not certain what to do, while his heart pounded with dread. "Should I call the ambulance?" he thought, but figured the time it would take for them to arrive might mean the difference between life and death for his wife. Shoving the bottle into his coat pocket, he scooped her into his arms, and hurriedly carried her to his pickup, placed her on the seat, then raced around and climbed in behind the wheel. Time was of the essence, and he lost none as he tore off in the direction of the hospital.

The drive before they would reach Emergency seemed endless in duration, but fate was being kind for the streets were unnaturally free of traffic, and there was no police in sight. Even if there had been Jonas did not care, for he had to get help for his wife, and fast. He tore through the city; luckily all the traffic lights were green, but even had they not been he would have run them. Any police that might stop him could very well see the reason why, therefore engage their siren and escort the pickup to the hospital. He roared crossed the Rideau River Bridge, and whipped his pickup onto Hwy 72 which would take him directly to his destination. Arriving at The Ottawa Hospital, he rushed his vehicle right to the Emergency doors. He tore round to the passenger door, gathered his unconscious wife in his arms, and then barreled through the automated doors.

"Please help her!" he called in frenzy. "She needs assistance and fast!"

A nurse came running, directing him into a small cubical to the right of the entrance, telling him she would secure a doctor immediately. "What did she take?" the nurse questioned, and accepted the brown bottle from Jonas' outstretched hand. He laid his wife upon a narrow bed, and pulled up a chair beside it.

Before long a man in a white lab coat appeared with the I.D. tag reading Dr. S. Roberts displayed above a pocket containing a few pens.

"I'm Dr. Sam Roberts. This is your wife, I presume?" the physician inquired as he proceeded to check the woman laid-out before him. "And her name is?"

"Willow Crosby, and yes, she's my wife."

As the doctor looked into the woman's eyes with a penlight, he said, "I see by the bottle's label handed me that your wife consumed the opiate Diazepam Benzodiazepine, a rather strong narcotic, often prescribed for depression and severe anxiety attacks. Do you know how many were in the bottle?"

Shaking his head, Jonas replied, "I don't know. I came home to find her this way. She's been fighting a cold for weeks, been tired, that sort of thing, but I never once thought she would do something like this. I didn't even know she had those Diaza pills - whatever you called them. Is she going to be alright?"

The doctor carried on his examination, as he said, "I should think so. You got her here in time. The pills have rendered her unconscious, but I don't believe she's been that way too long. The pills were not that strong - according to the milligram count on the label - but of course it would greatly depend on how many she took, and I would very much like to know that. I shall run blood tests immediately that will tell me what I need to know; in the interim I'll begin normal procedure."

Jonas' concern heightened, and he asked, "What is *normal procedure?*"

Concluding his examination, the doctor replied, "As she is unconscious her stomach contents will need to be removed mechanically. This is done through suctioning the contents via a tube whose movement is achieved by an electric pump. Once she has regained consciousness, which should be relatively soon after, she will have to consume our infamous charcoal cocktail to be certain nothing has been left behind. It is not the nicest, Mr. Crosby, but it is necessary.

You will have to step out during the first removal procedure. I'll let you know when you may return."

It was not long in the span of time before Jonas was given the green light to return. His wife looked pale and withdrawn, but considering the circumstances, it was to be expected. But treatment was not quite finished, for beside her bed, sat the doctor's drink of choice for overdose victims everywhere.

"Do I have to drink that?" a rather groggy Willow asked the attending nurse, who was standing aside her, recording her blood pressure.

"That's right, Mrs. Crosby," the nurse answered, "every last drop. Your husband may stay if he wishes, but it's not going to be pretty."

With a firm look in his eyes, Jonas said, "I'm staying. How can I be of assistance?"

"When things begin," the nurse stated, "you can hold back her hair from her face. I'll look after the other end."

"The *other* end," Jonas inquired, "you mean?"

Nodding her head, the nurse replied, "That's right. Are we ready?"

In less than five minutes Willow was emitting black water from every orifice in her body with such intensity she was amazed her internal organs remained intact. She was certain her stomach lining must be protruding from her mouth. And the force in which the black river gushed out her rear she was certain it was carrying her colon right along with it, as liquefied excrement landed in the awaiting bedpan with a mighty splash. She could barely catch her breath between stomach heaves, and just when she thought there was no more to come, she was handed the remainder of the bottle. This brought another onslaught to the vomit dish as well as to the bedpan holding vigil beneath her butt. It was amazing how fast it came, but even more amazing that the eruption of Mount Willow had been brought-on by something as simple as charcoal. Black water dripped from her reddened nose, she swore it was in the tears she cried, and she was definite about the disgusting color her bottom must be by now.

Jonas held fast, never once weakening in the face of the disgusting presentation before him. He stood erect, holding back his wife's chestnut hair from the swirling black water gushing forth. It was interesting how little odor there actually was, yet those presently concerned did not get away without experiencing some upheaval within their stomach. Maybe people actually witness this more often than is known about, and those that do never forget it.

Jonas felt drained as he sat by his wife's bedside. She was deep asleep, a blood pressure cuff secured around her upper left arm which activated every few minutes, sending its findings directly to the nurse's desk in Intensive Care. This latest development had almost become a way of life, and Jonas was not certain as to how much more he could handle. But he loved Willow, of that he was certain; therefore would rise to the occasion, and do what was required. Once she was out of the woods he would contact Patrick Doyle's secretary, have her contact her boss, and begin countersuit proceedings to be brought against Cailen and Declan Quinn for continued Defamation of Character, Harassment, and Manipulation of the Legal System as an Instrument of Abuse. "We shall see how *you* like it," Jonas thought, as their smug faces rose before him. This time there would be no mercy. This time they would pay.

Chapter 65

DEVASTATION, THY NAME IS NOT COLD

The early morning opened to glorious sunshine steaming through the hospital windows, as Willow, now out of danger, awoke in a newly assigned bed. The room was quiet, the only sound was that of the occasional announcement on the intercom, and even that had not as yet gotten into full swing for the day. Her current nourishment was that of the intravenous bag sending requirement on down the line into the thin arm hosting it. But she had been given the green light for the solid food, that of which had just arrived from the hospital's kitchen.

Visiting hours had not officially begun, but to her amazement, a hand, carrying a flaming array of red roses in a crystal vase, suddenly shot around the doorframe. Before she could say a word, her cousin Will popped his head into the opening, and happily exclaimed, "Delivery for a Willow Sutherland-Crosby! Could you, by any chance, be that lovely damsel requiring a delightful boost, that of which these beautiful offerings of nature are guaranteed to provide?"

Willow almost burst-out crying. She was speechless, overwhelmed with gratitude at the thoughtfulness her cousin always bestowed upon her.

Catching her breath, she cried, "Oh, Will, they are absolutely breathtaking! How thoughtful — then again leave it to you. Oh, I love you, cousin, and I am *so* happy to see you."

"Hey now, cousin dear, let's not get carried away. Of course you love me, I mean, what's not to love?" he audaciously remarked in a loving manner as he made his way to her bedside.

"Aren't you supposed to be working?" Willow inquired as she sniffed the sweet aroma of the roses. "It must be that time of day, though I don't think Jonas was going into work today — thanks to me and my latest screw-up."

"That will be enough of that, Miss Low!" Will exclaimed in a stern tone. "You did nothing to be ashamed of, so cut it out right now! I'm just thankful you're alright!"

"Yes, sir," Willow stated as her elated smile returned, "I'm glad I'm alright too - though I've felt better. I must look like I've been dragged through a knothole backward. That's about the way I feel but, I guess it could have been a worse."

"It could have been a *lot* worse. Thank God Jonas came home when he did. I already knew he was not working today. He's grabbing a few hours of shuteye, and then he's … well, you have to know about it sooner or later," he said, almost as if he were apologizing.

Surmising something was afoot, she asked, "What's he up to? Spill it, Willy, I know you know something. In many ways the two of you are like Siamese twins, joined at the brain. What's going on?"

Will had begun to sample the breakfast tray, totally devouring the raisin bagel smothered in cream cheese, before replying, "He's getting in touch with his lawyer today."

The surprise on Willow's face was astounding, as she cried, "He's what?!"

Will swiftly replied, "Yep. He managed to get word to Doyle wherever he was staying. The guy was flabbergasted! Apparently he's flying home this morning and told Jonas he'd have the requested papers drawn up by the time he lands. He expects them to be delivered via worldwide courier to the mighty House of Quinn no later than tomorrow morning. That rich bitch and her coward of a son best get ready. If what they did a couple of years ago wasn't enough, they damn well opened a can of worms this time, and if it's trouble they're trying to make then it's trouble they're going to get. That's the reason you took that overdose, isn't it?"

Willow felt totally ashamed of what she had tried to do, and if the prior night's activities hadn't been embarrassing enough, Will's inquiry now doubled it.

Holding her head in shame, she said, "Yeah. I'm so sorry; I just didn't feel as if I had any recourse. I mean, if they manage to push through those alleged allegations, how would that reflect on my family? None of you would ever be able to show your face in public without constant scorn brought on by my stupidity. I can't fight that woman, Will. She's won, and I cannot live with the shame she will bring down on us."

Taking her hand in his, Will said, "Low, you are the victim here, not them. I could never understand why you dropped the charges against that fucker. And that scum of a mother of his *needs* to be shown that her money and position cannot bully others. That's exactly what she's trying to do, Low. You cannot let her! You can't bow down to the kind of shit she tries to shovel. Doyle is nobody's fool, and she'll find that out very soon."

"I hope you're right, cousin," Willow replied as she let out a long sigh.

Nodding his head, and smiling, Will exclaimed, "Bob's your uncle I'm right! Now, you get busy on this food before I eat it all! You can do it, and you know I will if you don't get cracking!"

Picking away at a ramekin of fruit, Willow replied, "The doctor said I could go home this afternoon, but first he needed to speak with me. He said he's got the test results about this cold, and why it's not going away. But I should be ready to go by two or so. Tell Jonas I'll call him before I'm ready to leave."

"Sure will, girl," Will said. "Now you finish that plate, and have a nap if you get the chance. I'm glad the doc has found out about that cold; hopefully he'll have something that'll wipe it out completely."

"Yeah, me too," Willow agreed, and then began to consume her remaining breakfast as Will left the room.

The afternoon was not long in arriving and with it a visit from Dr. Roberts. He appeared most concerned, but Willow didn't expect him to be jumping for joy, considering the circumstances surrounding her reason for being there. She even found herself bracing for the reprimand he was sure to deliver, but instead he pulled up a chair, and sat down.

"Mrs. Crosby," he began, "I need to speak with you concerning something that was discovered in a test that was performed on your blood sample."

Taking a deep breath, Willow said, "It's this cold that doesn't seem to leave, isn't it? I should have seen a doctor about it quite some time ago, in-fact my mother has been on my back about it for awhile now but, well I figured it would run its course sooner or later. Summer colds are far worse than winter ones. Surely you have something I can take for it."

The somber look on the doctor's face grew morose, as he said, "I'm afraid there is nothing I can give you, Mrs. Crosby. You don't have a cold, you …"

He stopped, but Willow already surmised what he was trying not to say. Taking another breath, she said, "I'm not a stupid woman, Dr. Roberts, even if I sometimes conduct myself as such. I already know I don't have a cold. I kept telling myself that was what I had, it was what I was telling everyone else, but even I know that colds don't last this long. I have cancer, don't I?"

Dr. Roberts solemnly looked at her, and said, "No, you've tested positive for HIV."

Willow always thought she had a will of steel, but these words brought her world crashing down around her like a torpedo brings death and destruction when it hits its mark. She could barely believe it. It couldn't be true. How? When did this happen, and from whom?

"Mrs. Crosby," the doctor gently said, "I am sorry. It's never easy to deliver this diagnosis to anyone, and it gets harder each time I have to do it. But I must say this. Just because you tested positive does not mean that you will develop AIDS. It simply means you are infected, and that you carry the virus within you. It also means that you *must* divulge this to any sexual partner, and that you must use protection during intercourse. Because this virus attacks the immune system, it is vital that you boost your immune as much as you can. We have a good array of supplements for just that purpose. We have yet to find a cure, but we have learned a tremendous amount about this disease that at one time did mean a death sentence. In today's world it does not, and even should the virus develop, it can be controlled through diet and medication, and you can live a long, fulfilling life. In some cases it takes years to detect. In your case it is a good thing it has shown itself as quickly as it has. This way it can be controlled. I've no doubt you have questions?"

She was flabbergasted. "Yes, I have questions," she thought, "but the most important one is who gave this to me, and somehow that question needs no answer," as she said, "Dr. Roberts, how does one go about proving the source from where it came? I mean, I'm pretty sure I know who transferred it to me. How do I expose him?"

"You know who passed on the virus to you?" Dr. Roberts asked.

"Yes," Willow said adamantly. "I was raped a couple of years ago. I know it was my rapist. I never once experienced the way I now feel before that. I have had different sexual partners throughout my life, as well as unprotected intercourse, but I never once encountered the slightest problem until after I was raped."

"Did you report it?"

"It took awhile before I did. I was so ashamed, degraded, embarrassed and all that goes along with it. It felt hopeless, and I just couldn't bring myself to secure justice. I suppose the main reason for that was the humiliation and, well the stigma it carries, besides I didn't think the police would believe me; they very seldom believe a rape victim. My husband Jonas, and Will, my cousin, brought charges against this guy but it never got to trail. You see, the kid that did this to me got into an accident which left him in a vegetative state with no expected recovery. I just let it go. I felt it was useless."

The doctor's attention appeared to pique, as he said, "Are you certain that this person who raped you was infected with HIV?"

"I can't say for certain, Dr. Roberts, but I feel he is. Two years ago, before his accident, he was hospitalized, and I'm sure there was blood work done during his stay but, he comes from a very wealthy family in Ireland, and his mother has a way of overstepping the law. But I know he was sexually active because he told me about it."

"I see," the doctor said with amusement, "do you know if it was this hospital?"

"Yes," she replied. "The young man's name is Declan Quinn. His mother's name is Cailen O'Brian-Quinn. But they're back in Galway now. She had him transferred back there and I'm sure he's being taken care of at their home. The woman has scads of money to do just that."

"Well," the doctor said, "records cannot be tampered with, regardless of how much money she has. Not in this hospital. I shall have a look. May I send you the findings?"

Nodding her head, Willow said, "Of course. I'm currently being sued by Cailen Quinn for what she *thinks* I did to her son, and my husband is countersuing on my behalf. Information, such as what we have just discussed, would be extremely valuable, not only in the outcome of my case, but for public awareness and, well, protection."

"Definitely so, Mrs. Crosby," Dr. Roberts stated in compliance. "I shall have my nurse send the findings by courier directly to your home address later today. Now that I have a name it will not take long to search the archive records, but before I go, I have another issue to discuss with you."

"What's that?" Willow questioned as her anxiety rose.

The doctor briefly referred to his notes; then answered, "I would like you to consider speaking with a therapist."

"Why would I need to do that, Doctor?"

"When someone takes an overdose it is a sign of a serious underlying problem."

"Do you think I tried to kill myself?"

"Didn't you?"

Willow sat quiet, contemplating an answer. She had to admit to feeling defeated, so much so that she could see no way out except suicide, yet to admit to that would be admitting to an unbalanced mind, something else to bring shame and disgrace. She realized he was awaiting her answer; one that she was not truly sure about, but it did no one concerned any good if she kept it bottled up, least of all her, so she said, "I was tired, Doctor."

It was obviously not the answer he had hoped to hear, for he cleared his throat, and said, "What you did had nothing to do with feeling tired, and if you were being honest with yourself you would admit that."

"But I was tired," she said, trying her best to deter the inevitable.

"Willow, may I address you by your given name?" he asked.

"Certainly," she answered. "I'm not exactly sure what it is you're wishing me to say. I *was* tired, I'm *still* tired, I'm sure I'll feel that way the rest of my life, but to admit to suicide is a bit much, though I will admit to feeling defeated *and* at the end of my tether. I wanted to sleep, I wanted everything to just go away and leave me be, and at the time it wouldn't have mattered if I didn't wake up."

"Why then did you write a note to your husband?" he asked with compassion. "He brought it in to me during the night. He'd gone home for awhile and when he came back he had it with him. The note not only revealed your intentions, it cried out for help in the process. This is why I recommend you speak with someone trained to help you. I believe you have a lot of underlying issues, and I feel they have been there a very long time."

He had hit the nail squarely on the head, but how was Willow to explain the way she had felt from the time of childhood? Aside from what she now faced, things had finally started to get better, especially between her and her mother, and the rest of the left-over issues would also find their way to better days. She didn't want to rehash issues that could not be changed regardless of words spoken, tears shed, or medications that would alter her thought process in ways that were not her to begin with. She had to come to accept things on her own terms, not someone else's, and she would cling to this need however long it took to reach fruition.

Looking him squarely in the eyes, she said, "I am the first to admit I have problems, and I also realize that I have not always responded to them in the most stable of ways. But I was raised to solve my own problems, and carry on as best I can. Old habits die hard, and I know I have many strikes against me, but I will cope with them. I realize what I did was the wrong choice to have made and yes, I took those pills on purpose. It's done, still I am thankful to be alive, and I also know the heartache and needless stress I put those closet to me through, but no amount of therapy, or swallowed drugs will change that cold hard fact, nor will it remove the issues I still face. I alone must do that, and I will cope with whatever is to come."

Doctor Roberts had intently listened to this melodramatic confession, yet he knew that there was a lot more to it than what she was admitting. But he could not force her upon a psychoanalyst's couch, and since no internal harm had come from what she had done, he was not obligated to report it to the police.

"Willow, I really wish you would reconsider your choice, but it is your choice to make, I cannot force you; however I do hope you will keep in touch with me."

"Thank you, Dr. Roberts, I really do appreciate your concern, and I realize the reason behind it, but I will be fine. If it's any consolation, I will admit that a lot of my present problems began in my childhood, but I've also come to realize that the reasons where not what I thought they were. I blamed my mother for a lot of my misgivings and ill-placed choices because of her unfeeling, narrow-minded ways and views, but she cannot be blamed for doing the best she could based on her own unfeeling upbringing. It always bothered me, because as much as I adored and cherished my dad, I was always plying for my mother's attention and approval. I suppose the reason I tried so hard was because I was never receiving it, or anything anywhere near it. My dad was always there for me in every possible way he could. He always made a point of being sure my brother and I knew how he felt about us, but Mom was a different story. I suppose there are times when one has to be cruel to be kind, and maybe that was the way she viewed things, or the reason why she did a lot of the things in the way that she did. I used to think she did it merely to destruct, instead of construct, but never once did I ever think about her true intentions, other than they were never what I needed from her. I never once thought she loved me, and it was only a couple of years ago that we managed to actually bond. I know I was not an easy child - even more difficult as an adult - but I guess when you always try your best but to no avail you stop trying, and let the road lead where it may. None of this is any excuse for ill-judgment; it's only a view, and maybe not a very good one. So, Doctor, there you have it, my entire life in a nutshell."

"Thank you for sharing that, Willow. It would not have been easy to open up that way, but confession of the soul is one step closer to a healthier mind. I'll talk to you later."

The door closed behind the doctor, leaving a subdued Willow to contemplate her thoughts. She was still trying to come to terms with the hand she had been dealt. How would she tell Jonas, as well as the family? She could not, she must get away, leave everything, go to a place where no one knows her or has ever heard of her. But how could she leave those she so dearly loved, and not only that, how could she manage without them now, especially when she needed their support so much? "There must be an answer," she thought, "somewhere there has to be a way to cope with all of this, but right now I just don't know how." Turning on to her side, she let her eyes drink deep of the red roses her cousin had brought; now resting on the bedside table. As she did, tears suddenly came in full force, and she cried harder than she ever had before.

Chapter 66

WHEN YOU ADVANCE INTO BATTLE BEST BE SURE OF YOUR RESERVES

September twenty sixth was another lovely day at Quinn Manor. Autumn was a welcomed time of year, the heat of summer was gone, and the chilling cold of winter was still weeks away. Harvest had been good this year, and larders throughout the countryside would enjoy a full bounty throughout the coming winter. On the Quinn estate, flourishing for decades, were numerous varieties of apples, Orange Pippin being the most popular, but the rest of the tart, juicy varieties were fully as popular for munching on their own, or for sought after desserts. In the old days Bridget Donnigan's pies made from these scrumptious apples were to die for, and Declan Quinn was always her best taker. There wasn't a day throughout harvest that she didn't have to chase him out of her kitchen at least a half dozen times, but he usually got his way when he turned on the charm, that of which Bridget could never resist.

That was then. Today was far different, in-fact everything had changed, and not for the better. Matilda Prichard sat at the old kitchen table, deep in thought. By the slump of her backbone, usually as straight as an arrow, one could tell she was laboring. Life had changed for her, and changed greatly. Ever since Declan Quinn's accident, her duties, once respectable, were now diminished to that of errand girl, dumping drainage bags, and cleaning up after Cailen who remained glued to her son's bedside just in case his eyelids may flutter, his nose may run, or his intravenous required changing. Cailen's demeanor, once decent and kind, was now that of a rich ogre whose outrageous demands were nothing short of impossible.

Declan's bedroom had become a shrine to an earlier time. Pictures of his father were everywhere, while votive candles burned in designated rows throughout the room, giving the illusion that one should pause upon entry and light one. Cailen took her meals in this room at a table set for two in front of the massive stone fireplace, the mantle of which was lined with pictures of Cailen, Derek, and Declan. It was as if the rest of the family no longer existed. She had her desk brought to this room, where she conducted whatever business required her attention. She had even gone as far as having her bed and dresser relocated to this room. It had become Quinn Central, and it was a select few who were permitted entry.

Cailen was busy tending business when a knock came upon the bedroom door. "Who be there?" she inquired, not taking her eyes from the correspondence before them.

"Matilda Prichard," the voice answered.

"Enter!" Cailen ordered sharply.

"Mrs. Quinn, you have a special courier delivery that requires your signature," Prichard stated, and laid a paper, along with an envelope, upon the desktop. Stepping back, as if too close of presence to the desk might mean instant discharge, she said, "I signed for its delivery, but I am to return that paper to the courier along with your signature stating you received the envelope. He is waiting in the front entrance."

Looking up with daggers in her eyes, Cailen snapped, "A common delivery person be standing in me grand entrance? Ye knows very well there be an entrance around back for tradesmen and delivery! Why did ye even answer the door, where be the maid?"

"I don't know, Mrs. Quinn, possibly busy elsewhere. I happened to be passing through the foyer when the knock sounded at the door."

"Well ye had no business answering it when that be part of *her* duties. Very well! What be this, anyway?" and she began tearing the envelope with a sterling letter opener.

"I'm sure I wouldn't know, Mrs. Quinn, I am not in the habit of reading another's mail," Prichard replied sharply.

"Is that so?" Cailen stated cunningly as if Prichard's reply was anything but honest. "Tell me something I might be believing."

"Mrs. Quinn, I really must take issue with that. I —" But she was cut-off, when Cailen shrieked, *"What in the name of unfeeling Saints be this nonsense?!"* Scanning the words before her, she exclaimed, "Balderdash, how *dare* she move against me!?"

Prichard couldn't help but be intrigued, as she said, "What has gotten you so upset?"

"Look at this!" Cailen demanded, shoving the lily-white document toward her.

Upon reading it over, and none too surprised at its contents, Prichard peered over her spectacles toward her employer, and said, "I don't know why you're so surprised. I'm certainly not. Did you really think you could threaten the Crosby woman without some form of retaliation?" Inwardly Prichard was rather impressed by this move on Willow's part, showed backbone, something that she had felt lacking in herself for a very long time.

Cailen, ill-amused with what she considered an impertinent reply, snapped, "I not be finding yur insubordinate words amusing in the least, Matilda! How dare ye question me judgment?"

For quite some time Matlida Prichard had kept her mouth shut, and her feelings capped with regard to the way in which the Quinn matriarch had handled things leading up to their return home, not to mention the ongoing happenings since, and she certainly did not agree with the die-hard vendetta toward Willow Crosby. Knowing the courier was waiting on her return, she replied, "Mrs. Quinn, the courier is waiting for that signed paper. I will deliver it to him then immediately return as we have some issues that require discussion; hopefully a means to the end of this ongoing nonsense."

Cailen bristled, jumped to her feet, and exclaimed, "Nonsense!? I not be finding any move I make nonsense!" and began to pursue her employee, but she was out of luck, for Prichard had openly snatched the paper, turned her back, and left the room, leaving the fuming matriarch in her wake.

A good few minutes passed while Cailen, after having straightened the satin duvet over Declan for the umpteenth time during the hour, returned to her desk to await her employee's return. Before long Prichard entered, carrying a tray holding a teapot and two china cup and saucer sets. Placing the tray upon the table, she said, "I thought the heated circumstances might benefit from a few sips of tea, Mrs. Quinn. It always helped our cause whenever Bridget would deliver a tray, accompanied with her uplifting laughter of course. I know the laughter always settled me, and I've not a doubt that the tea also helped to ease the stress, which in turn helped us settle our differences. I hope it will do the same now."

Joining Prichard at the table, Cailen replied, "This be right nice of ye, Matlida, but ye not be swaying me intentions toward that Crosby dame. I find it appalling that ye would as much as consider forgiveness for what she did to me boy - yur boy in many ways - as ye always showed preference to him over the others."

Lifting the cup to her lips, Prichard replied, "Yes, I suppose I did, though it was never done intentionally. Maybe it was because Master Declan was the youngest, and in many ways required my guidance more than any of his brothers did. One cannot help but become attached, especially when you think of the amount of years that have passed since I was first approached by your husband in regard to this position. But I must say, Mrs. Quinn, your family was not the first that I cared for, but through the years I have become settled here. I had hoped to remain here until I retired, possibly after that, but I can no longer uphold nor support the way things have become here."

The cup slightly trembled in Cailen's fingers, while in a menacing tone, she replied, "And what way be that?"

Prichard instinctively knew by her employer's blatant mannerism that battle lines had just been drawn. "Should I retaliate?" she thought, knowing that if she did she must carry through to the bitter end, which would certainly mean dismissal upon completion, but she would not wait to be dismissed, she would resign before Cailen could have the satisfaction.

Setting her cup upon its matching saucer, she replied, "I believe you already know to what I refer without me having to state it. But since you've requested it, I shall speak my mind."

Cailen placed her arms on the table before her and clasped her hands together, as she said, "I believe I be knowing what ye are about to spout, but I must be reminding ye of yur longtime position with the House of Quinn and, should ye continue with yur *complaints*, it may well result in circumstances ye may not be prepared for."

Prichard shot a quick glance toward her young charge sleeping peacefully on his bed, the few moments that simple gesture took brought an imaginary knife through her heart, but she could not let that stop her. Everything that had happened since his unfortunate trek to Ottawa had to be brought not only to terms, but to justice. With the help of his mother he had escaped punishment for what he had done, though in certain ways was now paying. Prichard knew more than she ever divulged to Cailen, and it was time she let it all out.

Gathering lost courage, she said, "Mrs. Quinn, for quite some time I have been aware of more than you realize, but because of my affection for Master Declan, and for the family in general, I chose to look the other way, but I can no longer do that. You purposely, and without shame or decency, covered up any possible evidence of his despicable act upon Willow Crosby. He not only raped that poor woman, he beat her. Worse still, through his appalling act, he would have passed on the AIDS virus, which will undoubtedly infect her, ruining her life forever!"

Cailen, sitting with a Cheshire-grin on her face until hearing Prichard's latest remark, exclaimed, "What!"

"You heard me!" Prichard snapped. "Before we had left Ottawa, I received a report back from Master Declan's last blood test. The attending doctor, knowing I had nurses training and worked in that capacity for you, gave it to me because I had surmised something out of the ordinary a few days before Master Declan left for Ottawa. I kept it from you. It was wrong, I know, but I wanted to spare you further grief, yet I, more than anyone should have known better, and God help me to my dying day. I also happen to know a doctor on staff at Galway Clinic who gave me some very enlightening news about the dear Aednat Mulkearns, with whom Master Declan's continued dalliance with resulted in an enormous payoff by you, but not before she managed to infect him with HIV."

Cailen sat stunned. She had heard Prichard's words, but all she could do was shake her head in defiance. Casting her eyes toward her son, she snapped, "How can ye be so cruel?! How much can ye detest me to voice such wretched lies, simply because I am determined to bring that Crosby scum just what she deserves for enticing me boy? If he be infected, it be *her* doings! I not be stopping 'till she be rotting in prison for what she did. She will pay —"

Prichard cut her off, as she snapped, "You will do nothing of the sort, Mrs. Quinn! The woman *is* paying! She will pay for the rest of her life, however long that life remains! Your son, through his unfortunate encounters with that Mulkearn creature, has all but passed on a death sentence to Willow Crosby!"

"Well he shan't be infecting anyone else, will he, and how *dare* ye speak to me this way?" Cailen cried, doing her best to continue to absorb the upsetting fact of what her son may also face.

"I *dare* because you need to hear this!" Prichard exclaimed, no longer holding back. "I saw those repulsive photographs on Master Declan's cell – *the same as you did* – those lurid, odious images of what he was doing to that poor woman. He even had the blatant nerve to record it for his later enjoyment, and my God the horrendous bruising upon that women's body. We both saw it and *you*, taking it upon your high and mighty self to *exam* her while she lay unconscious, unable to protect herself. On top of that, for whatever plausible reason you might have pulled out of the air, you go to her home and attack her. And then you continue your self-righteous vendetta by bringing trumped-up charges against her, all of which are bolshie, totally so, in every way! You and your *son* have ruined that woman's life. And then you sit behind that desk over there and scoff because she dares to defend herself against your defamatory acts! I am so ashamed and disgusted with my involvement with any of it – any of you!"

"Ye just wait, Miss Prichard!"

"No! *You* wait, Mrs. Quinn!"

"Ye be through here as of now! Me boy and meself be no longer needing ye! I be blackballing ye name for any further employment on our beautiful emerald Isle! *Now get out me house!*"

Prichard pulled herself as erect as she could muster, and said, "I will go, but hear me. If you as much as push one more legal button, or pull one more legal string, I will *personally* go to both *your* lawyer, and Willow Crosby's lawyer and tell them everything, all of it! How back in Ottawa you bought off that drunk to discard of Master Declan's car in the river. How you skirted the Ottawa police, and the photographs on Master Declan's cell phone. And do not forget I know about all your dirty dealings over the years. The Quinn fortune is not as clean as you might like people to believe. The Crosby vendetta stops now, or I will do as I said I would. Your insane actions, and the way you continue to carry on is something that truly needs looking in to. I will be speaking with the doctor directly, and he *will* decide from here. As for me, I can no longer cope here, but I will be writing a letter to your lawyer that is only to be opened should you contact him with intent of continuing this madness. I knew this confrontation was coming, it was inevitable, and I will not be waiting around to contend with the outcome. I have recently secured a position with a young family back home in my dear England. I will be returning there within the week."

Walking to Declan's side, Prichard lay her hand against his cheek, leaned down, and kissed his forehead, as she said, "May God have mercy on you, and may He lead you every day of your life. I am so very sorry I could not avert all of this for you, and because of that, I have failed you. It is my hope that you may one day forgive me. I will forever remember our days with fondness. Goodbye, my dear."

As the door closed behind Prichard, Cailen stood watching, their words echoing in her head. In many ways she couldn't help but feel admiration for this woman who had become such a part of her life, her family's life, but mostly Declan's. She also knew that Matlida Prichard was nobody's fool, and that she would carry through. The serious words she had spoken made Cailen realize the actual extent of what she had done. There would be no retaliation toward anyone, as she quietly said, "Ye be right, Matlida Prichard, and ye have every right to go. Ye always did have one up on me. Pity I be too dense to realize that until now. I wish ye well, and like Bridget used to say, 'ye never know who be yur true friend 'till they be gone from yur presence'. Go well, Matilda. I will miss ye."

As she glanced around, she couldn't help wondering how she ever got so far off track. She walked to the mantle where she picked up Derek's picture. Gazing at it with fondness, she thought, "Oh how I miss ye, and how I've wronged ye. Through the loss of ye, I made our boy take yur place, and I was so wrong to have done that. I failed him; I failed ye, but I love ye both with all me heart as I do all me boys. I don't know if Declan will ere return to me, or if God will be kind to him in that respect, but I promise ye right here and now, Derek, I will do whatever can be done for him, if anything can, and if so, it will be done honestly."

Chapter 67

CLOSURE

October had opened to a chilly breeze and overcast skies. The weather channel was forecasting an early storm that was presently building over the prairies and heading east; it was destined to hit Ontario at some point within the next few days which did not leave a lot of time in which to prepare. The province was not yet ready for a major storm - should it happen - for it was far too soon for inclement weather of that nature to arrive. But it was autumn in Canada, the Great White North, where anything was possible. Jonas had batten down the hatches and had his shovel at the ready, as did most throughout the city and surrounding countryside, now all that was left was to wait and see if the storm materialized.

Jonas, along with his wife, sat on the sofa discussing the storm's possibility along with the early prediction of such, but aside from that, realized what this calendar date meant. But thanks to the cunning expertise of Patrick Doyle, the threat of losing everything, not to mention prison time for Willow, had passed, as Doyle had received notification from Shamus O'Riley stating that his client had mysteriously withdrawn her suit, and extended her sincere apologies for any inconvenience it may have caused. But the Crosby's were not privy, nor would they ever know the reason behind Cailen Quinn's sudden change of heart. All they knew is that the case was dropped, and for that they were thankful.

"I can't help but find her words a bit hard to believe though," Willow said to her husband as she continued to re-read Doyle's letter. "Hmm, *inconvenience*. Well, I suppose one could say she caused a bit, that is if pushing a person to the point of attempted suicide could be considered as inconveniencing someone."

Nodding his head, Jonas replied, "Yes, I really can't blame you for feeling that way toward her but, honey, what you did was a bit drastic."

"I know," Willow replied sadly. "But I just couldn't see any other way out. I mean, if she had managed to push through those charges, I just couldn't have that kind of disgrace brought upon you and the family. Heaven only knows I brought enough through my own discrepancies."

"Possibly," Jonas conferred, "but regardless of what you did *or* what you were facing, your life is invaluable to me and the family. I don't know how you could have ever doubted that."

Walking over to the table, Willow settled herself upon a chair, and replied, "I suppose, however much is left of it."

Settling beside her, and taking her hands in his, Jonas said, "I know your diagnosis, sweetheart, but I don't know a lot about the disease. I'm educating myself as I go. However I do know that just because a person tests positive doesn't mean it will develop any further."

"Doesn't mean it won't, either," Willow replied softly as her misting eyes stared straight ahead.

Clearing his throat, Jonas said, "No, this is true, but you mustn't lose faith, and you cannot give up hope. The woman I married would never throw in the towel, she would rail against adversity, regardless of what it was, and keep on the fight."

Willow got up and walked to the kitchen where she poured two cups of coffee. Handing one to her newly arrived husband, she looked him straight in the eyes, and said, "Is that what you think I'm doing?"

Realizing this was her answer to his assumption, Jonas replied, "I'm not sure. How *can* I be sure, Willow? How can I be certain that I won't arrive home from work tonight and find you the way I did a couple of weeks ago?"

Continuing her stare, she nonchalantly answered, "It can't happen. I haven't any meds."

The exasperation building within Jonas was immense. He could not get her unconscious vision out of his head, no more than he could wipe away the memory of her hurling black water in hope to dispel any left behind toxins that might further damage her liver. The fact that she could be so insensible was beyond him, but he realized that in her mind she had felt the necessity, regardless of how selfish it might have been, or the eternity of grief she would have brought the family. And this was not even taking into account the stigma that goes along with suicide.

"I'm going to overlook that last remark," Jonas said as he brought the coffee cup to his lips.

"I'm sorry," Willow replied before taking a sip of her coffee. Returning the cup to the counter, she continued, "I can't blame you for feeling as you do. All I ask is that you trust that I won't. I'm just trying to cope with things as best I can, Jonas, it sure as hell isn't easy."

The morning wore on, finding the Crosby's on their second pot of coffee, and deep in conversation. Words are required in order to solve problems, settle situations, but sometimes they are simply just words. In the Crosby's situation, words were the means to an end. The coffee continued to flow, as did the words.

"Dr. Roberts thinks I should speak with a therapist," Willow said, hoping to take the onus off her diagnosis and send it in a different direction.

Realizing his wife's intention, Jonas said, "I don't see how that could hurt. Expressing thoughts, regardless of how painful, can often be successful in solving issues."

"I suppose," she mused, "and I'm really not opposed to the idea per se, but even should I talk it out, it won't change anything, I'll still be sick."

"I know," he said in a gentle way, rubbing her hand, "but at least your feelings won't stay bottled up inside you. That can harm you just as much as sickness."

Willow suddenly rose from the table, placed the cups in the sink, and then requested Jonas come with her to their bed. He wondered at this, especially given her ongoing frigidity, but followed along. She lay upon the bed, and pat the immediate area of mattress beside her.

"What's this about?" he asked as he stretched out beside her.

"Don't worry," she answered, "nothing is going to happen. I would never put you at risk, besides I couldn't, even if I was healthy. I just want to explain things, if I can."

Knowing it was hard for her, he replied, "You don't have to explain anything."

"Oh, but I do," she said, and turned to face him.

Late afternoon had arrived by the time she had finished baring her soul. Once she got started she could not stop, and regardless of the way her words might be taken, she had to see it through to the end. Their entire future depended upon putting the past to rest. She told Jonas how she came to encounter Declan Quinn; how the friendship had evolved into what he thought was something that it wasn't; how she felt that she had led him to believe her feelings were the same as his, and how it all blew up in her face. "How was I to know he would come to Ottawa?" she questioned as she continued her validation. "It was under the pretense of attending a summer collage course, so he said, maybe it was, but he couldn't have been here all that long before he showed up on the porch that awful day. I didn't even know who he was; he looked nothing like his photographs. Then again that too was a ploy meant to snare me into paying attention to him. I don't begin to know who the guy in those photos is supposed to be, obviously a model, judging from the look of him. Maybe Declan somehow thought there was no harm in what he was doing. The things he told me of his life were things that touched my heart. He seemed vulnerable in ways, definitely young, yet the way he chased and spoke to me when we chatted made him seem years beyond his age, and those bogus photographs cinched it."

"Do you still have them?" Jonas asked.

"No," she answered, "I was so ashamed of the entire debacle that I deleted them. They would have gotten swept away the first time I cleaned the computer. It's just as well; you do not need to go there."

"Willow, I don't want you to blame yourself for any of this," Jonas explained. "If I had conducted myself in the manner in which I should have none of that would have ever happened. I realize the past cannot be changed, but I promise you the future will be as good as I can possibly make it. I hope you can believe me, and I hope you can forgive me."

Embracing her husband tightly, Willow cried, "Of course I forgive you but ... can you ever forgive me for what I did; what I've brought?"

"No one knows what life has in store for them, sweetheart," Jonas replied as he brushed the tears from her eyes. "I have something to ask you, and I want you to know that I truly mean it."

Brushing the hair from her face, she asked, "What would that be?"

"Maybe I should get down on my knee, but this mattress feels pretty good," Jonas replied, and taking her hands in his, said, "Will you marry me again?"

You could have knocked Willow over with a feather; she couldn't have been more surprised. Maybe this was the best medicine of all, and though it was coming out of left field, it brought her more joy than it had the first time he had said those words so very long ago. The stress she had been feeling literally melted away, and was replaced with a smile as broad as the side of a barn. For a few short moments she felt as if he might be teasing her, either that or she was dreaming, yet she knew what she had heard was indeed correct.

"Oh, Jonas!" she cried, fighting to hold it together. "I will! I will!!" she squealed, and then embraced him tightly.

Retuning her embrace, he jubilantly said, "I thought we could go away for awhile, have a long-over-do vacation somewhere warm with tropical breezes, and plenty of Mai Tais, rum, Piña Coladas, and BBQ up to our asses!"

"It sounds wonderful!" she exclaimed, the intensity of her embrace increasing, but she suddenly pulled back, and inquired, "Can we afford this?"

It would be tight, but Jonas was determined to carry through and bring to his wife some sibilance of happiness. She was way-past due, so was he, so he would do whatever was necessary to make it happen. Their celebration continued along with their new-found plans until a knock pounded upon the front door. Jonas and

Willow, arm in arm, made their way to the front hall where they were elated to see Will Sutherland, accompanied by a very petite, middle-aged lady, awaiting their inquiry.

It wasn't long before the couples were gathered in the living room, chatting up a storm.

"What brings you by, cousin - not that I'm not happy to see you - by the way we have some wonderful news!" Willow exclaimed, doing her best to remain seated.

"Weeeell, Cousin Low," Will replied, stretching his words to fit the growing happiness of the moment, "I'd like you both to meet Mandy Fellows, my fiancé! We just got engaged last night, but it was too late to come by, otherwise I would have been standing on your doorstep creating such a stir that the neighbors would have had me run in for disturbing the peace!"

Willow excitedly replied, "I am delighted to meet you, Mandy, and I am extremely happy for you both. Congratulations! You're getting yourself a fine man in my cousin. They don't come any finer, and he has certainly waited a long time for happiness. I couldn't be more pleased."

Will was looking at his fiancé with an expression on his face that would make one think he was either overly accepting of his cousin's praise, or extremely embarrassed by it, but regardless of what the chosen factor might be, it did not deter from his elation.

As she scratched her head, Willow said, "How long have you been keeping your lady under wraps, cousin dear?"

With a smile, Will answered, "Not all that long, actually. We met briefly a couple of years ago while you were hospitalized, but we continued to see each other ever since, now we're inseparable. Mandy is the granddaughter of the lady who babysits Dane's son. She is also a nurse, and a fine one at that," and as he spoke he slipped his arm around her waist and embraced her tightly, as he added, "Now I won't have to worry when I get myself in need of *care*, medically or otherwise," and he winked impishly. Returning his attention to his hosts, he said, "And what is your big news of the day? I take it's something super cool? I haven't seen you smile like this in a long time, Low."

"That you haven't," Willow thought, as she openly exclaimed, "Jonas and I are getting remarried! How is that for groundbreaking news?"

Jumping to his feet, Will quickly embraced his cousin, and then shook Jonas' outstretched hand in such a violent manner it was as if he wished to set a speed record for having done so. "This news is awesome, totally awesome!" he remarked with exuberance, and everyone concerned knew it was genuinely felt. "When is the big day?"

"We haven't discussed that yet," Jonas replied. "We've only spoken about places we'd like to go for a holiday."

Suddenly, as if she had been struck by a lightning bolt, Willow cried, "Let's all elope together! Mandy and I can stand up for each other, and Will and Jonas can do the same, and then we can all vacation together!"

Will looked at his fiancé, and said, "What do you think? I'm sure willing, but I'm not in this alone, and what about you, Jonas? I, more than anyone know the speed in which my cousin can come up with things, but I'm okay with it, if you both are."

The afternoon became evening, and with it completed plans. The ceremonies would take place in Cuba on the southwest beach of Old Havana. Each couple would witness the other's nuptials, and then following a wondrous feast, would retire to their respective cabana where they would listen to Latin rhythms all night long. It would be memories made in Heaven.

Willow lay awake in bed that night with every conceivable thought one could imagine running ramped throughout her mind.

For the first time in however long she was truly happy. She refused to let the past consume her any longer, and though she realized the time bomb within her body would forever remain ticking, she refused to let it dictate her life for the remainder of her time. One does not live life by the quantity of days given them, but rather the quality, and she was determined to cling to this knowledge whenever doubts filled her mind. Her children were grown and happy with successful careers and wonderful, loving families. Her mother, still determined and precise in her ways, successfully carried on the farm with the help of her hired hand. Willow was both grateful and thankful for the ability to have become a daughter to her in the ways in which it should be, and in return her mother could celebrate her in the way that God intended. Her brother, along with his wife and grown family, continued to live a peaceful life on their farm located just up the road from the old Sutherland farm in the Ottawa Valley, and whenever the chance presented itself, he and Willow got together.

In Ireland, Cailen Quinn continued to remain by Declan's side. His condition would forever remain unaltered; however the times of lucidity he enjoyed brought untold fulfillment to his mother in ways not many would understand. Throughout the entire ordeal of which they had faced, Cailen never once intended to let things get so far out of control. Her father had not raised a deceitful daughter with intent to bring anguish to others, and even through the circumstances of which had altered her course in life, they never really changed the person she truly was inside.

Though she thought of Declan Quinn and the family often, Matilda Prichard, throughout all her trials and tribulations, had finally found contentment through her new position. She was again in charge of a family of boys who brought out the best in her teaching ability. She celebrated this, for it had been a long time since she felt elation from her efforts. She fast settled-in, finding her new position to be all she had hoped it would be. However she was finding her youngest charge, a boy, who was shy and not certain of what might lurk behind the next door, challenging in every way, especially in ways she missed.

The night progressed. Jonas lay asleep at Willow's side as thoughts continued to ply her mind. She couldn't wait for their exciting plans to take place. Maybe everyone, regardless of their fears and uncertainties, would find peace and contentment. So many things had happened, so many unnecessary, cruel things which had altered the course of so many lives. Willow couldn't help but wonder that if things had turned out differently, would everyone still have found happiness in the way in which they had? She knew it was a question that could never be answered, but as she dwelled on this impossible fact, she softly whispered, "I don't know what's ahead for me, whether this disease will take me or not, but I refuse to sit around waiting to see, or waiting to die. I will stand on my feet and take what comes my way. I was not raised to accept defeat, and regardless of what hand I'm dealt, I'll cope with it as best I can. It's all I *can* do. Somehow, I think Winnie would agree."

Made in the USA
Charleston, SC
22 January 2016